Ben Elton's career as both performer and writer encompasses some of the most memorable and incisive comedy of the past twenty years. His work as a stand-up comedian hosting such ground-breaking television series as *Saturday Live* and *The Man from Auntie* has been hugely influential, as have his hit television sitcoms *The Young Ones*, *Blackadder* and *The Thin Blue Line*.

Elton has written three hit West End musicals, including the global phenomenon *We Will Rock You*, which he also directs, and three West End plays, including the multi-award-winning *Popcorn*. His internationally bestselling novels include *Stark*, *Inconceivable*, *Dead Famous* and *High Society*. In 2000 he wrote and directed the feature film *Maybe Baby*, based on his acclaimed novel *Inconceivable*.

www.**books**at**transworld**.co.uk

PAST
MORTEM

BEN ELTON

BANTAM PRESS

LONDON · TORONTO · SYDNEY · AUCKLAND · JOHANNESBURG

TRANSWORLD PUBLISHERS
61–63 Uxbridge Road, London W5 5SA
a division of The Random House Group Ltd

RANDOM HOUSE AUSTRALIA (PTY) LTD
20 Alfred Street, Milsons Point, Sydney
New South Wales 2061, Australia

RANDOM HOUSE NEW ZEALAND LTD
18 Poland Road, Glenfield, Auckland 10, New Zealand

RANDOM HOUSE SOUTH AFRICA (PTY) LTD
Endulini, 5a Jubilee Road, Parktown 2193, South Africa

Published 2004 by Bantam Press
a division of Transworld Publishers

A catalogue record for this book is available
from the British Library.
ISBN 0593 050959 (cased)
0593 050967 (tpb)

Typeset in 11/15pt Sabon
by Falcon Oast Graphic Art Ltd

Printed and bound in Great Britain
by Clays Ltd, St Ives plc

3 5 7 9 10 8 6 4 2

For my wife and children

PAST MORTEM

1

The victim died as he had lived.

Cruelly.

Except more so.

Seldom in the investigating team's experience had a murder scene howled horror in the manner that this one did. A brute had been slaughtered and the ugliest moment in an ugly life had undoubtedly been its passing.

'Good riddance,' they muttered up and down his street. 'Dying's too good for the bastard.'

The dead man's name was Adam Bishop and before an unknown hand had stripped him naked, taped him to his bed and inflicted upon him the many hundred skewered wounds from which his life had flowed, he had been a fifty-five-year-old builder, a self-made, wealthy man, married with six children, all of whom, like most people, were terrified of him.

It was perhaps the size of the man that made the tableau of his death so peculiarly ugly. The vastness of his surface area had allowed for so many, many punctures. And then there was his face, apparently untouched by the killer's instrument of torture, mean and bloated, cruel even in death. His neck was as wide as his head, and beneath each ear was a tattoo, 'Millwall FC' on one side and a crossed dagger motif on the other. Adam Bishop had the appearance of a man the wary might cross the street to avoid.

His had been an eye that sensible people endeavoured never to meet.

Now his eyes were closed, glued shut by a bloodied yellow crust, which had matted the upper and lower lashes together. Later, on a mortician's slab, when those lids were prised open, it would be discovered that the killer had used his skewer repeatedly on the victim's eyeballs. The last thing that Adam Bishop had seen on earth was the face of his tormentor in the process of blinding him.

'What goes around comes around,' people assured one another over celebratory drinks in the local pubs. 'As ye sow, so shall ye reap.'

Detective Inspector Edward Newson held a handkerchief to his nose and struggled to contain the nausea he felt welling up in his stomach. He must not be sick. He knew that. Puking on vital forensic evidence would not only hinder his investigation, it would inevitably lead to taunting from his colleagues. Newson was aware that he was already something of a figure of fun amongst the rougher element at Scotland Yard, and he dreaded provoking them further. Besides which, Detective Sergeant Wilkie was also present at the murder scene. Detective Sergeant Wilkie was a very attractive woman, or so Inspector Newson thought, and although he harboured no false hope that she could ever be his, he still did not wish to vomit in her company.

Natasha Wilkie had a new hairstyle that day, a short blonded bob which shone prettily beneath a rather rakish trilby hat. Newson thought it looked very nice and said so. Sergeant Wilkie replied that she thought the whole thing made her look like a boy, which was a ridiculous notion. Natasha Wilkie was not a girl who was ever going to look like a boy, no matter what hat she was wearing or how short her hair was.

Inspector Newson had been the last member of the investigation team to arrive at the murder scene, a large detached house in Willesden. The traffic had been slow and there had been a kerfuffle at the front door when he'd been required to show his warrant card in order to gain access. This was not an uncommon experience for Inspector Newson. He did not look like a policeman, or at least what people think a policeman ought to look like.

Particularly one who'd achieved such seniority at a comparatively young age. He was thirty-four years old and already a detective inspector, but at five feet four Newson was not just short for a copper – he was short for anyone. He was also pale and freckly. A ginger, in fact, but not ginger in a fierce Celtic-type manner, more ginger in a 'look at that ginger shortarse' sort of way.

Newson had kind eyes, and he always tried to smile when greeting people. He had been smiling when the constable standing guard at the front of the house had curtly asked him where the hell he thought he was going. When the constable realized his mistake he was embarrassed and apologized, but, as he explained, he'd been told to await the arrival of an important officer, and had not expected a man like Inspector Newson.

No one ever did expect a man like Inspector Newson.

When Newson finally gained access to the murder room he was pleased to see that the forensic pathologist in attendance was Alice Clarke, a woman with whom he was well acquainted. Newson always found it easier working with people he knew, people who had had time to get over the fact that they were taking their instructions from a mild-mannered ginger shorty. Besides which, Dr Clarke was attractive in a starchy, efficient sort of way, and the greatest pleasure in Newson's life (and of course the greatest pain) was attractive women.

'Hello, Inspector Newson,' said Dr Clarke. 'I was hoping they'd send you.'

'And vice versa, Dr Clarke, vice versa,' Newson replied. He peered at the purple and black cadaver.

'Nasty,' he said. 'When d'you think he died?'

'Between six and nine hours ago, I'd say. Early to mid morning,' Dr Clarke replied from behind the digital camera, with which she was recording every angle of the position of the corpse. 'As I think I've explained to you before, and contrary to popular myth, it's rarely possible to pinpoint an exact time of death.'

'We've already photographed the scene, Dr Clarke,' Sergeant Wilkie pointed out.

'I'm sure you have, Sergeant,' the doctor replied, 'but like most people these days I find it difficult to entirely trust the police. The mistakes made and the things overlooked, really it's quite astonishing. Sometimes I think there should be a judicial inquiry.'

'Ah, but who could be trusted to collect the evidence?' Newson asked.

'Good point, Inspector. A foreign force, I think. The Germans are good. Anyway, Sergeant, I prefer to collect my own reference materials so I know I've got what I want and can get it when I want it.'

'No need for me to be here at all, then,' Sergeant Wilkie said shortly.

'Certainly not on my account,' Dr Clarke replied.

Newson suspected that a small clash of authority must have occurred between his two colleagues before his arrival on the scene. He decided to ignore it and concentrated on the bloody mound that lay before him.

'His watch stopped at two a.m.'

The chunky imitation Rolex Oyster was still fastened to the dead man's wrist.

'Yes, I noticed that, and I imagine he was still alive when it did,' the doctor replied. 'If that's the cheap copy I think it is then it won't be waterproof. Mr Bishop probably bled into it and it stopped. Dead bodies don't bleed much because the heart isn't pushing the blood around, so he was almost certainly still alive when the watch stopped.'

'This man bled a lot.'

'Yes, he certainly did.'

The mattress on which the corpse lay had been sodden and had now dried almost completely into one enormous posture-sprung scab.

'Strange to lose so much blood from such small wounds,' Newson observed. 'I mean, I know there's a lot of them, but still . . .'

'Yes, I thought that. There seems to have been very little coagulation.'

'Perhaps he was a haemophiliac,' Sergeant Wilkie suggested.

The doctor pointed to a small shaving nick on the dead man's chin. 'That cut was healing perfectly normally. He wasn't a haemophiliac.'

'Just a thought,' said Natasha.

'But not a relevant one.'

'Whatever,' Sergeant Wilkie replied.

Newson wished that Dr Clarke would not be so snooty with Natasha. Natasha was a perfectly pleasant girl. In fact, as far as he was concerned, she was pleasantly perfect.

'Let me get this straight, Doctor,' said Newson. 'You're saying that the shaving nick healed but the stab wounds didn't?'

'At first glance it looks that way. It's almost as if the killer used some form of anticoagulant.'

'Ouch.' Newson grimaced. 'You mean he deliberately kept the wounds open?'

'I think it's possible. It's certainly what the evidence seems to suggest.'

'Deliberately bleeding this man to death?'

'Yes, over a considerable number of hours.'

'And Bishop would have been alive all the time that the blood flowed?'

'He would have to have been alive for the blood to flow.'

Newson removed the handkerchief from his nose and sniffed the air. He had thought when he entered the room that he'd smelled an extra element to the usual nauseating stink of death. At the foot of the bed a wastepaper basket had been upturned and its contents had spilt out underneath the bed. Newson lifted the bloody coverlet with a pencil. Scattered on the carpet were half a dozen bottles, which had contained what used to be known as smelling salts.

'So our killer quite deliberately kept his victim awake while he killed him?'

'Yes. Adam Bishop was forced to remain conscious as he was bled to death.'

2

Dr Clarke delivered her autopsy report at the case conference the following afternoon. She had probed the wounds, fossicked in the contents of the stomach, sliced the heart, measured the weight of the brain and scraped under the toenails, and now presented charts, graphs, photographs, and a plethora of clinically detached and carefully collated evidence that recorded body temperature, encroaching hypostasis, the processes of rigor mortis and liver mortis, marbling, liquefaction and putrefaction.

'The ophthalmic wounds are pretty unusual,' the doctor observed. 'I don't think there's ever been significant work done on how the globe of the eye reacts to repeated puncturing.'

'What's that?' Newson asked, referring to a photographic printout of the victim's mouth, from which a long orange ribbon of some kind had been carefully teased.

'Toilet paper.'

'I thought it was.'

'The killer stuffed it in his mouth.'

'Nice,' said Sergeant Wilkie.

'But the really fascinating development is that I was right about the killer keeping the wounds open. He used a compound commonly found in snake venom.'

'Snake venom. You're joking.'

'I don't joke about murder, Inspector.'

'But why snake venom?' Newson asked.

'Not actual snake's venom, a compound derived from it. Snake venom contains an ingredient that prevents the blood of its prey from clotting, thus making the wound it delivers more lethal. We know that he wasn't a haemophiliac from the evidence of his shaving cut. I was looking for an anticoagulant and I found one. Our suspect dipped his spike in it before insertion.'

'So he or she wanted Bishop to bleed to death?'

'Well, yes, but if that was all he wanted he could have taken a penknife and opened an artery. It seems to me that the killer wanted Bishop to die from damage inflicted by a *particular* spike, but he knew enough about killing to recognize that that weapon in itself would probably be insufficient for the purpose.'

'Really? You can't kill someone with a short spike?'

'You could, but it'd be difficult and you certainly couldn't do it in the way our suspect chose. I think he wanted Bishop to die slowly from as many cuts as possible and so deliberately avoided running the risk of delivering a knockout blow. Look . . .' Dr Clarke clicked on her computer and a diagram of the corpse appeared with coloured and shaded areas marking the intensity of the damage. 'For all the massed density of the wounds, the suspect clearly stabbed much more carefully around the main arteries than he did in the less sensitive areas of muscle and fat. What's more, he didn't puncture the heart or the brain and when he attacked the eyes he was careful to go in only an inch or so. He wanted to kill the man, but he wanted to do it slowly, on his terms and in his time.'

'And Bishop wouldn't have died from these wounds without the use of an anticoagulant?'

'Probably not, but I can't be sure. He *might* have bled to death, or the shock might have done it, I suppose, and also with so fat a man there would have been copious wound seepage. There are many other fluids in the body besides blood, and some are specifically produced during trauma. It's possible that Bishop might eventually have *oozed* to death, but it's not a given. That's why our killer needed the anticoagulant.'

'And this weapon, which was clearly so special to the perpetrator, what do we know about it?' asked Newson.

'I can't give you a factory and a serial number, I'm afraid. The wounds don't correspond with any stabbings I know. All I can say is it was a short, thin skewer exactly five centimetres long, mounted in a metal handle of some sort, the shoulders of which were approximately four millimetres across.'

'How do you know that?' Sergeant Wilkie enquired.

'Because I have eyes and I use them, Sergeant. The killer rarely pushed his spike all the way into Mr Bishop, but when he did and where the punctures are less densely clustered, it's possible to gain an impression of the hilt of the weapon from the bruising it caused around the wound.'

'Only asking,' Sergeant Wilkie said.

'The only other thing I can tell you is that I don't think this skewer was very sharp. The killer took great care to separate his thrusts but it can't have been easy using the weapon he chose. The edges of each tiny hole are slightly frayed. He had to punch it through the skin.'

'He used a blunt spike.'

'Yes, he did.'

'He didn't make life easy for himself, did he?'

'Certainly, given that this killing was clearly premeditated, the murderer could have chosen a more obviously lethal weapon. No doubt he had his reasons.'

'Or she,' Sergeant Wilkie added.

'Yes, that's true. These wounds could easily have been inflicted by a woman,' the doctor conceded.

'And this person,' Newson asked. 'What do the wounds he inflicted tell us about him or her? Anything?'

'Well, he's a thorough sort of a person, isn't he? Patient and painstaking. Those pricks were not made by somebody who was either careless or in a hurry. He's a cool customer, too. He was in that house for many hours. He must have known he could have been disturbed at any time. But this sort of observation is entirely speculative, Inspector. I'm not a psychological profiler, and if I'm honest I don't have a lot of patience with the practice. I prefer to confine my observations to what I can support with direct evidence. All I can say with any certainty is that the wounds were all made by the same right-handed person. Probably a man, bearing in mind that the victim was restrained, but possibly a woman.'

'Do you think that the victim might have allowed himself to be restrained?'

'Again I'd be reluctant to speculate, but I can tell you that there are no signs of a struggle.'

'What about the toilet paper?'

'Andrex.'

'He had Andrex in his ensuite, I noticed,' said Sergeant Wilkie. 'I'll check if it matches.'

'All I can tell you on that score,' said Dr Clarke, gathering her notes, 'is that the paper was mainly dry and in goodish condition when I retrieved it from the victim's throat, so I'm confident that it was pushed into his mouth after he died.'

3

Inspector Newson and Sergeant Wilkie stood together in the queue of a Starbucks in St John's Wood, shuffling past the muffins and the carrot cake.

'What do you think, then?' asked Sergeant Wilkie.

'Since the moment I walked into the murder room, I've been thinking that whoever killed Adam Bishop is going to kill again.'

'Why's that, then?' Sergeant Wilkie asked, and as she spoke she turned slightly towards him, causing him momentarily to lose his thread. A gap had opened up between the buttons of her blouse and he had inadvertently caught sight of her bra. Newson knew that he had only to shift his head slightly to catch a tiny glimpse of one of her breasts. But she would know, he was certain she would know. His eyes had already flicked downwards once. She was a detective; she was trained to notice things. Besides, all girls were detectives when it came to male weakness. He felt his face glowing hot. He was thirty-four, not fifteen. How *could* he be so pathetic?

Newson had been working with Natasha for nearly three years. He could not recall the point at which their spirited camaraderie and easy friendship had turned for him to this gruelling, secret infatuation. It had been quite quick, he knew that, for it felt as if he had been carrying the burden of it for ever. Looking back (as he often did) to the day when they had first met to discuss

Natasha's application to join his team, Newson did not think that it had been love at first sight. He definitely recalled that friendship had briefly preceded love, but love had come soon enough thereafter, love and with it an aching agony of longing, which had been present at every single meeting that followed.

He struggled to readjust his gaze to focus fiercely on a wicker basket filled with pieces of double-choc muffin that were being offered up for free tasting that day.

'I think he'll kill again because I think the scenario he created indicates that he's psychopathic, and being a psycho is not a part-time thing. Particularly if his problems are sexual, and, let's face it, in the end all problems are sexual.'

'Sexual? What's sexual got to do with anything?'

'I think it's highly possible that this assailant had sexual and ritualistic motivations.'

'Are all rituals sexual as well?'

'Sadly, Natasha, I've come to a rather depressing conclusion that everything is sexual . . . Just look at that advert.' Newson pointed to a framed poster on the wall featuring the coffee of the week, which boasted vanilla, coconut syrup and cookies 'n' cream. 'Read it: *hot, smooth, silky, frothy, warming, enveloping* . . . Freud would have had a field day.'

'Then Freud was a wanker.'

'I think that fact's well established.'

'A vanilla, coconut syrup, cookies 'n' cream latte is not sexual; it's a substitute for sex,' said Sergeant Wilkie.

'Well, you can't get much more sexual than a substitute for sex, can you?'

'What possible reason do you have for thinking that this was a sex crime?'

'I'm not saying it was. I'm saying it might have been. The killer bled his victim to death in a carefully prepared and highly specific manner. In my experience people who feel the need to do that sort of thing are driven to it by a very deep-seated urge, and deep-seated urges are, of course—'

'Sexual.'

'Exactly.'

They had by now arrived at the counter. 'One small latte,' said Newson to the arrogantly handsome French youth who was facing him across the counter, impatiently awaiting his order.

'One tall latte,' the youth replied.

'No, a *small* latte,' Newson corrected.

'Tall eez small,' the boy told him. 'Eet dozen get any smaller zan tall.'

'What do you mean, it doesn't get any smaller than tall?'

'Eet jus' dozen.'

'But that's a contradiction in terms.'

The boy shrugged. 'Maybe you should tell eet to somebody 'oo geeves a ferk.'

'Am I tall, then?' Newson asked.

'Eef you wan'. One pound seventy-five, please,' the youth said and turned to Natasha, who ordered a grande caramel-and-chocolate latte with mallows, for which Newson insisted on paying.

'Grande's medium,' she informed him as they collected their drinks.

'I know, I know, and medium is enormous. I have been in a Starbucks before, you know. I just think it's important to confront these things. I mean, since when did the British start drinking coffee in pints?' They found a table in the corner. 'For centuries you either had a cup of coffee or a cup of tea and cups were cups. Now everybody's walking round clutching a bucket of chocolate-flavoured froth with Smarties on top.'

'I think it's great,' Natasha said.

They sat down. Natasha dug in her briefcase and produced a sheaf of interview notes, which she placed on the table between them. The statements had been taken by ten constables, and the pile was a thick one. As Natasha leant forward to read the index her breasts touched the top of the pile. Newson stared at the ceiling and made a mental note to get a grip.

'Over two hundred people spoken to so far,' Natasha said. 'In the street, in the pubs, the local shops and at Bishop's yard. They divide into two groups: people who were terrified of Adam Bishop and people who hadn't met him.'

'Family?'

'Huge. All still connected and totally loyal.'

'Terrified of him too, no doubt.'

'Probably, but of course we haven't talked to them properly yet. The doctor says we can interview the wife tomorrow. She's all right, but a bit shocked.'

'Well, you would be, wouldn't you? Tied up in the kitchen all night listening to your husband being murdered.'

'Yes, and from what I can gather so far it seems like the Bishops had a strong marriage. They took family very seriously and if Adam Bishop loved anything at all I think he loved his wife.'

'And she reciprocated?'

'We've heard no reason to presume otherwise.'

'I suppose we should look into it.'

'If you're wondering whether she was involved, I think we're going to turn up about a million more obvious suspects than her. I have a profile from the local police. They knew Adam Bishop well and he sounds like an absolute bastard. He ran a petty fief-dom in and around the Kilburn High Road. Neighbours, colleagues, business associates – all either danced to his tune or paid the price. The Willesden Bill don't think this is a psycho thing at all, sexual or otherwise, and I don't either. It's a builder thing. Adam Bishop pushed his power too far and got done in by some angry rival or other.'

'I don't think angry rivals in the building trade do their killing with blunt five-centimetre-long spikes.'

'Look, Ed, I know you're very clever and all that, but don't you think you're being a bit *too* clever here? I mean, why don't we just pursue the obvious?'

'That's what I'm doing, and it's obvious to me that this is no ordinary revenge killing.'

'And it's obvious to me that it was. Adam Bishop was a

disgusting, ugly pig of a man. I refuse to believe that anybody seeking psychopathic sexual gratification would choose a lump like that to stick his prick into, or anything else for that matter.'

'Well, that's a very blinkered thing to say,' said Newson. 'You've been a policewoman long enough to know that it takes all sorts to make a world. Just because a person is ostensibly unattractive doesn't preclude them from sexual activity or from being sexually appealing. Otherwise where the hell would that leave me?'

If Newson had hoped that Natasha would instantly assure him that he was not remotely ostensibly unattractive he was disappointed.

'Look at the bloke, Ed,' Natasha said, producing 'before' and 'after' pictures of Adam Bishop from her bag. 'Tell me this killing is sexual.'

'You're being subjective. Go into Google and do a search on "torturing fat ugly men". I bet you score twenty hits straight off. In fact it's occurred to me that we may not be dealing with a murder here at all but a consensual sadomasochistic liaison that just went too far. Bishop may have *wanted* to be stabbed and milked of his blood.'

'Stabbed in the eyes?' Natasha asked rather too loudly, causing people around the café to look up from their frothy cups.

'Yes, very possibly in the eyes,' Newson hissed. 'Remember the case in Germany where some nutter agreed to have his penis cut off and then watched as his assailant cooked and ate it? It must have been total agony, mentally and physically, yet it was his choice and you've got to suppose he enjoyed it.'

'All right, it happens, but it doesn't happen very often.'

'Who knows how often it happens when it's consensual? That man in Germany answered an internet search appealing for a person who would consent to be murdered and eaten. The internet has opened the door for loads of activities that in the past would probably never have found physical expression. I mean, who would ever have thought that anyone would dream of such a thing as eating people, let alone advertise for it. But someone did, someone wanted a *hot, smooth, silky, frothy, warming, enveloping* human corpse to eat and he went looking for it. The only thing more astonishing is that he found a volunteer. The cannibal got an email from his lunch and in due course they met up. They both got their wish. The penis was merely an hors d'oeuvre.'

'All right, all right,' conceded Natasha. 'It could be sexual. It could be a black-magic ritual. Who knows? In a previous life Adam Bishop might have been a pincushion. There could be any number of motives, but surely the most obvious one is that this is a builders' tiff.'

'Tiff? He was stabbed three hundred and forty-seven times.'

'I *knew* Doctor Clarke would count them.'

'She's very thorough.'

'She's a very thorough pain in the arse. Look, those stabs were a warning. Bishop undercut someone, pinched one too many jobs, sold on a truckload of dodgy cement and offended the gyppos. Whatever. Someone needed to make him an example. That's what this is about. Hard men doing each other in.'

'You can't say gyppos,' Newson admonished.

'Tinkers, travellers, boys from the black stuff, call them what you like. There's a lot of very tough people in the building and associated trades. Bishop made the wrong enemies and they stabbed him to death to warn off others.'

'Stabbed him to death three hundred and forty-seven times with a five-centimetre-long skewer?'

'It would warn me off.'

'I just think it seems like a very mean-spirited little weapon to use to kill so big and violent a man. Not the weapon I'd imagine avenging navvies or double-crossed Tarmac cowboys would choose.'

'Perhaps they wanted to belittle him. You know, a little prick for a little prick, and we all know he did *have* a little prick.'

'We don't know any such thing,' said Newson. 'No six-hour corpse which has been systematically milked of nearly every drop of blood is going to appear well hung. Honestly, you girls, any opportunity to belittle the penis.'

15

'It's our job.'

'Look how many times the attacker stabbed the scrotum. You can't deny that the pricking is more intense there than on the limbs or back. And there's also a thick cluster of stabs in the anus. Bishop must have been face down for hours. Look at the photos.'

'Thanks, I've seen them,' said Natasha. 'I took them, and Mr Bishop's lacerated arse is something I'm trying not to remind myself of.'

Newson looked at the photos and was once again sickened to his stomach. These wounds were peculiarly horrible even to someone of Newson's considerable experience. The killer seemed to have taken such care with his pricks; this was no frenzied attack, it was *considered*.

'The killer *took aim*. He took aim *three hundred and forty-seven times*. He chose each new target carefully, took aim and drove in his spike.'

'That doesn't make it sexual.'

'No, but it makes it very, very weird, and in my experience of police work, weird rarely happens only once.'

4

Inspector Newson and Sergeant Wilkie drove to Willesden in Natasha's Renault Clio, and stood once more before the house in which the horror had occurred.

'I don't think I've ever seen stone cladding on a house as big as this,' Newson observed. 'I'm amazed they got permission.'

'The Bishops did exactly what they liked and got permission for exactly what they wanted. Guaranteed there's a bloke on the council planning committee who was given the choice between a handful of wedge or a handful of broken fingers. One thing's for certain, none of the neighbours were going to object.'

The master bedroom was at the front of the house, with large bay windows overlooking the drive.

'Bishop must have been in agony for the best part of twenty-four hours. Did nobody hear his screams?'

'No, because of the music.' Natasha referred to her notebook. 'The Bishops played music most of the time, and they liked it loud. Early seventies middle of the road, mostly, Brotherhood of Man, New Seekers, Tony Orlando and Dawn with "Tie A Yellow Ribbon". Demis Roussos. "Una Paloma Blanca" was a big favourite. Imagine that at full volume.'

'All night?'

'Not normally all night, but late. On the night in question it was on all day and then all night, but nobody had the guts to complain. Nobody ever crossed the Bishops, or at least if they did they only did it once. Last year a family that lived two houses down actually moved out without selling.'

Newson felt for these poor terrorized people. The possibility of noisy neighbours horrified him. He'd once lived next door to a family whose teenage sons tuned motorbikes all weekend and it had made him feel suicidal. 'Perhaps the neighbours did it,' he mused, looking up and down the quiet street.

'Well, I can assure you that not one of them's sorry he's dead.'

'It'd certainly explain why nobody seems to have seen anything.'

Newson took out his mobile phone and scrolled down to 'Clarke'.

'Sorry to disturb you, Doctor, but I just wanted to make sure that there's no chance that Bishop's wounds could have been delivered by different hands. You know – left and right, weak and strong, that sort of thing.' He had a vague memory of reading a novel or seeing a film in which the murder had been solved along these lines. 'It's just we've been wondering about the neighbours. They all hated Bishop with a vengeance. Thought they might have made a party of it.'

'I said to you at the time, Detective Inspector, it's my considered opinion that the wounds were delivered by a single suspect and I'm not in the habit of altering my conclusions to fit vague, arbitrary police theories.'

'What did she say?' Natasha asked after Newson had put away his phone.

'She said she thought it was a brilliant idea, but she still feels we're dealing with a lone suspect. Come on, let's go and talk to Lady Macbeth.'

Mrs Bishop was clearly a proud woman and despite the horror of what she'd been through it was obvious to Newson that she had no intention of allowing herself to appear vulnerable, particularly to the police. Her eyes were still red and swollen but her gaze was steady, as was the hand with which she lifted her teacup and lit her long white Kool cigarette. She'd taken trouble to have her great cloud of dyed blond hair redone and she'd applied heavy make-up to the marks left around her mouth by the duct tape. The Bishops must have been a formidable couple.

'Ad let him in, that's all there is to it. There's no way he could have forced his way through. Our house is Fort effing Knox. The only way in is the front door and no one gets through that 'less Ad or me wants 'em to. Ad's a very big bloke, you know. Or he was.'

Mrs Bishop's voice cracked very slightly as she made this last comment, and briefly she looked away.

'We can do this later if you'd prefer, Mrs Bishop,' Newson said gently, but his only reward was an angry snarl.

'There's never a nice time to talk to the police, is there?' she snapped back. 'Just get on with it.'

'You were saying that you don't believe it would have been possible for an assailant to force their way past your husband.'

'No effing way. Don't be fooled by the fact that Ad was out of shape. He was fat, but he was hard.'

'So you think that Mr Bishop might have known his assailant?'

'I just know he let him in, that's all. We've got a video-entry monitor. Nobody gets near us 'less we want 'em to.'

Newson seized upon the point. 'And yet this man got very close indeed to your husband. Mrs Bishop, forgive me for asking, but are you aware of Mr Bishop's ever taking any interest in . . . um . . . alternative sexual practices?'

'What?'

'To your knowledge, did your husband harbour any sado-masochistic or homoerotic instincts?'

For a moment Mrs Bishop's brittle confidence deserted her. She was genuinely shocked. 'Are you saying my husband was a poof?'

'I have to be open to all possibilities. You just said that nobody got close to Mr Bishop unless he wanted them to, but, as we know, his assailant got into his bedroom and tied him to a bed—'

'Take that back!' Mrs Bishop snarled, eyes flashing. 'Take that back, you little ginger wanker!'

'It would not be the first time that a death has resulted from sexual experimentation gone wrong, and the families in such instances are rarely aware of—'

'Now you listen here, you cunt—'

Natasha, who was standing behind Mrs Bishop, stepped forward. 'Mrs Bishop, will you please address the inspector as Detective Inspector Newson, Mr Newson, or nothing at all. If you carry on effing and blinding like that I'll caution you.'

'Caution me! I'm the fucking *widow*, love! You can't caution the fucking widow! Particularly seein' as how your little shortarse mate here just called my poor dead husband who ain't 'ere to defend himself a poof!'

'I shall take it, then, Mrs Bishop, that you do not believe your husband deviated from what might be called the sexual norm,' Newson said. 'Let's move on.' He smiled pleasantly but underneath he was angry. This woman did not have a solitary ounce of respect for him and why? Because he was five foot four and freckly. And Natasha, gorgeous Natasha, had felt the need to defend him.

'Please tell us what happened on the morning your husband was attacked,' he continued.

Mrs Bishop obviously felt that she'd made her point and calmed down. 'I'd been out at the shops and Ad was at home because he'd been on the piss the night before. Well, we all had. England–Turkey. Lovely night, it was. Ad hired the whole pub. Private function. Lock-in till three. Paid for the lot, food and all. Full buffet collation. Drink what you like, even champagne for the girls. Ad was like that.'

'England won that game, didn't they?'

'Of course we did.'

Newson wasn't interested in football, but everyone knew about England's famous victory.

'Anyway, Ad slept in the next morning and I went out at about nine while he was still asleep. I went down to Knightsbridge because Prada and Gucci were both having sales. I was gone about two hours. I took the Bentley because my little Merc was getting valeted. I let myself back in and was just shouting for Juanita to get my shopping in out of the boot when the bastard jumped me.'

'From behind?'

'Of course from behind. Otherwise 'e'd 'ave 'ad me fucking Jimmy Choos in his bollocks, an' mark my words, one day he will.'

'So you were unable to struggle?'

'He drugged me. Effing coward. Got a swab straight on me face. Next thing I know I'm all taped up in the kitchen staring at Juanita.'

'Who was also restrained?'

'Yes, not that you'd need to restrain her. Like a lapdog, that woman.'

'You didn't see your assailant?'

'I felt his arm around me neck, that's all. I can still feel it now. I reckon he was a fit sort of bloke, not big, but wiry. That's what I think, anyway.'

'And you're certain it was a man?'

'Yeah, I think so. Of course, these days you don't know, do you? There's some women down at my gym, muscles like navvies. Lezzers, I reckon, I mean it's the fashion, innit? Madonna an' all that, looks like a bloke these days. Turns your bleeding stomach.'

'And what happened after you came to?'

'Nothing. Me an' Juanita just had to sit there staring at each other all day an' all night listening to my own stereo which the bloke had put on in the lounge. Full bleeding bore, Everly Brothers and "Move It" and Del Shannon and the Platters over and over again. And whenever there was a gap between tracks or a quiet song we'd hear Ad screamin' in the bedroom upstairs. All night . . .'

Once more Mrs Bishop's impressive composure threatened briefly to desert her, but she recovered quickly, finding strength this time in the weakness of her maid. 'Juanita pissed 'erself an' all, on *my floor*. Dirty cow. She ain't staying, I can assure you of that. Anyway, in the morning Ad stopped screaming an' we could hear the bloke leaving and I was thinking that if I ever caught him I'd castrate him, and after that we just kept sitting till my Lisa Marie let herself in, bringing her kiddies round, and that was when we called you lot.'

The Bishops' maid was no more help. She testified that Mr Bishop had let the man in and shown him into the lounge. She'd gone in to ask if they required anything and had been dismissed. She recalled that Mr Bishop was serving drinks himself and, even though it was early, was offering whisky. The intruder had been sitting with his back to the door, and Juanita had only seen the top of his head. She could not recall the colour of the person's hair.

Newson noted that Juanita was in the habit of avoiding eye contact and focused her gaze instead on the ground in front of her. He imagined that the Bishops would not have been the kindest or most considerate of employers.

At the end of the interviews Mrs Bishop conducted Newson and Natasha to the front door, the same door through which she claimed no hostile intruder could have forced their way. Perhaps it was that that reminded her of Newson's speculative questioning.

'And I ain't forgetting what you said either, mate,' she snarled. 'Don't you worry about that. Adam woulda killed a bloke for less, and let me tell you there's an awful lot of family left who'd feel the same way if I was to tell them.'

'Are you threatening the inspector, Mrs Bishop?' said Natasha, and once more Newson wished she would not feel the need to fight his battles for him.

'Threaten *'im*?' Mrs Bishop sneered. 'What? Inspector Shortarse here? Bit beneath me, love. Maybe I'll get one of my little grandkids to do it. The eldest is only nine so that'd be about fair, wouldn't it?'

'I think I won her over in the end, don't you?' Newson remarked as he closed the garden gate behind him.

5

At the end of the second day of the inquiry Newson and Wilkie agreed to compare notes over a pizza.

'You don't have to get back?' Newson enquired. 'Aren't you seeing Lance tonight?'

'Lance is a dickhead,' Sergeant Wilkie replied.

'We all know that, but it hasn't stopped you going home to him before.'

'It's just amazing that he thinks he can say the things he says to me and get away with it.'

'It's not at all amazing, for the simple reason that he *does* get away with it, because you let him.'

'Not this time.'

'So you're finishing with him.'

'If he carries on the way he's going I will.'

'So you're not finishing with him.'

Newson and Wilkie had had this conversation or something very like it on numerous occasions and Newson could never work out how such a clever and apparently together girl as Natasha could be incapable of finishing with a man who was so obviously a waste of her time. Lance had been a shadow on Detective Sergeant Wilkie ever since Newson had known her, a boyfriend whose sole contribution to her life appeared to be to eat her food, spend her money and put her down.

Except, of course, Newson knew that Lance did far more for Natasha than that. He excited her. He thrilled her. He no doubt made love to her in a way that delighted her and left her gasping for more. To Newson it was a given that Lance was born to be sexually appealing to women in exactly the same way that he himself was not. Newson had met Lance once or twice and his charm had been clear. His mischievous smile and cocky manner were obviously what Natasha wanted. What girl wouldn't? He was tough and handsome. He made Natasha laugh and carried himself with a devil-may-care, don't-give-a-fuck swagger. In fact, the things that made Lance such a bad thing in Natasha's life – his arrogance and fecklessness – were exactly the things that Natasha liked and that kept her close to him. Newson often wondered what malign stars had been tugging at the firmament when nature had decreed that a man like Natasha's Lance would get a girl like Natasha while a man like himself never would. He knew that he could wait until the end of time and he would never see Detective Sergeant Wilkie naked. He would spend the rest of his life scavenging for the tiniest glimpse of some small part of her, while Lance, Lance who only made her sad, could glory in every inch of her almost any time he wanted. This thought truly and deeply depressed Newson.

It was his own fault, of course. When first he had realized that he fancied Detective Sergeant Wilkie he should have brought down the barriers. Experience had taught him that flames burn hotter when you fan them. He knew that he'd had a choice and that he'd made the wrong one. He hadn't been obliged to seek out Natasha's company. He could have prevented himself from looking forward to her entering the office in the morning, wondering what she would be wearing, hoping that it would be a skirt. He should have affected disapproval of her chatty, bubbly personality and her girlish penchant for gossip instead of exalting and basking in it. He shouldn't have shared jokes, sneaked glances at her legs when she crossed and uncrossed them, and he certainly should not have discussed her dreadful boyfriend with her, wallowing in the false and sterile intimacy that such conversations afforded him. He was the architect of his own obsession, but it was too late to do anything about it. He loved Natasha and the pain would simply have to be endured.

'So, d'you still think our bloke's a serial perv, then?' said Natasha now, oblivious to Newson's torment.

Newson hauled his mind back to the job in hand. 'I have absolutely no idea who or what our killer is. Let's look at what we know, shall we?'

'Right,' Natasha agreed. 'For me the most salient fact of all is that Bishop let his killer into the house and drank with him. Which tells us that he knew him.'

'Or at least was expecting him.'

'We know that Bishop had a million enemies. Almost everyone he knew thought he deserved to die. The local police have given us the names of any number of colleagues and associates who could potentially profit from Bishop's death. I don't see any need to drop some shadowy internet pervert into the mix.'

'Bishop has gone through his life being hated,' said Newson. 'He's been surrounded by enemies since he first drew breath. Nothing remotely like this has happened to him before.'

'You could say that about any killing. Nobody dies more than once.'

'The killer came prepared with his little skewer and his snake venom. How could he have known that he'd be invited in? If he was someone with a motive to kill Bishop, then Bishop would have been aware of that. He wouldn't have got into the house, let alone been served a drink. He certainly wouldn't have got Bishop up to his bedroom. We know Bishop was a sadist and lots of sadists are masochists too. Let's imagine that cruel, brutal Adam Bishop harbours secret desires. He wants to be punished, but he can't possibly risk exposing his perversion in his own circle, so he advertises on the internet for a torturer. Bishop lets the man into

26

the house, they have a drink, then he allows himself to be bound to the bed—'

'And invites this mystery man to repeatedly stick a skewer into his testicles, anus and eyes.'

It was at this point that the waitress appeared. She had clearly overheard Natasha's last sentence and her welcoming smile turned into a look of nervous alarm.

'It's all right,' Newson assured her. 'We're police officers . . . discussing a case.'

The waitress looked at Newson in disbelief. He toyed momentarily with the idea of producing his warrant card but dismissed the thought. It was embarrassing enough to have a girl think he was lying about being in the police without compounding the situation by pathetically trying to prove to her that he was.

'I'll have a mushroom pizza,' he said, and the waitress took their meal order.

'What about the maid?' Natasha continued after the girl had gone. 'What about the wife? One was in the house and the other was bound to return. If Bishop had a dirty secret he's not going to indulge it while they're around.'

'Who knows? Maybe arranging to have his wife brutalized is part of the fun. Maybe he wanted her to hear his screams.'

'To hear him die?'

'He didn't know he was going to die. That would've been part of the other fellow's plan. Or else it simply all went too far.'

'Honestly, Ed, this is just silly. It's like you're deliberately trying to come up with the least likely theory.'

'Look, of course there's a good chance Bishop was the victim of some terrible feud. And you'll no doubt see to it that everyone he ever knew is checked out until you come up with a psychopathic business rival with a blood-stained skewer buried in his back garden. But in the meantime you can't deny that this is a very strange case. The killing was so *specific*. I believe that if Adam Bishop hadn't died in the manner in which he did, the killer would have deemed his murder a failure and gone away un-satisfied. That suggests to me that this murder is as much about the killer as it is about Bishop. Something made him kill the way he did, and what worries me is it may drive him to do so again.'

The food arrived and as it did so Natasha's phone rang. Having glanced at the display to see who was calling, she excused herself and took the phone outside. When Natasha returned her face bore a defiant expression as if to say, 'Yeah, do you have a problem?' and Newson knew that, as usual, he would be dining alone.

'You have to rush? Aren't you going to eat your pizza?'

'Lance is cooking.'

'I thought you'd had a row.'

'He wants to make up. He's reaching out to me.'

'What's he cooking?'

'Steak.'

'That's nice.'

'If I can get any. Do you think they'd have it at Seven-Eleven?'

'So he's reaching out to you to bring him home some steak?'

'We're a couple,' Natasha responded angrily. 'We can do a bit of shopping for each other if we like. It's not a sign of weakness, you know.'

Newson borrowed an *Evening Standard* from the cash desk and read it while eating both pizzas and drinking a bottle of Chianti. The paper carried a report on the Willesden murder. Adam Bishop had been a major player in North London Tarmac and his killing was deemed news. It was a short article, tucked away on page seventeen. The horrific details had not yet found their way into the hands of journalists, so Newson didn't need to fear a copycat killing.

He finished his meal and, slightly drunk, asked the waitress for the bill. When it came he placed a credit card on the saucer and in so doing allowed the girl a glimpse of the police credentials dis-played inside his wallet. When the transaction was completed and feeling by now like a complete idiot, Newson absentmindedly picked up the copy of the *Standard* he had been reading and headed for the door.

'That's our paper,' the girl said, pausing before adding, '*Officer.*'

6

Newson lived in a small terraced house between West Hampstead and the Kilburn High Road. He had once shared it with Shirley, his ex-partner, but had bought her out after what they always called 'the divorce', although they had never actually been married. Shirley and Newson had split up when Shirley's infidelities had become too common and indiscreet even for Newson to miss. She claimed afterwards that seeing as how he was such a successful detective and all, she had presumed he knew and didn't mind. Newson had not known and he did mind.

They had met as students studying law at university. Their relationship had always been more mental than physical. Shirley was smart, but Newson was both funny and smart and she found this attractive. She used to tell people that when it came to brains, size really *did* matter, and that her boyfriend had a whopper. After a time Newson came to hate it when Shirley said this, because he felt that it implied that he had a small dick. He used to wish that Shirley would add 'and although he's short his dick's actually quite a decent size too,' but she never did.

During the death throws of the relationship Shirley informed Newson that she had faked every orgasm she had ever had with him. She explained that she had developed the deception early on in order to take the pressure off her in the hope that it would lead her to relax and thus encourage the real thing. Unfortunately,

Shirley felt obliged to report, it never had. Interestingly, she told him, she had not experienced the same problem with any other lover. He told her that he was thrilled for her.

Now Newson lived alone.

On arriving home after his solitary supper he took a can of Guinness from the pantry and went into his study. Newson kept his beer in a cupboard because of his belief that only lager should be served chilled. It was a point he had attempted to make to the bar staff at the Scotland Yard club, thus provoking more derision from his colleagues, who to a man believed that all beer should be served near freezing regardless of whether this rendered it tasteless. He sat in the darkness of his study for some time, thinking about skewers and snake venom and Detective Sergeant Wilkie's breasts.

After a while, at the point at which Sergeant Wilkie's breasts had forced all other thoughts from his mind, he decided to do something he'd been thinking about for months. He woke up his computer and dialled up the website Friends Reunited.com.

Until now he'd resisted the temptation. Something had always stopped him, but that something wasn't stopping him now. Later he would reflect on this and wonder what it had been that led him to finally surrender to the urge to visit that strange virtual world where fantasy could be made real as long as you stayed online and did not venture far from your computer. Perhaps it was just a simple twist of fate, but for a man with a first in law who had also been top of his year at Hendon Police Training College (in everything except fight training and all sport) that was no answer at all. The truth, which Newson hated to acknowledge, was that his infatuation with Detective Sergeant Wilkie had grown painful and obstructive. Perhaps, somewhere in cyberspace, he could displace it.

The Friends Reunited page was on his screen. Newson had already pressed the Union Jack and arrived at the British version, and now he had only to log on to join the happy throng of virtual teenagers. 'Christine Copperfield?' he whispered into the shadowy, screen-lit room, the booze giving voice to his secret hopes.

'Are you out there, Christine? . . . Hanging on the wind, crackling amongst the ions, walking in cyberspace? Dancing? Are you, Christine Copperfield?'

Or David, as the class wags had christened her on that memorable day when she had first walked boldly into Newson's form room halfway through their second year. Did she still wear a ra-ra skirt? He typed in the details of his school and his years of attendance. Such important years to him and to those with whom he'd lived them. The years when he was young. 1981 to 1988.

That skirt. That pure white ra-ra skirt. He could see it still, with its shiny red sash tied low at the waist, knotted across her hips, spread tight across her buttocks. Waists were low that season. How enchantingly she'd worn it, and with such natural grace. White and bright, scarlet for Christmas at the school disco in the deep midwinter, long, long ago.

Did she still wear pink pixie boots?

Probably not, Newson's logical mind told him, but he was quite sure that her legs would still be exquisite. They simply couldn't not be. It would take more than twenty years to mess with a pair of legs with the genetic advantages that Christine Copperfield's had enjoyed. Slim to the point of skinny, but to the point of skinny looks good at fourteen, and Christine's had looked so very, very good. December 1984. It simply did not get any better than that. Or, at least, in Detective Inspector Newson's case it hadn't.

Newson entered his name, credit card details and school information. Now he had only to push the search button to see if she was there. But instead he hesitated, fearful of disappointment, and allowed the screen to grow dim, stretching out the thrill of expectation for as long as he could. And so, as his details and dates stared back at him, challenging him to take the plunge, he closed his eyes and sought company in the ghosts of Christmas past.

In his mind's eye he could see his school once more, swathed in winter mists, the red brick cold, dark and unforgiving despite the coloured lights. He could see the sports field hard with frost, the prefabricated additional classrooms twinkling beneath the icy dust of a winter's night . . . And he could see teenagers, nearly a hundred and fifty of them, flocking to the Christmas disco, which was being held in the main hall, the hall which also doubled as a gym and which for one night only had been transformed into the home of dreams.

For the first time in Spewsome Newson's school experience the hall looked wonderful. The tinsel-laden tree, the trestle table heavy with plates of sausage rolls and bowls brimming with prawn-cocktail crisps, KP Discos and Monster Munch. There were rumours that somebody had spiked the bowl of non-alcoholic punch with vodka. In retrospect Newson was quite certain that this had not been the case, but at the time everyone believed it and it had lent a certain frisson to the sticky mix of fruit juice, Tizer, lemonade and chopped apple which they all guzzled. This was in the days before the Ecstasy revolution, ever since which, according to the press, every child has spent their entire school days permanently high. Certainly, one or two of the wilder spirits had managed a swig of booze or a puff of dope before entering the party, but in the main that night Newson and his classmates were straight and sober. Youth and Christmas were all the stimulants they needed.

Newson had arrived at the party with Helen Smart, a girl from one of the other forms in his year with whom he'd recently become friends. Helen was most certainly not one of the cool girls, the gang of which Christine Copperfield was the epicentre. Helen was one of the misfits, the post-punk goths whom the boys routinely accused of being lesbians. These girls wore baggy jumpers, steadfastly refusing to reveal the contours of their bodies, and knee-length skirts, and peered at the world from between split curtains of greasy hair. Newson had always got on better with this type of girl, and Helen was the prime example. She only listened to indie music, had recently read *The Outsider* by Camus, and hated Mrs Thatcher. Like Newson, she carried a certain status within her class for being a proper misfit. She and he were the radicals, being the only kids in the year to support the miners' strike. Helen had even been sent home on one occasion for refusing to remove the Coal Not Dole sticker from her jumper. Newson and Helen had begun to talk to each other during school Miners' Support Group meetings. They were the only fourth-year members and they had quickly become fervent co-conspirators against the world. They believed themselves to have a clear and uncorrupted overview of how crap everything was, unlike the idiots and fashion junkies who thought themselves cool. On the night of the Christmas disco Helen had surprised Newson by wearing a mini-skirt and some tinsel in her hair. The short skirt went well with her striped pink and black tights and monkey boots.

They entered the hall, walking past the forbidding figure of Mr 'Bastard' Bathurst, the much-loathed headmaster. Though he'd died in 1997, right now in Newson's wine-and-beer-soaked mind he was alive and well with a face like death, scowling grimly as he always did no matter what the occasion. 'Aha. Marx and Engels,' he said, and the lifeless smile indicated that Mr Bathurst was in humorous mode. 'Isn't a Christmas party against your principles, Helen? I thought the only party you approved of was the Communist Party.'

'I'm not a Communist, I'm a Socialist Worker, sir,' Helen replied, 'and in line with our policy of entryism I'm going to corrupt this evening from within.'

Beyond Bastard Bathurst, bathed in a golden festive glow, was Mrs Curtis. Curvy Curtis of cleavage fame! How all the boys had loved her kind smile, blond tresses and enormous tits. Newson could see her now as she had been on that special night, perched against the record table, long legs stretched out before her. No needle was ever jogged by a shapelier bottom than Mrs Curtis's.

Helen took one look at Mrs Curtis and growled that as far as

Mrs Curtis was concerned feminism might just as well have not happened.

'Yeah, that dress is really sexist,' Newson agreed, taking another long look just to be sure. Helen had stalked off to get some punch.

The computer screen seemed to grow ever dimmer with inactivity, but still Newson did not take the plunge. He was drunk and in no hurry to tempt the present, content to linger for a little longer in the safety of the past. To listen once again as the school DJ, an arse called Dewhurst from the lower sixth whose entire personality was based on the fact that he owned a double record deck, cranked up 'Do They Know It's Christmas' for the fifth time.

How happy Newson had been. How happy they'd all been, those long-since-grown-up boys and girls filled, at fourteen, with the endless optimism of youth.

Boy George, Simon Le Bon, Bananarama and all the stars of '84 sang plaintively about how hellish Christmas must be in an African famine zone. Boy George must have been happy too. He was the biggest pop star on the planet. Little did he know that his two lines on the Band Aid single would be the last time he'd ever see the Number One spot.

Boy George's were not the only dreams that would fade with the coming years. Many of the youngsters who smiled so broadly at that long-since-vanished Christmas party were destined to live lives filled with hurt and disappointment. Nobody could tell that night who would win and who would lose in life, but the years would reveal their secrets soon enough – sooner than any of those happy youngsters could ever have imagined. They thought they'd be young for ever but time was on the starting blocks, the long, lazy, sundrenched childhood stroll from the pavilion was nearly over and soon the sprint that was adulthood would begin.

The dance floor was slowly filling. One or two of the boys were even shaking a leg, having prised themselves from the walls to which they had appeared to be glued. Many of the girls had been dancing from the beginning, of course, the golden ones, the confident ones. Christine Copperfield was such a girl. The team leader.

In *that* skirt. That white ra-ra skirt with the crimson Christmas sash. And those legs. Christine Copperfield played tennis for the school. She also played hockey and netball and had won a disco-dancing competition at the local borough hall. In America she would have been named Homecoming Queen and the Girl Most Likely. She had sporty legs. Athletic. Balletic. Orgasmic. As a pubescent boy Newson had gone to sleep dreaming of those legs on so many nights. Legs that were a quantum leap out of his league. Legs that were most emphatically not for the likes of him.

Until the night of the Christmas disco in 1984.

On that night everything changed. All the rules were broken. The night the nerd got lucky. The night the princess stepped daintily and briefly from her pedestal and bestowed her favours on a member of the grubby underclass.

It had taken Michael Jackson to fill the floor. That, no doubt, and the effect of the additives in the Monster Munch, not yet known to the world as E numbers. DJ Dewhurst had put *Thriller* on to his left-hand side, dropping the needle with a flourish which was almost cool, and suddenly the party was on fire.

'Rock on, Tommy!' the young people shouted in the argot of the time as they spilled on to the floor. Everybody whooped, squeaked 'Ooh!', everybody tried to moonwalk and failed. The ones who were the worst at it were those who thought they could do it. Kieran Beattie, the class tub in an age when class tubs were rarer and hence painfully obvious targets, was actually wearing a single glittering glove. An eleven-stone, white, freckly, English Michael Jackson.

Michael Jackson was a hero then. Time would prove itself as cruel to the exalted as to the lowly.

Christine Copperfield was dancing with her girlfriends because that very afternoon she'd split up with her boyfriend, a lad called Paul from the year above. Paul and Christine were the golden couple of their years and their separation was the talk of the party. Paul was big, hard and handsome, the leader of his own little pack. He was sixteen and had a moped; what's more, he'd had the guts to remove the L-plate and carry a passenger as if he were already seventeen and had passed his test. He and Christine looked so cool as they swept up to school, he with that firm chin which clearly required regular shaving, her with those fabulous legs clamped round his muscular frame, her golden hair blowing from the edges of her helmet.

Now, it seemed, this famous relationship was history. Christine had seen Paul shopping in HMV Records with his arm round a girl from his village who went to the local comprehensive, which was known to produce nothing but slags. The girl wore white stilettos and, despite the winter weather, an electric pink boob-tube from which her frozen nipples protruded like bullets. Christine had watched Paul kissing her in front of the singles rack. She'd watched as Paul gripped her backside as they squeezed themselves into one of the listening booths. It was here that Christine confronted them as they shared a set of headphones.

Now Christine and Paul stood in very different parts of the room. Two bright and separate stars in the firmament that was the Shalford Grant-maintained Grammar School Combined Fourth and Fifth Form Christmas Disco. Two stars around which their respective posses revolved, Paul and his mates near the crisps, making plans to go to the pub, and Christine and her girl-friends bopping like wild things. A dozen cute, ra-ra-skirt-topped legs tripping, skipping and hopping about amongst their glittery little handbags, fancy party tights and clouds of Top Shop cotton, a whirl of colour and breathless delight. The lustful focus of so many male eyes, including Newson's. Six lovely girls making it noisily and exuberantly clear to one another, to the party and indeed to the whole world that they were *it*. Wild, beautiful and oh so happy.

What happened next surprised everybody. It surprised Newson

most of all. Helen had just brought two cups of fruit punch back to where Newson was standing and had asked him if he wanted to step outside for a cigarette. He'd been about to go when Christine Copperfield broke away from her group of cavorting friends and walked over to them.

'Hi, Helen,' she said.

'Hi, Christine,' Helen replied.

Then Christine turned her gorgeous violet eyes on Newson. 'Hi, Ed. Cool jacket,' she said.

Newson had chosen his ensemble with care. When you're only five foot two you have to make an effort, and he was wearing a tight-fitting grey leather bomber jacket, black button-down shirt and skinny piano-pattern tie.

'Thanks, Christine. You look amazing. Wow. Fantastic,' Newson spluttered.

'That was great about Simon Bates,' Christine continued. Newson had recently caused a huge stir by writing a spoof letter to the Simon Bates Radio One 'Our Tune' slot, in which listeners wrote in to tell the world of their heartache. Bates would read out these small sagas of tortured emotions to the accompaniment of lush backing music, ending with an appeal for true love to triumph: 'So, Sandra, if you're out there why not give Bob a call? Who knows, it could be the best five pence you ever spent.'

He'd invented a love story using the names of Mr Bathurst and Mrs Curtis, had sent it in and to the delight of the whole school it had been read out on the radio as the real thing. Even the hard nuts had had to pat Newson on the back for that one and he was briefly and happily famous.

'Yeah. I think Mrs Curtis heard about it, but she hasn't said anything. Imagine her and Bastard Bathurst shagging.'

'Yeah.'

They laughed together at the comically horrifying thought.

'Aren't you going to ask me to dance, then?' Christine said.

Newson was stunned. It was so unexpected. Helen was

surprised too, but Newson wasn't looking at her, he wasn't think-ing of her. Christine Copperfield wanted to dance! It could not have been any more surprising or indeed any more fabulous had Madonna herself walked into the party and asked him to treat her like a virgin.

'Um . . . do you want to dance?'

'"Girls just want to have fun,"' said Helen, using a phrase that was new at the time.

Newson's heart pounded, his senses on fire, but he was also cool, cool in his own quirky way. He put down the cup that Helen had brought him, bent his knees, went forward on to his toes, gripped his crotch, thrust his other arm skywards and went 'Ooh!' at exactly the point when Michael Jackson went 'Ooh!' over DJ Dewhurst's speakers.

Christine, with only the briefest of glances towards Paul, who was affecting not to notice, also punched the air and went 'Ooh!' And then they were together in the middle of the floor, leaping, jumping, punching the air and going 'Ooh!' The most surprising new couple in the school, Queen Christine and her court jester.

How the hardnuts gaped in astonishment. How they snarled. Roland Marcella. Ollie Dane. Collingwood, Reed and Simmons, and above all Paul. The tough guys of the fifth year, the ones who saw the fit birds from the fourth year as theirs by right because their own lush girls were going out with sixth-formers or lads who'd left and had real jobs, albeit crap ones.

They snarled, but there was respect there. Newson was funny, and he'd fooled Simon Bates and got something on the radio. Now he was dancing with the fittest bird in the fourth form, the fittest bird in the school, in fact. You had to respect that.

Wham! played and Newson and Christine jitterbugged briefly into each other's hearts. They shouted and let it all out to Tears for Fears, punching the air and stamping their feet. They agreed with Boy George that war was stupid and that people were stupid.

Relax, said Frankie. And relax they did, Spewsome Newson and the Golden Girl of the school. Newson the envy of every boy in the room save Gary Whitfield and Nicholas Perkins, who it was firmly believed were gay. *Relax*, the whole room shouted together. And everyone in the room wondered if Mr Bathurst knew that the song was about blowjobs.

Newson could hardly believe it when the time came to leave. The evening had passed in a thrilling blur and it was eleven o'clock. Outside Roger Jameson was puking in a flowerbed while his friend Pete Woolford finished off the half-bottle of Teacher's they'd stolen from the Pakistani supermarket. And at the front of the school parents' cars were beginning to block each other in as they arrived to collect their offspring.

Inside the twinkling hall DJ Dewhurst spun up his left-hand deck and put on 'Last Christmas', Wham!'s anthem to lost love, the Number One that never was, having been kept off the top slot by Band Aid with the single that claimed to save lives.

The final dance had arrived. And all the boys lucky enough to have secured themselves a girl to smooch with pulled their partners close and started to push the bone. Hands dropped down to close around bottoms and Fun-sized Mars bars were ground into the stomachs of those girls who would accept them. Christine accepted Newson's. He simply could not believe what was happening to him as the girl of his dreams allowed him to push his bulging Top Man trousers against her perfect tummy. Fortunately, he was wearing heels and Christine was only a few inches taller than him, so it was possible to work his quivering hips amongst the starchy folds of Christine's skirt. She even allowed him to place his face amongst the brittle, lacquered curls of her big hair and brush his lips against her adorable ears. Across the room Paul put on his motorbike helmet. For one brief moment Christine stared back before placing her face before Newson's and kissing him.

In another part of the room someone else was staring. Helen had told Newson on the way to the disco that she considered such parties bourgeois crap, and he assumed she had left hours before. But she hadn't. She'd watched all evening as Newson had danced with Christine.

In the darkness of his study Newson pressed GO and went in search of Christine Copperfield.

She was not there, of course. Why would she be? Christine Copperfield would have far better things to do at the age of thirty-five than sit alone in a dark room dreaming of kisses twenty years cold. Not Christine; she wouldn't have time, not with her undoubtedly full and successful life. Christine Copperfield did not need to look back.

But other ghosts had left their mark. Other voices from the class of '81 to '88 could be heard in the darkness.

Newson pressed 'Gary Whitfield'. Up came Gary's profile, his email and voicemail details, and the little paragraph of information that he had elected to leave.

> I hated school and it turns my stomach to return even in this virtual sense. But I had to do this because I wanted to let you all know that, yes, you were right, congratulations. I AM a poof! I am queer! Gay! Yippee, well done, you were right. And do you know what? I'm SO glad. I love my life. I love my partner, he's kind and sweet and everything that you all were not. You're shits, all of you and I HATE you! All of you. I hate the ones who tormented me and I hate the ones who let it happen. But most of all I hate YOU Roger Jameson and I hope you rot in Hell for what you did to me. Does anyone remember but me? Does anyone remember what used to happen in the changing rooms? Let me jog your memory . . .

Newson had not expected this. He'd been so swept up in post-adolescent fantasy that it had never occurred to him that the Friends site could be used as a medium for finally answering back. It was obvious, of course, when he thought about it.

41

Poor Gary Whitfield. Newson did remember what had happened to him in the changing rooms because he'd been one of the ones to let it happen. This shameful truth had been lurking at the back of his conscience ever since and now as he read Gary Whitfield's account of the torture he had suffered Newson felt his guilt keenly once more. Newson could still see a weedy little boy cowering in the corner of the changing rooms while Jameson and some of his toughs hemmed him in, whacking him with wet towels and chanting '*Poof! Poof! Poof!*' One day they'd taken Mr Jenkins' overhead projector pen and written 'I am queer' on Gary's forehead. Newson could still remember Whitfield being held down while Jameson wrote the words. The ink had been indelible and it had stayed on his forehead for days, faded but legible. Newson remembered Gary's red skin, sore from his mother's frantic scrubbing.

And he had let it happen. They had all let it happen. It was not good enough that he was small and Roger Jameson was big and tough. He could have done *something*. He should have done something.

And here now was Roger Jameson, also returned to class after twenty years. Another policeman of all things, just like Newson himself. Two in a class. It must have been Bastard Bathurst going on so much about respecting authority.

Maybe you guys remember I left at fourteen. My family went to the States and guess what? I ended up joining the NYPD! Yeah. Kind of a long way from Shalford huh?

Newson remembered Roger Jameson with very little affection. They had been friends at first. In fact, at eleven they'd been best friends, and a remnant of that friendship had remained throughout their time in the same class. But for Newson's part it had very quickly become a friendship based on unease. Jameson had a cruel streak, and he was tough. Newson had been scared of him; the whole class had been.

Currently I'm on an extended leave from the Department. In fact
I've been staying here in the UK, Rossiter Hotel, Marble Arch, if anybody wants to look me up. If I'm honest this stretch of leave is kind
of a medical thing. Being a cop is very stressful as you can imagine
and I guess I'm a little burned out right now. New York's a great city
but it's tough. Maybe you all heard about our zero tolerance thing.
Sometimes me and the boys think it's zero tolerance of cops. I was
married for a while to a sweet lady from New Jersey. We met when
we were just eighteen at a Springsteen concert, how cool is that?
I'm a big guy and she asked to get up on my shoulders. Well hey
that ain't something a girl has to ask this fellah twice! She left in the
end. Being a cop makes relationship stuff hard.

Newson wondered if Jameson had left his information before
Gary Whitfield left his. It must have been strange for him, logging
on in a spirit of melancholic self-pity and finding himself being
screamed at from across a chasm two decades wide. Newson felt
sorry for Jameson, which was the last thing he would have
expected. But Jameson was a lonely cop too. Of all the people in
Newson's class, Jameson was the last with whom he'd have imagined having parallel experiences.

Newson scrolled down the list of names. Most he remembered,
a few he'd forgotten; each one had a little story to tell, reaching
out for a sense of significance.

I did a degree in accountancy (boring I know!!) . . .
Yes I married Josh and we moved to Exeter but sadly we broke up . . .
I still see Karen and Nancy (Godmother to my three great kids!!)
and the other day I bumped into RYAN! . . .
I own my own sports shop and am SERIOUSLY into my music, so
no change there then . . .
I'm with Microsoft now and they've relocated me to Christchurch on
New Zealand's South Island . . .
I'd love to hear from anyone who remembers me . . .
If you remember me, drop me a line . . . Does anyone remember me?

Remember me . . . Remember me . . .

Was that what this site was about? Not so much a desire to remember as a yearning to be remembered.

Helen was there. He hadn't expected this one either. She'd always wanted to leave school and had done so two years earlier than anyone else, opting to do her sixth form at a tech. 1984–5 had been her last year at Shalford. Now, however, she was back. Newson wondered why. She'd left no biography, only her contact details. For a moment Newson thought about sending her a note; he'd been fond of her for those few months in the fourth form, her the angry punk and him the disaffected nerd. In the end he thought better of it. It was Christine he was after.

7

'Nothing. Absolutely nothing,' Natasha conceded.

'No shady tinkers lurking at the end of the drive, then?' Newson asked.

'No, if anyone was laying dodgy Tarmac it was the man himself, Mr Adam "Dead Bastard" Bishop, and if anyone was likely to be doing any killing and torturing it would have been him as well. The bloke was a complete shit and everybody's glad he's dead.'

'But nobody killed him.'

'Apparently not.'

All of the neighbours appeared to be off the hook. The killer had been in the house for nearly a day and a night, a long period to be without an alibi, and everybody in the street had one.

'On top of that,' Natasha moaned, 'the forensic search has turned up bugger all.'

The killer had been astonishingly careful. He'd spent nearly twenty hours in a strange house and appeared to have left no trace.

'Quite an achievement,' Newson said.

'He must have used the toilet,' Natasha said.

'If he did he was careful to leave it as he found it.'

'And he never went in the kitchen because Mrs Bishop and Juanita were in there.'

'The bastard must have brought sandwiches.'

Newson and Wilkie were sitting in Chief Superintendent Ward's outer office. Ward was the senior officer in charge of investigating unlawful killing. On the door beneath his name he had posted the legend 'Murder Room'.

'That'll have to say "Homicide Room" in a year or two,' Newson observed.

'What?'

'That's what the Americans call it, homicide, so we'll call it that pretty soon. Have you noticed how half the force has already started wearing baseball caps? What's all that about?'

'They look cool,' Natasha replied.

'They do not look cool. They look cool on Americans. We just look like farts who are trying to look like Americans.'

'American stuff's better.'

'It just looks better.'

'Well, what's wrong with that? I hated being in uniform, those stupid little girly hats.'

'I think they look nice.'

'You wear one, then.'

'Did you know that a large proportion of kids think the number to dial in an emergency is nine-one-one?'

'Then that's what they should change it to.'

'Oh, come on, Natasha! What about cultural diversity?'

'God, Ed, you can be a pain in the butt sometimes.'

'Bum! Bum! Not butt. Americans have butts; we have bums. I am a pain in the bum.'

'You said it.'

They fell silent for a moment. The superintendent's secretary brought them coffee. 'Won't be long now,' she assured them.

'Yes, he said it was urgent,' Newson said drily.

The gory details of the Bishop murder had made it to the front page of the early edition of the *Evening Standard*, and the Chief superintendent had requested that Newson personally brief him on the progress of the investigation. As far as Ward was concerned, murders that made it into the papers had to be solved. It was a pride thing. If the public were interested, Ward was interested.

While they continued to wait for the great man to receive them, Newson told Natasha about visiting Friends Reunited.

'Bit late, aren't you? Everybody else did that about two years ago.'

'Have you done it?'

'Of course.'

'Did anybody get in touch?'

'Mainly horny boys two years below me who I don't remember. Nobody you would actually like to contact you does. I think everybody plays the waiting game and doesn't want to look like they've got no new mates . . . or maybe it's just me . . . So, were you hoping to find anyone particular?'

'No, not really, just browsing.'

'Liar.'

'Not at all.'

'Of course you were. Was she there?'

'No, she wasn't, sod it. But next time I'm going to leave my profile just in case.'

'Well, don't get your hopes up,' Natasha said. 'Even if she looks at the site it doesn't mean she'll contact you.'

'Of course she will. I'm an old boyfriend.'

'If she does it could be even worse.'

'Why's that?'

'Because it'll mean she's as desperate as you and that's not the sort of woman you need.'

'What do you mean, desperate? Who says anyone's desperate?'

'Look, there're two types of people who go on that site. People who are bored and a bit curious about what happened to old classmates they can hardly remember . . .'

'Yes.'

'And people like you who haven't got a girlfriend and have got the hots in your mind for some chick who was a teenager twenty years ago. Actually, I think everyone's a mix of the two, really, it just depends on the degree. Even I was sort of hoping one particular boy might get in touch. I used to really tease and annoy him, but that was actually because I fancied him bigtime. He was a bit weird and took a lot of crap but it turned out he could play the guitar and then he started going out with an older girl from the local tech and we all realized he'd just been too cool for school and didn't give a shit whether we had a go at him or not. I often think I'd like to meet him just to tell him that I'm not actually an idiot.'

'But he's not on the site?'

'Not when I looked. He was just about the only one who wasn't as well. Like I said, too cool for school.'

'He's probably dead from a heroin overdose.'

'So, come on, admit it, this is sexual.'

'It's not sexual.'

'I thought you told me everything was sexual.'

'All right, then, it's a bit sexual.'

'There you go, and if she gets in contact with you, from her point of view that would be sexual too.'

'I'd like to think so.'

'Rekindling the fire and all that.'

'It might be nice.'

'Two lonely, needy people flailing about in cyberspace.'

'I'm not needy and I certainly don't flail about.'

'Ten to one she's in an unhappy marriage, she shags you and the next thing you know you've got an enormous, insanely jealous husband hammering on your door, and don't forget, you're only little. You don't need it. If you want sex on the internet look up some porn.'

'It's all very well for you to be all smug, Natasha. You've got a boyfriend.'

'No, I haven't. Lance is history. He's an arsehole.'

'You've dumped him *again*?'

'He dumped me. Literally. Last night.'

48

'But last night he was reaching out to you to cook his dinner.'

'Yeah, well, I couldn't get any steak, so we ate at the pub and they were having a karaoke night and I was brilliant and he was shit. You should never try and do Elvis unless you can really do it. It's just embarrassing.'

'You split up because he did a shit Elvis impression?'

'Basically. I wanted to stay and of course he wanted to go because everybody had booed his "All Shook Up", so we had a huge row outside the pub which was basically about him resenting my success and the fact that I've got my life together and he hasn't and then when we were going home on his bike he just suddenly stopped in the middle of bloody Hackney and told me to get off.'

'He just dumped you?'

'Yeah, he said everything wasn't all about me and that the world didn't revolve around me and that he was sick of it and then he just drove off.'

'In that case, forget Friends Reunited. Will you marry me?'

They both laughed and Newson wondered if he would ever in his life be capable of speaking to a girl about anything pertaining to his desire for her without pretending that it was all a ridiculous and hilarious joke.

'Don't take him back,' Newson added.

'What do you mean? Of course I'm not going to take him back.'

'I mean it. He's done you the biggest favour by being the one to do the dumping. He's the guilty party, you're the injured one. He's forfeited his rights over you. You have the moral high ground. Keep it. Don't let him back.'

'Look, of course I won't, and anyway he's not going to ask.'

'He will, he will ask. He'll realize what he's lost. He'll come back and say he was sorry, and because you're easily exploited you'll let him in. Don't do it.'

'Easily exploited? I am not easily exploited. What makes you say that?'

'Because you are.'

'I'm not.'

'You are. You've got a generous, open nature. Blokes like Lance feed on that.'

'Don't try and be nice now.'

'I'm not trying to be nice.' But Newson knew that in many ways he was trying to be nice. He was only telling half the truth. Yes, Natasha was generous and open, but she was also weak, at least as far as Lance was concerned. What was it that kept otherwise level-headed girls like Natasha locked in destructive relationships? Fear, Newson presumed. Fear of being alone.

Newson lived alone. It wasn't so bad. He wanted to tell her that. He wanted to take her hand and persuade her to be strong. He wanted to assure her that living alone was fine, it was more than survivable, it could even be good sometimes. No rows about the top on the toothpaste, first slice of toast out of the toaster every time. And, of course, no Lance.

'Don't take him back, that's all.'

'Look, he's dumped me, Ed. He's not coming back. That's it. Now shut up about it.'

'He'll be back.'

'I said shut up.'

'I guarantee it. He needs you. He'll be back.'

'He *won't*. Now shut up.'

At that point the chief superintendent's secretary invited them into the main office.

Newson had not been expecting a pat on the back, and he had been right not to.

'So, let's get this straight,' the chief said, reviewing the case notes in front of him. 'A man is tortured for half a day and a night in a quiet street. He's . . . stabbed how many times?'

'Three hundred and forty-seven, sir,' Newson replied.

'Three hundred and forty-seven times with a small skewer. The victim screams his head off, there's a complete bloodbath, the assailant has previously entered the house in broad daylight and physically restrained the maid, the wife turns up, he restrains her, he fancies a bit of music and makes free with the entertainment centre, yet he leaves not a single clue and you two don't have an idea between you.'

'I had an idea it might be a serial thing,' Newson said.

'What? One murder? How can one murder be a serial thing?'

'Nothing's emerged so far to suggest any opportunity or critical motive within the victim's own circle of influence. That suggests to me that the answer is out there in the broader community.'

'On the other hand, it could suggest that you simply haven't *found* anything yet.'

'That's clearly also a possibility, sir, although we've looked.'

'You might find it pays to try looking a bit harder before getting carried away with abstract theories. You're a copper, not a journalist, you have to be able to prove things.'

'Yes, sir. I understand that.'

'Yes, well, don't bloody forget it. I don't care what they might have taught you at law school. The majority of police work has got nothing to do with sitting around pontificating. It's about getting out there, getting your hands dirty and bloody well getting on with it.'

Ward, like many of Newson's colleagues, was uncomfortable with Newson, seeing him as a fast-tracked university arriviste. The chief had come up through the ranks and although he could see that Newson was clever he felt that such a young man could not possibly have gained the experience that his rank required. The fact that Newson had been successful with a number of seemingly unsolvable cases had, if anything, increased the resentment with which some officers regarded him. He was just so *unlike* a proper policeman. He was short, uninterested in sport and smiled too much.

When the meeting was over Natasha offered Newson a stick of her Twix. 'You shouldn't let him bully you like that.'

'I didn't think he was bullying me.'

'Of course he was. I wouldn't let anybody do that to me.'

'Ah, but you do,' said Newson. 'You've let Lance bully you for years and now you've even let him decide when the bullying stops.' As he said it he could see that he'd gone too far.

'That was horrible,' Natasha said, blinking a little.

For a moment Newson thought she was going to cry. 'I'm sorry. I did feel a bit put down, you know, by the chief and then you . . .'

'All the same, you shouldn't bring Lance into it. That's not your business.'

So many ways to feel bad all at once. Newson had hurt her, which he hated to do. He'd forced her to reveal how much Lance meant to her, which he also hated. He'd provoked her into reminding him that he had no right to make such an intimate observation for the obvious reason that she felt no real intimacy with him. Finally, he'd further undermined the true nature of their relationship, which was, of course, a professional one: two officers in the field, relying on each other in a potentially danger-ous game.

And it was also so unfair. There was no way that Natasha could claim Newson had no business bringing up Lance when she regularly volunteered information about her boyfriend and valued Newson's sympathetic ear. But then he fancied her and she did not fancy him. The playing field was not level, and unfair had nothing to do with it. When it came to an emotional stand-off right was on the side of the adored and he was always going to be the loser.

'Please forget I said anything,' Newson said. 'We have a killer to catch.'

'Well, the super isn't helping, is he?' Natasha replied. 'I don't see how much harder we could look. We've talked to everybody the bastard ever knew and come up with absolutely nothing. We don't know any more now than we knew at the scene of the crime.'

Detective Inspector Newson chewed his Twix. 'In that case I'm afraid we won't know any more until he, or at a stretch she, kills again.'

'Shit. That's depressing.'

'Unless . . .' Newson was speaking almost to himself, 'unless, of course, he's killed before.'

'Sorry?'

'Think about it. Adam Bishop's murder is already in danger of becoming an unsolved crime. Perhaps our killer has struck before and his crimes are still hanging about somewhere on the computer.

'You think we should type "short skewer in the anus" into the database and see how many matches we get?'

'I doubt it'll be as easy as that, but we could try a few searches, couldn't we? "Obsessive", "ritual", "left a very clean toilet", and see how far we get.'

Sergeant Wilkie looked at her watch. It was nearly five. 'OK, we could start now if you like. Let's face it, I'm not doing anything.'

'On the other hand, we could forget all about work, take a cab up town, get a table at the Savoy Grill, gorge ourselves on a huge and expensive dinner, then dance till dawn,' Newson said, leaving Sergeant Wilkie no time to reply before adding, 'You're right. Insane idea, madness, horrible place the Savoy, and anyway I can't dance, arse too close to the ground. Glad we've got that sorted out.'

8

'I expected someone older,' said Inspector Collins of the Greater Manchester Police when they met at Manchester Piccadilly Station. 'And bigger.'

Newson and Natasha's delving into the Police National Computer archive had unearthed three unsolved cases that Newson felt might fit the vague profile that had begun to form in his mind. The first had taken place a year earlier in the Manchester suburb of Didsbury. It was a peculiar murder featuring the same specific and repetitive attention to detail that had characterized the death of Adam Bishop. Inspector Collins had not been overjoyed to receive a request from the Metropolitan Police asking him to reopen one of his cases. He felt it cast a slur.

The victim was an army warrant officer, a twenty-eight-year-old unmarried man who had been home on leave visiting his parents. Both parents worked, and on the day of the murder had left their house together in the family car at approximately seven forty-five a.m. Warrant Officer Denis Spencer had been asleep in the spare room. His alarm was set for ten thirty and he had an appointment to meet an old friend in the pub at one thirty. Officer Spencer never made that appointment, because at some point between seven forty-five a.m. and approximately eleven a.m. Spencer had admitted his killer into the house.

'We reckon it couldn't have been any later than eleven because of the estimated time of death and the time it would have taken to do the killing,' Collins explained.

The police presumption was that the person Spencer had allowed into the house must have been armed because he or she was able to persuade Spencer, who was a big, fit man, to go downstairs into the kitchen and allow himself to be secured to a chair with duct tape. The police had not ruled out the possibility that there had been more than one assailant, but apart from the corpse and the blood splattered around it very little evidence of any intruder remained. As in the Bishop case, whoever had attacked Spencer had expertly covered his tracks. And, most significantly, the victim had been subjected to a strange and unusual torment. He had been hit on the head repeatedly, with a soft flat object, perhaps like a large rubber mallet. Warrant Officer Spencer was killed not by the force or weight of the blows, but by the number and frequency. He had been struck many, many hundreds of times over a period of between five and six hours, causing the vertebrae in his neck to become impacted and his brain to be slowly mashed from being bounced back and forth in the skull.

'The brain was massively bruised,' the Greater Manchester police doctor explained to Newson when they met at Deansgate Police Station. 'I remember the details well because it was such a very strange way for a man to die. I mean, I've dealt with any number of violently inflicted brain injuries in my time, but it's normally about one or two big blows. The harder the man is hit, the more damage is done. Poor old Spencer wasn't hit hard at all, not like with a hammer or a brick. The blows taken individually would not even have been particularly painful. I think of them as slaps rather than blows. The skull was hardly damaged, but the hair and skin on the scalp were completely worn away. I don't mean knocked off or torn out, I mean worn away. Imagine how many times you would have to slap somebody on the head to *wear their hair and skin away*. The scalp bleeds copiously, of course, and the man's face and shoulders were caked in it, as was the surrounding carpet. Eventually the man would have been in agony.'

'Was the victim conscious while he was being beaten?'

'Oh yes, conscious all right. The killer made sure of that.'

'Smelling salts.'

'Yes. Nasty bugger. Trying not to let him off until the final blow, although God only knows what sort of mental state he would have been in by then. Completely tonto, I imagine. His brain was literally rattling around in his skull.'

'And you have no idea what the murder weapon was?'

'Well, if you really want to know, I think it was a telephone book. That would certainly fit the profile.'

'But not the Spencers' own?'

'No, they were still intact. Besides, the killer would have needed more than a couple to do it. I conducted a little experiment at the time, whacking a Thomson's Local Directory on my stair post. It only took about twenty minutes for it to start to disintegrate. My guess is that the killer would have needed fifteen or twenty.'

'Twenty phone books? Not an easy murder weapon to carry about.'

'No, and you can imagine the mickey-taking I took at the time when I stupidly mentioned my theory. Assault with fifteen or twenty deadly phone books. Oh yes, I certainly paid for that one.'

'Maybe he wrapped one book up in the duct tape he used to secure the victim. That would've made it last.'

'I didn't find any trace of tape in the scalp, and there would almost certainly have been some microscopic residue.'

'But there was a trace of fabric fibre, wasn't there?'

The doctor scrolled through the forensic notes that he'd taken at the time, punching up jpegs of the wound showing ragged bits of blood-caked skin and hair lying across the exposed bone of the skull. 'The killer certainly did his best to clean out the wound, but of course he couldn't get it all, no one ever can, and, yes, there were twenty or so tiny threads of fabric.'

'Any ideas of what they might have been?'

'I thought that perhaps they came from the sleeve of his jumper.'

'Anything else?'

'Nothing that could help you.'

'Nothing unusual at all?'

'Well, apart from the funeral.'

'You went to the funeral?'

'Yes, I do try to attend them when I've had the deceased on my table, so to speak. Small gesture, really. I do it for the families. You see, they *know where I've been*.'

'Where you've been?'

'Inside their loved one. I've seen more of the person they loved than they ever did. I've been to every private place and looked at every little personal secret. I'm an intruder, another abuser, really, and I like to show that I always bear in mind that I am intruding on a fellow soul. Another human being who loved and who was loved.'

'That's an impressive point of view.'

'It's amazing how much they appreciate it. Never once has a family failed to thank me. Of course the funny thing about Spencer's funeral, the reason I remember it so well, is that I don't think he was loved very much at all, because I never saw a sorrier turn-out in all my life. Just me and his parents, his two brothers, the one surviving grandparent and the vicar.'

'A bit embarrassing, I imagine.'

'I'll say. What's more, I'd already agreed to do the sherry and sandwiches bit afterwards. I mean, what do you *say*?'

'"Lovely funeral," I suppose.'

'Except it hadn't been. There was a curious incident.'

'What?'

'It happened as they were lowering the coffin into the grave. Suddenly from nowhere this young fellow in army uniform appeared and played the Last Post. He must have been hiding behind a tree.'

'Well, that's quite nice, isn't it? Military man and all that.'

'He played it on a kazoo, you know, those things that sound like a fly farting. Not at all sombre or dignified. I don't think it was meant as a mark of respect.'

'Didn't anybody say anything?'

'The Last Post isn't very long, is it? I think we were all too taken aback. Anyway, the moment it was finished the man disappeared. Most embarrassing.'

As Newson took his leave the doctor asked to be remembered to Dr Clarke. 'We were at med school together,' he said. 'I always fancied her but she used to go with arty types.'

'Ah yes,' Newson replied. 'She ended up marrying a musician. A mandolin player.'

'You're kidding. Not a lot of money in that, I imagine.'

'I don't think she married him for money.'

'Or the size of his instrument either. Ha ha. A mandolin, eh? Not very rock 'n' roll.'

'In my experience very little in life is.'

'Well, give her my love, will you? Lovely girl. Lovely, lovely girl.'

Newson noted the wistfulness in the doctor's voice. Youth was so very fleeting, but what an impression it left. It was as if the rest of a person's life was merely a pale reflection of its promise.

9

The second case which Newson had discovered in the police database was one with which he was already familiar. Anybody who read the newspapers knew about this killing. It had been the stuff of tabloid dreams.

Angie Tatum, ex-page-three stunner, current celeb status D list slipping to E, one of the growing number of damaged identities of whom most people had heard but in whom no one was remotely interested. A woman who had briefly been the toast of a certain part of the town (notably Stringfellows nightclub) during the period in the eighties when page-three girls had been news. Now, nearly twenty years later, Angie was news only because she'd once been news, and had recently been lampooned in the press for being rejected by the producers of *I'm a Celebrity, Get Me Out of Here*, despite her promise to reveal again her once-celebrated breasts.

A sad story of a sad life. A little girl with big tits who had dreamt of stardom and who now, having briefly touched the hem of its garment, was stumbling towards anonymity. Then suddenly, against all expectations, Angie Tatum became major news again, when her rotting body was discovered six weeks after her soul had departed it, the victim of a brutal murder and mutilation.

The killing had occurred at Angie Tatum's home, one of the smaller, cheaper but still desirable flats that make up the residential developments lining the river between Fulham and Chelsea.

The crime notes taken at the time suggested that Ms Tatum probably paid for this accommodation from the proceeds of high-class prostitution. She herself would probably not have recognized what she did as such, but she was closely connected with a number of nightclubs, where she had many wealthy gentlemen friends. The CCTV surveillance cameras that covered the entrance to the block in which Ms Tatum lived recorded many comings and goings of these friends, and the police concluded that Angie Tatum's ex-celebrity and thrice-remodelled breasts still carried a market value sufficient for her to live in some degree of comfort. One of these visitors, a man who had taken care not to present any identifying features to the surveillance cameras, had killed her.

'She'd been dead a month and a half,' Dr Clarke said, for by coincidence it had been she who attended the murder scene, the Kensington & Chelsea police pathologist being fully occupied at the time with a train crash at Victoria Station. 'Obviously there had been a fair bit of damage to the cadaver. Six weeks is a fair time to rot.'

'Amazing how maggots just seem to materialize out of thin air, eh?' observed Newson.

'Yes. Like wheel clampers.'

Newson looked at the photographs of the dead woman, once such a cute, fresh-faced teen whose sixteen-year-old breasts had simultaneously charmed and outraged the nation. He and Angie were almost exactly the same age. When she had first revealed her double Ds to the nation he had been in the lower-sixth form doing French, English, history and sociology. He could remember masturbating over her pictures when they appeared in the *Daily Star*. Now he was looking at Angie Tatum's naked photographs again, pictures of a disfigured, maggot-infested corpse. It seemed to Newson that he ought to be feeling some sense of grave and dramatic irony about it all. Instead he shared with Dr Clarke the details of the Manchester murder.

'So, similar to this case in that the victim was secured to a chair,' Dr Clarke observed.

'Yes. And to the Willesden murder in so far as Bishop was secured to a bed.'

'But then murderers often tape up their victims,' Dr Clarke pointed out.

'Yes, sadly they do. By the way, the Manchester pathologist sends his regards. He says he was at medical school with you.'

'Not Rod Haynes?'

'That was his name.'

Dr Clarke reddened and smiled all at once. 'Good heavens. Roddy Haynes. I always fancied him, you know, but he used to prefer idiots.'

'He fancied you too.'

'No, really? Why didn't he say so? I thought he was lush.'

Newson had never heard Dr Clarke use a word like 'lush' before, and it sounded almost as though she was speaking a foreign language. In a way she was, because it was a word from her past, and the past, as has been observed before, is another country . . .

'How little we know, eh?' Dr Clarke mused. 'Rod Haynes wouldn't have had to ask twice. I'd have had him like a shot.'

'Well, he sends his best. You should look him up, you know, on Friends Reunited. Say hello.'

'Oh, I don't think I could be bothered doing that. It's all so long ago. Besides, I always feel uncomfortable about putting my details on the net.'

But Newson could see that Dr Clarke's imagination was flying. The years had slipped briefly away and once more the past was in the room.

Collecting herself, Dr Clarke brought out copies of all her case notes, which she presented to Newson in a neat folder. 'I'm afraid you won't find much there. Basically, the killer tied Ms Tatum up, then disfigured her and disappeared, leaving her to die.'

'Just the face?'

'Yes, just the face. No skewer wounds.'

'He split her lip.'

'Yes, very nasty, that. Sharp knife, straight cut from the middle

61

of her upper lip to her nose, then he folded one side of the lip across the other and stitched them together.'

'Without an anaesthetic?'

'Certainly without an anaesthetic. There was no trace of anything like that in her blood.'

'And he wanted her to see exactly what had been done to her.'

'Well, that's an inference which is your department, Detective Inspector, but it looks that way, doesn't it?'

It certainly did. The killer had secured Angie Tatum on her dressing-room chair, and had left her staring into the large three-sided mirror standing on the dressing table. Then to be absolutely sure that Tatum could not avoid seeing her reflection, no matter where she turned her head, he placed all the mirrors he could find in the house (and there were plenty) around her. He'd torn them from the wardrobe doors, brought in two large ones which had hung in the front hall, and prised the reflective tiles off the bathroom wall and attached them to the ceiling above her head.

Then he had superglued Angie Tatum's eyelids open.

'Tell me how she died,' Newson asked.

'Dehydration, starvation, deprivation. He knew she lived alone. He knew she was estranged from that awful mother who used to trot round the chat shows with her. He knew nobody cared a damn about her. The CCTV recorded that a few people tried to visit, but when they got no answer they went away. The killer left her bound and gagged, chair screwed to the floor, staring at her mutilated face until she died.'

10

The last of the unsolved cases that had caught Newson's eye was a kidnapping and murder in Stratford-upon-Avon. Newson took the train, which he always did when travelling outside London, because he preferred it to driving. This was another aspect of his character that his colleagues at New Scotland Yard found utterly baffling. On the journey Newson decided that he would enter his own profile on the Friends Reunited site. Perhaps Christine was doing as he had done, spying on the site without committing herself. He hoped that if he made an appearance it would flush her out. He took out his brand-new internet-connected mobile phone, opened up the tiny keyboard and began to type his message.

Hi, everybody. It's Period Head here. Yes, the Ginger Minge aka the Human Carrot, Spewsome Newson and, on very rare occasions, Edward. It was nice to hear news from those of you who've already signed up. Hi Gary, sorry you hated school so much. Hi Roger, I'm in the police too, as it happens. Not what I expected when we were all young but sadly Queen decided not to replace Freddie Mercury with me and there aren't many coal mines any more, so I never got to take over from Arthur Scargill. I'm with the Met, a detective in fact, which sounds more exciting than it is. I'd love to get in touch with anybody who remembers me, so why not drop me a line?

He considered adding a PS to say that he was single, but decided it might look a bit desperate, besides which the fact that he hadn't mentioned a partner would probably do the trick.

Newson had never visited Stratford-upon-Avon before. He'd expected an entirely half-timbered town filled with perfectly preserved Elizabethan buildings. Though there is much of this to be found in Stratford, it also has considerable modern developments away from the centre, and it was from one of these streets on a quiet Sunday afternoon that Neil Bradshaw had been spirited while walking home from the newsagent with his copy of *The Sunday Times*. From there he was taken to a seed shed on a farm two or three miles along the Birmingham Road, near a village called Snitterfield, and it was in this shed that he died.

Newson met Natasha at the gates to the farm. She had driven up from London earlier in the day to talk to the local police.

'They know when he was lifted because he'd been out to the newsagent and hadn't come back.'

'His family missed him?'

'No, there was no family. He was divorced, three times. He lived alone, between girlfriends, I suppose. The neighbour said he knows Bradshaw never came back because he was in the front garden waiting for him.'

'Sunday drink?'

'Hardly. They were in dispute over a hedge. Our Bradshaw had been growing one of those things that do a metre every five minutes and the bloke next door was going to have it out with him.'

'But he never got the chance.'

'No, because Neil Bradshaw never came back from the newsagent.'

The seed shed in which Neil Bradshaw had been found dead stood alone, isolated from the other farm buildings by a large field, and it was here that Newson and Natasha met Douglas Goddard, the farmer who had rented the shed to the killer.

'We never met,' Goddard told them. 'He only dealt with me over the phone. Said he was an artist, he needed privacy to work and apparently my shed had perfect ambience.' Goddard was standing in the shadow of a dilapidated combine harvester around which many weeds had grown, weeds that were now stealing their way up into its mechanism.

'He left cash in an envelope in my postbox down at the road and made it very clear that if he was disturbed he'd be off and take his money with him. I didn't mind a bit, a quiet tenant's a good tenant as far as I'm concerned, and he paid well over the odds. I'd like to add, Inspector, that I intended to declare the cash in my tax return, and I still do, of course, although it seems funny now, almost like blood money. I've thought about giving it all to charity, as a matter of fact.'

From the way this last sentence was left hanging in the air it was clear to Newson that thinking about it was as far as Goddard would ever get with his charitable instincts. Newson had already learnt from the original interview notes taken by the Stratford police that Mr Goddard had been at great pains from his first interview to stress his intention to declare the rent he had received. Indeed, he seemed to view the whole affair as an effort by an anonymous murderer to get him into trouble with the Inland Revenue.

'I was happy to let the seed shed out because I don't need any seeds at the moment, seeing as how the whole farm's lying fallow. Look at my combine, sunflowers in the cab. Strange sort of farming, I call it, but then these are very strange times. Did you know that the Department of the bloody Environment pay me to sow meadows? I mean, what's the use of a meadow when it's at home? You can't eat dandelions.'

'Meadows are an essential element in biodiversity,' Newson explained. 'The wild flowers bring the insects, the insects bring the birds.'

'And what do the birds bring? Bird shit,' the farmer replied. 'It's like with my hedges. I'm not allowed to tear them up. My own bloody hedges! Just so some hedgehog's got somewhere to sleep for the night. Who, I should like to know, gives a toss where hedgehogs sleep? You townies, that's who. You don't know the first bloody thing about country life, but that don't stop you making rules about it.'

'Excuse me, but you seem to be mistaking us for people who are remotely interested in your opinions,' said Natasha, who had a hangover and was in no mood to put up with the whining of reactionary countryfolk.

'Steady on, Sergeant,' Newson said.

'Well, just ask him what we need to know and then we can get out of this bloody field.'

'You can't talk to me like that, young lady,' Goddard complained.

'Of course I can,' Natasha replied. 'Just like I can check the tax discs on those two clapped-out old bangers I saw in your barn. You have to register all vehicles these days, you know.'

'Look, we won't keep you long, Mr Goddard,' said Newson in his most conciliatory tone. 'I just wanted to confirm that you only ever saw your tenant visit once.'

'Like I said, I never actually saw him at all, but on that Monday morning, the one after the Sunday when I now know that poor bugger got kidnapped, I saw there were a van parked down at the shed. As I told your blokes at the time, I think it were probably a Toyota Hiace, but I couldn't be sure 'cos like I say I'd been told to steer well clear and I did.'

'You weren't curious at all?'

'Why would I be? The bloke said he was an artist. I don't give a toss about art, do I? He paid. That satisfied my curiosity.'

'And the van was there all day?'

'Yes!' Goddard said with the exasperation of one who has had to tell his story before. 'It were there all through Monday and it were still there when I turned in that night. I remember because he was still playing his music . . .'

'You mentioned the music to the officers at the time, but

you didn't say what music it was. Do you remember?'

'I could hardly hear, what with it being so far away and that, but at night the wind changed and I caught the odd bit. Old stuff, from when we were kids. You know, Slade, glam rock an' that, least it could have been.'

Inspector Newson thanked the farmer for his help and he and Natasha made their way down to the seed shed that no longer contained seeds.

Despite the fact that the murder had taken place almost a year earlier, the scene remained very much as it had been when the starved and mutilated corpse of Neil Bradshaw had been carried from it. Either out of sloth or squeamishness, Goddard had elected to let things lie and the crude soundproofing with which the killer had lined the walls and ceiling was still in place, as were many of the planks, bolts and bars that had been installed in order to make the shed into a secure prison.

'He must have soundproofed the place just before he left, or Goddard wouldn't have heard the music,' Newson said.

'Maybe,' Natasha replied. 'Although if it had been on loud enough he might have heard it anyway.'

'Well, he certainly used the music to cover up the sound of Bradshaw's screams.'

'Which gives you a link to the Bishop murder, I suppose.'

'It's something, isn't it?'

Together they looked around the silent, empty shed. The air was heavy and stale and smelt of hay and dirt.

'If the killer hadn't stopped paying the rent I imagine the corpse would still be here,' Newson observed, for it had only been the absence for a week or two of his cash envelope that had led Goddard to investigate. 'I suppose our murderer knew how long it takes for a man to die of thirst, and once he knew his man was dead he didn't want to waste his money paying any more rent.'

The floor of the shed was bare now, but the scene-of-crime photographs showed that it had once been littered with instruments of torture: pliers, clamps, tweezers and a vice. An examination of the corpse suggested that these tools had been used to torment the victim's genitals and nipples.

'So the torturing didn't kill him?' enquired Natasha.

'No.'

'But it would have hurt.'

'It certainly would.'

The autopsy made grim reading. The killer had begun the torture using his hands, squeezing and poking at the victim's crotch and chest. The pectoral bruising in particular showed evidence of hard gripping and squeezing by both a left and a right hand, lots and lots of fingerpad bruising.

'He groped him?' Natasha said.

'Essentially, that's what he did,' Newson replied, 'and not very gently either. He really bruised the man's chest. Digging his thumbs deep into the pectorals. Bradshaw was quite a big man. He had tits, and the killer really went to work on them.'

Natasha grimaced. 'When I was fifteen I had a boyfriend who used to grope me too hard.'

Newson gritted his teeth and swallowed.

'He used to stop when I asked, but only after I'd asked a few times,' Natasha said. 'Years later I worked out that he had enjoyed the pain he caused me.'

'Why did you let him do it?'

'I didn't, I dumped him.'

'After how long?'

'Oh, I don't know . . . A month.'

'A month? You let him hurt you for a month before you dumped him?'

'It might have been less . . . Could have been a bit more.'

Natasha looked embarrassed. Newson did not pursue the point.

'After the groping, the killer began to use his tools.' It made Newson's own balls ache just to say it.

'Fuck,' said Natasha, for want of a more useful response.

'Then Bradshaw was sodomized. The pathologist was pretty

certain it was done with the handle of a claw hammer that was found with the pliers.'

'Nice.'

'Then he put a pair of knickers on his victim.'

'What, lingerie?'

'No, just white cotton girl's knickers from Marks & Spencer. Also a short, pleated tartan skirt.'

'So the suspect crushed Bradshaw's balls and then dressed him in knickers and a skirt? Do you think he wanted to turn him into a girl? Like some weird transsexual thing?'

'I don't know. That wouldn't explain him torturing the man's nipples.'

'So how did he finish him off?' Natasha asked. 'I'm sorry, I know I should be up to speed on all this, but I was pissed last night with the girls. It was a meeting of the All Men Are Bastards Club.'

'It's the men you choose to associate with who are bastards.'

'No, you're wrong there. It's actually been scientifically proven that all men are bastards. Not you, obviously, you get a special exemption.'

Inspector Newson presumed that this must be on account of the fact that he was short, mild and clearly in Natasha's opinion devoid of any hint of danger, sexuality or anything that she might find remotely attractive. 'I'm honoured,' he said.

Newson then explained that after the killer had had his fill of torturing Bradshaw, he had placed food and water on a little ledge, which he had secured to the wall about eight and a half feet from the ground. The killer had then put a chair below the ledge. By standing on the chair Neil Bradshaw would be able to stretch to within half an inch or so of the supplies but no nearer.

'That's just medieval,' said Natasha.

There were four holes in the floor just in front of the chair, where a television camera had been bolted to the boards, lens pointing upwards. The camera had been connected to a television monitor suspended on a bracket from the ceiling directly above the ledge.

'The camera had no recording function. It merely transmitted a live picture to the screen.'

'So Bradshaw had to watch himself reaching for the food.'

'Watch himself from below.'

'Weird angle to choose. You'd have thought the sicko would have wanted Bradshaw to stare into his own desperate face.'

'No, he wanted Bradshaw to stare up the skirt.'

'That is so weird.'

'Yes. At this point we presume that the killer left Bradshaw to it. Bradshaw died about a week later from his wounds, which by then were rotting and infested. You can see from the way the planks beneath the ledge are scuffed that the tormented man repeatedly stood on the chair and reached for the water which was forever beyond him. Those scratches on the wall below the ledge were made by his fingernails.'

After a half-hour or so inside the shed, which told Newson nothing more than he knew already from the crime reports, he and Natasha repaired to the Dun Cow, a nearby pub which promised basket lunches.

'The victim,' Newson explained after they had ordered their food, 'was probably kept in the van in which he was snatched for the rest of that first Sunday and was delivered to the seed shed under cover of darkness.'

'Well, then, this killer,' Natasha replied, 'and let's remember we still have no proof that these killings are connected, but if they are, this killer seems to have been pretty lucky in how little initial resistance his victims put up.'

'Yes, perhaps he knew them all.'

'Wide circle of friends. A north London builder, a Manchester squaddie, a Kensington slapper, and this bloke . . .'

'The curator of Anne Hathaway's Cottage, who incidentally owned the largest stash of pornography the investigating team had ever encountered.'

'Anything dodgy?'

'Dodgy, yes, but nothing illegal.'

'Why would our man know all these different people?'

'Why wouldn't he?'

'There has to be a motivation. Knocking off acquaintances from various parts of the country just because you know them isn't enough.'

'Well, he likes killing people, and it's easier to capture people you know.'

'Shit. With friends like that, eh?'

'On the other hand, perhaps he didn't know them.'

'In which case how does he get into their homes and lure them into vans?'

'I have no idea.'

'Possibly,' Natasha said, attacking her scampi and chips, 'because "he" is actually four different people who conducted four completely separate murders and we're wasting our time.'

At that point Natasha's mobile rang. Newson knew that it was Lance.

'I'm not going to answer it,' she said and let it ring.

Moments later when her phone rang again she did answer it, and retreated to the car park to conduct her conversation in private. When she returned she looked angry as she usually did after her conversations with Lance.

'I don't know why you bother going outside,' Newson said. 'You always tell me what he says.'

'He says I'm suffocating and possessive.'

'Why should he care what you are? He dumped you. You're finished. He has no right to be ringing you up to tell you what you are and aren't.'

Newson did not need the embarrassed pause that followed to work out that Natasha and Lance were once more an item.

'That didn't take long, did it?'

'I don't want to talk about it.'

'OK.'

'He came round last night.'

'I thought you were at a meeting of the All Men Are Bastards Club.'

'He was there when I got home, on the couch.'

'He had no right to let himself into your home. You should have arrested him.'

'Don't be stupid.'

'I'm serious.'

'You're being stupid. Anyway, he said he knew he'd been a prick. He was really nice and totally sorry.'

'I thought all men were bastards?'

'They are, but they're all we've got. Look, Lance has shit to deal with too, you know. He's uptight at the moment.'

'Oh, well, that's all right, then.'

'He said I had to give him another chance, that I owed him that at least.'

'You don't owe him anything. He owes you a lot of rent, but you don't owe him anything. I told you he'd come back. You said you wouldn't have him.'

'It's partly my fault. I mean, I do work a lot and I'm really into my job.'

'Which is commonly considered to be a good thing.'

'Yes, but perhaps I should've made more time for him and me. I mean, he's not working, is he, and I've got a pretty cool job, and that can be quite undermining for someone, particularly a bloke, and sometimes I don't think I'm sympathetic to that. I think I need to be there for him more.'

'I thought you were being suffocating?'

'Yeah, but he says I have it both ways. Like I want him to be a proper boyfriend, be faithful and not be out all night getting pissed but, on the other hand, I have this great job to do and I'm always going on about it and I need to give him some space but also be there for him, which I think is actually quite reasonable.'

Newson took a deep breath. He should not, absolutely *should not* be having this conversation. Even if he had not been remotely attracted to Detective Sergeant Wilkie it would have been inappropriate for him to be party to his subordinate's private life in this way. But he *was* attracted to her. He was in love with her. He thought about her when he went to sleep at night and he was thinking about her when he woke up in the morning. He was *obsessed* with her, and allowing himself to masquerade as nothing more than a sympathetic friend was simply feeding the obsession. He could not help it, though. Talking to Natasha about her boyfriend was the only intimacy with her that he had.

'I'm trying to understand his argument here,' Newson said. 'He's saying that if you don't want him to screw around and get pissed all night you need to take less interest in your work?'

Natasha did not reply.

'Natasha, this man is using you. He bullies you when you're together and when he drops you he bullies you into having him back . . .'

'I said I don't want to talk about it.'

'But we *are* talking about it.'

'I knew you'd be like this.'

'How else can I be?'

'I'm not hungry. I'm going to sit in the car. See you when you've finished.'

And Detective Inspector Newson was left alone with his chicken and chips.

11

Inspector Newson and Sergeant Wilkie spoke little on the drive
back to London, both of them lost in their own thoughts. Newson
sat in the passenger seat, staring out of the window in order to
avoid spending the entire journey taking sidelong glances at
Natasha's legs as she changed gear. Instead he tried to concentrate
on murder. He racked his brains, searching for a single name or
detail to connect conclusively the Willesden killing of Adam
Bishop with the three earlier crimes.

There was nothing. Of the thousands of names that had been
entered into various crime reports, the neighbours, friends,
colleagues and enemies of the deceased who had been interviewed, not a single name cross-referenced between one murder
and another.

Similarly, of all the tools, tapes, prints and microscopic threads
that had been identified and catalogued by the various forensic
teams, not one item was duplicated in any of the killings. Duct
tape was a feature of three out of the four crimes, but it was the
commonest type of duct tape. Rope had been present at the same
three murder scenes, but rope that could be bought at any DIY
shop or superstore.

Nonetheless, Newson persisted in his suspicion that the crimes
were connected and that he was dealing with a single serial killer.
The circumstantial similarities were too strong. Over a period of

not much more than a year, four murders had taken place in which the victims had allowed themselves to be subdued, held captive and then, while still conscious, were subjected to a lengthy, ritualized torture and killing. The victims had been *conscious* of their fate, not just the pain but the manner in which the pain was inflicted. It was important to the killer that they knew what was happening to them, that they *understood* what was happening to them and how it was going to end. Newson presumed that the killer's motives were sexual because he couldn't think of any other reason why someone would do these things except for the excitement, besides which, as he knew from his own experience, in the long run, everything came down to sex.

Eventually Newson tried to put murder from his mind and instead indulged himself further with stolen glances at Natasha's shapely legs. They were coming into London by this time, in dense traffic, and Natasha was forced to work the clutch of her little Renault Clio, causing the muscles in her legs to ripple attractively above her little boots. Natasha's legs were the part of her to which Newson felt most connected, they being the only part of her over which he could be said to have ever had any influence.

When he'd first known Natasha she'd rarely worn skirts or dresses, explaining that she had no high opinion of her legs, which she thought were too short. Newson had informed her that she was either mad, blind or both. He had assured her, in what he fondly deluded himself was a disinterested and offhand manner, that viewed objectively Natasha's underpinning was in the premier league, and that outside the world of *haute couture* it was well known that length was no substitute at all for shapeliness.

'Nobody really fancies those weird, skeletal, nine-feet-tall fashion models,' he told her. 'They're just there to make the dresses look long.'

Since then Natasha had 'got them out', as she put it, on a much more regular basis, and had been kind enough to give Newson some of the credit for giving her the confidence to do so. Newson could not decide whether this confession had caused him more pleasure or pain, since it was so obviously meant in an entirely sisterly manner. Eventually he concluded that it was too close to call.

Newson's mobile rang, returning his thoughts to murder.

'Inspector Newson? It's Dr Clarke.'

'Hello, Doctor.'

'That Manchester case, the man with the mashed brain. Rod said he thought it was phone books, didn't he?'

'Rod? So you phoned him, then?'

'Yes. Is there a problem?'

Newson could hear the defensiveness in her voice. 'No, no problem.'

'I looked him up on the Friends Reunited site as you suggested, and he sent me his number.'

'Right.'

'What do you mean, "Right"?'

'Nothing. I don't mean anything.'

'It was very nice to speak to him.'

'I'm sure it was.'

'What do you mean, "I'm sure it was"?'

'What do you mean, what do I mean? I don't mean anything. Why should I?'

'Exactly. There's no reason.'

'No, there isn't. You mentioned the phone books. I presume you discussed the Manchester unsolved?'

'Yes, we did, as a matter of fact, and those fibres he found in the scalp – I think they're from a book cover. Books used to be cloth-covered; they still are if you get them from the Folio Society. I reckon that's what the fibre was. Nothing to do with telephone directories at all.'

'You think that Warrant Officer Spencer was murdered with an old book?'

'Well, several of them, or new books with cloth covers.'

'I see. Well, thanks for that. I'll have somebody do a little research into book bindings. I'm sure you're right.'

'I'd have looked into it myself, but my husband's having three days at a folk and jazz festival so I'm a bit busy.'

'Three *days* at a folk and jazz festival? *Is* there that much folk and jazz?'

'They'll scarcely scratch the surface. I doubt they'll even get out of minor keys.'

Newson thanked Dr Clarke for her trouble and hung up. So her husband was away and the first thing she had done was look up Rod Haynes on Friends Reunited? Newson felt uneasy. He wished he hadn't passed on Haynes's message. He knew that Dr Clarke was a steady, sensible type, but Newson was discovering that the past exerted a powerful force. Its reach was long and its grip was tight.

When he finally arrived home its grip had tightened a little further over him. Two members of his old class had chosen to contact him, Gary Whitfield and Helen Smart. Sadly, neither of them was Christine Copperfield, but nonetheless it was pleasant to think that the class had begun to reassemble.

Newson opened Gary Whitfield's email first.

It was good to see that you had joined the class again, Edward. You always made people laugh, which is a valid and valued skill. My partner and I attend a clowning workshop and believe strongly in the therapeutic power of laughter. I'm writing to say that I'm sorry about saying that I hated you all. I didn't really hate most of the class and I certainly didn't hate you, you were always quite nice to me and let's face it, you got your fair share of crap from people like Jameson. Funny, you know, because cockney rhyming slang for queer is 'ginger' as in 'ginger beer'. Did you know that? I've occasionally been called a 'ginger' over the years and when it happens, I sometimes think of you. We're both gingers! We should be proud.

Newson did not think so. To him, being red-headed or homo-sexual was a symptom of your genetic make-up, something to be neither proud nor ashamed of. It simply was. He was happy for Gary Whitfield, though. Clearly adult life was for him a great improvement on childhood, which was surely the right way round. The cruelty of other kids had hit Gary much harder than it had hit Newson and the 'pride' that he had found was his way of fighting back. So good luck to him. Newson thought about writing back in ginger solidarity, but then he remembered the clowning workshop. Newson did not want to be in email contact with somebody who attended clowning workshops, even if he had been at school with them.

Newson harboured no special memories of Gary Whitfield, but he and Helen Smart had been real friends. She'd been his closest friend for some time and probably the best that he'd had at school. It had been twenty years since she and Newson had spoken to each other. Nonetheless her letter was couched in terms reminiscent of the familiarity they had once shared. Newson had noticed that about emails. They were so immediate, so spontaneous and personal, yet also so private and alone. Emails were dangerous things. Newson had a rule: never say something in an email that you wouldn't say to the recipient's face. It was a rule he often broke.

Hello, Ed, Helen wrote.
A policeman? A policeman? A POLICEMAN! Wow. Or were you joking? Maybe you were, I don't know. Maybe this E address is a hoax and I'm about to be groomed by an internet pervert who thinks I'm still a schoolgirl. Except I suppose we're all still at school on this site, aren't we? Fourteen forever. At least I'm fourteen because that's how old I was when I left you all. I imagine you left at eighteen. I always regretted that I never did the sixth, wearing jeans to school and swanking about in the sixth-form common room, but it was a small price to pay to get out of that dump. I've never contacted a stranger like this

78

before, by the way, so you don't need to think I'm sad or mad. Although of course you're not really a stranger at all, are you? Or are you? Has your life made you into a different person to the one I knew? I suppose if you've become a policeman it must have done. To be honest I thought there was a height restriction. I remember there used to be items in the papers about boys having themselves stretched in order to make the grade. Did you stretch yourself, Ed? I can't imagine you did. You used to say that you were normal height and all the other boys were freaks. Maybe the Home Office changed the rules. I expect it's illegal to discriminate against someone because they're vertically challenged anyway. Shit. I'm waffling. You will think I'm mad. OK, cut to the chase. I work for a charity and I live in London. Seeing as how you're with the Met (if it really isn't a joke) you live in London too. Do you fancy a drink? If you do then get in touch. Maybe we can work out why the miners lost. Perhaps it was our fault. I've got a kid but I can usually get a sitter. Bye.

She was the same Helen. Same old friend. Newson replied immediately.

Helen! Please don't worry if you hate me for being a copper. All my colleagues at Scotland Yard hate me for being a copper too. Some of them even call me Ginger Minge, so in many ways it's like I never left school. Anyway, what about you? Working for a charity? I remember you saying that Band Aid was aptly named because that's what it was, a little sticking plaster trying to staunch a great and terrible wound! I haven't got any kids myself but then why would I? I haven't had sex since 1987. I'd love to have a drink. Sieg heil. Detective Inspector Newson of the Nazi Party.

Helen must have been online as Newson wrote, because moments later she replied.

Great and terrible wound! Was I really that pious? No wonder you dumped me at the Christmas disco. How does tomorrow sound? Pitcher and Piano in Soho, eight? Ping back yes or no with alternative suggestion.

What a strange and uncharted planet was the worldwide web. To be conversing in such spontaneous intimacy with a ghost from the past who was nowhere to be seen but could be in the next room. It felt both exhilarating and uncomfortable.

Exhilarating? Of course exhilarating, because inevitably Newson's mind had turned to sex. It seemed to know no other route. Helen had scarcely been in Christine's league but she had been cute with her big bovver boots and cropped hair. Plump, certainly, but also pretty, and when you saw beneath her baggy clothes as on one occasion Newson had done, she had been shapely despite the puppy fat. Newson remembered her breasts particularly, for he'd held them once, and if he'd had to describe them the word he'd have used would have been 'perky'. Perhaps all fourteen-year-old breasts were perky. They probably were, but Newson wasn't sure, because he hadn't held enough of them at the time to mount any kind of statistically significant study. But Helen's had been very perky indeed. He closed his eyes and re-visited them across the years. Firm, despite her adolescent fat, taut, springy skin, he remembered, almost waxy to the touch, and puffy nipples. That had definitely been the most specific feature of Helen Smart's breasts, puffy nipples. Gorgeous in a quirky kind of way. Newson wondered what effect time would have had on perky nipples.

He pinged back 'Yes' and the date was made.

12

'Dumped you?' Natasha asked. 'So she was your girlfriend, then?'

'Not as I recall it. I mean, she was my *friend* and I'd kissed her, but I don't remember feeling that we were official in any way.'

'Had she let you grope her?'

'We-ll.'

'Aha. Thought so.'

'Only once. It was the night Arthur Scargill was arrested outside the Orgreave steel plant and we were feeling very angry and emotional.'

'Christ, I've heard some excuses.'

'Well, we blamed Mrs Thatcher for everything in those days.'

'Did she let you grope her upstairs, or upstairs *and* downstairs?'

'Only upstairs.'

'Inside or outside?'

'I'm not answering this.'

'Come on. It's important.'

'Oh, all right. Inside. Briefly.'

'Only inside blouse or inside blouse *and* bra?'

'I really don't remember.'

'Don't be pathetic, everyone remembers.'

'All right. Inside bra.'

'I have to say that letting a boy put his hand inside your bra is quite a big thing at fourteen, particularly if you're a serious, boring girl like this Helen sounds.'

'She wasn't boring. Just because your generation gave up on politics—'

'Were you pissed?'

'We didn't get pissed when we were fourteen.'

'Shit, we did.'

'The nineties were very different from the eighties. We blazed the trail, you reaped the benefits. Look, I was at her house and her parents were out. I'd gone round because we were planning to launch our own school magazine. We were having an editorial meeting.'

'Just you and her?'

'Yes. She was going to be editor and I was going to be principal feature-writer – well, only feature-writer, in fact.'

'God, you two must have been right pains in the arse.'

'We thought we were great. The only real people in the school.'

'Exactly.'

Newson remembered the night quite clearly. He and Helen had been filled with wild dreams of creating a fabulously successful and influential fanzine. Then they had turned on the news and it was filled with footage of policemen fighting miners, and famine in Ethiopia, and they'd got upset and righteous about the iniquities of it all, and suddenly Helen had asked him to hold her.

'She asked you to hold her?' Natasha said.

'I think that was how it happened, you know, like in fraternal solidarity, so to speak, and then one thing led to another, and . . .'

'Suddenly you had her boobs in your hand?'

'Exactly.'

'If it was her who asked you to hold her, then she fancied you bigtime.'

'Rubbish.'

'Not rubbish.'

'She just wanted a hug.'

'No one ever just wants a hug.'

They had returned to Kensington and Chelsea, but this time they were north of the river, walking past the gracious, white-pillared Georgian terraced houses of Onslow Gardens.

There was a scrum of press on the pavement ahead of them.

'It'll be Dr Clarke again,' said Newson. 'The Chelsea pathologist is still on that rail disaster inquiry so please try to control your irritation.'

'I don't have a problem with her. It's her who has a problem with me.'

The victim's name was Farrah Porter, and until her untimely death she had been a rising star in the Conservative Party. Attractive, blond and still under thirty, she had been the darling of the previous year's Brighton conference, living proof that Conservatism was youthful and dynamic once more.

'The only youthful thing about Farrah Porter was her age,' Newson remarked. 'Politically she was a Neanderthal. Hang 'em, flog 'em, eat their children then send the bastards back to where they came from.'

'I thought she was all right. I mean, at least she had a bit of style, didn't she? And you have to admit she wore great shoes.'

Once more Newson was ashamed to recognize that observations he would have found downright silly in others he found cute and feisty when made by Natasha. Why was it, he wondered, that having become attracted to a girl he ended up uncritically wallowing in every aspect of her?

'I can't take any politician seriously who works as hard on her tan as that woman did,' he said.

'It's a media world. Presentation's important. You've got to walk the walk, haven't you?' Natasha replied.

Farrah Porter had been famous for her tan; it was her trademark. When she won the Fulham by-election the *Sun*'s headline was TANFASTIC! She attended her victory party in a backless Versace mini-dress that was slashed at the front to below the navel, and at the sides from hip to armpit. Almost every square inch of her elegant, upright breasts was on full view, and it was quite clear that she sunbathed topless. Overnight, that dress turned Farrah Porter into the Conservatives' greatest asset, a politician of real significance, far and away the most recognizable figure in the parliamentary party, more so even than the leader himself. Her gorgeous presence sent Labour Party talent scouts scurrying out into the provinces in search of personable activists with whom to counter the Porter threat.

'She looked great and she was a laugh,' Natasha insisted. 'If I had the time and the money I'd probably have a tan like hers.'

'Well, don't. Your skin is just right as it is. You couldn't improve on it.'

There was a slightly uncomfortable pause. Newson had, as usual, gone too far, allowing his secret infatuation a momentary public airing.

'Thanks. That's nice,' Natasha said, looking at him quizzically.

The pause that followed lasted until they gained access to the building in which Ms Porter had lived and died. The victim was found by her mother, a woman who, having been married to a philandering cabinet minister, had spent most of her life dealing with painful public crises. It would be generally agreed later that she had risen to this most horrible of all her trials with real guts. Faced with the unspeakable sight of her daughter's body, she had nonetheless been able to alert the police and the Home Office in such a manner and at sufficiently high a level that the crime scene had been sealed very quickly and none of the appalling details of what had occurred had so far leaked out. The press mob that had assembled on the steps of the building were there only because they could see that the police were there. They did not know what had happened, that Farrah Porter, media darling and, due to her daring dress sense, potential Prime Minister, was dead.

Newson knew that Porter was dead, of course, but he had no idea of the manner in which she had died and was not prepared for the macabre horror that awaited him in the ensuite bathroom of the dead woman's bedroom.

'Brace yourself,' said Alice Clarke as they walked through the dressing room, past the many pairs of beautiful and beautifully ordered shoes. 'She's been bleached.'

'Bleached?'

'Well, I say bleached, because I think that was the intention. She's been soaked in a combination of trichloric acid and Phenol BP. Two very nasty skin-whitening agents.'

Farrah Porter's naked body lay in her kidney-shaped whirlpool bath, and she had indeed been bleached. Her famous rich tan had been replaced by a pale, red-raw, blotchy nightmare of ruined skin.

'He must have soaked her in it for hours,' Dr Clarke remarked. 'Probably sat on that toilet there and watched.'

'How do you know he stayed to watch?' asked Newson, mindful of the two cases he was looking at already in which the victims had been left to contemplate their fate alone.

'Because he hadn't finished with her.'

'The hair?'

'Yes, the hair. If he'd done that before he bleached her it'd be white too, and as you can see it certainly isn't white.'

Farrah Porter's blond hair had been almost as famous as her gorgeous skin. Now all that was gone.

Her hair was dyed bright orange. Even the tiny soft tuft of pubic hair, all that in life Farrah Porter had allowed to remain upon her waxed, polished and pampered groin, had been turned a sickly, electric, chemical orange.

Newson could not remember a stranger-looking corpse. It was like something out of a Batman comic.

'How did she die?'

'I don't know. I'll have to get her on the table. I doubt that the acid killed her. It would if you soaked in it long enough, but that would have taken days and obviously the killer just wanted to ruin her skin. It would have been pretty unpleasant, but at the point when the killer drained the bath Porter would still have been alive.'

Newson and Wilkie walked back through the dressing room, pausing to peek into immaculately constructed drawers and cupboards that stretched from floor to ceiling on all sides. It was not only shoes that Ms Porter had in abundance. Her dresses and suits hung in deep, glittering rows, and drawer after drawer was filled with exquisite lingerie.

'This was a girl who thought that matching bra and knickers were important,' Newson observed.

'I think most girls do,' Sergeant Wilkie replied. 'It's just harder for some of us to keep up standards.'

Newson wasn't sure Natasha was right about this. Shirley, his ex, certainly hadn't been concerned with such matters. But even in the midst of the horror that should have been consuming him, Newson could not help but grasp greedily this tantalizing snippet of personal information that Natasha had revealed.

In the sitting room all was in perfect order. Books and *objets d'art* were scattered about on the polished surfaces, giving an impression of exquisitely managed disorder. Two vast white sofas stood on either side of a low, carved-mahogany coffee table, upholstered with big, luxurious, down-stuffed cushions, the type that need regular plumping by a maid. On each sofa was an indentation that had yet to be replumped. It seemed reasonable to assume that Farrah Porter and her killer had sat here, facing each other.

On the mahogany table stood a half-full bottle of white wine. Two glasses had been poured, but only one remained; the other had been wrapped in newspaper and crushed heavily underfoot, a simple and effective method of dispensing with fingerprints. The killer had left the crumpled paper filled with tiny shards on the table.

'He's getting cheeky,' Newson remarked. 'Wants us to know just how easy we are to beat.'

'I *knew* the minute I saw her that you'd stick this in with the others,' said Natasha.

'Don't you?'

'I suppose so, but, God, I wish we could find some proof.'

'I think that perhaps he's getting frustrated too,' Newson mused, leaning over the table to inspect the other wineglass, beside which stood a small bottle, its screw top lying next to it. He hovered over the bottle and sniffed. 'No scent, but I think we'll find this is Rohypnol,' he said.

'You think he raped her?'

'Dr Clarke will check that out, but I doubt it. Rohypnol's good for more than date rape – it's a lot easier to restrain a person in preparation for torture if they're unconscious.'

Having checked that the table had been photographed, Newson put on a pair of plastic gloves and carefully replaced the lid on the little bottle. He then lifted it by the neck with a pair of tweezers and put it in a plastic Ziplock bag.

'Better check, although I imagine we can dust that bottle till it's worn away and it won't reveal any prints. Our man wants us to know how easy it is to kill and that we can do absolutely nothing about it.'

'Ed, there's no *he* yet,' Natasha remonstrated. 'We still have absolutely no proof whatsoever that the murders you've connected in your mind are connected in reality. We have five deaths. Don't you think it's strange that we've found no specific links?'

'They're connected, Natasha. The link is simply eluding us. Just look at what we have here: another effortless stalking followed by a grotesquely specific manner of death.'

'You don't know how this woman died yet.'

'My guess is that he made her drink the acid.'

'What makes you say that?'

'He manages to make every form of torture fatal. It's not always easy, but he puts in the effort. It's obviously important to him that how they suffer is also how they die. In Willesden he was forced to use an anticoagulant to make the spiking fatal. In Manchester the clothbound books killed a fit young soldier after what must have been many hours of effort. Angie Tatum died contemplating the effects of her torment, as did Neil Bradshaw, although I don't know whether it was the starvation or the fact that he was forced to stare up the skirt he had been made to wear that was the significant feature in the killer's mind. Now we have Farrah Porter turned from a tanned blonde into a pasty redhead by means of dye and bleaching acid. The killer wanted her dead but he couldn't simply slit her throat because slit throats weren't part of the punishment required. It has to be *connected*. Hence my guess that he finished her off with some of the bleach that destroyed her skin.'

'It always sounds reasonable enough when you explain it, but all this is still just conjecture.'

'Of course it is. That's all this killer leaves us with. Conjecture.'

They went into the bedroom. The large, expensive bed with its crisp, pink cotton sheets appeared to be untouched. The pillows were plumped and the covers had been smoothed by an expert at the job. Newson inserted a pencil into the drawer handle of the bedside cabinet and pulled it open. Inside were a packet of condoms and a vibrator.

'Very superior rabbit,' Sergeant Wilkie observed. 'You wouldn't find that in an Ann Summers shop.'

Once more Newson was unable to prevent himself from grabbing at this observation and storing it away in his mind for later. Another personal nugget to be savoured. She was familiar with vibrators. Did that mean she *had* one? He couldn't help finding that thought thrilling.

'These condoms are French,' Natasha added. 'Very exotic. Ribbed, assorted colours. She was one in-control lady.'

'Not in her last hours, she wasn't. Somehow this highly intelligent, super-tough politician was persuaded to give up all control.'

'The bastard drugged her.'

'But her guard was down, she let him in. Why? Who was he? Why do they always let him in?'

It felt strange to Newson, as it always did, to be party to the most private parts of a total stranger's life. Just a day before, Farrah Porter alone had known the contents of the drawer in her bedside cabinet. If she shared that knowledge with anyone it was at her discretion. Now two people she'd never even heard of were peering into it as if it was their own. Newson always felt uncomfortable with this. It left the victim with nothing. The murderer had taken the life, and the police then laid immediate claim to anything that was left.

He found himself thinking of Dr Haynes, the Manchester pathologist who attended victims' funerals. Then he thought of Warrant Officer Spencer with scarcely a soul to mourn him save his parents, his pathologist and some irreverent squaddie playing the Last Post on a kazoo.

They returned to the bathroom, where the initial onsite investigation had been completed and Dr Clarke was preparing to remove the body. Newson glanced around the spacious room. Farrah Potter had lived in luxury. The large double-basin unit had gold taps and the surrounding console was loaded with carefully arranged lines of expensive-looking bottles.

'Apart from around the bath very little has been disturbed,' Newson observed. 'She didn't struggle at all.'

'She may have been bound,' Dr Clarke replied, 'but the skin has been so damaged by the acid I won't be able to tell for sure without a microscope. You saw the bottle on the coffee table. Rohypnol, I should think. My guess is that she woke up in the bath and then the torture began.'

'She was conscious for that?'

'I think probably so. She seems to have thrashed her head about quite a bit.'

The floor at the head of the bath was surrounded by towels, all of which had been damaged by the acid.

'Why didn't she thrash about more?'

'I don't know. Perhaps he held her down with a broom or something.'

Newson glanced around the bathroom. He inspected the toilet with its thick polished-wood seat. Next to it was the bidet, which had more gold taps. Thick white towels hung from shiny heated chrome rails, and spotless mirrors gleamed within Italian mosaics.

'Whoever did this had tremendous nerves and the steadiest of hands. He's scarcely disturbed anything at all.'

'Perhaps he put it all back afterwards.'

'Either way, pretty cool.'

Newson opened the glass door of the shower cubicle, a luxury installation with both overhead and side-mounted faucets. All gold, all polished since the last time they were used, not a single dried watermark to be seen. A shelf held bottles of shampoos and conditioners and a soap dish, containing a brand-new bar of soap, a shell-shaped cake of perfect, pristine, untouched soap – except not quite perfect, because on it Newson discovered a pubic hair. Taking a small eyepiece from his pocket and looking more closely, he could see that someone had deliberately stuck this hair to the brand-new bar of soap.

The hair was orange.

Had the killer plucked it from his victim and planted it on the soap in the shower? It seemed the only explanation. If so, was this just another bizarre aspect of the murderer's ritualistic needs, or had the killer left it as some sort of message to the police? Was he trying to tell them something? Newson was a ginger. Was the killer trying to tell *Newson* something?

Behind him Dr Clarke had been supervising the police team's lifting of the body from the bath. When she spoke Newson noted emotion in her usually professional tones.

'Inspector Newson,' she said. 'I think I may be able to tell you why the woman did not thrash about in her bath, why only her head created a disturbance.'

Newson guessed what was coming. He knew about bodies on which only the head could move.

'I can't say for sure, but by the way this cadaver lifts I think the spine is broken.'

'Fuck.' Sergeant Wilkie had joined them in the bathroom.

Dr Clarke ignored the interruption. 'He wanted her conscious,' she continued, 'but he didn't want a struggle.'

'You're speculating, Doctor,' Newson reminded her. He had not seen Dr Clarke so visibly upset at a crime scene before, and it made him uncomfortable.

'It's not speculation, Inspector,' she continued. 'It's common bloody sense. I know a broken back when I see one. This . . . this animal . . . wanted a nice still body to soak up the acid. So he drugged her with Rohypnol and while she was unconscious he paralysed her.'

The room was silent for a few moments. Eventually Sergeant Wilkie spoke. 'I've found her appointments diary.'

She led Newson back into the sitting room, past the sofas to an antique dresser, which Porter had used as a bar. It was piled with bottles of single malt whiskies, ancient Cognacs and exotic liqueurs. In front of these lay an appointments diary, a beautiful one, of course, like everything else in Farrah Porter's life, with the exception of its end. The book was leatherbound, padded and richly embossed with the initials FP. Each page covered a single day, with all the very important appointments of a very important political life listed in Porter's confident scrawl: hair . . . make-up . . . television . . . radio . . . photoshoot . . . more hair . . . more make-up . . . more TV.

Except that the day of the murder was missing.

'He tore it out,' said Wilkie. 'Well, very carefully cut it out, in fact.'

Using the covered end of a pen Newson turned the pages and sure enough on close inspection he could just see the severed edge of a page nestling deep in the binding of the book.

'I never saw a man so neat,' Newson murmured.

'His name must have been on that page,' Wilkie observed.

'Or perhaps a number, an observation, something that might have identified him,' Newson replied. 'So he made an appointment with her. She noted it in her diary and let him into her home.

She either knew him or else he was able to produce a convincing reason for her to see him. Just like the others.'

Sergeant Wilkie stared at the diary. 'She made a date in her diary for her own death.'

13

She was there! Christine Copperfield was there! In the twenty-four hours since Newson had last looked, the Shalford Grammar School class of '88 virtual reunion had been increased by one. The most golden one of all. Christine had added her name to the list. Newson had not really expected this. He'd scarcely dared hope that someone as wonderful as Christine Copperfield, someone as cool, confident and popular as the class Girl Most Likely had not got better things to do with her fabulous, exciting, fulfilling life than log on to Friends Reunited. But she had. And what was more (Newson's hand trembled on his mouse), there was a little 'I' icon beside her name. She had left information. Newson had only to click on it to hear the authentic voice of the best-looking girl in school, the girl *he* had once got off with. Not wanting the moment to end, he waited a whole minute before clicking on the icon.

> Yay gang! I'm here! Yeah! I've been watching you guys for weeks, thinking about making myself known and when I saw that you'd joined up Ed well I had to get involved. How ARE you guys! Yes it's Christine here. Christine Copperfield, yeah that's right. DAVE! I'm STILL laughing at that one twenty years on. So what's been HAPPENING to you all??? I'm fine, I love my life. YAY! You remember I wanted to be in the media? Of course you do, I never SHUT UP

about it. Well guess what? I nearly made it, and I will yet! Yeah, I'm in PR which is the next best thing and TERRIBLY glamorous DAAAARLING! Who would have thought when I headed up the Christmas Disco Committees three years straight I'd end up coordinating VIP guests for way cool events like THE MOTOR SHOW at EARLS COURT! How cool is that! I love it and I get to travel loads, mainly in Britain but sometimes abroad. We recently did a corporate function on the Observation Deck of the QM2 which was soooo fabulous, it was only docked at Southampton but it sure as hell beat SHALFORD SCHOOL HALL! Ha! Yay! So. What else? Well I'm NOT married and I DON'T have kids (YET!!!!). There's been some significant others of course but sadly not the ONE. Hey, I can't help it. I'm choosy. Well I guess some of you boys remember THAT. Any old way, better go, lots to do. I'll keep looking at the site. Who knows, maybe I'll organize a reunion! Just don't expect the QM2!!! Byeeeeee!

Newson pondered this missive for some time.

Part of him felt disappointed. Christine had lived in his memory for twenty years as the personification of cool; beautiful, confident and effortlessly superior. A girl who stood casually at the apex of the prestige pyramid without appearing to try at all. Yet there was no denying that this long-awaited update on the progress of her golden life was not very cool at all. Viewed dispassionately, it was not the letter of a confident, effortlessly superior person. Newson knew that were Sergeant Wilkie to read it she would instantly dismiss his old flame as a prat. But then Sergeant Wilkie was going out with Lance, so what did she know?

After all, why shouldn't Christine want her old classmates to know how happy she was, how well she was doing? And she *had* mentioned him specifically. His had been the only name she'd picked out from that long-dispersed group of classmates. In fact, she'd only left her profile at all because *he*'d done so before her. Newson felt once again the ancient stirring. Christine Copperfield had picked him out just as she had done at the Christmas disco in

1984. Was this the cyber version of that moment when she had asked him to dance? Was he to get lucky again? It seemed too much to hope for, and yet she *had* picked him out.

As he stared at Christine's name on the screen with its 'I' for information, a second icon popped up beside it. She had added a photograph to her profile! She was doing it at that very moment! Eagerly he double-clicked on the icon and moments later Christine was smiling back at him. She was *gorgeous*. The same big, wide smile that had broken so many juvenile hearts. The clear blue eyes, long blond hair and tan were there too, but now they decorated a sophisticated woman instead of a girl. She was pictured at some kind of promotional party, standing in front of a board that said 'Gotex Aviation Fuel'. She held a champagne flute and wore a short black cocktail dress, and her legs were the same as ever! Slim and athletic, although if Newson had been honest he might have conceded that they had perhaps become a little bony over the years. Her cleavage was magnificent. The dress was clearly designed with big tits in mind, and it flattered Christine's beautifully. Newson did wonder about the tits, which appeared to have undergone some kind of late growing spurt. On the other hand, he didn't wish to jump to conclusions. Natasha had once told him that a good push-up bra could turn lemons to melons without the aid of the knife. All in all, Christine looked lovelier than ever. Cool, confident, stunning. A major player in the glamorous world of PR. The guys at the Police Club would certainly be surprised to hear that a girl like her had left a message in cyberspace for a man like Newson. Not that he would ever tell them, of course.

He looked at his watch; he'd have to hurry. He was due to meet Helen Smart at the Pitcher and Piano on Dean Street. He changed hurriedly and set off for the tube station. He'd been looking forward to the meeting with some pleasure, but he couldn't deny that now Christine Copperfield had re-entered the scene an evening with a thirty-five-year-old Helen Smart did not seem quite so exciting.

The Pitcher and Piano was a classic example of the new style of city pub, and Newson's heart sank the moment he entered. The guts had been torn out of whatever the building had been in its previous life and been replaced with a vast, soulless steel-and-plastic torture chamber in which hundreds and hundreds of people in their early twenties drank and shouted. They had to shout because they couldn't hear themselves speak, let alone anyone else, there not being a single soft or absorbent surface in the place, only steel, glass and more steel. It was like trying to hold a conversation inside an enormous bucket. Music blared on top of this. No one was listening to it, no one could hear it and yet on it played.

Newson was ten minutes late and he immediately despaired of ever finding Helen amongst the hundreds of braying, shrieking drinkers. He had no idea of what she looked like now. In the end he stood by the bar until she found him.

'Hello, Ed. It's me, Helen.'

He turned and focused on a small woman with cropped hair and a stud in her nose. He would not have recognized her in the street and even looking at her closely he had to struggle to discover traces of the plump girl with whom he'd briefly plotted to change the world. Her eyes had changed the least; they were still piercing, set wide in her petite face. As a girl Helen had had something of an overweight pixie about her and there was still that cute, impish quality to her face, but there were dark shadows beneath her eyes and she was thin. Too thin.

'Perhaps we should go somewhere else,' Newson shouted into an ear that was decorated with three studs and two rings. 'I think there's a slightly louder and even more unpleasant place just up the road.'

Helen smiled. She still had dimples. Newson had forgotten that.

'I couldn't think of anywhere else at the time,' she shouted. 'Do you want to leave?'

'Nothing would make me happier.'

'Finish your drink first.'

'No, I'll ditch it.' Newson wrestled an arm through the throng at the bar to put his full pint down on the puddled steel counter.

'They must pay you a lot to be a policeman,' Helen said as they left the pub. 'I'd never leave a drink like that.'

'Well, they give you a bonus if you're a racist and of course I take a lot of bribes.'

It was still early and they were able to get a table at the Red Fort Indian restaurant just up the road from the pub. The big room was hot and crowded and Newson removed his jacket. He noted that despite the tiny beads of sweat on her brow, Helen kept her cardigan on.

They ordered their food.

'Still a vegetarian, then?' Newson said.

'Yes, it's cheaper. But I do do dairy these days.'

'Sell-out. I can remember when you wouldn't even wear leather shoes.'

'I still don't. That's cheaper too.'

'I got an email from Gary Whitfield, you know.'

'Who?'

'He was in my class, not yours.'

'I left before the end of the fourth year. I don't remember every-body.'

'Did you see that Christine Copperfield left a profile? You remember Christine.'

'Yes, Ed, I remember Christine.'

'Did you read what she said? She sounds like she's enjoying life.'

'She sounds like a complete idiot. So, no surprise there, then.'

The food arrived and Helen probed Newson on the course of his life. He told her about his degree in sociology and his second degree in law and about his relationship with Shirley, except for the bit about her faking her orgasms.

'I suppose I ended up in the police because I didn't want to be a lawyer. Believe it or not, I don't find it a contradiction with all the stuff we used to talk about. I mean, I know we used to see all cops as Maggie's boot boys, but to me it's about doing the right thing. On the whole I think we do more good than harm.'

'I'll take your word for it.'

Newson didn't want to talk about himself. Two and a half bottles of Kingfisher lager were having their usual effect, and he wanted to ask Helen if she'd had anything else pierced besides her ears and nose.

'So come on,' he said. 'What about you?'

'I did English lit at Warwick, but I didn't finish it. And then I went to work for Oxfam. I spent a lot of the nineties in Africa working on aid programmes.

'Africa?' Newson said. 'I've never been out of Europe. That must have been amazing.'

'Amazingly horrible. I was only ever in famine areas.'

'Ah.'

'I came back ages ago. You can only do so much and then you burn out, and I've got Karl, of course.'

'Boyfriend?'

'Son. He's six now.'

'That sounds so incredible. You with a six-year-old son. It's amazing, I mean, you know, we were kids ourselves last time we met.'

'It's been twenty years, Ed. I had to do something in the intervening period, didn't I? I'm with Kidcall now. You know, the anti-bully helpline that all those celebrities support. Maybe you've bought one of our little tear-shaped lapel buttons. They weren't my idea, I hasten to add! I think they're revolting and pander to the idea of helpless victimhood. Kids don't need adults making them into victims, there're enough other kids doing that to them already.'

Newson was aware of the campaign she was referring to. It had a high-celebrity profile and there had been a huge poster campaign. 'They do amazingly, don't they? Almost as many famous faces as Comic Relief.'

'Well, it's for kids, for a start, which is always a good pull, and we're really lucky with Dick Crosby. He has the most incredible energy. He's transformed Kidcall. The trick with celebrity endorsement is to get a celeb to actually actively campaign on your behalf. You know, phone friends, write letters. Of course with someone like Dick they come running. People just love being close to money even when it isn't theirs.'

Of course Newson knew about Dick Crosby. Everybody did. He was the new Richard Branson. A handsome, swashbuckling entrepreneur who owned hotels, television companies, a cruise line, the world's largest commercial helicopter fleet. Anything that was fun, he was into. He'd been an early convert to the glories of the net and had bought thousands of computers for schools, leading to his being co-opted by Tony Blair himself as the government's 'computer tsar'.

Apart from joining Kidcall, his latest venture had been to acquire the National Telecom network, and in order to encourage people away from texting and back to conversation he had made a pledge to give one million pounds to whoever it was that made the billionth telephone call.

'Yes, he does seem like quite a good bloke,' said Newson.

'He's been great for us, but I don't know about his being a good bloke.'

'Why do you say that?'

'Because literally everything he does he does for publicity,' Helen replied. 'And I don't think it's any different for Kidcall. If he's this billionaire capitalist and he wants to show he cares, why doesn't he just give all his money away? I mean, all that bullshit about giving someone a million for making a call. Shit, he could give that money to us. He could give us a million every day for a year.'

'All wealth is relative, isn't it? I mean, we could deny ourselves this meal, couldn't we? The money would probably provide some African village with water for a week.'

'I don't eat out often,' Helen replied primly.

'Blimey, Helen, it must be hard work being you. Anyway, Crosby does loads of different stuff and it isn't all for PR. He's worked a bit with us, in fact, and that wasn't publicized at all. He came and addressed a fringe meeting of the Police Officers' Federation about the issue of problem families on housing estates. You know, when one gang rules the roost and terrorizes everyone else. You don't only get thugs at school, you know.'

'Yes, I do know, Ed, but I still think he's a bit of a fraud.'

'Well, what I think is that for somebody who's spent their life working for charity you're being a bit uncharitable.'

When the time came to pay the bill Newson insisted that the meal be his treat. Helen protested, but not for long.

'I suppose maybe you owe it to me for the way you dumped me at the Christmas disco.'

'You mentioned that in your email. I never felt I dumped you. I mean, we weren't . . . well, you know . . . We were friends, weren't we?'

'Hang on, we were more than just friends.'

'We were good friends, best friends, but . . . you weren't my *girl*friend, were you?'

'No, I suppose I wasn't. I just thought that was the way it was going, that's all.'

'Did you? Wow. I'm sorry . . . That would have been . . . well, it might have been great, but—'

'Princess Christine Copperfield wagged her little finger and I'm left standing beside the punch bowl feeling something of an idiot.'

They were just leaving the restaurant and for a moment Helen's voice had hardened. Out on the street Newson found himself apologizing for something he hadn't realized he'd done, more than two decades before.

'Look, Helen, I don't think I realized. I mean, we were mates, weren't we—'

Then Helen burst out laughing. 'For fuck's sake, Ed, it doesn't matter! We were kids. Who cares? I was only angry because I'd actually put on make-up for you and you *know* that was strictly against the rules of hardcore feminism *circa* nineteen eighty-four.'

They laughed together.

'All the same, Helen, I wish you'd said something at the time. I'd never just presume a girl was interested in me—'

'And would it have made any difference? Little dumpy Hellie trying to keep you from the school star? Come on, Ed, you were like a dog on heat that night. I watched you. Besides, girls didn't *say* in those days, even committed femmos like me. This was years before the Spice Girls, remember.'

'But really, it never occurred to me that you were interested in that way. I never do think that with girls. It never occurs to me that they might be interested. It's got something to do with the fact that I'm an ugly shortarsed ginger twat.'

'You're not ugly, Ed.'

'Oh, so just a shortarsed ginger twat, then?'

They both laughed. It was one of those moments and it went the way those moments usually do. They kissed on the lips, on the pavement on Dean Street, and Newson said, 'Would you like to come back for coffee?'

'I can't. I've got a sitter and it's already late. But I've got coffee. Fairtrade, too.'

Newson hailed a taxi and went with Helen to her flat in Willesden. During the drive they kissed again. As they walked up the path, through the untended, unloved communally owned front garden of the big dark house, Newson realized that Helen lived barely five minutes' walk from the scene of the Bishop murder. He'd driven past her house many times and not known it.

As Helen searched for her keys Newson noted the extraordinary number of bells by the front door. It must have taken some architectural ingenuity to squeeze so many dwellings into a house built originally to contain only one.

They made their way past the bicycles stacked up in what had once been rather a fine hallway and up the stairs to Helen's flat.

There followed an excruciating period while they sat waiting in Helen's tiny front room for the babysitter's minicab to arrive. The three of them, trying to make polite conversation, plus the sleeping figure of the sitter's own baby, which she had brought with her in a carrycot.

Newson made an effort to maintain his excitement. He must surely go to bed with his old schoolfriend, but the desire was draining. He was certainly no kind of snob, but Helen's life was so *drab* it made him sad, and sadness is not a good stimulant for sex. He tried to conjure her breasts up in his mind – he had no clues as to their current condition because she had still not removed her jacket, but he recalled her nipples from another age and tried to imagine what they would be like now that the puppy fat was gone.

Eventually the babysitter left.

Before Newson could speak Helen put her finger to her lips and disappeared into what Newson soon discovered was her bedroom. She returned a moment later carrying a small sleeping boy, whom she placed upon the couch and covered in blankets.

'This is Karl,' she said softly. 'His father's Samoan.'

Again Newson felt his sex drive slipping away. The tiny flat, the tiny boy . . . It was all too *intimate*.

'Look, Helen, I hate to kick Karl out of—'

'Ed. I don't have a lot of money. I only have one bedroom. So what? Does that mean I have no right to a sex life?'

'Well no, of course not. I just thought—'

'He's fine. He'll sleep.'

Helen took Ed's hand and led him into the bedroom. He noted immediately that not only was there only one bedroom, there was also only one bed. He was going to have to make love to Helen in Karl's still-warm bed.

She closed the door and then quite suddenly in the total darkness she was kissing him, working at his mouth with semi-drunken fervour. And he kissed her back. Now her jacket was finally off and her small, bony body was taut and strong against his. Newson's energies returned as he resolved to take his luck where he found it. Together they fell upon the bed and once more after a gap of over twenty years he held her breasts in his hands. They were smaller now, tiny in fact, but the nipples were as he remembered them, big and fleshy, and they felt quite exquisite in the heat of his passion and the rarity of the moment. As his hands explored the rest of her body Newson discovered with excitement that both her navel and her vulva had been pierced, something he hadn't encountered before.

'Nice,' he said, anxious to break what had become a rather intense silence.

'I love being pierced,' Helen said. 'I want to do my tits, but it's hard with nipples like mine, they're so fat. I'll do it one day, though. All the way through.'

'Ouch,' Newson murmured.

'Yes!' Helen replied with enthusiasm.

When the crucial moment arrived Newson whispered that he had a condom in his wallet. 'I don't think it's quite past its shag-by date yet,' he said, 'although it may be getting close.'

'Use it if you want. It's up to you,' Helen replied.

This was not something Newson wanted to hear. If there was one thing he did not like it was a girl who was casual about sexual hygiene. But he was too excited now. Her skinny body felt good and, anyway, he was committed. As long as he wore his condom he would be fine. He struggled in the darkness for his jacket. 'Can we have a light on for a moment?'

'No,' Helen replied. 'I like the dark.'

Eventually Newson found what he was looking for and began to fumble with the little packet. Of course by this time his erection was collapsing at speed, but fortunately Helen sensed the danger and made moves to rectify it. Ed reflected as her head descended that if she always made men try to apply condoms in total darkness she would be used to this problem. Eventually all was ready and they made love.

It had been many months since Newson had last scored and he

endeavoured to make the most of it. The feeling of a lithe, hungry female body moving beneath him was a pleasure indeed. Nonetheless, as he finished he could not rid himself of a slight feeling of unease. Try as he might, he could not quite abandon himself to the moment.

Later, as they lay together, half propped on the pillows, Helen with her arms across Newson's chest, the door opened.

It was Karl, asking for a drink of water.

This is not a situation that any man revels in, but Newson was not thinking about Karl. The light from the doorway had flooded the small room and as he blinked and his eyes readjusted he saw Helen's thin white arm on his chest. She hurried to cover it with a sheet, but he saw in time that it was crisscrossed with cut marks, too many to count. The badges of honour of the dedicated self-abuser.

Helen knew that he had seen them. 'Shut the door please, Karl,' she said. 'I'll be through right away.'

Once more the room was black and Helen said, 'It was a long time ago. I don't do that stuff any more.'

But Newson had been around cuts, scars and scarring all his adult life. Even in that brief bright moment he had seen that some of the marks were still ruddy and fresh. Not immediate, he thought, but recent. Helen put on a dressing gown and went to attend to her child. When she returned she put the light back on.

'I've ordered you a cab,' she said. 'You've got work tomorrow and so have I.'

Newson tried not to show it, but the relief was considerable. He'd been dreading the possibility of having to stay the rest of the night for politeness' sake with this girl who clearly had more problems than he did.

She put Karl back in his rightful place in her bed and while they waited for the taxi she made coffee.

'I still can't quite believe you went off with Christine Copperfield that night,' she said from the tiny kitchen that led directly off the living room.

'I've told you, Helen, I had no idea you were interested.'

'I don't mean because of me, idiot,' she said. 'I mean because of her. I mean, you were kind of cool and she was just a complete shit.'

'Me, cool? She was the one who was cool. She was Queen of the Year.'

'She had power but she wasn't cool. She was an arrogant, smug, nasty cow and secretly most of the girls hated her.'

'Come on, she was incredibly popular.'

'Bollocks. She wasn't popular. All the boys fancied her, sure. That's different. As for the girls, most of us were scared of her. I know I was.'

'You weren't scared of anybody.'

'I was scared of everybody, Ed. Except you.'

'Oh.'

'Of course I tried to look tough and act tough, but, believe me, Christine Copperfield could have destroyed me any time she wanted. All she had to do was turn the other girls against you. Mostly it was just words, making you feel fat, ugly, useless, dead. Occasionally they'd get physical. I saw her and her gang force a tampon into a girl's mouth once.'

'I had no idea.'

'In the girls' changing rooms after netball. The girl had just started her period. She'd sat on the bench and when she got up there was blood. It was like that scene from *Carrie*. Christine Copperfield laid into her. Laughed at her. Called her "filthy bitch" and "dirty slag", made the other girls get some tampons from the vending machine and then they stuffed one in her mouth. That was golden girl Christine fucking Copperfield. And you went off with her, Ed.'

'I didn't know anything about any of that, Helen.'

'No, you just knew about her tan and her hair and her tits.'

'Yes.'

The doorbell rang. Newson's cab had arrived. At the door he kissed Helen goodbye.

'That girl who had the period,' he said.

'What about her?'

'That was you, wasn't it?'

She didn't reply before closing the door behind him.

14

Newson got home shortly after two in the morning, feeling very uncomfortable indeed. He had enjoyed the sex, he couldn't deny it, but he'd definitely not enjoyed the sudden and intimate immersion in someone else's life. Someone who, if he was honest, meant nothing to him any more. Helen was clearly an unhappy woman. Her life was difficult and her self-harm was evidence of a low and damaged self-esteem. He didn't need that in his life. He had enough trouble maintaining his own confidence without seeking out the company of sad, embittered single mothers. He felt guilty because he'd had sex with her, and now he never wanted to see her again. He imagined she could get a lot of that sort of thing from men if she wanted.

He had a long shower and thought about Christine and what Helen had said. It didn't surprise him that Christine had been cruel to Helen. She'd been cruel to him, dropping him after a week with the same casual presumption with which she'd picked him up. But beautiful people played by different rules. Surely everybody knew that, and if Helen didn't then she needed to grow up. Newson couldn't hate Christine. Christine was beautiful, and for a brief moment she had chosen him. For that he would always be grateful.

Newson's computer was on broadband and so constantly online. After his shower he noticed that he'd received mail. Despite the lateness of the hour he couldn't resist going to his inbox, partly in fear that Helen might already have sent some grim accusatory post mortem on their evening together.

There was nothing from Helen, instead two emails concerning the Farrah Porter murder. The crime had of course instantly become big news. The minicab driver who picked Newson up from Helen's place had given him his copy of the late-edition *Standard*, and the MP's death had been splashed across four pages. Newson knew that there would be immense pressure on him to come up with something fast.

The first message was from Dr Clarke.

Well, we are a brainy pair.

The killer did indeed break Farrah Porter's spine in order to paralyse her. He did so by bashing it with a heavy instrument, probably a clump hammer, while she lay unconscious from the Rohypnol. I think he (or she) caused the injury with a single blow, which suggests either great skill and steadiness or a lot of luck. I incline to the former. The only point I can raise to miti-gate the horror of this case is that by breaking the woman's back the killer rendered her largely insensitive to the pain of the acid-bleaching, although of course the mental agony would have been almost beyond endurance.

Newson stopped reading and thought for a moment. This was an interesting point. The killer was not principally interested in inflicting pain. It was what he was doing to Farrah Porter that counted – the bleaching, not necessarily the pain it caused.

Next point. You were right about the cause of death.
He made her drink the Phenol BP acid. An extremely clever guess. Her insides were rotten with it.

Newson took no pleasure or pride in his assumption. He knew he was on the trail of a single killer and he knew that this killer tortured first and then finished off the victim in a way that developed directly from the torture. But that was all he did know, and, as he had guessed when he stood before the corpse of Adam Bishop, more people were bound to die. How many was down to him. He felt utterly helpless.

I've been experimenting with skin and acid in an effort to determine how long the killer worked on Ms Porter. This is clearly not an exact science, since the victim's skin was alive and I necessarily used a section of dead skin. Nonetheless I can make an educated guess that he let her soak for approximately one hour. During that time Porter was gagged with a cloth stuffed into her mouth – there's soft bruising on her tongue and her throat. Unfortunately I've been unable to retrieve any evidence of what the cloth was made of, so he must have cleaned out her mouth thoroughly. After the killer deemed his bleaching process sufficient he killed her by forcing as much as a pint of acid down her throat. She might have been able to scream briefly at this point, between the removal of the gag and the administering of the acid, but her larynx would have been dry and damaged. Nonetheless, perhaps a neighbour heard something. It's not possible to say whether the killer dyed her hair and pubic hair before or after he killed her. Unlike skin, hair is basically dead cell matter and hence would react to the dye in a similar manner whether the victim was alive or not. There was a minuscule growth in the hair, creating tiny blond roots, but hair of course continues to grow after death so that tells us nothing either way.

Newson knew the answer to this issue. He was certain of it. The killer dyed Porter's hair before her death and made sure she saw it too. Having got Farrah Porter where he wanted her, he would have been anxious for her to understand every aspect of her fate. He could not leave her staring at herself as he'd done with Angie Tatum. Farrah Porter was a very different woman from Tatum. She was in demand, dynamic, busy, the centre of a vast, adoring circle both personally and professionally. She could not be left to die alone, staring at her ruined self; she would have been discovered in hours and saved to tell her tale. No, Farrah Porter was one that the killer had to finish off before he left, but Newson was in no doubt that she died in the knowledge that she departed her life with ginger hair.

The second email was from the forensic laboratory at New Scotland Yard confirming that the pubic hair Newson had found on the soap had indeed come from the victim.

Newson's mind spun with the possibilities of what this might mean. It was such an out-of-character thing for the killer to have done. Normally he left no trace at all. In fact, that was perhaps the most compelling feature of all the murders. Why change now? Why be so careful to leave no sign of your presence save the corpse, and then deliberately plant this very specific clue? And then there was the killer's shattered wineglass, and the Rohypnol bottle. Newson sensed that the killer was developing, heading for a change.

He looked at the clock in the corner of his computer screen. It was late and perhaps he was no longer thinking straight. It was surely arrogance to imagine that the killer was talking to him? Yet he *was* a ginger and he *was* the only person making any connection between the murders. Perhaps the killer was giving him a pat on the back, encouraging him to keep going. But how would the killer know that he was making the connections? Were his emails being intercepted? Was he going mad?

Finally, at three a.m., Newson went to bed. Despite the fact that only hours before he had been having sex with Helen Smart it was, as always, Detective Sergeant Wilkie who occupied his thoughts before he went to sleep. Perhaps this was the reason he was so determined to keep faith with his memory of Christine Copperfield. He did not care whether she had bullied Helen as a girl or not. She was beautiful, she was a woman and she was not Natasha Wilkie. Newson felt that as long as there was a corner of his mind in which there was room for a woman other than his secretly adored colleague, he was not without hope.

15

Newson needed all of his resources of fortitude the following morning as he approached the front entrance to New Scotland Yard. Ahead of him he could see Sergeant Wilkie being dropped off to work by the dreaded Lance. There she was, climbing girlishly from the pillion of his great big motorbike like a lovestruck teenager. Why, Newson wondered angrily, on top of everything else, did Lance have to ride a motorbike? Who did he think he was with his leather jacket and steel-capped boots? And his brawny forearm forever reminding the world that punk was not dead? Newson knew that he could never have a tattoo; tattoos would look terrible on his thin white arms. And were he to mount that big Kawasaki his feet would not even touch the ground. Not like Lance, sitting effortlessly astride the stationary machine; those long denim-clad, big-booted legs were all he needed to keep the gleaming black 1000cc of pure grunt upright while Natasha reached up to lift his visor and kiss him.

Newson watched in agony as Lance grasped her slim waist, enfolding her body with a single, casual, proprietary arm and pulling her on to her tiptoes so that the short summer dress she was wearing rode up her body. Newson's heart leapt as he devoured the sight of Natasha's legs thus exposed, hoping that the rising hem would not stop its upward trajectory, until . . . Then his heart sank at the recognition of just how pathetic he had become.

'Morning, Natasha. Morning, Lance,' he said brightly.

'How's it going, geeza? Yeah, nice one. Whatever,' Lance replied, fulfilling his entire conversational obligations in a single non-negotiable sentence. He gave Natasha a final squeeze, firmly staking his claim over her before adding, 'Later, 'Tash. Don't be all night, eh? Else I'll only end up going down the pub and eating no dinner, which is so not a good thing.'

'I'll be back by seven at the latest, gorgeous,' Natasha replied.

'Yeah well, watch out for them sickos. Don't go coming back with no different-coloured pubes, eh? I'm serious, girl. I worry about you. It's fuckin' sick, all that.' Lance glanced at Newson almost as if to suggest that somehow it was Newson who was responsible for the sick sights that Natasha was forced to witness in the course of her duty as a policewoman. He sparked his machine into life and roared off.

Newson felt he had to say something. 'Natasha, it's completely out of order to discuss our cases when you're off duty.'

'Oh, come on, Ed, everybody does. How could you not?'

'Very easily. The last thing we need is copycats.'

'Lance isn't going to tell anyone, is he? It's all right for you – you go home alone, nobody asks you what you've been up to or whatever. Lance wants to know. What boyfriend wouldn't? It's too weird to say "Sorry, I'm not at liberty to discuss it." You can't say that to your boyfriend, can you?'

'Yes, you absolutely can.'

'Yeah well, wait till you get a girlfriend and see how long you manage it.'

'I have *had* girlfriends, you know. I was a copper when I was with Shirley.'

'Whatever.'

'And I did *not* share classified scene-of-crime details with her.'

'Only because you never talked to each other. You told me that yourself.'

Newson bit his lip. She was right, of course, it was easy for him. He didn't have a girlfriend and when he had had one the

113

relationship had been so tired that he might as well not have had it. The only thing missing from Natasha's comprehensive understanding of his pitiable personal and social inadequacies was that she did not know that he was in love with her. He found it extremely difficult to thank heaven for small mercies.

The entrance to New Scotland Yard was more crowded than usual. Farrah Porter's murder was of course huge news. The press were desperate for information and had turned out in force. Newson hoped that he and Natasha might push their way through the throng unnoticed, but in the rarefied world of crime reporting Newson was already gaining a certain reputation. A number of the crime writers outside the famous glass doors had encountered him before, and always on tough, often high-profile cases. The physical characteristics that made Newson anonymous to most people made him distinctive to them. A youthful, mild ginger shorty heading up a Scotland Yard murder squad was always going to be remembered, and they already knew from his presence at the murder scene the previous day that once more Newson was in charge.

'Inspector Newson,' they shouted. 'How did Farrah die?' 'Was it political?' 'We hear sex was involved! Was it a sex crime?'

'We'll no doubt have something to tell you in due course,' Newson replied as he ushered Natasha into the building.

'Wow,' Natasha said once they were inside. 'You're really getting quite famous, aren't you? How cool is that!'

'I don't know. How cool is it? Do you think it's cool?'

'Of course I think it's cool.'

'Oh, right . . . good.'

And it did feel good. Newson definitely liked Natasha to think he was cool.

'Of course, if we don't crack the case they'll know it was you who screwed up and they'll say you're crap.'

'Well, that's the press for you. They build you up and they knock you down.'

Newson's first appointment of the morning was with Chief

Superintendent Ward. Because of Farrah Porter's profile, Ward had decided to speak to the press himself and wanted to be well briefed on the progress of the investigation.

'Tell me exactly how far you've got,' Ward demanded. 'I'm not interested in theories or suppositions at this stage. We should keep that sort of thing to ourselves. The only thing you can safely give to a journalist is facts, and that's what I want. What exactly do we know about the person who killed Farrah Porter?'

'In terms of undisputable fact, sir?'

'Yes.'

'Nothing.'

Newson was not surprised to find himself facing the press alone.

'All that I can say at this stage,' he announced, standing at the entrance to the building, 'is that Ms Porter was murdered by a person or persons unknown and that we are pursuing a number of lines of enquiry. Thank you and good morning.'

'Brilliant,' said Natasha as he re-entered the building.

'Thank you.'

'But I really think you should have done up your flies.'

He looked. 'I knew you were lying.'

'Then why did you look?'

'Because . . . I have a reason, but I've decided to withhold it.'

They spent the rest of the morning together fruitlessly cross-referring the names and associates of Farrah Porter with those on the file of Adam Bishop the builder. Nothing matched.

'Not really surprising,' Natasha observed, 'her being a posh-tot Tory superstar and him being a well-dodgy Tarmac cowboy. No connection. Sorry, but there it is.'

'They both let the killer into their home and shared a drink with him. In my opinion, we now know how Adam Bishop ended up helplessly taped to his bed.'

'You think Rohypnol?'

'I'm sure of it, and I'll bet the same goes for Warrant Officer Spencer and Bradshaw and probably Angie Tatum too.'

'Well, it sounds more plausible than your last theory – that Bishop took his killer to his bedroom because he got his rocks off being repeatedly punctured with short spikes.'

'It wasn't a theory, it was a supposition.'

'If Bishop's killer did slip him a Mickey, then he's a strong bloke. It wouldn't have been easy to drag that man upstairs.'

'Hmm, unless he or she had an accomplice, we're looking for a fit man.'

Around midday the first batch of transcripts of beat interviews pertaining to the Porter murder was delivered. Ever since the body had been discovered a large squad of constables had been roaming the surrounding area endeavouring to discover if anyone had seen anything suspicious. Of course, this being such a celebrated case, the press had already spoken to everyone but had found nothing of interest to print, so Natasha began leafing through the intimidating pile of paper with little enthusiasm. As expected, nothing had been turned up. What Natasha did notice, however, was the similarity between the way the dead woman's neighbours described her and the accounts Adam Bishop's neighbours had given of him.

'She may have been the darling of the Tory Party,' Natasha noted, 'but she was not a popular bunny in her building.'

Even a cursory glance at the transcripts revealed that Farrah Porter was in dispute with just about everybody who lived near her. The old couple below her, who had lived in their flat for nearly fifty years. The young marrieds above with their twin babies. The lady at the top who had the difficult job of chairing the residents' association. They had all in their various ways made it clear to the interviewing constables that they were glad Farrah Porter was dead. Even the newspaper vendor on the corner of the street remembered her with nothing but ill will.

'Everyone says she made their lives a misery . . . A right bully, in fact.'

'Just like Adam Bishop.'

'Yeah. Different class. Different sex. Same shit.'

'Perhaps we should pop down to South Kensington and speak to these people ourselves.'

They decided not to travel from New Scotland Yard by car because West London had recently become a designated traffic nightmare due to changes in the application of the congestion charge. They took the tube, and Newson noted that the station was plastered with posters for a pop concert due to take place in Hyde Park. It was to be a big eighties revival gig entitled 'How Cool Were We?' The *whole* of Duran Duran were top of the bill, supported by half of Spandau Ballet, two out of three Thompson Twins, one New Kid on the Block, all three Bananaramas (the second line-up rather than the original), four Specials, one Man At Work, a Flock of Seagulls and Dannii Minogue.

'God, was Dannii Minogue going in the *eighties*?' Natasha asked, looking at the poster as they descended on the escalator at St James's Park.

'Just. Not *my* eighties, the early eighties, the glory days of New Wave and New Romantics. She sneaked in at the tail end of the decade, riding in her sister's slipstream. Quite a perky debut single, as I recall, called "Love And Kisses". It might even have been 1990 – they cheat sometimes with these shows. It must depend on who they can get.'

'Your detailed acquaintance with the minutiae of girly pop is quite scary.'

Newson and Natasha sat next to each other in the baking hot tube. Natasha was not wearing tights, and her bare legs were so close that Newson could watch them in relative security as he pretended to read case notes. Such sweet legs, stretched out straight, scarcely reaching halfway across the aisle.

'How do you get your legs so smooth?' He'd asked it before he even knew that he was going to.

'Just soap and a Bic,' she said. Her voice was perfectly friendly but she *must* have thought it a strange question to ask. She drew her legs in, tucking the feet beneath the knees. Now she knew he had been looking at them. But it had been worth it. Closing his eyes for a moment, he imagined Detective Sergeant Wilkie in her bath, shaving her legs with soap and a Bic.

Stop it. *Stop it.*

Newson distracted himself by focusing his thoughts on the other women in the carriage. None was a patch on Natasha. He thought about Helen Smart with her skinny body and funny little breasts. Fat puffy nipples, they were cute, she had been cute . . . but damaged. Not like Natasha.

Detective Inspector Newson threw back his head and stared at the ceiling. *He had to stop this.* Christine! That was who he needed. Christine – strong, confident and happy Christine. Not mad like Helen, not *damaged* by the years. No, Christine had been *enhanced* by time, in the case of her boobs, it seemed, quite literally. Christine, in her cocktail dress with her glass of champagne, queen of all she surveyed. Perhaps, Newson thought, if he could only win her once again, punch above his weight in the battle of love for a second time in his life, then maybe, just maybe, he could shake off the chains with which he had bound himself to his detective sergeant. Could Christine do it? Could she save him from the agony of love and lust into which his life had collapsed?

Natasha's voice interrupted his thoughts. 'I'll have to jump ship at six,' she said. 'I suppose you'll work on all night, unpaid as usual.'

'Ours is not a nine-to-five job, Sergeant.'

'Yeah I know, but Lance says I'm being exploited.'

'You are being exploited. By him.'

'No I'm not, he's my boyfriend. I owe him my time. I don't owe it to the Home Office.'

'What about the victims of crime?'

'Look, Lance and I have made an agreement. We're going to be there for each other in a much more meaningful way.'

'I see.'

'We think that the reason our relationship reached a crisis point

118

was because of a shortage of "us" time.'

'He said that, did he?'

'No. *We* said it, smartarse.'

'You can't call me smartarse. I'm your commanding officer.'

'All right, Detective Inspector Smartarse.'

'Thank you.'

Newson did not like holding conversations on the tube. He felt the proximity of strangers too keenly. Natasha, on the other hand, was the sort of girl who didn't mind who knew about her boyfriend problems.'

'So no more unpaid overtime for me,' she said loudly. 'Sorry, but I'm going to be less career-focused until my relationship's self-inflicted wounds have healed.'

Newson waited until they were on the escalator at South Kensington before replying.

'Tell me, Sergeant, on the subject of your career focus and the promised reduction thereof. Exactly what lifestyle adjustment will Lance be volunteering as his contribution to the nurturing of your new togetherness?'

'He's going to . . . well, I suppose he's going to be nicer.'

They were walking down the Old Brompton Road now. Natasha was annoyed with Newson and picked up her pace in a defiant manner, moving a few paces ahead of him. The sun shone on her bare shoulders and glowed on the delicate dusting of soft hair on her forearms.

For a moment he found himself thinking of those other forearms. Of that flash of light in the darkness on the night before when the shape of a little boy had appeared silhouetted in a doorway and he had seen the scars that the boy's naked mother had inflicted upon herself.

'I see,' he said, hurrying to catch Natasha up. 'So *he* chucks *you* and calls you all sorts of names, and *his* price for *your* taking *him* back is for *you* to give *him* more "us" time.'

'Yes, as it happens,' Natasha snapped, without looking back. 'And I think he's right. I've been selfish.'

'For God's sake, Detective Sergeant Wilkie! Listen to yourself.'

Natasha stopped and turned. Her dark eyes flashed in her small face and her chest heaved in anger. 'Look, Ed, just back off, OK? Lance has promised to stop being a bastard and that's fine by me. All right? Just because I love my bloke does not *make me a victim . . .*'

'I never said you were a victim.'

'You imply it all the time! And just because you're not getting any doesn't give you the right to give me all this shit, OK?'

Newson felt as if Natasha had kicked him in the stomach. She was right, of course. His position in her life gave him no rights at all.

They were standing beneath one of the scaffolding erections that seem to encase every busy pavement in London and on which builders sit during the lengthy periods when they are not doing any building. 'That's right, gel!' one shouted down. 'You give the little twat what for.'

In an instant Natasha had pulled her warrant card from her shiny black leather bag. 'Shut your ugly face, you prick, or I'll nick you for being an arsehole! *Capisce?*'

The man shut his ugly face and it being lunchtime Newson and Natasha went into one of the many patisseries that litter the streets of South Kensington.

'*Capisce?*' Newson enquired, ordering coffee and a *croque monsieur*.

'Yes. It's what they say in *The Sopranos*.'

'Which is of course why it sits so well on the lips of a London police sergeant.'

They sat down at a table, squeezing themselves between the huddles of rich old ladies of Continental origin. Natasha's remark about not getting any had hit home with Newson and he toyed with the idea of telling her that on only the previous night he had most definitely got some, and what's more he reckoned that if he felt like it he could get some more. But he thought better of it. Screwing a lonely ex-schoolfriend whom he'd pulled over the internet was scarcely proof of great skill or insight in the game of love.

Lunch was consumed mainly in silence, and when it was finished Natasha slapped four pounds on the table and walked out, leaving Newson to pay the bill. He caught up with her outside the house in which Farrah Porter had died.

'Let's get on with it,' Natasha said curtly, and they made their way past the constable on the door and down the stairs to the basement flat, which was situated below Farrah Porter's.

Mr and Mrs Geldstein were two of the oldest people Newson had ever met. Both in their mid-nineties, they had lived in their flat in Kensington for nearly fifty years. They sat together in their stuffy, heavily draped living room awaiting Newson's questions.

'Tell us about Farrah Porter,' he asked.

'We've always been happy here.'

'Until Miss Porter moved in.'

'We never knew such a woman,' Mrs Geldstein said, rolling her eyes to the ceiling.

'What was it about her that you found so objectionable?' Natasha asked.

'I do not like to speak ill of people who are dead, Sergeant, but she was a bully. She wanted us out, you see. Her dream was to create a ground-floor maisonette connecting her flat to ours. The landlord was on her side, of course. You see, we are on a fixed rate and he has wanted us out for years. We have cost him many many thousands, but that is not our fault.'

'He thought we'd be dead twenty years ago,' the old man chuckled.

'So Miss Porter and the landlord together have been trying to intimidate us. She makes complaints, she says that there are noise and smells and although this landlord knows the complaints are rubbish he takes them seriously and so we are given warnings.'

'She said it was obscene that she should pay nearly half a million for her flat and that we should have ours for two hundred a week and that she had to live with dirty immigrants ruining her

121

property. Immigrants! I have lived in England for longer than she's been alive, I told her. We experienced life under Hitler and came here with nothing but the clothes on our backs. She didn't scare us.'

'But she did, of course.'

'Not any more, though!' the old man said, and he was unable to hide his smile. 'To think that we were angry that night with the music,' he added.

'Yes,' his wife agreed. 'We thought we would make our own complaint. Of course in the morning we discovered there was nobody left to complain about and that while we had banged on the ceiling to stop her noise she was actually being killed.'

'There was music?' Newson enquired.

'Yes, it's the first time we heard any from her.'

'Do you remember what the music was?'

'It was pop music. Not good music at all.'

'What type of pop music?'

'Good heavens, Inspector. There is only one type, isn't there? Rubbish.'

'So you don't remember what was being played?'

'If you mean what singer was it, I have not the faintest clue.'

Newson and Natasha took their leave of the Geldsteins and stood in the stairwell discussing what they'd heard.

'So there was music,' he said. 'As with Bishop and Neil Bradshaw in the seed shed. Maybe the others too, we don't know.'

'Well, he played it to cover up the screams, didn't he?'

'Yes, except that Farrah Porter was gagged. You know, there was something about that music that always struck me as strange in the Bishop case.'

'What's that?'

'We had any number of statements testifying to the Bishops' musical taste. The whole street knew exactly what they listened to.'

'Middle of the road, easy listening.'

'Exactly. Early seventies, as I recall.'

'It's a common aberration, and what's more it's on its way back.'

'And yet on the night of the murder the music coming from the house was late fifties rock 'n' roll.'

'Which tells us?'

'Ah, that I don't know.'

They made their way up the stairs past Farrah Porter's flat and on up to the one above it. This was occupied by a young stockbroker and his wife and their baby twins. Farrah Porter's natural constituency, without doubt, but in this case there had been no love lost.

'The first time the baby cried she just went berserk,' Mrs Lloyd reported while the nanny served tea. 'I must admit they are loud babs – both boys, you see. They're asleep at the moment, thank God, but what can you do? Babies are noisy creatures.'

'I couldn't believe it the first time she complained,' the nanny added. She was a confident Australian girl who clearly felt entirely at home butting in. 'I was on my own with Harry and William, the doorbell goes and there she is, ranting and raving, saying that an apartment block is no place for babies and she was entitled to an adult environment to work in and we should move to a detached house.'

'Can you believe the nerve?' Mrs Lloyd added.

'I said to her, I said, listen, darling, I'm just the nanny, but I've got two screaming babies to deal with already so I can do without another one storming up here and ringing on the doorbell.'

'Which may have been a *little* confrontational, Jodie.'

'And Mr Lloyd?' Newson enquired. 'I presume his relationship with Ms Porter was as bad as yours?'

Newson had not really been probing but instinctively he could see that he had hit on something. The embarrassed pause that followed and the way the two women glanced briefly downwards was enough to tell both Newson and Natasha that while Farrah

Porter objected to the Lloyd babies, she had not objected to their father.

'My husband has had very little to do with Miss Porter since . . . Well, for some time.'

'She was a total bitch,' Jodie added.

'Did either of you hear anything going on downstairs on the night of the murder?' Newson asked.

'No, Inspector. As I told your constable before, with two small babies in the house one has quite enough to listen to.'

'I was thinking in terms of music. Did you hear any music playing?'

'I really couldn't say.'

'I did,' the nanny said. 'Definitely. Someone was playing music down there. I'll tell you why I remember it, too. One of the tracks was "Love And Kisses". You've probably never heard of it.'

'Dannii Minogue's first single, apparently,' Natasha said.

'That's right. First record I ever bought. I was six. Haven't heard it in fifteen years. I noticed it because it seemed like such a weird choice for an up-herself, oh-so-sophisticated bitch like Farrah Porter to be playing.'

'Yes,' said Newson. 'It does, doesn't it?'

The lady at the top of the house who ran the residents' association had no better opinion of Farrah Porter than had the Geldsteins or the Lloyds, and both Newson and Natasha were relieved to get out of the house. As they stood on the sunny pavement they reviewed the situation.

'I admit that the victim profile is very similar to Bishop's,' Natasha conceded, 'in that in both cases the victim has been deeply unpopular with their neighbours.'

'And the reason for that is the same. Both subjects were powerful, brutish personalities, domineering, selfish and cruel.'

'You think we've got a killer who's got it in for bastards?'

'I think we have to consider the possibility.'

'Then why the weird methods? They seem to've come from nowhere.'

'Except I bet they didn't.'

'And then there's the other three murders that you've unilaterally decided to credit to our single killer. What about those victim profiles? Were they all bastards?'

'Spencer was a warrant officer in the army, wasn't he? I don't wish to speak ill of non-commissioned officers or lump them all into the same category—'

'Particularly seeing as I'm a sergeant.'

'Yes, exactly. But it certainly offers job opportunities for the bullying type, and there were no mourners at his funeral, were there? He must have been pretty unpopular.'

'You can bet there'll be plenty of people at Porter's funeral, and Adam Bishop may have been hated but he still rated a full-scale old-style cockney cortège.'

'Hatred can take different forms. I think a lot of people wanted to dance on Adam Bishop's grave.'

'Well, what about the other two? Angie Tatum was a model and Bradshaw was a museum curator.'

'That doesn't preclude them from being intimidating and anti-social, does it? I think we need to find out.'

There was a roar of motorbike engine in the quiet street and Lance's Kawasaki screeched up. Natasha had asked him to pick her up in Kensington.

'Come on, doll. If you've got any money I'll buy you dinner.'

Natasha laughed prettily at Lance's sledgehammer wit and put on the big full-face helmet he offered her before daintily climbing aboard the bike behind him. Newson noticed that Lance did not even glance back to see if his girl was properly seated and settled before kicking down, twisting the throttle and roaring away, causing Natasha to wobble alarmingly as they swerved into the traffic. If she had fallen off and been injured, Newson swore that he would have spent the rest of his life making Lance pay.

16

When he got home Newson poured himself a drink and sat for a long time thinking.

He was emotionally and sexually dysfunctional. He had no girlfriend and no life. He was in love with someone who did not love him, and the only sex he'd had that year was with a woman he'd dragged up out of his past who was even more dysfunctional than he was.

He had to get a grip. He *had* to sort himself out.

He also had to find a serial killer. A serial killer who in Newson's opinion had already murdered a minimum of five people.

It was early evening and Newson resolved that the best thing he could do to put pointless thoughts of Natasha and Lance from his mind was to get straight back to work. He brought out his file on the Bishop case, picked up the phone and dialled. A nervous foreign voice answered the phone.

'Meeesis Beeshop 'ouse.'

'Oh, hello. Is that Juanita?'

'She no here no more. Goodbye.'

The phone went dead. Newson dialled again.

'Hello, I'd like to speak to Mrs Bishop, please. This is Detective Inspector Newson.'

It took some time, but eventually he heard the hard estuary

tones of Adam Bishop's widow on the line. 'Yeah. What is it? You caught the bastard yet?'

'Sadly not.'

'Then what you doing phoning me for? I'm being sprayed.'

'I was just wondering, Mrs Bishop, whether your record and CD collection contains much music from the fifties or early sixties?'

'Are you having a laugh? I'm having an all-over treatment.'

'This is a police inquiry, Mrs Bishop. Just answer the question, please.'

'Oh, I see. So I'm still getting treated worse than you lot treat the villains, am I? Well, let me think, then. We chucked a lot of that stuff out when we went over to CDs. We preferred more modern sounds. We've got Elvis, of course, you know, greatest hits and that, and I suppose a couple of compilations for parties.'

'Do you own any Everly Brothers?'

'No.'

'Early Cliff Richard?'

'Piss off.'

'So you don't have "Move It"?'

'Oh, I see what you're getting at. What the bastard who done Adam in was playing? Yeah, that weren't our stuff. I coulda told you that at the time. He brought his own bleedin' music with him. Can you imagine! What a *cunt*.'

Newson thanked Mrs Bishop and put the phone down. He went to his computer with the intention of searching the files on the Spencer and Tatum murders again to see if there had been mention of music that he'd so far missed. However, something was waiting for him that required instant attention.

There was an email from Christine Copperfield.

Disappointingly it was not a personal message. His name was only one of many on the list in the address box. She was contacting the whole class. Nonetheless he was included, and she was definitely back. After twenty years Christine Copperfield and he were sharing the same environment. Even if it was only a virtual one.

Hi Guys! How's it GOING! Christine here. Yeah! Looks like once you start with this Friends Reunited thing you just can't STOP. Look, I had a thought OK! Did you see that they're having a big Eighties concert in Hyde Park? YAY! It's called 'How Cool Were We?' and weren't we just!! It's an incredible line-up too! Duran, The Thompson Twins, Spandau!! I mean COME ON GUYS! This one was made for US! And, more importantly, it's all for charity! Kidcall! Yeah, it's being organized by Dick Crosby, isn't he the greatest? I SO admire all the brilliant stuff he's done. Anyway I was thinking why don't we use it as an excuse for a reunion! Yeah! We could meet somewhere cool like maybe Pizza On The Park (gotta eat! Don't want to get TOO pissed!!!) and then go on to the gig! How cool would that be? I'd be happy to organize the tickets (might even be able to get some concessions through my PR job daaaaarling), so I only need to know the numbers. INTERESTED??? Get back to me. And hey, Roger? Gary? If you're around you guys HAVE to come, can't hold grudges, LIFE'S TOO SHORT!! See ya!!

Newson wrote back immediately.

Dear Christine, You ask how cool would that be? My answer is WAY COOL! Count me IN! It's wonderful of you to offer to organize this, I must say, but then you always were rather wonderful, weren't you? Particularly during the period between the 12th and 18th of December 1984 which still ranks for me as the best week of my school days. I THINK you know why. Listen, I'm SO glad you're an admirer of Dick Crosby, I think he's great too. In fact I sort of know him! Yeah! Jealous? Get OVER it. Yeah, he's done some work with the Police Officers' Federation. He addressed our last conference and I got chatting to him. Maybe I'll be able to introduce you at the Hyde Park thing, although no promises! Hey, it's so great that you've broken into the media! You really followed your dream, didn't you? And I thought I had an exciting job as Senior Murder Detective with the National Crime Agency working out of New Scotland Yard, and yes, before you ask, I am cleared to carry firearms, but I promise not to bring a gun to the gig. HEY! How cool are we! GOLD! as Spandau Ballet used to say. I guess you can't put it better than that, can you?

Feeling rather ashamed but very pleased with himself, Newson pressed 'send' before his conscience had a chance to stop him.

Almost immediately he had mail, but it wasn't from Christine, it was from Helen. He'd been expecting to hear from her sooner rather than later. There was no way he was ever going to have been able to simply walk away from that one. What he hadn't expected was for the note to have a jpeg attached to it. Helen had sent him a photograph.

The subject in the title bar said 'This Is Me' and when Newson opened the jpeg it was a picture of Helen naked. She was standing in her flat with her arms held slightly apart, the palms of her hands turned outwards to show the cuts. Apart from the scarring it was in fact a very pretty photograph. Helen's body did not look as skinny as Newson had expected it to and her legs were shapely with nice calves. Her pubic mound was bushy, natural and unwaxed, which Newson remembered from when they had slept together and rather liked, and those tiny, weird little breasts stuck straight out from her ribcage in an engaging manner. Helen wasn't smiling, but she wasn't frowning either. There was just enough quizzical curl at the corner of her mouth to bring out one of her dimples, and her short cropped hair had clearly had some product put in it. Newson considered that Helen must have been quite pleased with this photograph, for overall she looked very cute.

He opened the email.

Dear Ed,

So now you know my weakness. My shameful secret. I cut myself. I know. I know. Get a grip, girl. Get a life. I wasn't lying when I said that I don't do it often, but I was lying when I told you that I hadn't done it recently. I expect you knew that, didn't you? You're a detective after all. I expect you know all about scars. Anyway, I just wanted you to know that the fact that I'm a self-abuser is not all of me, in fact it's not much of me at all . . . just a tiny part, something that comes upon me from time to time, a kind of self-hate. I suppose when I'm down I get this kind of idle curiosity about how much worse I can feel. It's almost like doodling. I don't know what to do with myself so I make marks on my arms. But most of the time I'm not like that at all. I love my boy and I love my job. I told you that I was bullied and it's really important to me to help other kids who find themselves in the same situation. That's why I work for Kidcall. You wouldn't believe the things that happen, the pain that's caused. Kids, as they say, can be so cruel. But the positive side is we can help and we do help. That's what I hang on to, always accentuate the positive.

I hope you like the photo and I hope you don't think that sending it to you is too weird a thing to do, but having made such a point about the darkness last night I wanted you to know that I am not ashamed of who I am or for you to see me in the light.

This Is Me.

Love and love, Helen.

PS Karl is with his grandmother tomorrow night. I could come to you if you like. No pressure. Don't even feel that you have to reply. I promise I won't slash myself. H. xxx.

It was a very nice note to go with a very nice photo. Newson looked at the picture again.

When he'd left Helen's flat the previous night he'd been quite sure that their new relationship such as it was would end right there. Too much baggage, as they say, far too much baggage. On the other hand, who was he to be so proud? He was a lonely man of thirty-four who was quite gruesomely obsessed with his entirely attached and equally uninterested sergeant. He drank too much, occasionally used pornography and was having rings run round him by a mysterious psychopath. He was useless.

Helen, on the other hand, was all right. So she had her problems? Just because he went to bed with her did not make those problems his. She was lonely, he was lonely. What was more, he imagined that she, with her dimpled smile and pixie eyes, would find it a lot easier to meet people than he did. And yet she wanted him. That was nice. He felt flattered.

> Dear Helen,
> I thought the photograph was a lovely gesture and also a very lovely photograph. Forgive me if I don't reciprocate with one of my own, but I'm not sure the net is ready yet for my naked ginger sauciness. It would be very nice to see you tomorrow night. Do you eat fish?
> Ed

Newson toyed with the issue of how many crosses to add for some little while. How many? If any? In his suddenly fired up and horny state he was tempted to put about ten, but he knew that the sensible thing would be to go easy. Because of a combination of their ancient intimacy and the curious familiarity that emailing allowed, they'd come a long way very quickly. This woman was effectively a stranger, and yet he had already slept with her once and was now arranging almost immediately to do so again. Ed put one cross beside his name.

Ed. x.

Then he added another. And another.

Ed. xxx.

*

The following day was a Friday, most of which Newson spent at the Home Office in various political briefings and self-consciously cloak-and-dagger meetings. He had been told to proceed there urgently by no less a figure than Chief Superintendent Ward, because for all her youth Farrah Porter had been a high-profile MP.

'A chance to redeem yourself on this one,' Ward had said. 'Don't want another unsolved Tory politico on your record, do you? They'll be giving you honorary membership of Sinn Fein.'

Ward was referring to what had been without doubt the most significant failure in Newson's career to date. It involved the disappearance eighteen months before of a leading figure from the Tory front bench of the House of Lords. The highly reactionary hereditary peer had disappeared without trace, and Newson still hoped one day to find him. The case was never far from Newson's mind because it had been so frustratingly baffling and utterly inexplicable. Lord Scanlan-McGregor had been wealthy, powerful and enjoying his recent third marriage to an elegant ex-model. One afternoon he had answered the door to an unnamed old friend. His butler stated that His Lordship had insisted on answering the door himself and that none of the servants had seen the visitor. Scanlan-McGregor had left the house shortly thereafter, presumably with the friend, and had never been seen or heard of since.

'Lord Scanlan-McGregor's absence from the House had a significant effect on the fate of both the Northern Ireland Police Bill and the blood sports second reading,' Ward said. 'In my opinion it seems a near certainty that he was abducted for political motives, and I don't think we can rule that out in the case of Farrah Porter's murder.'

Except, of course, in Newson's mind it could be ruled out because as far as he was concerned it was quite the stupidest idea he had heard in a long time. He said as much to the lady from MI6 with whom he had been instructed to liaise as they sat opposite each other in a featureless, windowless basement room in Whitehall.

'Why would a terrorist or maliciously motivated foreign power murder an opposition back-bencher, bleach her skin and dye her hair orange?' he asked.

'She was no longer merely a back-bencher,' the woman replied. 'Porter had just been co-opted on to the Shadow Cabinet steering committee for Northern Ireland.'

'The parliamentary Tory Party isn't as big as it used to be,' said Newson. 'Most of their MPs are on some standing committee or other.'

'Orange. Very emotive colour in Northern Ireland, don't you think?'

'You're kidding me, of course. This is a joke, isn't it?'

'Not at all. Porter was an unashamed Unionist, reactionary even by Northern Irish standards. Opposed to the Good Friday Agreement, opposed to any form of power-sharing with Sinn Fein. Apart from the fact that she was born in Basingstoke, she was an out-and-out Orangewoman. Perhaps somebody decided to actually turn her into one.'

'You think some loony Republican dyed her hair orange to show what happens to people who oppose a united Ireland?'

'We have to be alert to every possibility.'

'In that case you should be alert to the possibility that this is completely insane.'

Newson left the meeting promising to keep MI6 closely informed of any developments in his investigation and went in search of rainbow trout. He intended to microwave it with butter and herbs and offer it with new potatoes and a summer salad.

This was going to be a nice evening. He was going to enjoy himself and hopefully get laid again. He was careful choosing the wine. A Margaret River Chardonnay.

Helen arrived almost exactly on time, having walked from West Hampstead tube station. She had with her an overnight bag. This took Newson slightly aback. While he realized that there could be little doubt about the nature of their intended liaison and that it was perhaps sensible of Helen to bring a toothbrush and a change of pants, nonetheless it made him feel a little uncomfortable. After all, sex had not actually been discussed, and if Newson was honest with himself he had rather hoped that at some point in the night Helen would return to her own home.

Clearly she did not feel the same way.

'Hello, you,' she said when Newson opened the door. She had on a tight white T-shirt from DKNY, white baggy combat pants with lots of bits hanging off them, and pink Doc Martens. She had obviously made an effort and looked sexy in a politically aware, feminist sort of way.

'Hi,' Newson replied. He too had done his best and was sporting chinos and a blue silk shirt.

They kissed in a slightly self-conscious manner in the open doorway and Newson showed Helen through the little house to the kitchen/dining room at the back, where he had been preparing the meal.

'I brought some vodka,' Helen said. 'I hope you like vodka, because it cost fourteen pounds. It's still pretty cold. I've had it in the freezer and I wrapped it in newspaper for the journey.'

'Yes, I like vodka,' Newson replied. 'Shall we have it with orange juice? We could sit in the back garden. I'm rather proud of my garden.'

Newson's kitchen opened on to a tiny garden, which lay between his house and the North London railway line. He loved this little oasis of nature and had been toying with the idea of doing the trout on his barbecue.

'No orange juice,' Helen said. 'The whole point about vodka is you take it pure. You hit it back and then chase it with beer. Do you have any beer?'

'Yes, loads. D'you want cold lager or Guinness at room temperature?'

'Cold Guinness.'

'That'll take time.'

'We don't have time. Cold lager.'

There was undoubtedly something sexy about Helen's brisk,

almost urgent manner. It created a tension between them but one of expectation. Newson reached into the fridge to get the beer, and without asking Helen took two glass tumblers from a shelf. She filled each of them three-quarters full with Stolichnaya vodka.

'That's a lot of vodka, Helen,' Newson remarked, putting the beer on the table.

'If you want to get high on alcohol you have to drink it strong and fast. I hate the way most people drink. They drink just as much as this – more, lots more – but they take all evening doing it and all the time they get more stupid and more brought down. If you take a big shot early and then relax into it, you get sharp and high. It's a spin-out.'

'Is it?'

'Yes. And it saves time.' Helen picked up her near-full tumbler of vodka, put it to her lips and began to gulp it down. In moments she had finished. She slammed it down with a mighty gasp.

'Fuck,' she said. 'Now you have to do it too or else we'll spend the whole evening on entirely different levels of reality.'

Helen seemed more fun than she had done on their previous evening together, and much prettier too. The sudden alcohol rush had brought a pink hue to her cheeks.

Newson picked up the glass and drank the vodka down. 'Fuck, fuck, fuck, fuck, fuck, *fuck*!' he gasped, although scarcely able to raise a sound from his larynx. Then he began to gag.

'Of course, you can't be sick,' Helen said. 'That ruins it.'

'Thanks,' Newson replied, fighting with his stomach for mastery of his body.

'The beer'll taste good now,' Helen said.

And it did. Having won the struggle to keep the vodka down, it was already having a marvellous heady effect on Newson. Helen was right, he thought. Getting drunk quickly at the start of an evening was much more fun than drinking slowly and ending up sozzled at the end. He was already enjoying a wicked, liberated feeling, the same sudden rush of *joie de vivre* that he got on occasions like his birthday when he allowed himself to drink at lunchtime. Of course, as with lunchtime drinking, Newson knew that there would be a price to pay later, but for the time being he was determined to live for the moment.

Helen drank most of a can of Stella and burped hugely. For some reason Newson found this amusing and also very attractive. He drank his own beer in two or three big gulps and belched.

'Right,' he said. 'Now that the tone has been suitably lowered, dinner.'

Newson turned towards the chopping board, attempting to stay upright and conceal the fact that his head was spinning around somewhere close to the ceiling. 'I'm doing rainbow trout. Mish is what ficrowaves were made for. I mean, fish is what ficr . . . Fircoowaves. Shit, you know what I mean. It's what they were made for. That and porridge, as long as you have a big enough bowl, because it expands alarmingly.'

'Really? Rather like you, as I recall,' Helen said.

'Ah. Yes. Well . . . um . . . Dinner.'

'I'm not hungry.'

'Got to eat.'

'I'm not hungry,' Helen repeated, crossing the kitchen to stand directly behind Newson at the workbench. Then she put her arms around him and began to undo his belt buckle.

'Helen, I've already put the potatoes on.'

'I *said* I'm not hungry.'

She had her hand inside his trousers now. The touch of her urgent, lively fingers trying to find a way inside his underpants was a welcome feeling, but the speed and intensity of her desire had taken him by surprise. And then there were the potatoes. They'd soon be boiling. Perhaps he should turn them off? Except that they really ought to eat. He felt as if his body contained nothing but alcohol, which was of course pretty close to the truth.

'Helen . . .'

But her hand was already inside his underpants. She had hold of him now and further protest was useless. He was already expanding alarmingly like microwaved porridge, and as he hardened in her grip she began to jerk at him roughly.

'Ow,' Newson said. 'That hurts.'

'Good,' Helen replied, and she pulled him around to face her. Clamping her mouth on his and using her free hand to pull open her own trousers, she grabbed at one of Newson's hands and thrust it down between their bodies. It was the hand with which Newson had been about to chop some spring onions.

'For Christ's sake!' Newson gasped into Helen's mouth as the sharp cook's knife clattered on to the floor. He had only had a second to let go of it before his hand was buried deep into the thick hair of Helen's groin.

'I was holding a knife!'

'That's nice,' Helen said as she adjusted her legs to welcome Newson's hand between them, pushing herself against him as he leant back on the workbench. Their trousers were round their knees now and as they kissed they tossed each other off in the kind of awkward, rough-and-ready manner that is all that such a position will allow. In fact it was Helen who was masturbating them both, for there could be no doubt who was driving the ship. She held Newson's hand firmly in her groin while with her other she pulled at his straining dick, stretching the skin back unforgivingly with each aggressive stroke. Newson was happy to be led. He did not suffer from macho pride, and did not mind at all as Helen ground his trapped hand against the ever-loosening lips of her vagina, working her groin over his fingers.

Just as Newson began to fear that things for him were about to reach a climax, Helen let go of his penis and removed her mouth from his. Continuing to keep his hand clamped between her thighs she pushed him down to his knees with her free hand and then on to his backside so that he was sitting on the kitchen floor before her. He presumed that this was his cue to perform oral sex and leant forward, but Helen pushed his head back, knocking it against the kitchen unit, and continued to hold his hand to her groin, clasping it now with both of her hands and thrusting it hard against herself.

Newson felt her fingers closing over his. He realized that she was making his hand into a fist and was pushing it harder and harder against herself.

'Aha,' she said. 'This should move things along a bit.' Helen reached over Newson's head and picked up a bottle of olive oil with which Newson had earlier been preparing a salad dressing.

'Extra virgin. How ironic,' she said, upturning the bottle and splashing oil liberally at her groin and over Newson's clenched hand. 'Yummy.'

Being rather a tidy person, Newson might have objected to the fact that somebody had emptied half a litre of olive oil down the sleeve of his best shirt and over his kitchen floor, but he was drunk and in the grip of passionate arousal, and thought it confusingly erotic.

'Now push,' said Helen.

Newson had never fisted a girl before, but clearly this was what Helen required of him as she kicked violently at her trousers, which were now around her ankles, trying to spread her legs far enough apart to allow him in. Her thick shoes made it impossible for her to free herself completely from the trousers, but she was able to turn one leg of the garment inside out to make sufficient space between her thighs for her to work Newson's fist slowly but surely into her vagina. It was fortunate that Helen was in control, because this was new territory for Newson, but he was an easy-going sort of fellow and as he sat with his bare buttocks on the kitchen floor, his back against the pan cupboard door, his legs stretched out between Helen's feet, his trousers and pants round his ankles, his cock stiff as a broomhandle and his right hand buried up to the wrist in the hot, wet, hairy vagina that hovered a few inches from his face, he reflected that there were worse things that he could be doing on a Friday evening.

'Punch me,' said Helen through gritted teeth.

Newson presumed that she was referring to the fist on which

she was grinding herself and that she wanted him to thrust it in her harder. He decided not to do so and kept his arm still. Olive oil or no, he was already surprised at her body's capacity to accommodate him and did not want to push his luck. If Helen wanted to be damaged internally she could find someone else's hand to sit on.

Seemingly indifferent to his lack of ready co-operation, Helen continued with both hands to hold Newson inside her, grinding down on him until his wristwatch had half-disappeared within her. Then suddenly she gave a guttural scream and leant forward over him, grabbing at the bench with both her hands to support herself.

Looking up at the agonized expression on her face and with her almost primeval shriek ringing in his ears, Newson feared for a moment that Helen had indeed injured herself, but then the grimace turned to a smile and, looking down at him, she blew a kiss. 'Mmm, lovely,' she said. 'Very nice.'

She stood up, slid herself from Newson's gleaming, oily hand and shuffled backwards with both feet still caught up in the legs of her sodden trousers. She was still wearing her T-shirt, but now she pulled it up over her head to reveal once more those fascinating breasts, which were really nothing much more than big fat nipples. Newson wanted to put them in his mouth and tried to struggle to his feet in order to do so. Unfortunately his trousers were also round his legs and his leather-soled shoes skidded in the oil on the floor. He hit the ground hard but could not help laughing, and Helen laughed too as she sat down in front of him, sliding her bottom about in the oil, naked except for the crumpled trousers and her body jewellery. She seemed utterly un-embarrassed to sit like that, naked, crosslegged in front of him, tugging at her trousers and shoes, which were now hopelessly stuck around her feet, proudly displaying the three metal rings that surrounded her clitoris.

'Fuck it,' she said, unable to remove her feet from the trousers. She grabbed the knife that lay on the floor beside them and stabbed it violently into the crutch of the oil-stained combat pants, hacking them into halves along the seam. 'I shouldn't wear such big shoes.' Finally freed, she stood up with half a pair of trousers attached to each ankle and pulled Newson to his feet.

'What now?' he said. Things were going so well with Helen in charge, he felt perfectly comfortable taking his orders from her.

'I need a pee.'

'It's upstairs.'

Newson was learning fast about Helen, and he wasn't surprised when she grabbed his hand and took him with her. He kicked off his shoes as he went and with a bit of hopping about got his trousers off as they climbed the stairs, arriving at the top naked apart from his shirt and socks.

'I want to piss on you,' she said.

'Um . . . oh . . . OK, then.'

'Can I do it on your bed?'

'No.'

'All right.' She took him into the bathroom and pushed him down into the bath. Once more he found her standing over him.

'That shirt needs a wash anyway,' she said as she let loose, squirting pee at his chest and then his face. This was another first for Newson. He was surprised at how hot it was and at how excited he felt. He'd never seen a girl pee close up, in fact he couldn't remember seeing a girl pee at all.

'Now me,' Helen said, slipping down into the bath as Newson took off his sodden shirt.

'Bit of a problem,' Newson said, indicating his achingly erect penis.

'I said piss on me! For Christ's sake! So just *do it*, will you?' Helen grabbed at the shaft of Newson's dick and bent it down towards her face.

Newson yelped in pain but none the less did his best to do as he was told, leaning forward, supporting himself with his hands against the wall. He slowly began to pee over Helen.

'Harder,' Helen spluttered.

'I can't do it any harder,' he said. 'I'm in bloody agony as it is.'

'Good.' She reached out and bent Newson's erect penis further towards her.

Newson watched as she played the hot stream over her face and mouth and into her spiky punky hair.

When he'd finished Helen stood up and kissed him. This was not something that Newson wanted to happen. He was not and never had been interested in water sports. At a pinch, being very drunk, he might have been just about happy to taste a smidgeon of Helen's urine, but his own was something in which he had no interest whatsoever, and Helen's mouth was dripping with it. If she noticed his closed mouth as she worked her face against his she did not seem to mind.

'OK. I'm ready again,' she said.

Newson wondered what would be required of him now, as once again she took his hand, this time leading him into the bedroom. He'd been rather hoping that a shower might be part of what she had in mind, but he was disappointed.

'Fuck me,' she said, falling on to the bed, her body and hair glistening wet, while Newson tried with all his might not to worry about the sheets.

'Fuck me.'

'Fine. All right. I can do that.'

'And do it without a condom this time.'

'No.'

'Why not?'

'It's just a rule I have.'

Helen shrugged. 'OK. I bought some with ribs on.'

'Lovely.'

Despite her own preferences, Helen had come prepared. Lying on her back on Newson's bed, she raised one knee in order to bring half of her sodden trousers within reach. She probed in the pocket and produced a packet of three exotic-looking condoms and tossed them at Newson.

For the briefest moment Newson found himself thinking of the exotic condoms that he and Natasha had discovered in Farrah Porter's bedside cabinet. Then he thought of Natasha, and a dizzying wave of drunkenness swept over him.

'Bag it up if you must,' Helen snapped, 'but I really think you're a sissy.'

Fumbling with the packet, Newson did as he was told and then fell upon his old schoolfriend, determined to put all squeamishness regarding the fact that they were both covered in piss and olive oil from his mind. His sexual preferences were pretty conventional and he had never before had what might be described as a truly dirty shag. He reckoned that he was having one now, though, and he decided that he owed it to himself to get over his reservations and quite literally go with the flow.

Now, however, he encountered a problem. Perhaps due to her taste for fisting, Helen was very loose. She was also very oily and Newson simply could not gain enough purchase to maintain the required state of arousal. Even as he entered her he was horrified to feel the imminent danger of everything collapsing beneath him. He couldn't believe it. He'd been as solid as a rock moments before, running at fever pitch, desperate to ejaculate, and now this.

Helen realized the situation at almost the same moment. Perhaps she was used to it. Anyway, she had a solution. 'Stick it in my arse,' she said.

'Pardon?'

'You heard what I said. Stick it in my arse. It's tighter and I like it either way.' She rolled over on to her knees and, dropping her chin to the sheets, arched her back, offering her prone backside to him, cheeks spread wide.

Newson hesitated and Helen looked back at him over her shoulder. 'Come on!' she snapped, 'stick it in.'

She reached back, grabbing at him, and Newson allowed himself to be guided. He pushed for a moment as her muscle resisted and then, all of a sudden, he popped through and in so doing chalked up yet another sexual first. Anal sex was something else that until now Newson had managed to get through life without.

In the space of one crazy half-hour debauch Helen Smart had increased his sexual experience more than he had been able to do himself in the entire twenty-two years that had passed since his puberty.

'Go easy,' she said. 'It's been a while, it hurts.'

'I'll stop, shall I? Should I stop?' said Newson, ever the gentleman.

'Don't be so fucking stupid. Just let me loosen up for a second, then go hard.'

Once more Newson did as he was told, and shortly thereafter, with a head spinning out of control on beer, vodka and confusingly hardcore sex, he finally climaxed, collapsing forward on to Helen's back.

'You finished?' Helen asked, somewhat tetchily.

'I'm afraid so.'

'Suck the cum out of my arse and then kiss me with it.'

'No.'

'Just do what I say.'

'No.'

'Do it!'

'I'm sorry, Helen, but I said no.'

'It's called felching.'

'I don't care what it's called. I'm not doing it. As it happens, I couldn't anyway, not that I would, but I couldn't because I'm wearing a condom.'

'No, you're not. I took it off when I was guiding you into my arse.'

'What!'

'I told you, I don't like them. Don't worry, I'm perfectly clean.'

It took a moment or two for this to sink in. What Helen had done was so wrong on so many levels that Newson hardly knew where to start.

'Perfectly clean!' he spluttered. 'You've just had me fist you, piss in your mouth and bugger you without a condom. How can you say you're perfectly clean?'

'I mean I'm clean physically, healthwise.'

'You can't possibly know that for sure—'

'I don't do this with just anybody, you know.'

'What? Deliberately put them at risk of contracting STDs?'

'All the things we did. I'm usually celibate.'

'*Usually?* You can't be *usually* celibate . . . You either *are* celibate or you're not! Anyway, it's completely irrelevant. You've . . . you've . . . *Fucking hell*, Helen!'

Suddenly Newson felt completely sober and desperately stupid. What had he done? It was horrible, disgusting. There was piss and semen all over his sheets. He stank, she stank. The spuds would be boiled to a pulp. He felt like he was going to be sick. 'That was an incredibly stupid and irresponsible thing to do. You can't just secretly remove a person's condom!'

Helen began to cry. 'I'm sorry. I just wanted to feel closer to you.'

'But Helen, you're a grown-up woman. You've got a kid, you know the rules. You just can't go around doing that sort of thing. You've abused me. Betrayed a trust.'

Helen drew the sheet up to her chin. 'I've said I'm sorry,' she said, before adding in a small, quiet voice, 'But then you'd know all about abuse and betrayal of trust, wouldn't you, Edward?'

'What the hell are you talking about?'

'You dumped me, didn't you?'

'Oh, please!'

'You made me look like a complete arse in front of the whole school.'

'Helen. That's just insane! We were two fourteen-year-olds who'd had one snog and fumble. And also could I remind you that it was *twenty* years ago?'

'You never tried to find me, did you? When I didn't come back after New Year.'

'I phoned you. You told me your parents were moving.'

'They weren't. I went into hospital.'

'Because I'd got off with Christine Copperfield?'

144

'Because that was when I first started to hurt myself.'

'Which is not my fault.'

'I felt worthless.'

'Which again is not my fault.'

'It all started around about then.'

'Surely you're not suggesting, Helen, that because I left you standing by the fruit punch while I went and danced with Christine I'm responsible for what appears to have been a lifelong instability? We were just schoolmates, for Christ's sake!'

'I thought you loved me. I thought it was us against the world.'

'And you're saying that until the night of the Christmas disco you'd been completely fine, a well-adjusted girl?'

'No, I'd always hated myself.'

'Exactly.'

'Which is why when I thought you liked me I felt happy, and when I found out you didn't it was ten times worse.'

'Oh, *come on*, Helen. This isn't fair. I never gave you any reason to think we were together.'

'You said you loved me when you held me that night. You said mine were the nicest tits you'd ever seen.'

'They were just about the *only* tits I'd ever seen.'

'I hated them! The other girls called me Jelly Tots. Christine fucking Copperfield came up with that, Edward. Your girlfriend! But *you* said you liked them!'

'And I did! I do! They're very nice. But Helen, we were fourteen. We were in the same year at school. We were friends, that was all.'

'You never called me once after school broke up.'

'It was Christmas. Who calls their mates in the Christmas holidays? I called you when you didn't show up at school in the New Year.'

'After a week.'

'Look, I can't believe we're having this conversation. I think we need to clean ourselves up, have a shower and then maybe we can sit down and talk properly.'

'I like feeling dirty.'

'Well, I don't and you're in my bed.'

'And you were in *my* arse!'

'What the fuck has that got to do with anything!'

'You've had what you wanted, Edward, and you can't just give me orders now that you've finished.'

Newson decided he'd better stop talking for a moment. He knew that he was in dangerous waters. He and this woman from his past had just done things that could not be ignored and yet clearly she had come to him with a very specific agenda.

Had he been *stalked*?

'I'm going to take a shower,' he said.

The bath was still puddled with urine, and Newson felt dizzy with self-loathing, hating himself for what he'd done with this strange woman. And she *was* a strange woman. He now recognized that he hadn't known Helen Smart the *first* time around. And now, unbeknownst to him, she had fixated on him as the solution to her secret pain and self-doubt. He got into the shower cubicle and was finally and copiously sick.

He washed himself with pointless vigour, paying particular attention to his penis, which he soaped and rinsed six or seven times. If Helen Smart was in the habit of having unprotected anal sex, then there was every chance that she was not as clean as she thought she was. He studied his dick. He reflected that he had not been inside Helen for long, and of course the risk was far greater for her in that position than for him. Nonetheless Newson knew that he would see his doctor in the morning and once again in three months, and only when that was clear would he entirely relax.

When he could wash himself no longer, he wrapped a towel around his waist and stood for a moment, gathering his thoughts in preparation for facing Helen once more and negotiating her out of his house and out of his life.

It was then that the bells and sirens started to ring. For a moment in his semi-drunken, traumatized state Newson imagined that this was one more element in Helen's perverse sexual repertoire. Perhaps she liked to end a sticky conquest with an earsplitting cacophony of noise. Then he smelt burning and remembered the potatoes. He rushed downstairs. The kitchen was filling with smoke, which, of course, had set off his smoke alarms. Naked and advancing across the kitchen to turn off the gas, Newson skidded on the puddle of olive oil. Arms flailing, his legs disappeared from under him and he hit the kitchen floor with a thud. His head and lower back took most of the impact and on later reflection he realized that he must have blacked out momentarily. Certainly when the telephone began to ring he had trouble distinguishing it from the agonizing noise of the smoke and fire alarms.

Struggling to get himself upright, he racked his brain to orientate himself sufficiently to locate the telephone. He had to answer it, he knew that. He *must* answer it, because he knew that it would be his alarm monitoring service, and if he didn't they would send the fire brigade, and above all else Newson did not want them to send the fire brigade. There was very little clear in Newson's mind at that moment but of one thing he was certain: he did not want half a dozen large men trying to force their way into his house with axes.

He grabbed the phone and heard Helen's voice. She must have picked up the extension in his bedroom.

'Yes, I can smell burning,' she was saying. 'I think there must be a fire in the kitchen.'

'No!' Newson blurted into the phone, 'there isn't!'

'I think there is, Ed,' Helen replied. 'I can definitely smell burning.'

'Well, yes, there is, but—'

'So there *is* a fire?' a third voice interjected.

'A small one . . .'

'Do you require the fire service?'

'No!' Newson shouted.

'The lady said she smells burning, sir.'

'Of course she smells burning. That's why the alarms have gone off.'

'So there is a fire?'

'It's just the potatoes. They boiled dry.'

'So there's no fire,' the third voice said.

'No,' Newson replied.

'No, there isn't a fire? Or no, there is a fire?'

'THERE IS NO FIRE. IT'S THE POTATOES.'

'I'm not deaf, sir. You understand I have to be sure.'

'Yes, of course. I'm sorry.'

'It's extremely easy for misunderstandings to arise under stress.'

'I understand.'

'And if there was a fire and I failed to respond to an alarm alert, and death or injury resulted, you would hold me responsible and you would be right to do so.'

'Yes, I see. You have to be sure.'

'Yes, I do, sir. But in this case, there is no fire?'

'No . . . I mean, yes! Yes, there is no fire. However, unless I go and turn the gas off immediately there will be.'

The woman at the monitoring service thanked Newson and he heard a click as she put the phone down.

'Come back upstairs,' said Helen, who was still listening on the extension.

Newson turned off the gas beneath his charred cast-iron saucepan and returned to the bedroom.

Helen was lying exactly where he had left her, except that she had thrown off the sheet and was once more completely naked. 'I want more,' she said. 'The night is young.'

'Helen,' Newson replied. 'I really think you should get up and get washed now. I have to strip this bed.'

'It's fine.'

'It isn't fine.'

'We'll only mess it up again.'

'No. No, we won't.'

'Yes, we will. I want you to do it all to me again.'

'Helen. I think we should go downstairs now and I should make us something to eat, and we should have a talk, and then I can take you home in a taxi.'

'I haven't got any trousers. I cut them off so that you could get into me more easily.'

'Helen, we both know what we did. We had enthusiastic consensual sex and I don't appreciate these implications that somehow this has been just for my benefit.'

'Well, hasn't it been? Just like before, you have your bit of fun and then walk away when you feel like it.'

'Get up, Helen. I have no intention of buying into a guilt trip of which I've been unaware for twenty years. I'm really sorry that you felt that way then and I'm sorry you feel this way now, but I was a fourteen-year-old boy and fourteen-year-old boys get off with whoever they can. Besides which, I had no idea that you felt the way you say you did.'

'You just dropped me. Even as a friend you dropped me.'

'Look! I was excited, all right? I was besotted with Christine. I had been since the second year. She was the dream girl and I was a horny little nobody. As for you, I'd have called you in the end. I thought you'd be back and that we'd get back to our magazine and rolling back the frontiers of Thatcherism. But you didn't come back, Helen. You left, and that was it. We all moved on. Now get up, have a shower and I'll find you some trousers and a fresh T-shirt.'

To Newson's intense relief Helen got up and went into the bathroom. Moments later, as he was pulling the damp sheets from his bed, he heard a groan of pain. Not a shout, but a low, resigned groan.

The bathroom door was half open and when Newson opened it he saw Helen looking at herself in the mirror, still naked but for the absurd rags of trouser that remained attached to each ankle. There were tears running down her face and blood streamed down the side of her body. She had stabbed herself in the nipple with Newson's nail scissors, pushing the blades all the way through, where they remained, while she stood with her scarred arms hanging limply by her side staring at herself with abstracted curiosity.

Newson was not a man to panic easily. He was a senior police officer and good in a crisis. Without saying a word, he went to the open bathroom cabinet from which Helen had taken his scissors and grabbed a bottle of Dettol and some cotton wool.

'I'm sorry,' she said quietly.

The blood was now running off her foot and on to the floor. How much more could she mess up his house? He took hold of the scissors and with one quick movement removed them from Helen's nipple. She grunted with pain but did not move and allowed him to pour Dettol over the wound. Next he put a wad of cotton wool on either side of the bleeding nipple, covering the streaming cuts.

'Try to pinch those together,' he said. 'Push and pinch, put some pressure on it while I try to tape them down.' Helen held the swabs and Newson dried her chest with toilet paper so that he could tape down the makeshift dressing.

'A nipple is not the most convenient thing to dress,' he said, 'even a protruding one.'

'I'm sorry,' said Helen for the second time.

Eventually Newson managed to attach the dressing to Helen's chest and the blood flow began to slow. 'We have to go to Casualty,' he said.

'No, that's stupid.'

'Helen, I don't know the first thing about the anatomy of a nipple. You've impaled yours with a pair of scissors, and I don't know what damage you've done. It may need a stitch, it may need cleaning out. If you ignore it and it goes septic you could be in big trouble.'

'Can't I just stay here? You seem like a good doctor.'

'No. I'm taking you to hospital.' He rang for a minicab and then, having sponged Helen down to wash off the blood and urine, found her a baggy shirt and some trousers. He dressed himself and while they waited for the car to arrive he made coffee. It was less than an hour since he had been about to prepare dinner.

'Helen,' Newson said gently, 'you have to see someone. You need to speak to a professional about this.'

'It's fine. I'm fine.'

'You've got to think about Karl. You have a child. He's your first responsibility. I'm going to be very frank now, Helen. From where I'm standing I have a duty to report this situation to the social services. You're a single mother given to self-harm.'

'I never do any real damage.'

'What if you made a mistake one day? What if you were alone at home with Karl and you went too far and he found you bleeding on the floor?'

'I won't. I never have.'

'Will you try and get help?'

'I can't afford therapy.'

'If you talk to your GP he should be able to refer you on the NHS.'

'And run the risk of him doing what you've just threatened to do? Take Karl? No thanks. I'll be fine. Are you going to report me to anyone?'

'No, I suppose probably not.'

'Lucky for you, Ed, because if you did I'd make up stuff about you and what you did to me that would stick to your record for ever.'

The cab arrived and Newson was relieved when Helen picked up her overnight bag and got into it without further protest. 'You don't have to come with me. I'll be fine,' she said.

'I want to,' Newson replied, which they both knew was a lie.

'All right.'

In the car Helen asked Newson if he had replied to Christine's email about the reunion.

'Yes, I thought I'd go,' Newson said.

'After what I told you about what a bitch she is?'

'Look, I'm sorry, Helen, but I had different experiences at school from you and I have different memories. I can see that you were unhappy then and you're unhappy now, but that's you, it isn't me. I'd like to go to the reunion and I'd like to see Christine again. If you think that makes me a terrible human being, then I'm sorry but there it is.'

'And by comparison you never want to see me again in your entire life, do you?'

'Helen, I don't need this. I'm sorry.'

'Don't be sorry. It's understandable. And don't worry about me. Like you say, I have Karl. I have to keep things vaguely together for him, don't I?'

'Yes, you do.'

It was still relatively early in the evening so there was only a two-hour wait in Casualty before Helen could have her wound dressed properly.

'The doctor agreed with you,' said Helen as they waited at the hospital cab rank, Newson having insisted on taking her back to Willesden. 'He said I should get my GP to refer me to a psychiatrist.'

'Will you?'

'Perhaps.'

'Please try. You really should.'

'I might. Don't worry about the condom thing. You're the first man I've been with in more than a year.'

'You really shouldn't have done that, Helen.'

'Will you come in?' she asked. 'We really could just have coffee.'

'Helen . . . I'm sorry.'

'But you really do want to get away from me as quickly as possible.'

All Newson could do was shrug pathetically. It felt so cruel, but whatever she might believe, this woman was not his responsibility.

'Bye,' she said and got out of the cab.

Newson arrived home shortly before eleven and spent the following hour cleaning up his house, mopping the kitchen floor, washing the sheets, disinfecting the bathroom. It was all so horrible he almost had to laugh. There he'd been, planning a polite supper for two, and here he was now cleaning up olive oil, urine, pools of congealed blood, ripped and sodden clothing and a stinking bed. It had been the strangest evening he had ever spent. He thought on balance he would probably not tell Natasha about it.

Helen had said that she would not contact him, but in fact she did inasmuch as his address was included on a general email that she had obviously composed and sent immediately after he had dropped her off.

Hello everybody
Maybe some of you remember me. I'm Helen Smart.
I left halfway through the fourth year. I see that Christine Copperfield is planning a reunion. Well, I thought I'd get in early with my reminiscences so as to give you something to talk about. Christine Copperfield was an evil bitch . . .

She gave a detailed description of the tampon story she had told Newson on their first evening together.

17

Newson had woken up the following day feeling depressed. It was a Saturday and he'd been intending to lunch with friends, but instead he'd phoned to cancel. He was hung over, he felt queasy and he was overcome with feelings of disgust and self-loathing. Every time he closed his eyes one aspect or other of Helen Smart's spreadeagled anatomy rose up before him. His dick was red and sore from having been so roughly pulled about.

It was not like Newson to feel so low. He had a naturally optimistic disposition and had never been prone to depression, but his evening with Helen, shocking both in itself and as evidence of his own empty personal life, had really brought him down. He decided that he needed a break.

'You're *where*?' Natasha said when he phoned her on the Monday morning.

'Fort William. It's in Scotland. I took the sleeper up on Saturday night. I can't tell you how good it feels. The air's like champagne.'

'What are you doing in Scotland?'

'Right now I'm walking up a mountain.'

'Why are you walking up a mountain?'

'I'm having a day off.'

'In Scotland? You've gone six hundred miles to have a day off?'

'Well, I had Sunday too. It's what you call a mini-break.'

'It's what I call bloody barmy. Why didn't you go to Brighton?'

'No mountains in Brighton.'

'But sea.'

'Yes, but no mountains.'

'What about our duty to the Home Office and to the victims of crime?'

'It's only a day. I'll be back tomorrow morning. There's a six a.m. flight from Glasgow. Besides, I'm thinking while I walk. Working on the case. Like Richard Hannay in *The Thirty-Nine Steps*.'

'Who?'

'He used to go for a long tramp to clear his head. By the time he got home in the evening he'd usually cracked an entire German spy ring.'

'Have you cracked any spy rings?'

'No, but I've had one thought. Could you look at the murder scene inventories and see if there was a CD or cassette left in the sound systems at Spencer's or Angie Tatum's?'

'Are you looking for anything in particular?'

'Compilation albums.'

'You mean like *The Greatest Air Guitar Anthems*, or whatever?'

'No, I'm thinking more of compilations based on year. *Now '84*. Something like that.'

'Any specific year?'

'Sergeant, I don't think we need to go into that amount of detail at the moment. If you find that there was a music cassette or CD in the stereo at the Spencer or Tatum murder locations tell me, OK?'

'OK.'

'Right then, I'll see you tomorrow.'

'Have a nice walk. Ring me if you have any more brilliant thoughts.'

'I won't hesitate.'

That evening as Newson sat in the tiny bar of his guest house, nursing a single malt whisky of startling intensity, he reflected that taking a couple of days out of London had been a sensible idea. He felt sharper and was sure that the keen winds blowing at the summits of the three Munros he'd climbed had done something to clear from his mind the grimmer aspects of his evening with Helen. He'd even felt sufficiently himself again to order the trout with new potatoes.

Newson looked up to discover that the landlady was standing before him.

'I'm so sorry, Mr Newson, could you possibly repeat your order?' she said. 'I'm afraid I'm rather distracted. You see, Craig has not come home from school yet and it's nearly six.'

Newson had noticed Craig, a small, shy boy who cleaned the guests' boots at seventy-five pence a pair. He was a ginger, like Newson, but of course in Scotland that was less noteworthy.

'I'm sure it's fine,' Newson said. 'When's he supposed to be back?'

'Well, it's not normally later than five. John's been out looking, but he's just phoned to say Craig's not to be seen anywhere on his usual route.'

'In the police we don't normally think of an hour late as being cause for alarm. Kids are dreamy types and so often it turns out that the child's just been distracted and lost track of the time.'

'You don't think I should call the local police, then?'

'You could, but I'd give it another half-hour. I'm sure Craig'll be back by then.'

Just then the door opened and Craig walked in. He looked dishevelled and had clearly been crying. His mother turned on him, half in relief and half in fury.

'Craig! Where have you been? Your father's out looking for you. I was about to call the police! What's been going on? Why have you been crying?'

'I haven't been crying.'

'Where have you been?'

'I haven't been anywhere.'

'We've been worried sick!'

156

While the landlady went to call her husband with the good news that Craig had returned, Newson studied the boy. Something had happened to upset him. He was obviously hiding something.

'What's wrong with your arm, Craig?' Newson asked. The boy was gripping his arm as if in pain.

'I fell over,' he replied. 'My shirt got ripped and I grazed my arm.'

He was lying. Newson wondered why, and a picture flashed into his mind of Gary Whitfield cowering in a corner while Jameson and his cronies closed in with their indelible marker and he, Newson, stood by, doing nothing.

'Bit of trouble at school, eh?' Newson suggested.

'No, I just fell over.'

'Let's see.'

'Yes,' said his mother, coming back into the room. 'That shirt's nearly new. If you've ruined it I shall be furious.'

Craig slowly removed his blazer. One of his shirt sleeves was bloodstained, and he had clearly been trying to wash it.

'I fell over,' Craig repeated. 'I'm sorry, Mum. Is the shirt totalled?'

Newson looked at the boy's sleeve. 'It doesn't look torn at all.'

'It's only tiny,' said Craig.

'I can't see anything. Why were you bleeding?'

'I told you.'

The boy's mother took hold of Craig's arm and inspected it. Now Newson could see that in the middle of the bloodstain were two small nicks in the fabric of the shirt.

'Funny sort of tear,' she said, unbuttoning the cuff and rolling up the sleeve. There on Craig's arm were two tiny puncture marks.

Newson stared at the boy's arm. He'd seen wounds like that before, hundreds of them. He'd seen them on the body of a dead builder in Willesden.

*

The following morning Newson got up at three thirty in order to be in Glasgow in time to catch the first flight back to London. He sat in his room drinking tea, watching the glorious first light creep its way over the edges of the mountains. He had been writing a note for Craig.

Dear Craig,

You don't really know me, but I know you because I recognize in you a boy I used to know. Me, in fact. I was very like you when I was a lad. Like you, I always tried to be pleasant to people around me, but I discovered as I think you are doing that not everybody is as nice as we would like them to be. I don't know how bad things are for you at school, but just in case the going is tough, I wanted to say something to you.

The most important lesson that anyone can learn is to respect themselves. If you think of yourself as a victim, then the bad kids will see your weakness and treat you like one. It's all down to you, Craig, because bullying is about power, and you have the power to beat them by simply maintaining your self-respect. Yes, of course they can hurt you physically, but a dog could do that and if you can just believe in yourself and your own inherent value as a person then eventually they will see that in the truest sense they can't hurt you. They'll realize that they have no real power over you and they'll leave you alone.

And that's where the real challenge begins, because when the bullies do move on and you see another kid in trouble, you have to help them. I mean it, even if it means getting hurt. Stand up for the kid who's in trouble. You'll never ever regret it, I promise you. On the other hand, if you stand aside it'll stay with you all your life. I stood aside once and I'll always be sorry. Of course I wasn't strong enough to stop the bullying, but if I'd just gone in there and stood beside that kid, his torment would have been halved. Find the power inside yourself, Craig. Are you going to be a victim or a hero?

Natasha met Newson at the airport. As he emerged into the arrivals hall and saw her waiting he indulged in the fantasy that she was meeting him because she was his girlfriend and couldn't wait to see him, rather than because she was his subordinate and tended to do the driving. Two days in Scotland certainly had not cured him of that.

'You were right about the compilation albums,' Natasha said, 'although I don't know where it gets us. Nothing from the Spencer case but the investigating cops in Kensington and Chelsea were pretty thorough and they noted that there was a cassette in Angie Tatum's machine. It had been set on play and the tape inside was broken. The machine had an auto-reverse capacity and would have kept playing the tape back and forth over and over again, and in the end it just wore out. The volume was not set loud so no neighbours would have heard it. It was a compilation from 1984, Culture Club, Wham!, Tears for Fears, very much your era, eh?'

'Terrific stuff.'

'Not much fun for Angie Tatum, though, sitting listening to it, staring at her stitched-up lip, waiting to die.'

'No.'

'Of course, it *could* have been set before. I mean, by Tatum rather than her killer.'

'What? Run a tape on auto-reverse until it breaks? Hardly.'

As they sat in traffic on the Westway Newson called Dr Clarke. The phone was answered by her husband, who said that she no longer lived at that address. He sounded tetchy and rude, not the sort of attitude Newson would have expected from a mandolin player, and refused to take a message. Next Newson tried Dr Clarke's mobile, which was switched off, but he left a message and soon enough she called him back. They agreed to meet at her office.

When Newson and Natasha arrived at Dr Clarke's office she was just letting herself in. She carried a takeaway coffee and looked tired and slightly unkempt, not at all her usual smartly turned-out self.

'Yes, we're having a few weeks apart,' Dr Clarke admitted in what she clearly hoped was a matter-of-fact, noncommittal voice. 'He has the children most of the time because, surprise surprise, the call for mandolin players is at its usual zero.'

'Oh,' said Newson, not really knowing how to respond.

'Yes. So. Enough about me. It's not interesting and it isn't remotely germane. You say you have a murder weapon for the Bishop case. I'd be fascinated to know what it is.'

'It's one of these,' said Newson, producing a small steel and copper instrument from his briefcase, a piece of equipment familiar to schoolchildren the world over. 'A pair of compasses.'

Dr Clarke stared with surprise and disbelief. 'Oh, my God,' she exclaimed. 'It's so obvious.'

'Well, not really. It did, after all, take a genius to work it out,' Newson observed.

'No, it is obvious! A five-centimetre spike mounted on tiny shoulders four millimetres across. It's exactly as I described to you and it could not be a description of anything but the business end of a compass. It fits perfectly.'

'Well, I certainly think so.'

'Our killer murdered Alan Bishop with a school compass!'

'I'm impressed he found a use for one,' said Natasha. 'I carried mine in my pencil case for six years and I don't think I ever got it out. I mean, how many times do you need to draw a circle?'

'They're not for drawing circles,' Dr Clarke informed her. 'They're for creating right angles and bisecting lines.'

'Another really useful thing you need constantly throughout your adult life,' Natasha retorted.

'They're for stabbing people,' said Newson. 'Every schoolboy knows that, and so did our killer.'

In order to be absolutely sure that Newson's hypothesis was

right, Dr Clarke measured the diameter and shape of the compass spike that Newson had brought and compared it to the notes she'd taken on the numerous wounds that had killed Adam Bishop. She had even created a three-dimensional computer image of the average shape of the holes she had found in the victim and by typing in the data on the spike she was able to create its virtual twin. Staring intently at the screen of her computer, she moved her mouse about until she had popped one into the other.

'Perfect fit. Like a sword in a scabbard. Well done, Inspector.'

'A bit of luck, really,' Newson conceded. 'I saw similar wounds to Bishop's on the arm of a schoolboy. It turned out he'd been attacked by another lad with a compass.'

'God, kids can be bastards, can't they?' Dr Clarke opined.

And with that Dr Clarke bustled Newson and Natasha out of her office and rushed off to deal with a life that had clearly spun somewhat out of control.

As Natasha and Newson drove back to New Scotland Yard they considered the significance of the new information.

'It certainly justifies your going to Scotland,' Natasha said. 'I mean, you didn't crack a German spy ring, but not bad all the same.'

'As I said, a bit of luck, being there when that kid got bullied.'

'Of course, the Bishop murder weapon being a compass doesn't preclude the suspect's being an angry business associate,' Natasha said, but without much conviction. She knew that in the Tarmac community school compasses were unlikely to be a weapon of choice.

'No, it doesn't,' Newson replied, 'but I'm absolutely certain that the compass was central to the motivation for the murder. It seems reasonable to at least experiment with the assumption that at some point in his life Adam Bishop himself used a compass in anger and that eventually it came back to haunt him.'

'Well, the last time I laid eyes on one myself I was at school.'

'Exactly. Me too. Of course he *might* have used one since. He was a builder. Builders talk to architects. Architects do geometry.'

'Yes, I suppose we'd better take a look at that.'

'Otherwise, it's a school thing. He stabbed some kid and now the kid has stabbed back.'

'But Adam Bishop was fifty-five! Something like that would've happened over forty years ago.'

'The mills of God.'

'What?'

'The mills of God grind slowly but they grind exceeding small.'

'Shit, Ed, you think someone waited forty years before taking revenge for being bullied?'

'Perhaps. I know someone who waited twenty.'

'Who?'

'A girl I knew at school—'

'Christine? Your old pash?'

'No, the other one. Helen.'

'Ah, the one you titted off because the miners were losing their strike.'

'Yes, that's right, if you must put it like that. I never knew it, but Christine bullied Helen and got some of her gang to stuff a tampon in her mouth.'

'Nice.'

'And now that Christine has decided to arrange a class reunion over Friends Reunited Helen has decided to tell the class all about it.'

'Wow! Good goss! How did that go down?'

'The reunion hasn't been cancelled, so I suppose most people don't see it as their problem.'

'D'you think this Helen girl will go?'

'No, I very much doubt it. She certainly didn't say she was going.'

'Oh yes, of course! You met her, didn't you? So how did *that* go? Did you get any further than upstairs inside this time?'

'Don't be ridiculous.' He said it, but he wasn't quite quick enough. The tiny hesitation was enough to give away the truth.

'You did! You did! You scored, didn't you?' Natasha exclaimed. 'You pulled an old girlfriend over the internet!'

'Look, we had dinner. Now, can we please move on—'

'Look me in the eye and tell me you didn't shag her! Come on, look me in the eye and say you just had dinner.'

'Natasha, we have a very—'

'You did! I know you did! That's amazing. *Fast stuff*, Ed! Good *work*, fellah! Come on, tell me everything. How was it? Was it great, or was it completely complex and weird?'

Newson gave in. 'It was completely complex and weird.'

'I warned you. I told you only sad people get into this sort of situation.'

'I got into that sort of situation, Natasha.'

'All right, maybe not sad . . . Just a bit . . . well, you've got to admit it, it *is* a strange way to get laid. Anyway, never mind that. I want to know *how* weird and *how* complex.'

'Very, but it's over and done with now. I don't want to talk about it.'

'You *hope* it's over and done with, but I'll bet it isn't.'

'It is.'

'She may be a bunny-boiler. Unbalanced and vengeful.' Natasha put on an American accent. 'What? So you think you can screw me then just *walk away*! Think again, Detective Inspector Newson! Eeee, eeee, eeeeh!' Now she was doing the shower scene from *Psycho*.

'This isn't a movie and it's definitely over.'

'So come on, you have to tell me. What happened?'

But Newson would not be drawn. 'All I can say is that when you crash your plane on to the deck of someone else's life after an absence of twenty years, it's hardly surprising that you encounter a bit of damage. Helen had plenty, her life is complex and difficult, and I think that perhaps momentarily she hoped my appearance might provide some solutions for her.'

'And you just wanted a shag.'

'Exactly.'

'Bummer.'

'The very word I was thinking of myself.'

The conversation lapsed for a moment. Newson felt uncomfortable. He did not really like Natasha's knowing that he had slept with Helen. Certainly he was happy for her to understand that he was not entirely sexless, but he also suffered from irrational feelings of infidelity. In sleeping with Helen he had been unfaithful to his fantasy relationship with Natasha, and although she would never know how much he loved her he was still prone to a kind of perverse private guilt.

'Everything good with you?' he asked, breaking the silence. 'Lance well?'

'All right. He's not happy with me working so hard.'

'As far as I can see he's not happy with anything you do at all.'

'He's dealing with a lot of issues. He's a complex bloke.'

'He's a very lucky one, that's all I can say. He should be on his knees with gratitude that you even give him the time of day.'

'Oh, you don't know me. I can be a right bitch.'

'Oh, I know *that*.'

Natasha smiled. Newson wanted to kiss her so much it hurt.

'I . . . I missed you while I was away,' he said. 'I mean . . . it was nice when you called.'

'I thought you wanted to get away from everything.'

'Yes, work, of course, but not from . . . Well, it was just nice to hear from you, that's all.'

Natasha turned to him and smiled, but then looked away. There was further silence. Every fibre of Newson's being yearned to declare his love. To throw caution to the wind, fall on to his knees next to the gear stick of Natasha's Renault Clio and plead with her to forsake Lance for him. But he didn't.

'Yeah, well. Anyway,' Natasha said.

Newson opened his briefcase and fossicked pointlessly with papers, trying to refocus his mind on what they should have been discussing.

'Right,' he said firmly, 'we need to discuss what to do about the Bishop case. It seems clear to me that we have to take a look at who he went to school with.'

164

'Shit, that's a hell of a job. Forty years is a long time. People could be absolutely anywhere.'

'Fifty years. If he's fifty-five now he first went to school in about 1954 or five.'

'I don't think they have compasses in nursery school.'

'That's true. I reckon we should start by taking a look at who was at school with him in 1958 and '59.'

'Why particularly then? They left school at fifteen in those days, so he'd have been there till at least 1964.'

'Just a hunch. Cliff Richard released "Move It" in 1958.'

'Any good?'

'Fantastic. It's generally considered to be the first genuine all-British rock 'n' roll record. Cliff was cool in those days.'

'Was he really around in *1958*?'

'Yes, he was.'

'And the killer was playing "Move It" while he punctured Adam Bishop with a school compass three hundred and forty-seven times.'

'Yes, that and the Everly Brothers, the Platters, all terrific stuff, all from the last two years of the fifties. Elvis was in the army, you see. The field was wide open.'

'I suppose it does seem kind of likely that the killer chose that music for a purpose,' mused Natasha.

'Well, we'll see, won't we? Besides that, we need to keep going with cross-referencing our five murders. Look at the backgrounds on Spencer, Bradshaw and Tatum. It'd be interesting to see if they were all viewed with the same degree of animosity in their circles as were Adam Bishop and Farrah Porter.'

Natasha dropped Newson off at New Scotland Yard. She was to return to Kensington to supervise further forensic work on Farrah Porter's flat. The police had been forced to vacate the apartment while MI6 went through it, and only now was the investigation back in police hands.

Newson stood on the pavement, watching as he had done so often as Natasha disappeared into the traffic. Even her little Clio seemed cool and feisty to him. A spunky, independent little car for a spunky, independent little lady. Red, of course. Red meant don't mess with me. Newson despaired. He was even in love with her fucking car.

With head bowed, he made his way into the office, thinking about the forthcoming class reunion. Perhaps he might find a cure for love there, or at least some distraction from it.

18

The week passed slowly, with the frustrating business of going through the motions of an investigation. Newson was convinced that in the Bishop and Porter cases he was looking for the same killer, and that the motivation for murder was an as yet unidentified element that they had in common – an element that they also shared with the three previous murder victims. However, he had no proof to support this assumption and so was clearly required to pursue his investigations with an open mind.

Farrah Porter had many political associates and rivals, of course, all of whom had to be interviewed, and her recent contacts and activities required investigation. Adam Bishop's numerous enemies within the building trade and the wider Willesden community all had to be laboriously traced and eliminated. Computers were impounded, bank accounts searched, cupboards opened and skeletons rattled. All was to no avail, as indeed Inspector Newson had privately predicted.

And still the only factor with which Newson was able to link the two victims, one a violent builder, the other a celebrated junior politician, was the fact that they both appeared to have been loathed by those who knew them. In this aspect, at least, Natasha had been able to draw some parallels with the earlier three victims Newson had chosen to lump into his investigation.

'Angie Tatum wasn't popular,' said Natasha, 'but she wasn't

hated in the way Bishop and to a lesser extent Porter were hated – or at least not recently.'

Natasha and Newson were holding an unofficial end-of-week briefing in a Dunkin' Donuts on Piccadilly Circus. 'Most of the people who knew her just thought she was a bit sad.'

'Hanging on to a glory that was long gone?'

'Exactly, and, let's face it, it was a pretty tawdry glory in the first place, wasn't it? I mean, getting your tits out, what sort of job is that?'

'Quite.'

'I did speak to a couple of girls who knew her when she was queen of page three, and they said that in those days she was pretty nasty, cocky and a bit spiteful, but even they weren't glad she was dead.'

'What about the others?'

'Neil Bradshaw was different again. At first you wouldn't say that he was particularly disliked, but, reading between the lines, people were wary of him. They didn't trust him. It's all very political.'

'Political? He worked at Anne Hathaway's Cottage, didn't he?'

'Ah, but it turns out that the heritage museum world is a very small one. Small, incestuous and as prone to bitching, jealousy and backbiting as any other walk of life. Very intense lot, curators.'

'Who'd have thought it?'

'It's the world, isn't it? Everything's the same. Same crap, different toilet.'

'Nicely put.'

'Bradshaw was a manipulator and a stirrer,' continued Natasha. 'He got on to all the committees and spoke at all the conferences, constantly building little power bases and forging and reforging alliances. Weird, eh? He was the Stalin of local tourism. It's all about funding, of course – who gets it and how much, and Bradshaw was master of bullying committees into putting cash into his area. It made him enemies.'

'All the same, I can't see anybody torturing a man and starving him to death because he managed to win a local council tourism grant.'

'People have killed for less. A lot less.'

'True. D'you think there's any actual food in these donuts, or is it all E numbers?' enquired Newson.

'Don't be ridiculous. Why d'you think they taste so nice?'

'But the gap between "This is delicious," and, "Oh God, I wish I hadn't done that," is so short.'

'All the more reason to enjoy it while it lasts,' Natasha replied, selecting her second, a pink one with green sprinkles. 'Anyway, apart from the whole tourism political thing, we also picked up one or two accusations of sexual harassment. I got put on to a seventeen-year-old girl who'd had a Saturday job at the bookstall. She claimed that Bradshaw started off giving her gifts and things, but then pretty soon he asked her to email him some holiday snaps of her on the beach. When she refused he turned sinister and set her up, or so she says. She reckons he planted money and a book in her bag and then accused her of stealing them. He also tried to blackmail her into giving him naked photos of herself, even offered to lend her a webcam to do it with. She just left her job and that was the end of it. She never heard from him again. But guess what her parting shot was to me?'

'"I'm glad he's dead"?'

'Her very words. How many times are we going to hear that in this investigation?'

'So neither Bradshaw nor Tatum's a particularly pleasant person. What about Warrant Officer Spencer?'

'Well, his old outfit is in Afghanistan at the moment, so we haven't been able to conduct any interviews face to face, but I emailed some questions to the local redcaps and they've been quite helpful. Quite glad to be involved in a bit of proper policing, I think, instead of just dealing with drunks. Anyway, yet again we have a picture of a man who was by no means everybody's cup of tea. He was admired as a tough soldier, but also loathed and feared by the men under him. It seems he believed the only way to toughen a soldier up was to half kill him. You know the sort – if they can survive me, they can survive anything.'

'Not such a popular attitude in our modern caring and inclusive armed forces.'

'No, and Spencer nearly lost his stripes on a number of occasions for brutalizing squaddies. The bloke who played the kazoo at his funeral had been forced to lick the entire squad's boots clean for allegedly turning up on parade with a scuff on his own.'

'Nasty.'

'So, anyway, that's it. Overall, I'd say that your hunch holds up, although much more with Bradshaw and Spencer than with Tatum.'

'But nonetheless all five of our victims were to a greater or lesser degree shits.'

'Yes. What we seem to have here is a serial killer with taste.'

19

The following day was the day of the reunion, which had been arranged most efficiently by Christine Copperfield, who had sent numerous round-robin emails with questions and instructions. She still had not mentioned Helen Smart's internet attack on her, so clearly she had decided to ignore it. Everyone else must have done so too, because Christine was promising a fine turn-out at the Hyde Park Hilton, where the gathering was due to take place from one o'clock.

Check this out, guys! I got the room for NOTHING. Yay!
How cool is that? They're happy to give it us for the profit
on the bar. So NO Bring A Bottle please or they will chuck us
out! I'm thinking of YOU, Pete Woolford. I remember the way
you used to sneak booze into school parties. Mind you, I
shouldn't complain, you always gave me a swig (what WERE
you after??) Anyway, as I say, the room is free but there will
be a ten pound charge for lunch nibbles. I chose their Number
Two Corporate Finger Buffet: mini Yorkshires with beef,
scampi bites, prawn tartlets with crème fraîche, Tai spring
rolls and assorted sarnies. Hope that's cool. Finally, for those
of us who are going on to the 'How Cool Were We?' concert
(and most of us ARE – yay!), the tickets were forty pounds
each. SORRY to be going on about money but hey gotta

do it! Dannii Minogue is due to kick the show off at four so we'll have LOADS of time for embarrassing reminiscences. See ya THERE!

Newson walked into the foyer of the Hilton Hyde Park, keeping his sunglasses on and hoping that he looked cool. Glancing about, he tried to give the appearance of a man who knew exactly what he wanted and where he was going. What he was hoping was that there would be a felt board on an easel with little letters stuck to it saying 'Class of '81 to '88 reunion'. There being no such sign, Newson approached the receptionist.

'Hello, I'm looking for a room booked by Christine Copperfield? It might be under the name "Shalford Grant-maintained Grammar School Reunion".'

For some reason Newson felt embarrassed just saying it. Admitting the purpose of his visit. Perhaps it was because the girl behind the desk looked about seventeen and so would no doubt look on a school reunion as something that happened to geriatrics.

'Yeah, I know,' he said, for no particular reason. 'Crazy, right. Rule numero uno, don't look back. Never look back.'

The receptionist either did not know what Newson was talking about or did not care. 'Two hundred and three. Second floor,' she said, directing Newson to the lift.

As he turned away he bumped into a large man with a vaguely familiar face.

'Edward?' the man said. 'It's Ed Newson, isn't it? Got to be. Can't mistake that hair! Spewsome Newson. Jesus H. Christ. The man himself! Rock on Tommy!'

Newson peered at the man. 'Kieran Beattie?'

'That's right. Eatie Beattie,' he said, slapping his substantial stomach. 'Still on the large side, I'm afraid.'

'Yes. I'm still on the short side.'

'The boy is the father of the man, they say.'

'Good to see you, Kieran. How long is it?'

'Ay ay, oo-er, missus!'

'What?'

'How long is it? Very long indeed, mate, ha ha.'

'I meant how long is it since we met?'

'Yeah, I know. Eighteen years.'

'Wow. Seems like . . . about eighteen years. How are you?'

'OK, good, yeah, really good. Fine. Rocking. Really rocking.'

Newson knew instantly that Kieran was not fine and most certainly not really rocking. 'Come far?'

'Just from Dagenham. I'm with Ford. Great company.'

'Yeah.'

'I don't think, ha ha.'

'Well, shall we go up, then?'

'I suppose we'd better. You're a policeman now, aren't you? That's great. I always thought there was a—'

'Height restriction? Yes, everybody thinks that. Not any more, though.'

'A detective inspector. That's pretty good, isn't it? I mean senior.'

'Sort of. Not really. Well, I suppose it's quite . . . Shit, is that Sally Warren?'

A woman in her mid-thirties had just entered the hotel, heavily pregnant and pushing a small child in a buggy. Sally Warren had been second only to Christine Copperfield in the golden-girl stakes, undisputed number two in the hot-babe gang. The hair was still blond but that was the best that could be said. The rest of her looks had deserted her. Some women blossom when pregnant, but it did not seem to suit Sally Warren. She looked tired, drawn and drab.

'Sally?' Newson said, approaching her.

'Spewsome!' Sally shouted, too loudly for a public place, her face lighting up at the sight of an old friend. 'I mean, Edward! Amazing to see you. I'm *so* glad you came. Have you seen anyone else yet?'

Kieran Beattie was grinning widely only a metre or two behind Newson, but Sally had looked right through him.

'I'm here . . . Hi, Sally, it's Kieran. Kieran Beattie.'

It was obvious that Sally only vaguely remembered him. 'Oh
. . . oh, *right*. Kieran, yeah. Hi, Kieran.'

'We didn't know each other very well then,' Kieran added
unnecessarily.

Because you were a fat nerd and she was a class beauty,
Newson thought. The playing field had levelled somewhat since
then, but Sally Warren was not going to admit to it. As far as she
was concerned she still ranked way higher in the pecking order.
She turned immediately back to Newson.

'So, Ed, how *are* you? You said you're a policeman now. A
senior detective. How cool is that? What are you investigating at
the moment?'

'Oh, nothing much.'

'Wasn't it *terrible* what Helen Smart wrote about Christine!
Actually, I remember when it happened. I was there, and it wasn't
anything like as bad as she says it was. We were only having a bit
of fun. She always was a bit self-important was Helen Smart with
her politics and all. At least you had a sense of humour about it,
Edward.'

'Yeah, Ed was a right laugh, wasn't he?' Kieran added from the
distant sidelines of Sally Warren's world.

'This is *Josh*,' she said, referring to the child in the buggy. 'I had
him naturally at home.'

'Great. Maybe we should move on up.'

'Like a sex machine,' said Kieran Beattie.

'Yes. It's on the second floor. The lift's over there.'

'Cool bananas,' said Sally Warren.

'So how *are* you?' Sally asked again, pushing the buggy
towards the lift, but further conversation was suddenly rendered
impossible by Josh, who exploded without warning like a
grenade. Newson, who was not used to children of any age, had
never heard such screaming. It was horrible and horrifying, as if
the little boy's life was draining from him.

'Josh, please,' his mother pleaded. '*Please* don't do this. What's
wrong, darling? What's wrong? Please don't do this.'

174

All over the hotel foyer people began to turn and look. Kieran Beattie grinned supportively. 'I've got two of my own. It's awful when they go off in public, isn't it? I mean, you're not allowed to hit them, so what can you do? I suppose I'm lucky because I only have them every other weekend.'

If Sally Warren could hear Kieran Beattie above the screaming she was not interested in what he was saying. Squatting her pregnant bulk down on to her haunches, she pushed Marmite sandwiches at the little boy, who thrust them away, hurling them on to the spotlessly carpeted floor.

'Want! Want! Want!' it was possible to discern him screaming.

'What, darling?' Sally said, trying to transfer the brittle calm she was affecting across to her hysterical child.

'Go back! Go back! Don't want go that way! Go back!'

'I think he didn't want to be pushed into the lift,' Newson suggested.

'He's doing this all the time at the moment,' Sally said. 'I try not to give in.'

'I think perhaps you'd better.'

'All right, then, darling, you want to go back.' She tried pushing the buggy back to where it had been, but clearly this was not right either, because the screaming redoubled to truly deafening proportions.

Newson presumed that the infant must surely have reached the edge of his envelope, but suddenly he seemed to have found a new stock of decibels that he'd overlooked before.

'I had to bring him,' his mother said miserably. 'Babysitters cost double at weekends, and if I didn't take him with me I'd never go out at all, would I?'

The child was now writhing and shrieking alarmingly. Hotel staff were beginning to hover.

'Is there anything we can do to help, madam?' one asked.

'No, thank you. He'll calm down in a minute.'

For a moment Newson shut his mind to the screaming. He half-closed his eyes and remembered a gorgeous, leggy girl of fifteen.

A dancer, a runner, so cool, so confident. At fifteen she had known exactly what she was doing and where she was going. Not any more. Sally Warren did not know what to do or where to go, because her screaming child would not tell her. She was desperate. Everyone wanted her to shut her child up, and she couldn't. 'There's nothing you can do when they're like this. Nothing.'

'I know. I know,' said Kieran Beattie.

'I'd better take him out, I suppose. I'll see you up there. Wish me luck.' She turned the buggy towards the exit doors, causing the screaming infant to find yet another notch on its volume control to make it clear that leaving the building was not on his agenda either and he didn't care who knew it. Sally Warren looked close to tears as she smiled grimly and waddled away.

Newson and Kieran shared the lift to the second floor. There they were directed along carpeted corridors to a room in which a chattering throng of thirty-four-year-olds, who had been thrown arbitrarily together nearly twenty-five years previously, had already assembled.

It was indeed a good-turn-out. Christine had done well. Of the seventy or so kids who had made up the two classes in Newson's year, about half had now returned as adults.

Christine was at the door. Her PR training served her well and on the little table next to her were neatly ordered name tags. 'Steven Wilmot, right?' she said to Kieran Beattie. 'Hi, Steve! How *are* you?'

'Kieran Beattie.'

'Of *course*! Kieran! Of course.' Christine gave Kieran his badge before turning instantly away from him to concentrate on Newson.

'Now *you* are unmistakable. The very amusing and rather dashing Edward Newson. I could never forget *you*, could I?' she said with a smile that would have flashed even in a darkened room.

'That's because I haven't actually got any taller,' Newson replied.

She looked good, at first glance almost radiant. While the years had ground Sally Warren down, they had lifted her old friend up. Her blond hair was still long and silky, her eyes were still violet blue and her skin was still a glowing shade of copper and gold.

For a moment, but only a moment, Newson's mind flashed on the bleached-white figure of Farrah Porter lying in the bath. That happened to Newson a lot, murders flashing across his mind. His was a difficult job to get away from.

Christine's breasts had certainly grown, there was no doubt about that. He had held them briefly when she was fourteen and had last seen them (clothed) when she was eighteen, and although he remembered them as being quite lovely, nothing about them had suggested the size to which they would eventually expand. They were just about contained within a stretchy halterneck top, which made her shoulders look even more skinny than they were. The whole look was of course a bit obvious, and would not normally have been to Newson's taste. But this was Christine Copperfield and on her it somehow looked just right. He would not have wished her to grow up any other way. She was still way out of his league, of course, but then she'd been out of his league in 1984.

'You know, if you hadn't said you'd come, Edward, I think I would have cancelled the whole thing. You were the first to reply, you know. The very first. It was almost like you read my mind.' She leant across the table to pin his name tag to his lapel. She could scarcely have been unaware that by leaning forward she was making the most of her wonderful cleavage and that once again every boy in the class was straining for a peek. Just as they had always done.

Just then a big man approached the table. Newson glanced at his name tag. Paul Thorogood. The boy whom Christine had split up with at the Christmas disco of 1984. The boy Christine had caught in Guildford HMV canoodling with a slapper from the local comprehensive.

'Can I get you a drink, then, Chris?' Paul asked.

'*Paul*, you remember Ed, don't you? Ed Newson. *Detective Inspector* Ed Newson, I might say. Phew,' she said, fanning herself. 'Two old boyfriends at once. What *is* a girl to think?'

'Hello, Paul,' said Newson, noting that this was probably the first time in his life that he had ever actually spoken to this person. Man or boy.

'Yeah. How's it going, Ed? All right?' Paul replied.

'I know I cheated inviting Paul,' Christine said, 'because he was in the year above, but you don't mind, do you, Ed?'

'No, of course not.'

'So,' said Paul to Christine, 'do you want a drink, then, or not?'

'Oh, that's all right, Paul. I *think* Ed was about to offer me one.'

'What? Oh, right,' said Newson as Paul shrugged and turned away. 'Um, can I get you a drink, Christine?'

'I thought you'd never ask. A glass of champagne, please. It *has* to be champagne today.'

A table in the corner of the room had been set up as a bar. As Newson made his way towards it he found himself greeted on all sides. People seemed genuinely pleased to see him, something he had not really expected.

'Ed!' said a balding man with a pleasant face. 'Graham Brooke. Remember me?'

'Graham! Of course, of course . . . Didn't your profile say you were working in New Zealand?'

'Yes, that's right. South Island.'

'You've come a long way, Graham.'

'No, no. I was back anyway. I'm afraid my mother died . . . You remember my mother. She worked part time in the library.'

'Oh yes, of course,' Newson lied. 'That's very sad, Graham. I'm really sorry.'

'Yes, it's been an awful shock. She was only fifty-nine, you see. Cancer, of course. It seems to claim so many of us, doesn't it? The best of us, I sometimes think.'

'Mmmm. Sadly.'

'She fought it. It was amazing how she fought it. Like a tiger, I used to say. When it was diagnosed she said she wouldn't let it beat her, and she was right, it didn't.'

'Oh, it didn't? But that's great! I misunderstood. I thought she was dead!'

'Yes, she is dead.'

'Ah.'

'She beat it in spirit.'

'Oh, right, that's wonderful. Well done her.'

'In the end she just said no to the treatment they were offering her on the NHS and fought it with the power of positive thinking. She gave it a name. She called it Candy, you know, instead of Cancer. She'd say, "Oh dear, Candy's really giving me a hard time today, but I'm not going to let her get me down, I'm going to stand up to her. Candy's not going to get the better of me, the minx."'

'And that helped, did it?'

'Immensely. That and diet. Absolutely no dairy, obviously, that goes without saying, and only fruit and vegetables in season. It's quite impressive, actually, because you can get a lot of good organic stuff in the big supermarkets these days, which has to be a positive development, don't you think? I'm a member of the Soil Association, you know. Prince Charles is our patron.'

'Look, um, I'll be right back, but I promised I'd get Christine a drink.'

'Oh, right. I never really spoke to her when we were at school.'

'Hmmm. Right.' Newson got to the bar, having failed to avoid catching Kieran Beattie's eye as he stood alone against the far wall.

'Um . . . two glasses of champagne, please,' he said.

A sweet-looking girl in a Hilton waistcoat reached into an ice bucket and fossicked for a bottle of Moët. There was a pop as she opened it and everybody turned to see the flash git ordering champagne.

'Pay well in the police, then, Ed? Ha ha,' said a man who

Newson thought may once have been Roland 'piss stain' Cuthbert.

'Ha ha, yeah,' Newson replied. 'Gotta do it, eh? Yeah.'

'Piss stain', if indeed it was he, rewarded Newson with a raised glass. 'Good work!' he said. 'Rock on, Tommy my son!'

'Fifteen pounds, please,' said the girl in the waistcoat.

'Wow. Seven fifty a glass?' Newson enquired.

'Yes. It's champagne.'

'Yes, right, of course.' He picked up the small flutes and started to make his way back towards Christine.

'Ed? Ed Newson,' said a woman, whom Newson knew had once been Sheila Keaton, a bookish, swotty sort of girl who had organized knit-ins for Oxfam.

'Hi, Sheila,' Newson said. 'Don't have to look at your tits to remember who you are, ha ha.'

'Sorry?' said Sheila.

'The name tags,' Newson said quickly. 'I find them really embarrassing. It means you spend your time peering at people's chests, you know, to find out who they are . . . Except, of course, I knew who you were, and not that I'd have minded anyway . . . I mean, peering at your chest . . . Happy to.'

'Oh . . . good. Well. Any time.'

'Ah, goodoh.' Newson did not know whether this was a joke or not. He flicked his eyes down comically for a moment before looking up again. 'Lovely,' he said. 'Very nice,' and Sheila laughed loudly.

'Same old Edward Newson. Always made us giggle. You've done well, haven't you?'

'Oh, I don't know. I suppose I'm doing something I enjoy, which is important.'

'Yes, you're lucky. Not many people can say that they're doing something they enjoy, can they?'

'Can't they? I don't know. Aren't you enjoying . . . um.'

'Online travel. I assemble cheap flight packages for Lastminute.com.'

'Oh, great. Well, that sounds interesting, all those exotic places . . .'

'I don't go to them, I just assemble the packages and we sell them over the net. It could be toilet rolls or frozen peas.'

'Yes . . . I suppose you're right, but . . . Look, I promised this drink to Christine.'

'Ah yes, beautiful Christine, eh? Still gorgeous. Good luck to her, I say. Some girls just have it, don't they? You got off with her once, didn't you?'

'As a matter of fact I did. Long time ago, though.'

'I remember it happening. Everybody was talking about it and Helen Smart crying in the loos.'

'Was she?'

'Yes, sitting in a cubicle sobbing for ages. I suppose it must have been a shock. We all thought you were an item.'

'Well, we weren't.'

'We all thought you were.'

Newson excused himself and began again to make his way back to Christine. He did not get far before he was stopped by two extremely well-groomed men who were rather self-consciously holding hands.

'Ed?'

'Hello, Gary. Long time no see.'

'I suppose you could say that to anybody today, couldn't you? This is Brad. I know we weren't supposed to bring partners, but I decided sod that. Didn't we, Brad?'

Newson sensed that perhaps Brad was not quite as enthusiastic about attending Gary's grammar school reunion as Gary would have liked him to be.

'I'm glad you came, Gary,' said Newson.

'I was a bit nervous after what I said on the web, blaming every-body for me getting bullied and all. I feel embarrassed about it now.'

'It was perfectly fair,' Newson assured him.

'Yes,' said Brad. 'I told him he shouldn't bother to see any of you bastards ever again.'

'Brad! Behave!' Gary scolded. 'He's more defensive for me than I am. No, really he is. Which is lovely, of course.'

'Brad's right, we were bastards. And I just want to say, Gary, that I'm sorry I stood by while Roger Jameson bullied you.'

'That's all right.'

'It isn't really all right. Bullies only get away with what they do because everyone else ignores it, and I've always felt guilty about ignoring what happened to you.'

'I never said anything when they called you "period head", though, did I?'

But Newson knew that it had been different. He had not been a victim and Gary had.

'Anyway,' he said, 'I was really pleased to hear how happy you both are.'

Finally he found his way back to Christine.

'Coo, a girl could die of thirst,' she said, taking the glass he offered her. 'Mmm, just *love* champers.'

'Sorry, people were saying hello.'

'Of course they were. Everybody's talking about you, Ed. You're the class success.'

'Don't be silly.'

'No, really. You seem to be the only one of us who's doing anything interesting, apart from me, of course. I mean, let's face it, being a detective *is* pretty cool. That arsehole Paul Thorogood was pretending to be all distant and up himself, but I could see he was jealous of you. He used to think he was so great and what is he now?'

'I don't know. What is he now?'

'A warehouse foreman at Tesco. Can you believe it?'

'What's wrong with that?'

'It's not very cool, is it, Ed?'

'In my experience, Christine, when you come down to it, very little is.'

Christine shrieked as if Newson had just said the wittiest thing imaginable. Newson thought her a ridiculous snob, but

182

there could be no doubt that she was paying him a gratifying amount of attention. And she was right, people were certainly treating him differently from the way they'd done at school. On the status market his stock was trading much higher than expected.

'Hang on a minute,' said Christine. 'Don't go away.'

There was a chair behind Christine's little admin table and she now stood on it, giving every man in the room the opportunity to appreciate the fact that her tanned legs were still slim and attractive and every woman the opportunity to be jealous.

'Ching, ching, ching,' she said, pretending to tap a glass. 'Hi, everybody! Christine here! I just wanted to say a few things before we all get *too pissed*! First of all, it's just *so* great to see you all here. Yay! And yah boo sucks to all the boring ones who decided not to come. All right! Now, for all of you who're attending the concert I've got your tickets here and as you know they're forty pounds each, but I would remind you that I managed to negotiate this room and the staff for free, so thanks for that, Cindy.' Christine nodded at the girl behind the bar as if she was in charge of the Hilton's hospitality pricings rather than being one of its wage slaves.

'I should hope the room is free at four pounds a Heineken,' said a voice from the back.

'Well, that's fine, Pete,' Christine replied, 'but if anyone thinks things could have been better organized then they're welcome to tell me how.'

'No, no,' Newson said. 'You've done great, Christine.' He led a small round of applause and Christine smiled at him prettily.

'Now look, everybody, the thing I really wanted to say was this. Obviously everybody here checks out the Friends Reunited site or else you wouldn't be here, and so you all know that a few days ago a girl from our year, Helen Smart, posted up a notice and sent a circular email making some very unpleasant allegations against me and some of the other girls.'

Silence fell in the room. Nobody had expected Christine to

183

tackle this situation so head-on. Newson understood and could not help but admire Christine's nerve. She'd spent time and effort arranging this reunion, of which she clearly intended to be the star, and at the last minute some half-remembered nobody had tried to spoil it. If she ignored the accusations they would hang over the whole day and therefore ruin it. Somehow the boil had to be lanced and she had the *chutzpah* to go for it.

'Now, what I wanted to say was this—'

The door swung open and Sally Warren appeared with her huge stomach and baby buggy before her. Josh, for the moment, was quiet, having been rendered briefly submissive by the application of sweets and crisps.

'*Hi, everybody!*' Sally said as she barged her way in. 'How *are* you? This is Josh! Hope you like kids . . . Oh . . .'

Only now did Sally notice Christine. 'Wow, Christine, you look fantastic! Did I interrupt something?'

'Well, yes, kind of. Hello, Sally.'

'You mean you've started without me?'

'Well, I was just—'

'You said one o'clock in your email, Christine. It's only twenty past now. You could have given me a chance to get here, you know, at least waited till half past.'

'I just wanted to say a few words, that was all.'

'I have got a kid, you know. It isn't easy.'

It was clear to Newson that Sally Warren was a woman on a very short fuse. Hardly surprising, he thought, considering the state she was in and the kind of volume that Josh was capable of generating.

'Why don't I get you a drink, Sally?' Newson said. 'I think Christine just wanted to get something off her chest.'

There was a general good-humoured 'Woooaar' at this from the men in the room. Christine reddened but did not let herself be thrown. Sally thanked Newson and said that she'd have a gin and tonic, and finally Christine was able to continue.

'I was talking about Helen Smart and what she wrote on the

internet. What I wanted to say was that it didn't happen that way and I know that all the other girls will back me up. Yes, Helen could be a bit of a pain and I'm sure we teased her quite badly, which was wrong, but I don't remember anybody ever actually attacking her, and certainly not with a . . . well, in the way she says we did. Anyway, as you know, Friends Reunited is self-regulating and so I've contacted the organizers and asked them to remove the note from the noticeboard because I consider it libellous, and they've agreed to do so. So that's it, I'll say no more about it. We're all here to celebrate the class of 'eighty-one to 'eighty-eight, so I suggest we charge our glasses and drink to our decade, the one we grew up in, the best decade of the last century! The eighties!

Everybody cheered and Christine got off her chair. Newson wondered if she believed what she had said about Helen. He thought that she probably did. People who feel guilty will jump through any number of hoops to justify themselves. Perhaps there was even some truth in her protestations of innocence. After all, in his own case Helen certainly thought that he had done her far more harm than he believed he had.

Just as Newson was about to rejoin Christine a loud voice rang out from the doorway.

'I'd like to say something if I may.' The voice was deep and the accent pure New Jersey, but there was no doubting who its owner was. The big American standing in the doorway had once been an English schoolboy. Roger Jameson had come to the reunion.

'That's right, everybody, it's Roger. Roger Jameson, sometime of New York City Police Department, currently on extended vacation.' Jameson did not need to stand on a chair to command attention. He was six foot four and his fancy leather boots had heels.

'Now, we all know that Christine isn't the only person who's been accused of stuff on our little page of the Friends site. Oh yeah, I copped a whole heap of it too. I'm sure you all know what's been said and who said it, so I guess there's no need for me to ask Gary to go repeating it now. Hi, Gary.'

Newson turned to look at Gary, who had been standing at the front of the group. The years had fallen away and once more Gary was terrified. It was as if he expected Jameson to pull out a ruler and start prodding him again right where he had left off more than twenty years earlier.

'I don't know what happened between Christine and this Helen Smart girl, to tell you the truth I ain't even sure I can remember who Miss Smart was. But I do know about what happened between me and Gary here and also who else was involved. I see Kieran Beattie there. How's it going, Eatie? And one or two of you other guys too. Hi, Pete. Remember us getting puke drunk that time on stolen Scotch? Jeez, we felt bad, huh? Anyway. I guess what me and you boys all know is that every word of what Gary Whitfield wrote about us tormenting him is true and more besides, and what I want to say is that I've come here today to ask Gary Whitfield's forgiveness. I did what I did and I can never undo it, and I will feel the guilt of it until the end of my days. Like I say, I became a cop and in the course of my duties on the streets of New York City I've come to recognize what it feels like to be a victim. What it feels like to live in fear of the violence of people to whom you mean nothing. I know the fear Gary suffered and I am ashamed. I was a shitty, heartless bastard, Gary Whitfield. And I do not deserve your forgiveness, but that is what I'm asking for. If you can't find it in your heart to grant it to me, just say the word and I'll leave right now so you can get on with your party in peace. But if you can forgive me, then I'd like to stay and share a drink with you.' There was a moment's pause before Gary stepped forward with tears in his eyes, reached up and hugged the big New Yorker.

'Thank you, Roger,' he said. 'Now I think we both have closure.'

Clapping and cheering broke out around the room.

'Let me buy this man a drink!' Roger Jameson shouted. 'Hell, I don't care if the dollar's gone through the floor. Let me buy everyone a drink!' He put his arm around Gary and Gary's partner, and together they all headed across the room to the bar. Christine hit the music. She had arranged for the hotel to put a stereo in the room and had brought along some eighties compilation albums. Whatever faults there may have been with her memory, there was no denying that she was a superb organizer.

'These are Friends Reunited albums,' Christine explained. 'They do their own compilations. Isn't that great? I've got all our years.'

Suddenly the little room was jumping. It was partly the music and partly the booze, but there was no doubt that the real catalyst had been Roger Jameson and his extraordinary *mea culpa*. Until his arrival Newson had felt only tension in the room, a group of virtual strangers all concerned for their own fragile egos, anxious not to be thought sad, anxious not to be left leaning against a wall talking to Eatie Beattie, all vaguely and uncomfortably aware that their very presence at a gathering of this kind might indicate inadequacy. Might mean that things had been better for them before they had had the chance to screw up their lives. Jameson had changed all that. He had created an event, a positive and empowering moment in the *present*. They had all somehow moved on. The day was no longer simply about nostalgia, it was about closure and a better future, which meant that they were now safe to wallow in the past freed from the secret fear that it was all that they had left.

'That was some speech,' Newson said to Jameson when they bumped into each other on the way back from the toilets.

'Yeah, I guess. Good to see you, Spewsome. We were pretty good pals for a while back then, weren't we?'

'I was scared of you, Roger.'

'I know. I'm sorry.'

'Don't be. I think what you said to Gary did for us all. It was very brave. Very generous.'

'Nah, it wasn't generous, it was selfish. I needed to get through that for myself. Gary was the generous one to accept my apology the way he did.'

'He'd have ruined the party if he hadn't.'

The two men did not return immediately, lingering instead in the corridor together. Jameson lit up a Marlboro from a softpack of reds.

'Wow, you really have turned into an American,' Newson said. 'They'll tell you to put it out, of course.'

'When they do I will. I don't want no trouble with the English authorities. Hell, I guess the English authorities is you, isn't it, Ed? A detective inspector, no shit, that's like a chief for us. I never got up offa pounding the sidewalk.'

'Ah, but you're an *American* cop. You see, to us that makes you cooler and better whatever the rank.'

Jameson laughed. '*Was* an American cop. I ain't actually left yet, but I very much doubt I'll ever get back into service . . . There's issues, you see.' Newson sensed that Jameson had more to get off his chest than the speech he had made about Gary Whitfield. 'Do you ever get like conflict of interests and loyalties at work, Ed? Like times when you know you should do one thing but you do the opposite because of other cops on the team or whatever?'

'Well, I'm in love with my detective sergeant. I suppose that creates conflicts of interest, and it certainly makes life a bit complicated.'

'Oh, boy. I imagine that would be,' Roger laughed. 'So . . . is he like gay too, or what?'

'She's a woman, Roger.'

'Of course, right. Yeah . . . Ha ha. My mistake.'

'No problem.'

'Does she know about what you feel, Ed?'

'No.'

'I'll bet you a hundred bucks she does.'

'We weren't talking about me. We were talking about you. What conflict of interest were you talking about?'

'Whistle-blowing. That's why I doubt I'll go back to the Department, see. I blew the whistle. I copped an immunity plea and sang.'

'You've lost me a bit here, Roger. What happened?'

'It was one of those pack things, Ed. You know, when guys act one way 'cos they're all together? Act like they never would if they was on their own. I was in a pack.'

'Kind of like with poor old Gary Whitfield, you mean?'

'Yeah, I guess. Except a little more serious, and this time I wasn't the leader, right? That was our sergeant.'

'You beat up a suspect?'

'Shit, he wasn't even a suspect, Ed. He was just some poor fucking guy from Somalia who didn't have papers and didn't have a home. We clear them offa the streets all the time.'

'Yes. I've heard about that. Zero tolerance.'

'Exactly. You know the theory. City Hall reckoned that if you clean up all the vagrants you're gonna make the streets nicer, which is something I guess you can't argue with. But, shit, what a job for a cop, eh? Dragging skinny black guys outa cardboard boxes and ferrying 'em round town trying to find a cell with five square inches of breathing space to stick them in. Man. It gets to you. It really does get to you.'

'I imagine it does. And one of these skinny blokes paid the price for your collective frustration.'

'We'd lost a man that week. Knifed by a guy that our man was waking up in the street. I guess he just woke up on the wrong side of the doorway. Feelings were running high at the precinct and when this Somalian guy started telling us about his rights, some of the boys just flipped.'

'You killed him?'

'Yes, we did. Oh, we killed him all right. It was like a kind of frenzy. We stripped him and beat him and the boys was just shouting and going crazy and then the sergeant shoved his night stick up the guy's ass.'

Newson winced. 'Jesus, Roger.'

'Yeah. Don't some ugly shit happen.'

'I suppose that's one way of putting it. I think I read about this case.'

'Yeah, those media parasites really went to town on it. Making out like every cop in town was a sadistic racist. Huh. Let me tell you now, those guys on the papers are the first to tell us that their wives are afraid to ride the subway and that we need to clean up the streets and protect honest citizens.'

'And when Internal Affairs came down on it you testified against your sergeant?'

'It wasn't just to save my skin, Ed, I swear it. I was truly sickened by what'd happened. I hadn't taken part, well, I had at first, shouting at the guy and pushing him around the room, and I gave him one good punch. But as the pace began to pick up I could see things was getting stupid and so I hung back. A coupla the other guys did too but most of the squad just laid into this screaming little fucking skinny guy. They was like a pack of dogs moving in on a piece of meat. I wanted to pull out my gun and fire it in the air and say that this has to stop right now. I really did. But I was too scared. Scared of the sergeant and of the other guys and of what they'd think of me. So I didn't say nothing and the truth is, on reflection, I've come to the conclusion that it ain't good enough that you weren't involved, you have to try and stop it.'

'Yes. Yes, I know what you mean.'

'Anyway, after the guy died everybody calmed down and the sergeant got real scared and started arranging his cover-up and telling everybody just how we'd say he resisted arrest and had a gun or whatever, but I knew I wasn't going to go along with it. I knew that what had happened was wrong and people had to be punished.'

'An attitude which didn't go down so well with your colleagues, I presume.'

'No, they want to kill me, obviously. That's why I'm here. I'm on leave until the trial comes up and once it's done I guess I'll have to leave town for good. Those guys I'm going to put away are popular guys. They got a lot of friends in the department who don't appreciate a snitch. I'm a marked man.'

'But you're still doing the right thing, Roger. You know that.'

'Yes, I do. I really do. I've seen bullying and I've been a bully and I know it's wrong. People have to fight it. I'm telling you now, Ed, it ain't good enough to stand around shaking your head saying what a terrible, terrible thing it is. *You have to do something about it.*'

20

'Ladies and gentlemen, Dannii Minogue!'

The class of '81 to '88 had left the hotel and made their way into Hyde Park, where in the beautiful sunshine fifteen thousand thirty-somethings were all having the time of their past lives.

'I can't believe it's Simon Bates doing the compering!' Christine shouted excitedly at Newson. 'It was you writing that thing for his radio show that first made me fancy you. Isn't this so *great*?' She threw her arms around him, and he felt her strangely un-yielding breasts pushing against him as Dannii sang about love and kisses.

'Doesn't Dannii look great?'

'I'm afraid I'm something of a purist,' Newson said. 'To me the eighties were over musically when Wham! split up. Everything after they played The Final at Wembley in 'eighty-six is really just the nineties waiting to happen.'

'You are so *funny*,' Christine said, taking out a can of ready-mixed gin and tonic from her chiller bag.

'This is *so* cool!' said Sally Warren, dancing over with Josh. She had not had a ticket, claiming a prior engagement, but when Christine had offered to try and blag her in with the rest of the crowd she had readily agreed. There were thirty of them and when Christine had handed over the large wedge of tickets at the gate in her best media events co-ordinator manner the

192

security man had not bothered to count the crowd.

'Spewsome could sneak in between Roger's legs!' Pete Woolford had shouted to much hilarity when the plan was hatched.

Now that Christine had got Sally Warren into the gig Newson could see that she was regretting it. Sally was overexcited and clingy. Clearly a day out was a rarity for her. What was more, she'd brought a small child and there was simply no denying the apartheid that existed between people who bring children to gigs and the rest of the civilized world. Three-year-olds cannot be ignored and Josh Warren was no exception. He whined, he wanted crisps, he screamed, and whenever his mother tried to speak to anybody he forced himself between them, smearing his snotty face on whatever legs got in his way.

'I just want to show Ed something,' Christine said, taking Newson's hand. 'There's a gang of girls all dressed as Nick Rhodes. Thirty-five-year-old Duranies. It's hilarious.'

'We'll come,' said Sally, picking Josh up, but Christine pretended not to hear her ex-best friend and quickly dragged Newson away, leaving Sally to dance intensely with her child. When he glanced back a few minutes later Sally was talking with great animation to Kieran Beattie. The status market had gone into freefall for her and she was grateful for the social lifeline that even an outcast like Eatie Beattie was able to throw her.

Up on the stage Dannii Minogue was finishing her set and Simon Bates was reminding the crowd what the gig was about. 'You all know why we're here, of course,' he said, 'apart from in order to have a fantastic time! And aren't we doing just that, all right! We're here because of Kidcall. As you know, all the artists performing here today have given their services for nothing and every penny from the ticket sales will go to where it's needed most, which is helping kids deal with the cancer of bullying.'

Newson realized that Graham Brooke was standing at his shoulder.

'I hate the way people use cancer as some kind of catch-all

phrase to describe anything bad,' he said. 'My mother formed the opinion that the only way to beat cancer is to welcome it into your life as a kind of friend, a difficult friend but a friend none the less. You have to try to learn from it.'

'Shhhh,' said Christine.

'I'm sorry, Christine, but my mother's just died from cancer.'

'I know, you told me. Shhhh.'

Newson found himself admiring Christine even more. He'd never have had the front to shut Graham Brooke up like that.

'Now we all know who we have to thank for this great afternoon of terrific pop music,' Simon Bates continued from the stage.

'Look! Look!' said Christine with excitement. 'Behind the drum kit! That's Dick Crosby! Isn't he just the coolest guy alive?'

Sure enough, if Newson stood on his tiptoes he could see the distinctive gingery mullet and goatee beard now flecked with grey of the great hippy entrepreneur himself.

'Yes, that's right,' Simon Bates was shouting. 'I'd now like to welcome to the stage the man who has personally underwritten all the costs for today's show so that your money goes where you want it to go. Helping kids here in London and all over the UK. Please welcome the President of Kidcall, Dick Crosby!'

There was a huge cheer and the still boyishly good-looking billionaire skipped on to the stage. 'All *right*!' he shouted. 'How cool is this or what!' Having paid tribute to the acts that were appearing, Dick Crosby went on to make a brief but moving speech about the curse of bullying.

'It's the feeling of helplessness and isolation,' he reminded the crowd. 'Since I joined Kidcall I've met loads of kids who've been bullied and I know now that it's not only the physical pain that it can cause. It's the isolation. The feeling that you're alone and beyond help.'

Newson looked around and he could see Gary Whitfield nodding gently, his eyes filmed with boozy tears.

'Kidcall is there to show those tormented children that they are *not* alone. That help is out there and that somebody *can* do something. All they have to do is pick up the phone. It's free, of course, and they'll be immediately talking to a trained counsellor. A counsellor who'll give them the help and advice they need to break out of the cycle of lonely despair.'

'God, I just think he's so great,' said Christine, and Newson could only agree with her. Looking around, he could see the effect that Crosby was having on the crowd. He spotted Roger Jameson, staring intensely at the stage, an almost evangelical expression on his face. For a moment Newson felt a shiver as he recalled the terrible story that Jameson had told him. '*You have to do something about it*,' he'd said.

Looking at him now, Newson felt that Jameson would probably be prepared to do anything.

Christine's voice intruded on his thoughts. 'I'd so love to meet Dick Crosby,' she said. 'I've done a couple of corporate things for some of his companies but he's never actually been there, of course.'

Newson had had a few drinks now and Christine was looking better and better by the minute. It wasn't just that he fancied her, either. Despite himself he rather liked her too. He knew she was a bit silly and no doubt in her youth she'd been as unpleasant as any kid can be. But there was something invigorating about her high spirits and her determination to have a good time. And then there were those tits. Newson had never felt cosmetically implanted boobs before and in his half-drunk state he was fascinated to know what they were like. Was it possible that if he played his cards right he might find out that very evening?

Christine's hand brushed against his. This had happened a number of times now. Perhaps it was time to make his move. As he pondered this, Newson realized with a thrill that he had not thought about Natasha since he'd mentioned her to Jameson in the hotel corridor, hours ago. This was something of a record and Newson felt liberated.

'You did *say* you might try and introduce me,' Christine said, and his heart leapt into his throat as she slipped her hand into his.

He was on! He must be! All he had to do now was not screw up and it seemed more than possible that Christine Copperfield, *the* top babe in school, would once more be his. He'd been expecting Christine to bring up his internet boast about introducing her to Dick Crosby all afternoon and had been intending to brush it off when it arose, saying that it wasn't the right time to go bothering the great man. Now, with a belly full of booze and the greatest conquest of his life standing so close to him, he knew that he was going to have to go for it. Faint heart never won fair lady and Newson *so* wanted to pull Christine Copperfield for a second time. 'You know it's possible that Helen Smart'll be backstage,' he said. 'She works for Kidcall.'

'So?'

'Well, you know, you might not want to bump into her, that's all. She's still obsessing on what she said you did to her.'

'Oh yeah, like I'd *really* pass up the chance to meet Dick Crosby because some sad weirdo doesn't have a life.'

Newson procrastinated no longer. 'Come on,' he said and, giving her hand a squeeze, he led her towards the large gang of fluorescent-yellow-clad security men barring the way backstage. Standing nearby were a couple of uniformed police constables. It was towards these that Newson made his way, having first taken the precaution of swallowing a couple of mint Tic Tacs to take the booze off his breath.

'Good afternoon, Constable. I'm Detective Inspector Newson, New Scotland Yard, Murder Investigation Unit,' Newson said, quickly producing his warrant card and photo ID. As usual, he could sense the reluctance of the constables to accept that he was indeed a senior officer, so while they inspected his credentials he ploughed on with all the authority he could muster. 'I'm off duty, as it happens. However, this young lady's in a bit of trouble. Diabetic, lost her insulin, someone nicked it along with her purse. A drug addict, most likely. Bastard. Anyway, I need to get her to the first-aid backstage.'

'There's a St John Ambulance post over there, sir. It's closer.'

'Backstage is quieter, Constable. The lady's upset.'

Christine fluttered her eyelids.

'So will one of you please shift your arse and take us through. I don't have a uniform and I don't want to be having this conversation with every private security thug we meet.'

There was no denying Newson's warrant card and so one of the officers did as he was told and escorted Newson and Christine into the backstage area.

Christine was thrilled. 'Oh my God. Oh, my *God*!' she said. 'I'm like . . . We're backstage! There's Simon Le Bon! He looks fantastic!'

'Doesn't he? Let's get something to eat.'

'Oh my God. Do you think we can?'

'Of course we can.' Newson led Christine to the catering tent, noting with pleasure that various members of the stage crew turned to admire her as they passed. Real live rock 'n' roll roadies were checking out the girl *he was with*.

Inside the tent the food was spread out like a king's feast: cold collations, hot dishes and a fully stocked bar.

'Crew ticket?' the serving lady asked.

'Police,' Newson said, once more showing his warrant card and ID. 'We're with Mr Crosby.'

'Of course, Officer.'

'Wow,' said Christine. 'Do you do that all the time?' She piled her plate high with every kind of exotic salad.

'No, not really. Using your warrant card to gain special privileges is generally thought to be entirely illegal and an ethical nightmare.'

'How *boring*. It doesn't do anybody harm. It's not as if they're short of food around here, is it?'

'It's not so much a catering issue as a matter of principle.'

'God, don't you *hate* the way people go on and on about crap like that? Why can't they just *chill*? This is just *incredible* . . . Look, there's Dannii!'

It was true. There she was, actually standing nearby.

'She's done *so well* with herself, hasn't she?' said Christine.

'I preferred early Dannii.'

'Too tubby. Can't be tubby after eighteen, Ed. Puppy fat is *strictly* for puppies.'

'Right.'

Christine was staring around, wide eyed. 'Thank you. Thank you,' she said. 'This really is an amazing treat.'

'No credit to me, Christine. All I did was abuse the confidence and trust that Her Majesty has placed in me in order to gain favours to which I have no right.'

'You are so *funny*, Ed. You always were.'

They were sitting in the dining area now. The sound of part of the Thompson Twins could be heard from the stage, but Christine was more than happy to remain where they were, surrounded by roadies and musicians looking confident and cool. Occasionally there appeared from a dressing trailer someone who had once been a huge star and for this afternoon at least was once more.

'The truth of the matter is,' Christine said, 'I shouldn't have dumped you, should I?'

Newson swallowed hard. Christine was moving so fast. Was she joking? 'That was certainly my opinion at the time.'

'We had a nice week, though, didn't we?'

'We had a lovely week. I took you to the pictures, we went Christmas shopping, we ate hamburgers, watched videos and on three glorious, never-to-be-forgotten occasions—'

'I let you have a bit.'

'You let me have a bit.'

'Not too much, though. I wasn't cheap. Bad but not cheap. Do you remember when we went to see *Beverly Hills Cop*?'

Newson would never forget it as long as he lived. What a Christmas treat it had been. Walking up Guildford High Street to the Odeon cinema, they'd been so snug and happy, wrapped up in winter coats on that frosty, sunny afternoon in the Christmas holidays of 1984. Christine had worn a long scarf and a knitted hat and Newson had made her laugh from one end of the High Street to the other. A forlorn-looking group of miners were collecting money outside the cinema, and Newson put fifty pence in their box and raised a clenched fist in solidarity. 'Coal not dole!' he'd shouted.

The big, tough, sad-looking men smiled and thanked him. 'That's right, lad. You tell 'em.'

Christine could not help but be impressed, even though she strongly disapproved of the strike. 'You know they get loads of money from Russia, don't you?'

'That's a Tory lie,' Newson replied. 'The Russians don't have loads of money.'

Newson paid for the tickets and bought choc ices and Kia-Ora orange juice, which Christine informed him was for babies and nerds and sent him back for a Coke.

'I'm a traditionalist when it comes to eating at the flicks,' he informed her. 'Gotta be a choc ice, never mind all that King Cone crap. That's all wrong, that is.'

Christine laughed. She laughed at almost everything Newson said, and his reward had been a snog. A genuine full-on, back-seat snog and fumble. She'd let him put his tongue in her mouth and his hand up her jumper. She'd even placed her hand in his lap and rubbed a bit, although only on the outside of his trousers. He'd never been more excited in his whole life.

When they emerged from the cinema it was dark and the High Street Christmas lights were on. They'd stopped by the church's Christmas crib and listened to the Salvation Army band playing carols. 'I hate the way Christmas has been overtaken by religion,' the young Newson had quipped. 'People seem to have forgotten that Christmas is supposed to be a commercial festival about getting pissed and spending too much money.'

'You are so *funny*,' Christine had said and kissed him again.

He could still recall the exquisite feeling of her cold face against his. They'd had supper in McDonald's, which was still relatively new and exciting, and then took the bus to Godalming, where

Christine lived. He walked her to her house and received one last lingering Christmas tonguey under the mistletoe that hung above the door. Then her dad called her in and she was gone. He floated home as if the return bus was a hovercraft. He'd never been so happy.

The next day Christine rang him up and told him he was dumped. It was tough, but he was not as devastated as he might have been. He'd known that he was in a dream and that sooner rather than later he would wake up.

'I didn't really *want* to dump you, Christine said now, pouring more wine. 'I just sort of *had* to.'

'Because I was Spewsome Newson and you were Christine Copperfield and there are rules about these things.'

'Yes, I suppose so.'

'That's OK, Christine. I was amazed you bucked popular opinion for as long as you did.'

'Well, you *were* cool, you know, sort of. Everybody thought that, even if you didn't yourself. I think that was always part of your attraction, that you were kind of cool but you obviously didn't think so . . . You just weren't *sexy*, that's all.'

'Well, clearly not.'

'Not then, anyway.' She smiled prettily and looked into Newson's eyes. 'Who'd have thought you'd end up a detective and Paul Thorogood would end up in Tesco?'

'I don't understand your problem with Tesco.'

'Oh, come on, Ed, *you know*.'

'No, I don't.'

'Well, I didn't dump you for Paul, anyway. I already knew he was a loser. I dumped you for Pete Congreve.'

'Yes, he was a sixth-former, wasn't he? I didn't know him. You were pretty brutal when you did your dumping, Christine. Once out of the circle you were well and truly out. Do you know, I think we hardly ever spoke to each other again.'

'God, I must have been *such* a *bitch*. I still see Pete occasionally when I go home at Christmas. He's a postman.'

'I suppose you think that's uncool too.'

'Well, postmen aren't licensed to carry guns, are they?'

'I very rarely carry a gun.'

'You see!' she squealed. 'I can't believe that *Ed Newson* is even *saying* that! No one would ever have thought it.'

The bottle of wine they had been sharing was nearly empty, and they were both quite drunk. Christine leaned forwards, resting her elbows on the table and her chin on her hands. Her surgically enhanced, horizontally mounted attachments hung in the air like two big guided missiles, frozen in flight. It had to be said that they did not look very natural, or even *comfortable* ... Not like Natasha's. For a moment Newson found himself thinking of Natasha.

But then Christine kissed him on the lips. 'That's for making today so special,' Christine said.

'You did it, not me,' Newson replied, his heart flying and his groin straining. 'You organized everything. Anyway, it's not over yet. We still have to meet Dick. Come on,' he said, getting up.

They left the catering tent and made their way to the stage. Dick Crosby was standing at the side talking to Simon Bates. Newson boldly led Christine up one of the trolley ramps, at the top of which they were stopped once more by the omniscient security figures, but once again Newson's badge worked its magic. 'Police,' he said curtly, and they were allowed through.

'Are you sure you're not going to get into terrible trouble doing this?' asked Christine.

'I might, if I was caught. But as I'm pretty certain I'm the most senior officer present on the site I don't really see who's going to do the catching.'

'Ed! Will you *please* stop being so cool!'

But he just couldn't help it. He was on a roll.

They had arrived side stage and they paused for a moment to take in the view. The whole east side of Hyde Park was a seething mass of people, fifteen thousand of them at least, all hopping and bopping to 'Down Under' performed by one Man At Work.

'So this is how it feels to be a pop star,' Christine said, squeezing Newson's hand once more and pressing her thigh against his.

Just ahead of them Dick Crosby was checking his notes before making another appeal.

'Come on. I said I was going to introduce you to the main man, didn't I? Let's grab him before he goes back on.'

With only the tiniest pretence at shy resistance Christine allowed herself to be dragged through the mass of cables, flight cases, large men in black and women talking earnestly into headsets.

'Mr Crosby? ... Dick,' Newson said. 'Newson. Detective Inspector Ed Newson, New Scotland Yard.'

Crosby looked up. 'Yes, Inspector?'

'This is Christine Copperfield, a friend of mine,' Newson said and Crosby turned his smile on Christine, which she returned with a dazzling combination of teeth, bust and fluttering eyelashes. Crosby was famous for his womanizing and for a moment Newson wondered whether introducing Christine had been a mistake. The last thing he wanted was for Crosby to pull her. He need not have worried. Crosby obviously liked the look of Christine but he seemed more interested in what a detective inspector was doing backstage at his gig.

'Police business,' Newson explained. 'Nothing to concern you. An event like this is always going to attract lowlife and my officers and I like to keep our eyes on it. I just thought while I was backstage I'd say hello. We spoke at the FPO a couple of years back ... The Police Officers' Federation ... You were working on initiatives around urban bullying. You know, neighbours from hell.'

'Ah yes, I remember,' said Crosby, who was obviously pretending that he recalled Newson, to whom of course he'd never actually spoken. 'We thought we were facing up to a massive social problem, and it turned out we were just researching a reality TV programme.'

They all laughed at Crosby's quip and then once more the

afternoon's biggest star was called upon to cajole the audience into making further donations to Kidcall.

Newson and Christine descended the trolley ramps with Christine prattling ecstatically about what a thrill and an honour it had been to meet Mr Crosby.

And that was when they bumped into Helen Smart. She was heading towards the stage-right stairs and they quite literally bumped into each other. Helen was holding a large sheaf of papers covered in figures and graphs and she was forced to bend down and pick them up. Newson tried to help her, but she pushed him aside.

'Helen!' he said. 'Wow. Hello . . . um. Christine, Helen, you remember each other . . . you know, from school. Yes, of course you do.'

'Helen!' Christine squealed. 'Helen Smart! I can't believe it's you. You look *great*. I *love* your hair. So funky! No, really, I just love it.'

'Hello, Ed,' Helen said, refusing to look at Christine.

Christine ploughed on. 'But, Helen, this is great! You're here! Ed told me you might be. I was really hoping we'd bump into you, that's really why we came backstage, isn't it, Ed? I mentioned you when we had our drinks. Didn't I, Ed?'

'Yes, you did.'

'So now you just *have* to come and see everyone, join the reunion, because I think it's time to move on, don't you, Helen? I mean about the things you wrote—'

'I'm not coming – to your poxy fucking reunion, you disgusting bitch.'

Newson was taken aback by the ferocity of Helen's tone.

'Oh!' said Christine. 'There's hardly any call to—'

Helen turned to Newson. 'So you've pulled this slapper again, have you? *Well done*, you. Don't let those tits get too close to the microwave, though. They might go pop.'

'Now hang on a minute,' Christine said.

'No, you hang on. What the fuck are you doing back here, anyway? Where are your passes?'

'We were just going, Helen,' Newson said gently.

'Good idea. Piss off.'

'Look, Helen,' Christine protested, 'this is silly. If I said I was sorry, would that help? Because I am. I—'

'I *said*, piss off.'

'Well, I think that's pathetic.'

'And I don't give a flying fuck what an airhead slag like you thinks, Christine.' Helen turned back to Newson. 'I presume you used your warrant card to get back here because there's no other way you'd have got through. That's an abuse of authority and you'd better leave now or I'll make a complaint against you. I will, Ed, don't think I'm joking. I just can't believe you brought *her* back here. After what you know she did to me . . . You must have *known* I'd be here.'

'I thought you might be, Helen, but we wanted to meet Dick Crosby. Sorry, but there it is.'

'Whatever. Who gives a fuck? Just go.'

'No,' said Christine, 'I'm not going anywhere yet. In fact, I'm going to have another drink.'

'You don't have a pass. I'll call security.'

'Tell-tale tit, your tongue shall split. *I'll call security . . . I'll tell teacher . . .* You always were a bit sad, weren't you, Helen? Call who you like. Ed's the most senior policeman here and I'm with him. Do you think his own cops are going to nick him? Who are you going to call? Ghostbusters?' Christine turned on her heel and headed back to the catering area.

'Look, Helen,' said Newson. 'We'll drink up and then we'll go.'

'Christine Copperfield. Jesus, Ed! *Christine Copperfield*. How could you?'

Newson was getting bored with Helen Smart, bored and annoyed. If everything she had accused Christine of was true then she had every reason to be angry and unforgiving. But she did not have to be so completely *grim* the entire time. And she did not have to continually try to offload the whole thing on to him. He had not stuffed a tampon in her mouth twenty years before. On the other hand, less than two weeks previously she had tricked him into having unprotected anal sex. That was almost certainly a criminal act if it could be proved. If it had been the other way round and *he* had played the same trick on *her*, it would have been called a serious sexual assault, and quite rightly so. Helen Smart had no call to be so high and mighty.

'Helen. Please. Do yourself a favour. Get over it. You only get one life. You should be getting on with yours. We'll be out of here very soon. All right?' He turned away.

'My nipple's fine, thanks for asking,' Helen said bitterly.

'I didn't cut you, Helen. You did that yourself and I'm telling you now, you really need to get some help. Think of Karl.'

'You know something, Ed? One thing I've learnt working for Kidcall is that with bullying it isn't enough to stand round shaking your head. You have to *do something about it.*'

'I've made a donation, Helen. Isn't that what we're supposed to do?'

'You make me sick. Bye.'

Newson walked away and joined Christine in the catering tent.

'I've got us a drink and some pudding,' she said. 'Pavlova. The meringue is *lovely*! I really admire people who do mass catering, don't you?'

Newson smiled at her. There was something about Christine's emotional resilience that he found refreshing. Yes, she was a little shallow, but she was happy being shallow, so why try to be anything else?

'Poor old Helen,' Christine said, daintily wiping cream from her lips. 'You really would *not* want to be her, would you? She so needs to get over herself! I mean, *come on*, Helen!'

'That's exactly what I said to her.'

'And you were right. Anyway, let's forget her, she's not going to ruin my day, which is turning out to be just the *best*. The only question is, what can we do to top it?' Christine looked Newson steadily in the eye. He knew that the time had come to make his move.

'Christine?'

'Yes, Ed?'

'Can we go somewhere?'

'Where?'

'Maybe your place. Or mine. Or a hotel?'

'OK.'

'Great.'

'My place, if that's OK. I have to feed my flatmates' cats. They're both away.'

'The cats?'

'*You are so funny!* The flatmates. That's why I have to feed the cats.'

'Right. Great. Do we need to say goodbye to the old gang?'

'No. I collected their money. And you were the only one I really wanted to see anyway. God, didn't Sally Warren look *awful*? If ever I have kids I will simply *not* let myself go like that.'

They finished their drinks and made to leave. As they passed the security barrier Newson glanced over his shoulder and saw that Helen was watching them go, tears streaming down her face. He prayed that there were no sharp objects to hand.

21

Newson had been surprised to learn that Christine lived in shared accommodation. From the way she'd spoken about herself and her job on the Friends Reunited site, he'd thought that she would be able to afford her own place. This might have been the case had she been prepared to live in Barnet, Watford or Morden, but Christine was a city girl who put location before space and comfort. She lived with two friends in a very nice but very small flat in a thirties-built apartment block on Abbey Road.

'It's nearly Swiss Cottage, daaaarling,' she joked in the taxi going up the Finchley Road. 'Which is almost Hampstead.' Soon they were pulling up outside the imposing listed-entrance porch of Christine's block.

'Both of my flatmates are air crew,' she said as they entered the building and stepped into the old-fashioned lift with its big metal grille. 'I love them, but I also love the fact that they're away so much. They're serving drinks and bits of shrinkwrapped cheese at thirty thousand feet while I get this fantastic flat all to myself. Mind you, they can't complain. They make heaps of money.'

Newson could not help but reflect that this said something about what Christine must be earning herself, because he knew that flight attendants did not make 'heaps of money'.

The flat was solidly built, with what would be described by an estate agent as period features, including big old-fashioned radiators and proper, decent-sized skirting boards. There were two bedrooms, a double and a single that was more of a large cupboard, a living room, a tiny kitchen and a bathroom.

'When we're all here together it's a bit crowded for sure. I have to share the double with Maureen, because it was Sandy who found the flat. Her name's on all the forms. Boys love it when I tell them I sleep with a girl! I tell them we snuggle up together with our cocoa and talk about sex. It's all good fun, though. We have a great laugh. The *Sex and the City* girls, that's us.'

It was a very girly flat, filled with magazines, paperback books and biscuit-packet wrappers. There was an old piano that was clearly never played because its lid was covered with numerous framed photographs of bikini-clad air crew having a fantastic laugh around pools in foreign hotels. The dining table that stood in the window bay and at which it was obvious no one ever ate was piled high with photos, CDs and cassettes, Nurofen boxes and more magazines. There were cushions strewn everywhere, and a huge television surrounded by DVD boxes. In front of that was a big saggy sofa on which, Christine explained, all three girls would sit and watch television together.

'You should see us. Pjs, red wine, choccy biccies. We're terrible. We have a rule that if ever we're all single at the same time, we get a bottle of Baileys and do *Dirty Dancing* and *Grease* on DVD as a double bill. Who needs real men when you've got Patrick Swayze and John Travolta? By the time we get to "We'll Stick Together" we're singing every word. The neighbours hate it.'

Along one wall was a bookshelf filled with stuffed toys.

'Most of them belong to the others, Christine explained. 'They get given them by Japanese businessmen . . . This is mine, of course. My bestest and most precious friend in all the whole world.' She plucked an ancient stuffed figure of the lazy-eyed cartoon cat Garfield from the group of simpering fabric monsters. 'Say hello to Inspector Newson, Garfield. Do you remember him?'

Newson could scarcely believe it. 'Christ, Christine. That's not—'

'Yes it is, Ed. I've still got it.'

He had given her that stuffed toy himself. Christine had loved Garfield, as had lots of her post-Snoopy generation. She'd had a Garfield pencil case, a Garfield ring folder and a poster on her bedroom wall about being allergic to mornings. Newson had bought her the toy as a Christmas present and had sent it to her after she had dumped him in what he hoped was a dramatic gesture. He'd enclosed a note with it that said, 'I'd been hoping to give you this personally, but it was not to be. Merry "heart-broken" Christmas from one who will always love you.'

Newson had last laid eyes on that Garfield twenty years before and here it was, grinning at him again.

'I never thanked you for it, did I?' Christine said.

'No, you didn't. But that's fine.'

'Thank you, Edward.' She dropped the toy to the floor between them and put her arms around him. A moment later they had collapsed together on to the squashy sofa, locked in a passionate embrace.

After a long and jaw-breaking kiss in which Christine worked her mouth and tongue as if trying to unblock a toilet, she disengaged her face, smiling the big, pretty smile that she had perfected at the age of eight. 'That nice?' she said, in a slightly babyish voice.

'Um, yes, lovely.'

'Just picking up where we left off, really.' Christine's hands went behind her back and she began to unfasten her halterneck top.

Newson gulped. 'That Garfield isn't really your favourite thing, is it?' he asked.

'Well, let's put it this way, I always kept it, didn't I? And I've had a few presents in my time, I can tell you.'

'I'm sure you have.'

'I don't keep them all for twenty years, you know. But I thought it was cute. Like you.'

Her top was off now and Newson could not help but stop and

stare in amazement. They looked so *strange*. Not unattractive, by any means, but strange. Of course, he'd seen pictures of breasts like these before, two perfect domes attached to a chest with that slightly weird location of the nipples, sitting unnaturally high. But he'd never seen a pair for real, and they were without doubt fascinating objects. Christine had not gone obscenely far with hers: these were not grotesque caricatures of breasts as beloved by tabloid newspaper editors, but she'd certainly opted for big ones, and they were staring at Newson like two entirely independent entities.

'You like?' said Christine, now affecting a sort of Italian accent.

'Lovely,' Newson replied.

'Obviously, I've had them done.'

'No! Really? Honestly? That's amazing. I had no idea.'

'A couple of years ago. I think they look fantastic. I'm really proud of myself for doing it.'

'Yes, yes. And so you should be. They're lovely. Absolutely lovely,' Newson said, although he was not sure that he was telling the truth.

'They were pretty big before, anyway. Well, you'd remember, I expect, you naughty boy.'

'Oh yes. I remember.'

'So I had to have a lot put in or else it wouldn't have made any difference, would it?'

'No. I'm sure not.'

'I know of girls who've spent *thousands* and when they came out their boyfriends have asked them when they're going to have the operation. That's no good, is it?'

'No, certainly not.'

'I'm thirty-five, Ed. In my job image and looks are everything.'

Newson wanted to tell her that she didn't need to justify herself to him, but he knew that if he said that she'd be offended. So instead he remained silent.

'Nobody wants birds with saggy tits fronting up their corporate dos. The company I work for bin you the second you start looking even slightly rough. We had a girl let go because she came back from holiday with brown sunspots on her face. Don't talk to me about employment rights. They get round them. They're bloody ruthless.'

Newson was learning a little more about Christine's life all the time. He had presumed that she worked for herself. Now he knew that she did not, that she was paid to stand around being a blonde with a pretty face. Not a career at all, but a job and a job with a sell-by date on it.

'You look fantastic,' he said.

'I tried to claim them against tax,' she said, looking down at her breasts. 'No go, though.'

'That's a pity.'

'So do you want to feel them, then? Of course you do, every-one does. Even girls. Go on, I want you to.'

Newson reached out and began to caress Christine's firm breasts.

'You've got lovely gentle hands,' she said. 'You always were a gentle person, weren't you, Ed?'

A great surge of pleasure and affection swept over Newson. He was drunk, and it was all so very erotic. Christine sat next to him on the sofa, her long blond hair falling on her tanned shoulders, her feet tucked under her long legs, a happy smile on her face. She looked like a caricature of a cartoon teenager, and he felt like an adolescent, fumbling and fingering away.

'OK,' she laughed. 'Now you've got to know them you don't need to be scared of them.' She leant forward and unzipped Newson's trousers.

'My *my*, Ed!' she exclaimed with comical shock. 'Have you had *this* cosmetically enhanced? It's *most* impressive. Well, you know what they say about short men!'

They laughed together. Christine's frank, open manner was relaxing to be around. Perhaps it was her PR training, but she knew how to make a man feel at ease.

'I don't think I ever saw this the first time around, did I?' she enquired.

'No, we didn't get quite that far.'

'Such innocent days. Special, special days. I'll just get something to put on it, shall I?' She got up and went to the bathroom, walking across the room in her little mini-skirt with her breasts leading the way. Moments later she returned. 'Have to do the right thing, don't we?'

She slipped a condom on to Newson, then stood up, reached under her mini-skirt and pulled down her knickers. Then, stepping daintily out of them, still wearing the skirt, she placed herself astride Newson, one golden thigh on either side of him, and lowered herself down. Newson could not help but reflect that Christine for all her silliness was a girl with a fair degree of natural class. He certainly preferred this to Helen Smart's taste in lovemaking.

And so began a wonderful, long, relaxed evening of gentle, unselfconscious, undemanding adult sex. They did it together on the sofa with Christine on top. Then they drank a Bacardi Breezer, which was all the booze that Christine had in her fridge, and went into the bedroom where they made love again, but this time for a long, long time in the big soft old double bed with its pink sheets and picture of Betty Boop on the duvet cover.

By the time they had sated themselves it was past ten o'clock. Christine turned off the shaded lamp that had illuminated their lovemaking and they fell asleep. It had been a long time since Newson had actually *slept* with a girl, spending the night in her bed, and he relished the experience. He gloried in the soft skin so close to his, the gentle breathing, the hint of perfume in the room, and the warm, cosy luxury of a woman's presence, in a woman's room. He woke up several times in the night but was happy to lie there listening to Christine sleep. At about four a.m. she stirred and they made love again. Her tastes were as conventional as Helen's had been strange, and Newson much preferred it that way.

Afterwards, Christine smoked, something that normally Newson would not have liked, but even this now seemed sexy and feminine and intimate.

'I'm thinking about that woman,' she said.

'Which woman?' Newson said with a start.

'Helen Smart.'

'Ah, her.'

'We did do what she said we did, you know.'

'I thought you had.'

'It was a fucking terrible thing to do.'

'Yes, it was.'

'There were six of us, and a nasty tease got out of hand. We made her put that tampon in her mouth. It was my idea, too. I just suddenly did it. I called her a disgusting cow and told her next time perhaps she would remember to stick it where she was supposed to stick it and then she wouldn't mess up the changing room.'

'Because she'd left blood on the bench?'

'Well, we said that was why, but I think we did it because she thought she was better than us. She was some intellectual bloody communist and we were airheads.'

'I don't think she had that much confidence.'

'We thought she did, and, anyway, it happened. I've always known it was terrible and it shows I'm not a good person. I've thought about it over the years and it always makes me feel bad.'

'But not bad enough to have owned up to it yesterday.'

'Like Roger Jameson did?'

'Yes.'

'Well, I sort of tried, didn't I, when we bumped into her backstage. But she was so nasty, same old self-righteous Helen Smart. I thought, who knows, maybe she deserved it.' Christine put out her cigarette and rolled over to go back to sleep. 'Maybe I'll send her something, some flowers or a bottle of champagne,' she said sleepily. 'John Lewis do a nice basket with a half bottle of Australian and some muffins.'

Newson wondered whether she was joking, and decided that she was not. In Christine's world a nice basket of muffins was significant currency.

He closed his eyes and, unbidden, Natasha was with him. She was with him every night before he slept, although on this occasion she had taken a little longer than usual to turn up. He tried to force her from his mind and replace her with the girl lying next to him, but he could not.

When he awoke the following morning he had a hangover. It was Sunday and Christine was all cuddly smiles and giggly excitement. She seemed unaffected by their day-long binge and wanted to go and buy coffee and croissants in the traditional manner.

'Come on,' she said, grabbing a dressing gown and heading for the shower, 'it's what you're supposed to do after a first date. Although this isn't our first date, is it? We just broke up for a while, that's all . . . Hey! How about this? We could go up to Hampstead and have breakfast at Louis'. They're normally absolutely packed, but you could flash your card and get us in, couldn't you? Oh, *sorry*, I expect that's against your principles, isn't it? But we could at least get some carry-out and go and sit on the Heath. Why not? The sun's shining and we've got all day . . .' She was shouting from within the shower now, and her words were soon lost in the sound of the water. Nonetheless, Newson could hear that she was continuing to prattle.

He sat up in bed and considered the situation. '*We just broke up for a while, that's all.*' Had she really said that? Did she really think that they were back together? He rather thought she did.

This was extraordinary.

For so long Newson had lived the life of a monk and now suddenly he was fighting girls off. Not only that, but the girl whom he had long seen as the very definition of the phrase 'out of his league' was tilting her cap at him and setting the pace. And the pace was fast.

Too fast for him.

He should have been pleased. It was everything he'd hoped for when first he went online to find her. A gorgeous, fun girl, great sex, a relationship even. A way to break his cycle of dependence on the fantasy of Natasha.

Why not go for it? He'd had a good time the day before, and an even better night. Christine was an easy girl to be with. Why not have Sunday breakfast with her? Why not hang out with her for the rest of the day? Why not arrange to meet tomorrow and see where it all went from there?

Because it was already clear to Newson that Christine was expecting more from him than he was prepared to give. She was not a girl looking for fun, sex and a few romantic dinners. A girl like Christine would never need to look for that. She was looking for a relationship, for Mr Right. And Newson knew that he was no Mr Right. Not for her anyway.

It was quite shocking, Newson reflected, how time had changed everything. He was not a vain man. He had never considered himself any kind of catch for a girl, but he could see that the tables had been turned. For twenty years his status with Christine had remained frozen at the low point in 1984 when she had dumped him for a sixth-former. Now, things were different. For all his unrequited romantic obsessions, Newson was happy with his life, and Christine wasn't. Her brittle self-confidence and expensive breasts could not hide the fact that she was a single woman in a dead-end job paying rent to a flight attendant for half a room in a tiny flat. He could now see that when Christine contacted Friends Reunited she too had been reaching back into the past for a way to break the cycle of the present. Newson was successful, he had status in the community. And that was what Christine craved: status. Once, she'd had it in abundance, she'd been the golden girl of the school.

'Isn't it fantastic that neither of us have any *fucking kids* yet?' Christine said, emerging from the bathroom, a towel knotted across her ledge-like breasts. 'I've been out with loads of guys with kids and, believe me, their kids are never out of the picture. Particularly on Sundays. It's so boring. You either can't go round because *she's* there and doesn't want to meet you, or you have to sneak off early in the morning because she's coming round to drop them off and has insisted that the precious infants aren't corrupted by meeting the slag who's shagging her ex. You end up feeling as cheap as if it was you that walked out on his family, not him. But you haven't got kids, have you, Ed? And neither have I, so we can do just what we *fucking well like*.'

Newson knew enough about life to know that as the years went by the number of unencumbered singletons diminished. A girl like Christine could get herself laid twenty times a day if she so desired, but to find a man whose life had so far not been claimed, that was harder. A lot harder.

'So. Breakfast?' said Christine, drying her hair.

'Yes, fine, great,' said Newson.

They took a cab to Belsize Park and then walked up Haverstock Hill to Hampstead. The sunshine was glorious, the air was fresh, and Newson was still trying to work out what he felt. Perhaps he was being too hard on himself, and on her? Could he not simply take his luck where he found it? He would be quite happy to spend the day with her and indeed the night. She was pretty and fun, and he had been lonely for so long. But he *knew* that he had nothing more to offer than that, that he would not wish to develop anything remotely serious with Christine Copperfield. He liked her, but he could never love her, not in a million years.

Besides which, he was in love with Natasha Wilkie, and he always would be. He knew, therefore, that he should not sleep with Christine again, no matter how much he might like to.

They did manage to get a table at Louis', but shortly after they had sat down and ordered the famous croissant, Newson's mobile rang. It was Natasha.

'I think I have something,' she said, 'from Adam Bishop's past. I'm at UCH. Where are you?'

'Not far. Hampstead. I'll be there in half an hour.'

Newson explained to Christine that he had to go. 'Sorry,' he said, 'I may not have kids, but I do have an ongoing murder investigation, and something's come up. I can't let it wait, either, because the man's still out there and there's always the chance that he'll, as they say, kill again.'

'How exciting,' Christine said. 'I suppose that's just one of the down sides of hanging out with a big tough cop. Oh well, nothing's perfect, is it? Will you come round later? I could cook you dinner. *Or*, much more fun, you could take me out to dinner. I *love* eating out.'

'I don't know how long I'll be. You never do with this sort of thing.'

'Well, I'll be at home. Come if you can.'

'Yes, certainly.'

'Ed, you *will* call me, won't you?'

'Of course.'

They exchanged mobile numbers and Newson left the café. He took the Northern Line down to Warren Street and walked a couple of blocks west to University College Hospital. Detective Sergeant Wilkie was waiting for him in the gloomy entrance to the Victorian building.

'I did what you suggested,' she said, 'and got a list of Adam Bishop's schoolmates in 1959. He was at a state junior in Catford, near Lewisham. There were thirty-eight in the class. After that I thought I'd run the names through whatever hospital archives remained for admissions in that year.'

'Christ, how many of those records still exist?'

'A surprising number, actually. I brought Campbell and Levaux in from their Sunday off and we got stuck in. We started with Great Ormond Street, but nothing checked out there. Then we spread out across the London hospitals and, bingo, we got lucky. One of the names on Adam Bishop's class of 'fifty-nine list was admitted at UCH in February of that year. A lad called William Connolly.'

'How do we know it's the same William Connolly?'

'He was a nine-year-old boy and, get this, he was seriously ill due to blood poisoning caused by . . .'

'Infected puncture wounds?'

'Exactly.'

'Wow. That sounds like the real thing, doesn't it?'

'Certainly does. But if it was Bishop who stabbed him I don't think Connolly ever snitched. I've checked the school records and there's no mention of an expulsion or suspension. And we've gone through Hampstead, Bromley and Lewisham police archives and they don't record any juvenile arrests. If it was Bishop—'

'Come on, it has to be Bishop.'

'If it was, he got away with it.'

'He may have got away with it then, Natasha. But forty-five years later I think it caught up with him.'

'Well, maybe. Anyway, I've tracked Connolly down. He's still alive, still living in south-east London. What do you reckon?'

'I reckon let's hope he's in.'

William Connolly lived with his wife in what had once been a council house just behind Blythe Hill, scarcely three hundred metres from where he had been to school. The little house smelt of old-fashioned Sunday lunch, boiled cabbage, Bisto gravy and proper grey meat. Grandchildren swarmed all over the place. Mr Connolly showed Newson and Natasha into the parlour.

'Yes. I remember Adam Bishop,' he said. 'Anybody who was in our class'd say the same. I doubt anybody who ever met him forgot him.' For a moment Connolly said no more. He stared into the distance. Newson and Natasha waited.

'He was a bastard,' Connolly said finally, before again lapsing into silence.

'Could you elaborate, Mr Connolly?'

'That's the best I can say of him. An absolute bastard. He made our lives a misery, ruined our schooldays. I read he was dead and I hope he rots from now until the end of time.'

The brief spasm of hate that had registered on William Connolly's features subsided into a mask of weary sadness, a sadness that over the years appeared to have seeped into the lines on his face and the reflection in his eyes. 'I don't often get drunk,' he said. 'But I certainly did on the night I read that he'd been killed. I went up the pub at six and I didn't leave till closing time and

218

with every pint I cursed the bastard's memory and prayed that there's a hell, because if there is he's burning in it.'

'Do you know how Mr Bishop died?'

'I know what I read in the *Standard* the next day, and when I read it I went out and got drunk again. My missus wasn't too pleased, but she knew how much it meant to me so she let me go.'

'He was stabbed.'

'That's what I read. Stabbed loads and loads of times.'

'Do you know what he was stabbed with?'

'It didn't say in the paper.'

'That wasn't what I asked you, Mr Connolly.'

There was a pause. 'Well, I did wonder. Wonder whether he'd done it to somebody else. And whether that somebody else didn't roll over and take it like I did.'

'You were admitted to University College Hospital in February 1959 with blood poisoning caused by small puncture wounds, Mr Connolly.'

'You've done your homework, haven't you?'

'You never said at the time who stabbed you or what with.'

'No, I didn't. I was too scared. Pathetic, eh? I nearly died because of that bastard and yet I protected him. I wouldn't say a word. Kids didn't in those days.'

'So tell us now what happened.'

'You obviously know.'

'We need to hear it from you.'

William Connolly undid the cuffs of one of his shirt sleeves and drew it back to reveal a series of tiny white scars in the weathered brown skin. Then he pulled out his shirt flap to reveal similar tiny scars on his stomach.

'Adam Bishop held me down behind a desk one day during break time and stabbed me with a dirty compass and nearly killed me. It wasn't the only thing he did to me in the five years I knew him, but it was the worst, the only one that actually put me in hospital.'

'Mr Connolly, I'll need to know details of your whereabouts

219

on the evening of Tuesday June fourth of this year,' said Newson.

'Is that the night the bastard died?'

'Yes.'

'To be honest, one evening's much the same as another in our house. I would've been at home. I'm home every weekday evening. We only go out Saturdays. Bingo or the pub.'

'Can anyone corroborate that?'

'Only the wife. It's just me and her in the week. The grandkids come over on Sunday.'

'Have you ever told the story of what Bishop did to you to anyone else?'

'Only to my wife. Isn't that funny? In all the forty-five years I've woken up in the night sweating and remembering what happened to me, you're the only other people I've ever told. I've always been ashamed, you see, that I never stood up to the bastard.'

'So apart from us, your wife is the only person who knows about how, when you were ten years old, your classmate Adam Bishop attacked you with a pair of compasses?'

'Oh, no. Plenty know about it, don't they?'

'Who?'

'My bleeding classmates, that's who! It was a wet break, see. This didn't happen in no dark and quiet corner. Oh no, at least half the class was in the room watching. Not one of them raised a finger. Not one of them said a word. He even made one of the girls go and get some paper from the toilets 'cos I was crying. When she brought it he told me to stop blubbering, dry my eyes and mop up the blood, but instead of giving me the paper he stuffed it in my mouth.'

Newson and Natasha exchanged glances.

'Tell me, Mr Connolly,' Newson said, almost as an afterthought, 'do you and your wife use the internet much?'

'The internet? Blimey, Inspector, we ain't even got a computer. What the hell would we want one of them for?'

'Fine. Just wondering.'

As William Connolly showed them to the front door Newson

turned once more. 'One thing I would say, Mr Connolly. Don't feel ashamed about not fighting back. Adam Bishop was exceptionally violent, and all through his life people were absolutely terrified of him. Nobody stood up to him.'

'Except one person, eh? The hero who did for him.'

'Well yes, except for him. Anyway, he was a big man. I expect he was a big lad too. You have nothing to be ashamed of, so you can stop letting him live in your head rent-free.'

'Particularly seeing as how the bastard's dead.'

'Exactly, particularly since the bastard's dead.'

22

Newson and Natasha sat together on a bench at the top of Blythe Hill, glad to be away from the smell of cabbage and the rawness of a pain long past that was still as livid as if it had only just been inflicted.

'I don't think William Connolly could have drugged Adam Bishop and dragged him up a flight of stairs, do you?' said Natasha.

'No, I don't,' Newson replied.

'He has two sons. They could've done it. Perhaps he's lying to us about never having said anything. Perhaps he told his sons and they took revenge.'

'Perhaps, but I doubt the Connolly boys bleached Farrah Porter or cut Angie Tatum's upper lip.'

'Perhaps we've been deluding ourselves and none of these murders is actually connected.'

'They're connected. Although I must say I'm disappointed that the Connollys don't own a computer.' Newson yawned, suddenly dog-tired.

'Up late, were you?' quizzed Natasha.

'As it happens, I was.'

'How was the reunion?'

'It was a huge success, thanks for asking.'

'And now you're tired and yawning . . . Hmm.'

'What do you mean, "Hmm"?'

'Just hmm. So?'

'What do you mean, "So"?'

'So *what happened*? Come on, you've got to tell.'

And Newson did tell her, not about his doubts, but about his triumph. He couldn't resist it. He wanted her to know that he was not entirely without sexual magnetism.

'You mean you copped off with the best-looking girl at the class reunion?'

'Yes, I did, and she wants me to go back tonight.'

'Are you going to?'

'Perhaps.'

For a moment Natasha was quiet. She turned away, and then she smiled at him. 'Be careful, Ed,' she said. 'Remember what you said about crash-landing your plane on to the deck of someone else's life.'

'I know, I know. It certainly wasn't a happy experience the last time I tried it . . . Look, I don't suppose I could buy *you* dinner instead, could I? You know, just to keep me out of trouble?' There, he'd asked her out.

'I'd like to, Ed, but—'

Newson leapt upon her refusal before she had the chance to complete it. 'Fine, fine. No problem, none at all. Stupid idea. You're right. Absolutely. Forget it. Sorry I asked.'

'Don't do that, Ed.'

'What?'

'Mention something nice, then go into some huge joke thing about how insane it is as if you're a complete nerd.'

'Do I do that?'

'Yes.'

'Oh.'

'I'd have liked dinner, but I've been working all weekend and I owe Lance some "him" time.'

'Of course.'

'Otherwise, it would've been very—'

223

'No problem, no problem at all. Give Lance my best wishes, will you, and tell him he's a lucky sod.'

Natasha smiled. 'You don't know me, Ed. He's not so lucky.'

But Newson knew that he was.

Natasha walked off to her car, leaving Newson alone on the bench. He turned on his phone, which he had switched off during the interview with William Connolly, and saw that he'd been left a message. It was from Christine. Despite his doubts, he was pleased that she had called so quickly.

'Hi, Ed. It's me! Yes, Christine, she of the recently concluded night of passion. How weird was that? Weird but good, I think. Yes, definitely good. Hope you think so too. Hope you're pleased and not messed up about it. What a drag about you having to rush off like that. Look, I meant what I said about tonight, not about you having to buy me dinner but definitely about seeing you. I'd love it if you wanted to come around again. No pressure, but hell, were we good together or what! You are a stud! *Please come round, Ed, any time you like, whenever you finish with your big important police stuff. I'd love to see you . . . I don't know. "Us" just feels sort of right. Anyway, that's it, but . . . Oh, hang on, that's the doorbell . . .'*

As Newson listened to the message he could see Christine in his mind's eye walking across her flat.

'Ju-ust checking through my little spyhole . . . Well, well, well! This is *a surprise. Wow, Ed, will I have something to tell you. You'll have to come round now! Gotta go . . . Byeee.'*

Newson wondered. She wanted more from him than he did from her, but why was he making such a big deal of it? All she was doing was asking him round. She wanted to share dinner and perhaps once more share a bed. What was wrong with that? Sitting alone on a park bench in south London, watching Natasha get into her car at the bottom of the hill, Newson could not think of a thing. He decided that he definitely wanted to have sex with Christine again, and to laugh with her, and to feel her body sleeping close in the night.

Of course, he didn't love her like he loved Natasha, but Natasha had gone off to Lance, just as she would always do. What was he to do in the meantime? Deny himself a life for fear that he might fail to meet up to the expectations of a woman who had merely asked him to dinner? Christine was a grown woman, responsible for her own feelings, as he was responsible for his.

There being no chance of a taxi on a Sunday afternoon in such an area and no sign of a minicab office, Newson took the over-ground train to Waterloo. There he bought flowers at the flower stall and two bottles of Veuve Clicquot from Victoria Wine before taking a taxi up to St John's Wood. Suddenly he was excited. He was not making a commitment. He was going round to see a girl. That was all.

When he arrived at the mansion block Newson was disappointed to receive no answer. Thinking that perhaps the doorbell was broken, he called Christine's mobile, but received only her outgoing message in reply. 'Hi, Christine,' he said into his phone, 'I've come round like you said . . . I'm outside on your doorstep. Um, not sure what to do now . . . Maybe your bell isn't working.'

Just then a little old gentleman emerged from the ancient lift inside the building and let himself out of the door. Newson used the opportunity to slip past him into the entrance hall. 'Yeah, meeting someone. Their bell's broken,' Newson said.

The old man looked a little concerned, but Newson couldn't help that. He took the lift up to Christine's floor and knocked loudly on her door. Still there was no answer. Standing in the gloomy corridor, he wondered what to do. Then the inevitable thought struck him, inevitable at least to a man like Newson. Perhaps she too had been having second thoughts? That was probably it. She'd changed her mind. Suddenly the anguished dilemmas that he'd recently been indulging in seemed arrogant and foolish. There he'd been, fondly imagining that it was he who was in the emotional driving seat, and now it seemed that perhaps *she* had cold feet. Maybe she was behind the door right now, not answering, trying to keep quiet, hoping he would go away.

Newson resolved to go home. Perhaps he'd hear from her later. Either way, he sensed that the moment was spoiled. He bent down to put the flowers by her door and thought of the last gift he'd given her, the stuffed Garfield that she'd kept for twenty years. It was a tradition now. She dumped him and he gave her presents.

Then he heard it. Very, very faintly, but he heard it. Somewhere close by, somebody was playing music.

Wake me up before you go-go.

Newson looked around. Where was it coming from? He put his ear to Christine's door. There was no doubt about it. The music was coming from inside her flat. It was Wham!'s huge number-one hit, from the late summer of 1984. George and Andrew's triumphant return after a year in the wilderness fighting their record company.

He knew instantly that something was wrong. Dread gripped his stomach, and a cold sweat prickled on the palms of his hands. He hammered his fists upon the door. 'Christine!' he called out. 'Are you in there?'

He remembered that, apart from two deadlocks at the top and bottom of the frame, the door was closed with only a simple latch. If it was only latched . . . He put his shoulder to the door.

Newson was small, but he was strong, and the seventy-five-year-old doorframe was weak. It splintered on his third attack and the door swung open into Christine's flat.

Inside all was in darkness. The heavy drapes were drawn, but from the light that flooded in through the doorway Newson could see that the sitting room was empty and all seemed in order.

'Christine,' he said, and then, louder, 'Christine!'

The music was coming from the little stereo unit on top of the girls' television. On the previous evening Newson had loaded CDs into that very machine: Dido, Sophie Ellis Bexter, Jewel. Christine favoured female easy-listening of the more sophisticated lounge variety. The Wham! track was finished, and the stereo was now playing Bananarama. It was clearly a compilation album. An eighties' compilation album.

Newson felt for the switch and turned on the lights. Everything in the room seemed normal, the pleasant clutter undisturbed from when he had last seen it only a few hours earlier. There were cushions on the floor and magazines scattered on the furniture. Garfield was back in his place amongst the teddies and Beanie Babies.

'Christine. It's me, Edward.'

Newson picked up his champagne and flowers and stepped into the room, walking over to the table that stood in the window. He found a space and put them down on it.

'Christine?'

Then he noticed the first of the marks. It was on the big soft sofa where he had first made love to his old school flame. A rust-coloured stain on the yellow upholstery. Newson knew that colour well, having seen it many times in the course of his duties. It was the colour of dried blood. The sight of it made his own blood run cold.

He glanced about. One of the chairs that had been tucked under the table had been moved out. Somebody had sat on it, sat on the worn, threadbare cloth of the upholstered dining chair. That cloth had once been a rich shade of cream, but it had grown grubby with age. It was grubbier still now, for Newson could see that it too was stained with blood. A thin smear in a shape vaguely reminiscent of a spearhead.

From where he was standing beside the table, Newson could see into the tiny kitchen and the bathroom. Both were empty. The bedroom door, however, was closed. Being careful to disturb as little as possible, he crossed the room towards it. As he pulled a handkerchief from his pocket in order to turn the bedroom doorhandle, he noticed that there were drops of dried blood on the polished wooden floor just outside the door. The drops led his eye to the piano. The four deep indentations in the rug in front of the piano indicated where the stool normally stood and that it was rarely moved. Someone had moved it now, though. The upholstery was dark green, and Newson could make out a darker patch in the middle of it. More blood.

227

He opened the door to the bedroom. Somehow he already knew what he would find, and yet he was completely unprepared for it. The girl with whom he had spent the previous night and upon whom his mind had lingered on and off for the previous twenty years was dead. She lay naked on her back, on top of the Betty Boop duvet, with her hands awkwardly stuffed behind her. Newson supposed they had been tied. Her legs were parted and between them the bedcover was stained with blood. As Newson stepped forward to check her pulse, knowing already that he would find none, he noticed that from Christine's half-open mouth there trailed a short, thin piece of white string. Newson was not particularly familiar with this type of string but he knew immediately what it was and what it was attached to.

He took out his phone and reported what he had found. Then he retreated from the flat, attempting to retrace the steps he had previously taken. Once in the corridor outside, he closed the door behind him and leant against the wall to await his colleagues. For the moment, at least, this brief display of professionalism represented the limits of Newson's composure. Crushed by the terrible weight of sadness bearing down on him, he slid down the wall until he was sitting on the floor.

Newson knew that he had only minutes to mourn. Or at least only minutes before the gruelling hours of police work that would now follow. Once Natasha and the forensic team arrived, the investigation would begin and Christine Copperfield would necessarily become one more murder victim whose killer he had been tasked with finding. For Newson knew absolutely that Christine had become a part of the series of killings he had first encountered at the house in Willesden when he arrived to investigate the Bishop murder. The thought caused pangs of anguish to shoot through him. Had he been a better detective he would already have caught the lunatic and prevented Christine's death. But he wasn't and he hadn't. She was dead and he had minutes to say goodbye to her before focusing on her killer.

'I'm sorry, Christine,' he said under his breath. 'You did not deserve this. Some bastard thought you did, but I know you didn't. You were just another person, and we all make mistakes.'

What mistakes had he made? It was a short step for Newson from reflecting on his own shortcomings to speculating on whether he might have caused Christine's murder. Was the killer focusing on him? Could it be that by murdering his old friend – his lover – the killer was speaking directly to him? It was a horrifying thought and Newson struggled to force it from his mind. He *knew* what the connection was now. He *knew* how the killer found his victims, and it had nothing to do with him.

It had nothing to do with him.

23

'Whoever it was didn't use Rohypnol to subdue her,' Dr Clarke said. 'It was chloroform. There are residual traces around her mouth.'

Newson had specifically asked for Dr Clarke to be contacted when he had alerted the local police and his own office at New Scotland Yard to this latest murder. She had attended three out of five of the previous murders and Newson felt that there might be some benefit in continuity. Besides which, in his shaken state he did not feel up to having to convince any new colleagues that he really was in charge.

'And it was you who found the body this time?' the doctor asked.

'Yes, it was me who found her.'

'A friend of yours?'

'Sort of.'

Newson caught Natasha's eye. She'd been looking at the champagne and flowers standing amongst the clutter on the table in the window.

'Yours?' she enquired.

'Yes, mine,' Newson replied.

'Flowers and *two* bottles of Veuve. It must be nice being your friend,' she remarked.

Newson felt hot and deeply uncomfortable. He hated the way

230

Natasha was looking at him. It was clear that she must think he'd bought these clichéd and expensive tokens with the sole purpose of exchanging them for sex. But he *hadn't*. Not entirely, anyway. He had *liked* Christine and he knew that she would have *loved* to be brought flowers and two bottles of good champagne. He'd been looking forward to seeing her smile when he handed them over.

He also felt excruciatingly exposed professionally. Christine had been brutally murdered, and shortly thereafter he had turned up bearing romantic gifts. It was a profoundly awkward situation for anybody, but particularly so for the chief investigating officer.

'You're completely convinced that this is part of the cycle?' Natasha asked.

'Absolutely,' Newson replied. 'The victim allows her killer to walk into her home where he promptly drugs her, restrains her and inflicts on her a macabre death while playing music that was popular during her schooldays. He then departs leaving scarcely any trace that he was ever there. It's the same killer. I've no doubt of that.'

'Seems very strange, doesn't it,' Natasha said, 'that he should kill a friend of yours? I mean, apart from the fact that you're in charge of the team that's pursuing him, what possible connection do you have with the killer? Do you think he's trying to tell you something? Warn you off, maybe?'

'Well, it'd be giving me a great deal too much credit if he was, since I have absolutely no idea who he is.'

'So is he interested in you as a person, then?'

'Do you mean, have I become part of his motivation? Of course I've wondered about it,' Newson said, trying to assume an air of cool and efficient confidence. 'But, frankly, I very much doubt that that's what this is about. This thing was going on long before I became involved, and either I'll stop it soon or I'll be removed from the case, and then I'm quite certain it'll go on without me.'

'So what happened here, then?' Natasha asked. 'How did he kill her?'

'Somebody stuck a tampon deep into her throat and she choked to death,' said Dr Clarke.

'And whoever did it gained access to her flat without encountering any resistance,' Natasha said.

'Yes,' said Newson. 'She knew her killer.'

'We can only presume that,' Natasha replied.

'No, this time I know for sure. I have a recording of Christine's voice on my mobile answering service. She was leaving me a message at the moment when the killer turned up. Talking to me while she looked through her spyhole. I heard her saying, "Well, well, well, this *is* a surprise," and that she'd have a story to tell me.'

'So *you* know the person, too?'

'She certainly thought it'd interest me, so I suppose I must do.'

'Fuck. If that's true you *know* the killer,' said Natasha.

Dr Clarke broke into the discussion testily. 'We need to deal with the scene of crime, Inspector. You can discuss it all later. It's a Sunday. I'm supposed to be with my children.'

Newson had forgotten about the changes taking place in Dr Clarke's life. She seemed harassed and on edge. Could it really all be down to his having told her about her old passion from medical school? Had that been the spark that exploded her marriage? Was the past really so powerful that it could comprehensively ruin the present?

Christine Copperfield's corpse lying in the next room was proof that it could. Something she did twenty years before had come back and brought her present to a sudden and brutal end. The present. Newson knew that he must focus on the present. Christine was dead. More people were likely to die unless he could find the perpetrator.

'The killer acted quickly this time,' he said. 'Christine only left her message with me a couple of hours ago. He entered the flat and since there seem to be no signs of hostility I imagine he subdued her immediately with the chloroform.'

'I think he stripped her while she was unconscious,' Dr Clarke added. 'I've had a good look at the body and there are only two sets of bruises on it. Big heavy ones just below the shoulders of each arm. If she'd been aware of his taking her clothes off I imagine she'd have struggled and we'd see more evidence of it.'

'Unless he held her up with a knife,' Natasha suggested. 'The knife he cut her with.'

'Maybe, but if so why bother with chloroform at all?' said Dr Clarke.

'That's right,' Newson said. 'I think he stripped her while she was out of it and bound her wrists, then waited for her to come round. In the past he's always made some effort to ensure that the victim understands their fate, and I'd be surprised if he let Christine Copperfield off any of the details.'

As he said it he was trying to remain calm and dispassionate, but inside an immense anger was building. He'd been having breakfast with this girl only hours before. She had not deserved what had been done to her.

'When she woke up I think he must have acted immediately. I think he pushed the tampon into her throat at this point,' he continued.

'Before he cut her?' Natasha asked.

'Yes. Once she was bleeding we can tell where she went and what she did simply by following the stains. If he'd waited till she was on the bed to choke her she would have thrashed around and we'd see a great deal more staining on the duvet instead of the simple neat puddle between her legs. By the time Christine hit the bed, I think she was nearly done for. She was choking while she was being moved around the room. What's more, nobody heard anything. These are solid flats, but if the tampon hadn't been acting as a gag, I think they'd have heard her scream when he used his knife on her.'

'So, she woke up naked, he pushed the tampon into her mouth and then he cut her,' Natasha said.

'Yes, a single slash across the vulva,' Dr Clarke said. 'It's not a deep cut, not life-threatening at all.'

233

'It didn't need to be deep,' Newson said. 'It just needed to bleed. He needed her to bleed from that particular place in order to complete his scenario.'

'Which was?'

'He wanted to mark the seats. Mark them with blood. So, having made her bleed, he grabbed her by the upper arms in what would have needed to be a very firm grip because of course she would have been struggling, and he hauled her about the room from one seat to another, pushing her down and leaving a bloody imprint wherever he took her. The sofa, the dining-room chair and finally the piano stool. Then, as her resistance began to lessen because of oxygen starvation, he marched her backwards into the bedroom and pushed her back on to the bed, where she breathed her last, but not before having been fully conscious of the detail and hence the reason for her terrible fate.'

'He wanted to mark the furniture with blood from the wound in her groin?' Natasha asked.

'Yes, he did.'

'So this is sexual, then?'

'No, it isn't sexual.'

'I thought everything was . . .' Natasha had clearly been about to quote Newson's old adage, but she stopped before it was completed.

'Yes, Natasha. I know what I once said, but this was not sexual. None of the murders are, except in the very broadest Freudian sense of the word. You see, I know what this killer was doing and so do you. I told you about it. Do you remember? The killer was aping an episode of bullying. Just like he was doing when he killed Adam Bishop.'

'So this is all about bullying?'

'Yes. The blood he forced Christine to leave on the furniture in the last minutes of her life represents menstrual blood. It is a macabre recreation of an incident that happened more than twenty years ago when Christine Copperfield bullied a girl for unwittingly starting her period on a bench in the girls' changing rooms at their school. Which was also my school.'

The room fell silent. The busy police officers looked up from their cameras and their fingerprint dust to listen to Newson. Even careworn Dr Clarke seemed to forget that she was in a hurry.

'Who was the girl?' Natasha asked. 'Whose menstrual blood do these stains represent?'

'The woman I told you about. Helen Smart.' Newson looked away from Natasha, but not before he had noted in her eyes the clear thought, 'Ah, your other recent lover.' Newson had had sex with only two women in many, many months, Natasha knew that. She also knew that one of the women was the murder victim and the other looked to be shaping up as the principal suspect.

An hour later the on-site investigation was complete, and the body of Christine Copperfield was removed, leaving the flat she shared with the air crew for the last time.

Dr Clarke was preparing to leave with it. 'You know something, Edward,' she said, using his first name for the first time that he could remember in their long association. 'You really should remove yourself from this case. You're too connected now. You discovered the body. You were the last person to talk to the victim alive. You're compromised. It could look very bad for you. You need to hand it over before Ward tells you to. If you wait till it's forced on to you it would look pretty bad.'

'These murders have nothing to do with me,' Newson said.

'From where I'm standing you seem to have an awful lot of inside information. Only you could have worked out the menstrual blood thing and that's because you knew the people involved. Nobody could have come up with that theory simply from the evidence available.'

'On the contrary, Doctor, all the information required is in the public domain. Anybody can access it at any time.'

'How?'

Newson crossed the floor of Christine Copperfield's living

room and stood in front of the television, on top of which sat the stereo. One of the constables had turned off the music some time before. Once more taking his handkerchief from his pocket, Newson pressed the CD eject button. The disc emerged.

'By going online and going to the address printed on this compilation CD,' he said. 'All you need to do to find the motivation for this murder is visit Friends Reunited.'

24

'I'm sorry, I can't help it. Part of me's glad she's dead.'

Helen Smart was sitting on the same threadbare sofa that she had sat on while making smalltalk with the babysitter on the evening when she and Newson had first had sex. Inspector Newson sat in the same chair that he had sat in while waiting for the babysitter to leave. Newson could not decide whether he found Helen's flat more or less depressing in the daytime. Had it really been less than a fortnight since they'd sat there together? It seemed like a lifetime ago. Helen was fiddling with a pair of scissors, cutting shapes out of children's coloured card. The scissors were not the blunt children's type, though, they were big, sharp adult ones. He wondered whether she was playing with them for his benefit.

'I can't mourn her,' Helen reiterated. 'I'm sorry, of course, she was a human being after all, but it'd be hypocritical to pretend I'm upset. She ruined my life. Now someone's ruined hers.'

Natasha was leading the interview. 'Do you have any idea who that person might be, Ms Smart?' she enquired.

'No, of course not. How would I?' Helen replied.

She did not look well, Newson thought. Her eyes were hollow and there were bags beneath them. Her hair, which had been so cutely moussed and spiked when she'd come to visit him, was flat and greasy. She had clearly just got up and wore only a big shirt and slippers. Her legs were unshaven and somewhat bruised.

'Because,' Natasha continued, 'whoever killed Christine Copperfield appears to have done so in order to avenge an incident that happened to you while you were at school.'

'I have no idea what you're talking about.'

Newson watched Helen closely. Was she lying? Did she really not know how Christine had died?

'We thought that perhaps you might,' Natasha said.

Helen turned to Newson. 'Why's she asking all the questions, Ed?' There was a hard, sarcastic edge to her voice. 'I thought you were supposed to be a big important policeman. Who's in charge, you or her?'

'I'm in charge, Helen,' Newson replied gently, 'but Detective Sergeant Wilkie is my colleague. You can treat her as you would me.'

'I slept with you, then you dumped me.'

There was an embarrassed silence before Natasha resumed her questioning. 'Ms Smart, can you tell me where you were and what you were doing between noon and four o'clock this afternoon?'

Newson's discomfort was plain for all to see. It was certainly not lost on Helen.

'What's the matter, Ed? Embarrassed? Haven't you told her, then? Look, he's going red. I think he fancies you, Sergeant.'

'Please stick to the questions, Helen,' Newson said. 'What were you doing this afternoon?'

But Helen was in no mood to be told what to do. Newson wondered if she had been drinking.

'What's he like to work with?' Helen said, turning to Natasha. 'My old mate Ed Newson. Has he abused his position of authority with you? Flashed his warrant card where he shouldn't? That's how he pulled Christine, you know. Getting her backstage because he's a copper, gatecrashing the hospitality and getting her pissed for nothing on the strength of his warrant card. How crap can you get?'

Newson said nothing. What Helen was saying was true.

Natasha's expression did not change. 'I'm going to have to

insist that you answer our questions, Ms Smart. I don't want to have to arrest you for obstruction.'

'She was with me. All day.'

A man had emerged from Helen's bedroom. He was skinny with long dirty hair, and wore only his jeans, which were not fully zipped up. Though fit-looking, he was also wasted. Newson noticed needle track marks amongst the tattoos on the man's arms. They did not look recent. He hoped that they weren't.

The man walked across the room with an arrogant swagger and went into the kitchen to put the kettle on. 'Don't tell me you've got no fucking milk, girl,' he said.

'This is Kevin,' Helen said.

'*Kel*vin, darling, Kel-vin, with an l in it. All right?'

'Yeah, all right,' said Helen. 'This is Kelvin.'

'So, Kelvin,' Natasha enquired. 'You say that you and Helen have been here all day?'

'Yeah, in bed. We only got up when you came round.'

'Where's Karl, Helen?' Newson asked.

'What's it got to do with you?'

'I'm concerned about his wellbeing.'

'Oh, please *do* fuck off, Ed. Like you care a toss.'

'I was simply asking where he was.'

'Karl and I were fine before you barged back into my life for a quick couple of shags and then fucked straight off again, and we're fine now, OK?'

Newson noted that Natasha's expression still did not change. She was giving a perfect impression of being supremely un-interested in Helen's remarks about Newson's private life. She was a good police officer and a good friend. Newson hoped that he too was maintaining a calm exterior. Inside, he was mortified. 'I'd like to know where Karl is,' he said.

'He's at his nan's. Now, is there anything else?'

'Yeah,' said Kelvin. 'Is there anything else? Because it's Sunday afternoon and we was chilling.'

'Shut up, Kelvin,' said Natasha, before turning back to Helen. 'When did you place your description of Christine Copperfield's bullying of you on the Friends Reunited notice-board?' she asked.

Helen looked at her for a moment, her face a blank. Then a strange smile lit her face and her dull eyes shone. Newson had never seen Helen with such an expression before. A weight seemed to be lifting from her. 'Oh, my God!' she said. 'You're not saying . . . You're not saying that someone choked her with a tampon? I don't believe it! Please say yes!'

Natasha persevered with her questioning. 'When did you place your descrip—'

It was enough. Helen had heard all she needed. She leapt to her feet and punched the air. 'They did! They did! The bitch died as she lived. Fuck me, that's incredible, that is just fantastic. Oh my God!'

'I know when Ms Smart placed the notice, Sergeant,' Newson said, 'and it'll be dated on the site. Let's leave it for now.' He felt a terrible sadness. How desperate and distorted must Helen's world be to take comfort from such a perverse and terrible victory? But he also felt guilt. He did not *think* Helen had killed Christine, but if she had not, whoever did kill her had read her notice on the Friends Reunited site. She'd only placed it there because of her anger that he intended to attend Christine's reunion, and Christine had only organized the reunion after he had visited the site. The conclusion was unavoidable: if Newson had not been plotting to find a way to sleep with Christine Copperfield, she would never have been murdered.

Natasha took Kelvin's details, which he gave with enough reluctance for Newson to form the impression that Kelvin's was a name that already featured on the police computer, and then he and Natasha left.

There was silence for some time as Natasha drove them back to New Scotland Yard. Eventually Natasha spoke.

'That must have been a bit hard, Ed. I'm sorry,' she said. 'That woman really put you through it.'

'Yes, it was pretty grim. With the benefit of hindsight I can see that it was a very bad move to sleep with her.'

'But that's so often the case in life, isn't it?'

'I don't think I've had sufficient experience to comment. All I can say is that she didn't seem half so weird at the time.'

'I warned you about looking into your past for sex.'

'Well, I have to look somewhere.' It was a flippant comment. Too flippant, considering the brutality of what had occurred, and Newson knew it. Silence returned, until once more Natasha broke it.

'Ed, listen to me. Do you want to know the reason why you haven't had a proper girlfriend since Shirley dumped you?'

'Because there are not sufficient bargepoles in London with which girls can refuse to touch me?'

'Exactly. Comments like that. You're the problem. *You*. You've decided that you're not going to get a girl, and so you don't. You joke about and act like you're this total no-hoper, and it's kind of funny, which is OK, but it gets boring after a while, and I can assure you it's not very sexy.'

They were interrupted at this point by a call from Chief Superintendent Ward, who had been notified about the Copperfield murder at the end of a long lunch at his golf club.

'Newson, is it the case that you *knew* the victim of this grotesque crime? That you were in fact probably the last person to see her alive?'

'Apart from whoever murdered her, sir, yes.'

There was a pause before the chief superintendent replied. 'Well, that doesn't look very good, does it?'

'It's a coincidental complication I'd have preferred to avoid, sir.'

'I'm damn sure you would. What were you doing breaking into her flat, anyway? Why'd you gone to see her?'

Newson was conducting the conversation using the conference facility on the car's hands-free phone, and the chief's voice boomed around them. He could sense Natasha's embarrassment.

'I was paying her a social visit, sir. We'd attended a school reunion on the day before—'

'Did you sleep with her?' The chief's voice was angry.

'It isn't relevant, sir.' Newson's face burned.

'Of course you did, and of course it's bloody relevant, you damn fool. This girl was stripped and cut on the sex organs. That makes the murder a sex crime as far as I'm concerned, and your DNA will be all over her flat and I don't doubt all over her.'

'Sir, her death doesn't have anything to do with me.' Newson said it, but he knew that it wasn't true. The murder *did* have something to do with him.

'Oh, doesn't it? You meet her, you sleep with her, and you leave the following day. You return a few hours later and break into her flat. In the meantime the woman has been horribly murdered.'

'Yes, sir—'

'Why did you break into her flat?'

'Because I was suspicious. I'd been invited round but there was no answer.'

'Would you normally break into someone's flat simply because having made an appointment they failed to answer the door?'

'No, sir, but there was music playing.'

'There was *music playing*?'

'This killer plays music relevant to his victims while he murders them.'

'For Christ's sake, Newson! You broke in because there was music playing! Have you any idea how that sounds?'

'Excuse me, sir, but may I ask what you're suggesting?'

'I'm not suggesting anything at the moment, Detective Inspector, but I *will* tell you that I find it all very strange.'

'It's a very strange case, sir, but I think I may have finally established a proper link between the murders.'

'You *think* that you *may* have established a link.'

'Sergeant Wilkie and I are heading back to the office now, sir. I hope to have something to show you first thing tomorrow morning.'

'Ten o'clock. In my office. Goodbye.'

The drive continued in silence. Ten minutes later the chief superintendent was back on the line. 'Who's Helen Smart?' he asked.

Newson and Natasha exchanged surprised glances.

'She figures in the Copperfield case, sir.'

'Is she a suspect?'

'The details of the murder tally directly with a note that she left on the internet describing a childhood experience of bullying.'

'Have you slept with her too?'

'Um—'

'I've just received a disturbing call from my office saying that Helen Smart has made a complaint against you. Says you've been round at her place harassing her.'

'Sir,' Natasha interjected, 'Detective Sergeant Wilkie here. I attended the interview, in fact I conducted it, and I can assure you that there was absolutely no question of harassment.'

'She says that it was inappropriate for you to be interviewing her since you and she have recently been sleeping together. Is this true?'

'Yes, sir, it is.'

'*My God*, Inspector Newson! What's wrong with you? Are you ill? How much bloody sex do you need? You've slept with the victim, you've slept with your suspect. Perhaps if it ever comes to court you can work your way through the women in the jury! Just how compromised do you feel you need to be in this case?'

'I don't believe I am compromised, sir. My recent involvement with these women is not relevant to the case.'

'Detective Inspector Newson, let me assure you, this does *not look good*. I'll see you in the morning.'

After the chief had rung off Natasha clearly felt she had to say something. 'Don't worry about what that madwoman has said about you, Ed. I was there, don't forget. And I hardly think that bloke Kelvin is going to want to involve himself in trying to frame police officers.'

'No. No, you're right. There isn't a problem . . . Still, not pleasant, eh?'

'No, definitely not pleasant.'

'Shit!' said Newson. 'Shit, shit, shit. This is so unfair. *So* unfair. I have sex with just *two* women in about a trillion years . . .'

'And they turn out to be the victim and chief suspect in the case you're investigating. Good work, my son.'

Newson was in for one more massive embarrassment that day in front of Natasha, and, as always, he was the architect of his own misfortune.

They had returned together to the office they shared at New Scotland Yard.

'The answer to all this lies on the Friends Reunited site,' Newson said. 'Let's take another look, shall we?'

Natasha sat down at her computer and logged on while Newson went off to fill the kettle for tea.

'I presume you used your home email address,' Natasha said when he returned.

'Yes, of course.'

'What's your password?'

Newson froze. The private password he had chosen with which to gain entry to Friends Reunited was 'Natasha'.

It had not seemed foolish at the time. On the night on which he had joined Friends Reunited in pursuit of Christine Copperfield he had felt a moment of weird infidelity. His love for Natasha was so real to him that he had almost felt that in lusting after his old school flame he was being unfaithful to her. Stupidly, drunkenly, in order to assure himself that his fantasy relationship with Natasha was indeed real, he had entered her name into the little box marked 'password'. Now he was paying the price.

'My password?'

'Yes. What is it?'

'Maybe you should be the one to log on. You're a member, aren't you?'

'I don't know. I haven't done it for so long I presumed it had lapsed. Anyway, I've put your address in now.'

'I don't think their memberships lapse.'

'What difference does it make?'

'I don't know . . . You know, the fact that I'm connected to the last victim . . . Maybe I shouldn't be accessing the site.'

'That's ridiculous. You've accessed it loads of times.'

'I just think we should try and use your membership.'

Natasha was an astute woman. Her expression showed that she knew Newson was hesitating because he was embarrassed about his access code. What was more, she had clearly decided not to let him off the hook.

'No, it's your theory and your investigation. I don't have to let you use my personal membership.'

'I could order you.'

'No, you couldn't, any more than you could order me to lend you my kettle.'

'So you're not going to let me access the site via your membership?'

'No. What's your password, Ed?'

The game was up. He needed to get on to the site and quickly. The bullet had to be bitten. 'Natasha.'

'Yes?'

'No. Natasha, that's it, that's my password.'

'My name?'

'Yes, I don't know why I used it. It was just the first name that came into my head, that's all.'

'Bit weird, Ed.'

'I don't think so. I just needed a word, any word that I'd remember.'

'And you chose my name?'

'Yes.'

Natasha said nothing.

'Right,' said Newson, putting her tea down on the desk and attempting an airy tone, 'better get on with it then, shall we? Bang it in, Natasha. Do you need me to spell it?'

Still she said nothing as she typed in her name and the seven little black blobs appeared one after another in the box. Newson could not remember the last time he had felt such an idiot.

25

Newson began by informing the site that he wished to pursue his investigation by the name of a school. When the box appeared he typed 'Brockley Rise Junior', the school attended by Adam Bishop and William Connolly from 1955 to 1960.

'Connolly said he'd never spoken or written about what happened to him at the hands of Adam Bishop, but perhaps somebody else did.'

There were twelve names entered for the year that moved on in 1960, but neither Bishop nor Connolly was amongst them. Six of the class members had left information about themselves.

Marjorie Bartlett wrote:

Like lots of us from Brockley I went on to Lewisham Secondary Modern as was! I believe it's a sixth-form college now. After that I worked in Woolies on Catford High Street where I met John and married him within a month! We are still together after thirty-three years and have two lovely grown-up girls. I would love to hear from any of the old gang if anyone remembers me.

'They all want to be remembered,' Newson remarked.

Lucy Seman wanted to be remembered, as did Donald Cornell and Patricia Powers.

I ended up joining the Navy! That was in the days when we were still Wrens. No ship board duty for us, more's the pity! I would have loved to have gone to sea like the girls do now. I wonder if anyone remembers me? If they do I'd love to hear from them.

Jason Hart's name had the word 'NEW' next to it.

I had to join this site now. I just had to tell someone and you of course are the only people who would understand. Has anybody heard? Adam Bishop got murdered! Yes! Ding dong, the bastard's dead. It was in this evening's Standard. He's dead! And I for one can find nothing in my soul but delight. That bully damn near ruined our schooldays. He did ruin poor old Bill Connolly's and I hope he rots. Vanessa, if you're reading this, well done for what you wrote on the noticeboard. I suppose it's only us that will ever read it or care. But at least somewhere there is an account of his cruelty. A cruelty I stood by and watched happen for which I'll always be ashamed.

Rebecca Wilkinson was also new.

Thank you for joining us, Jason, and for saying something that I have not had the courage ever to say. I stood by too. I watched Adam Bishop hold little Billy down and stick that compass into him. Seventeen times, it was. I remember the number. He was always sticking it in him, wasn't he? But not like he did that day. I've always said that because I was a girl there was nothing I could have done. But that's not true. I could have spoken out. But I didn't and like you Jason I've always been ashamed.

'Jesus,' Natasha said. 'So much pain in the world. Little slabs of it hanging about in the air, unnoticed and ignored.'
'Not ignored this time,' Newson said. 'Somebody else was reading this website.'

'Helen Smart, do you think?'

'No, I don't think. This all started some time ago, maybe with Warrant Officer Spencer. Who knows? Maybe even before that. Let's see what Vanessa wrote on the school noticeboard, shall we?'

Vanessa Cuthbert had left no information about herself, but had made a contribution to the Brockley Rise junior school noticeboard.

Ours was a good school, but even good schools are not immune from the cancer of bullying. I've decided to say something here that I have waited forty-five years to say. When I was ten years old I witnessed an incident of violent bullying that has lived with me ever since. Anyone from my class will remember what happened because it resulted in a boy being hospitalized and nearly dying. Yet we did nothing about it at the time and nothing was done subsequently. Adam Bishop was a big, cruel, violent boy from a cruel, violent family. Everybody knew the Bishops and everyone was scared of them. Adam made the lives of all of the kids in his class a misery, including mine. He used to touch the girls even though we were all only ten and he would hit the boys. One boy above the rest was the main victim of this vicious bully. William Connolly suffered at his hands from the age of five, and slowly but surely the bullying got worse. Adam Bishop got into the habit of stabbing William with his compass, just little scratches and pricks at first, but one day it got out of hand. I will never know what it was that sparked Bishop's fury that day and I doubt that William will either. I'm sure he did not know at the time. Just something in Bishop's psychopathic nature flipped and one breaktime he literally threw William to the floor behind his desk. Then Bishop fell upon him and began to stab him with the compass, mainly in the arms but at the end he pulled up his shirt and gave him several in the stomach. Bishop was cunning as well as cruel, and he only let the thing go in at most half an inch. I can still remember him holding the spike between his finger and thumb about two thirds up it so that it would not go too far in. It was over in five minutes and then Bishop made William clean up the blood on the floor. He sent a little girl to get toilet paper. I was that girl and I did what I was told. After I handed the paper to Bishop he stuffed it into William's mouth. Then he told him to clear out of school for the rest of the day and never say what happened. William ran out of the room and that evening he was taken into hospital with severe blood poisoning. There were about fifteen kids in the room when this attack took place and not one of us lifted a finger to help William. What's more, when we were questioned later by the school and by a police constable not one of us was prepared to say a word. None of us wanted to become Bishop's next victim and we should all be ashamed. Well, I've told the story now. It's probably just between me and cyberspace and perhaps one or two of the old gang who like me look back in shame. Perhaps Adam Bishop himself will read it. If you do read this, Adam Bishop, then know this. You are hated. You were hated then, you are hated now and you will always be hated. What you did scarred us all.

Vanessa Cuthbert's public soul-searching was dated two months earlier and had preceded all the other mentions of Adam Bishop on the Brockley Rise pages. She had been the first to break the silence.

'Just a few weeks before Adam Bishop was killed,' Natasha noted. 'Why do you think she spoke up when she did?'

'Who knows? This whole Friends Reunited thing is only three or four years old. I suppose there are going to be a lot of worms slowly crawling out of the woodwork.'

'So the killer read what she wrote and decided to act upon it?'

'I can't see any other explanation,' said Newson. 'We now have both the Bishop and the Copperfield murder described in detail on the internet before they even occurred. What we need to do now is take a look at the schooldays of Warrant Officer Spencer, Angie Tatum, Neil Bradshaw and Farrah Porter.'

'It's Sunday evening, Ed. How do we find out where they went to school?'

'Farrah Porter won't be difficult, it'll be listed in her *Who's Who* entry, and I'm sure there's any number of internet hits to be found on Angie Tatum.'

There were indeed. Like anyone who has been in the public eye, Angie Tatum had her obsessives, people who had set up sites in tribute to the girl whose breasts had caught the public imagination twenty years before. Since her death these sites had proliferated. There was even a goth rock group called Angie Tatum's Dead.

The first site they opened revealed that Angie Tatum had attended a large comprehensive school in Essex.

Sergeant Wilkie entered the name of the school on to the Friends Reunited site. 'I presume we're looking at 1984 because of the compilation tape they found in her machine.'

'Yes.'

'The same as for Christine Copperfield.'

'My guess is that's a coincidence. I think it's possible that the eighties generation is the one that figures most highly on the Friends site.'

'Old enough to be feeling discontented with the way your life's going but young enough to still think you might want to shag the people you were at school with?'

'Something like that, yes.'

'It'd be interesting to do the research.'

Angie Tatum had joined Friends Reunited and despite the fact that she was dead her entry remained on the list. The message of a dead girl who had posted it in the hope of being remembered made uncomfortable reading.

'You'd think they'd have removed it,' Newson said.

'Nobody's asked them to take it off, I suppose.'

Remember me? Of course you do. Everybody does, don't they? I was 'it' for a few years back then wasn't I? So there's no point me writing what I've been up to since I left like the rest of you have all done because you know all about me. Let's face it I was already modelling and getting in the papers in my last year wasn't I? I remember some of you girls calling me a slag and a slapper because you were jealous and had fried eggs for knockers. But some of you were really supportive about my dream which I will never forget. And of course the boys didn't mind did they? I didn't get any O levels of course but who cares I had a couple of excellent Double D's so I didn't need any exams did I? Anyway just to say contrary to what has been said in the press I'm not thick and what's more I'm really proud of what I did and the fact that I used what I had to follow my dream and make a success of myself. I am strong, in control, and I have no regrets.

'Written late and pissed, if you ask me,' said Natasha.

After reading a number of innocent messages from other people who had been in Angie Tatum's class, Natasha and Newson found what they were looking for.

Hello. My name is Katie Saunders. I wonder if any of you remember me? I expect some of you do. Well actually I doubt that you remember ME as in a person. I doubt that you remember somebody who, like you, had a heart and a soul. Somebody who needed friendship and felt the pain of isolation. No, I doubt anybody remembers that. Perhaps you don't even remember my name. You certainly never used it, not to me in my memory anyway. What some of you will remember is that somewhere lurking on the edge of your school days there was a small, skinny, ungainly, ugly girl with a harelip.

'Oh my God,' said Natasha.
'Bingo,' said Newson.

Yes. I was born pretty much without a thing going for me physically. They tried to correct my lip a couple of times but made a mess of it. I looked awful and I sounded worse. I had the classic harelip speech impediment. Not that you'd have heard it much since I scarcely ever said a word at school unless I absolutely had to. What you may remember hearing quite a lot was Angie Tatum's impression of me. Funny isn't it that our class contained both the least and the most fancied girl in the school? Maybe it was that which made you do what you did to me, Angie. You were so cute, weren't you, such a sweet face, even before you grew those extraordinary breasts. You were the classroom star with that pretty face. And then there was me with my harelip, lost alone in almost complete isolation except for you Angie. I wasn't isolated from you, was I? Because for five long years you never let one day go by without doing your famous impression of me. The mong. The spaz. The saddo. You were so vain, Angie, so incredibly proud of your teenage beauty, that I think you used me as a way of constantly drawing attention to it. By always being near me and doing your little impressions you were able to keep the focus of the entire class on you, weren't you? Well we all moved on in the end and you managed to make yourself into a focus of attention for the whole country. I never managed to move on fully from the problem of my face. They never did get it fixed up. Things improved of course. Adults are perhaps not as cruel as kids, or at least they don't have the same opportunities to practise cruelty that the classroom presents. I've made friends, and believe it or not I've even had boyfriends, despite the fact that you assured me many times that that could never happen. But I've never been able to form a long-term relationship. Something in me pulls away. I don't feel worthy of it, and I don't want to be hurt. I have to say that I don't think I'm overstating the case when I say that your cruelty, and the way that for five years you crushed any spark of hope or confidence that might have grown in me, has burdened me throughout my life and will do so until the day I die.

Katie Saunders' entry had been made five months earlier. 'Two weeks before Tatum died,' Natasha observed.

253

Newson took up a pen and paper and created two columns, one headed 'Victim', the other 'Victim's victim'. In the first column he wrote the names of all those who had been killed, and opposite these he wrote the names of the victims' victims that they had so far discovered.

VICTIM	VICTIM'S VICTIM
Adam Bishop	William Connolly (compasses)
Neil Bradshaw	
Christine Copperfield	Helen Smart (tampon)
Angie Tatum	Katie Saunders (harelip)
Farrah Porter	
Denis Spencer	

'God, Katie Saunders must have had a terrible time,' said Natasha.

'Somebody obviously thought so, and to exact "justice" they thought it necessary to create a harelip on the face of Angie Tatum and glue her eyes open so that she was forced to stare at it for every second that remained of her life.'

'Do you think that Katie Saunders was involved?'

'She's certainly involved, but what part the victims' victims played in the murders I can't say. Did one of them do it? Did they all?'

'Perhaps they clubbed together and hired a hitman.'

'But how would they have *found* each other? Has somebody been spending their time trawling through the vast Friends Reunited archive?'

'They have ten million members.'

'Well, anyway. Let's take a look at Farrah Porter. Where was she at school in 1989?'

'1989?'

'"Love And Kisses", remember. Dannii Minogue's first single. The Ozzie nanny heard it playing in the Onslow Gardens flat.'

Newson was right about *Who's Who*. A quick glance revealed that before going to Cambridge University Farrah Porter had boarded at one of the most expensive girls' schools in the country. Armed with this information, it did not take long to find the entry on the school site of one Annabel Shannon. Annabel had been a housemate of Farrah Porter, a fact which appeared to have condemned her to a school life of abject misery.

You were so beautiful, weren't you? You still are, of course, and don't you milk it? I feel sick every time I put on the news and see you there preening yourself as if butter wouldn't melt in your mouth. I want to scream LIAR LIAR LIAR at the screen. Because I know you, Farrah. I know you for the evil, cruel, racist shit that you are. You made my life and the life of any other girl who was poor or foreign or stood out in any way a complete and utter misery, didn't you? I was poor and foreign in so much as I was a scholarship girl from the Irish Republic, and I curse the day my parents ever thought it would be a blessing to send me anywhere I would find myself at the tender mercies of the likes of you. What chance did I have? A pale, white, freckly potato head from the bogs of Ireland? And you with your blond hair and Caribbean tan? You made my ginger hair and freckles the joke of the whole school, didn't you? All the girls had to be in on it or they knew you would cut them adrift too. I'll never forget as long as I live the misery of my accursed colouring. White skin and orange hair. You actually made ME hate it! As if it was my fault! I wanted to scrape off my freckles with sandpaper and shave my head! I tried tanning in the holidays, but of course all that happened was that I got burnt and blistered. Shower time was the worst, and getting ready for bed. When I had to reveal my body to your ridicule! You stole my nightie nearly every night. I remember standing alone, naked and helpless at the centre of your pack, while you all taunted me. And of course it was my flame-red pubic hair that seemed to enrage and delight you most, wasn't it, Farrah? How you loved your favourite joke of pretending to find strands of it on the soap and taunting me, throwing the soap at my head, pretending to be sick at the sight of what I was.

255

I hope you die, Farrah Porter. I hope you die a slow and horrible death. But in the meantime I'll do anything I can to harm your career. I've tried on a number of occasions to interest journalists in stories of what you were like at school, but so far they've declined to risk the wrath of your lawyers. That's why I've decided to put this letter on the Friends Reunited site. Perhaps someone of influence will read it. Perhaps some of the other girls who have achieved positions of authority may read it and remember. Remember in shame their failure to stop you. They did not speak out against your appalling bullying then, so perhaps they will now. Speak and denounce you for the evil devil that you are. Speak out and save the people of Fulham from electing the most poisonous viper that ever destroyed another person's life.

'Fuck,' said Natasha, when they had both read Annabel Shannon's letter. 'So now we know what that pubic hair on the soap in Porter's shower was about.'

'Yes, we do. A little extra detail. Our killer seems fond of them.'

'Reading that almost makes you feel the woman deserved it,' Natasha added.

'Nobody deserves to be bleached in acid, however awful they were at school.' Newson took out his pen and added 'Annabel Shannon (ginger)' to his 'victim's victim' column opposite Farrah Porter's name.

It was late, and Newson and Natasha decided that they had achieved all they could for the day. They would track down Warrant Officer Spencer's and Neil Bradshaw's records in the morning.

'I suppose you'll need to be rushing back,' said Newson. 'Please apologize to Lance for intruding on his Lance time.'

'He's dumped me,' Natasha replied. 'When you called me back in for the Copperfield murder he told me that I wasn't to go. He said that I wasn't obliged to—'

'Which is true.'

'And that if I loved him I'd tell you to shove it.'

'Ah. And you didn't.'

'No, I came into work and he said I was a dysfunctional workaholic and that there was no point our being together if it was all going to be about me, so we should split up and I said fine.'

'Since you didn't tell him to shove it, does it mean that you don't love him?'

'Of course I love him. He's my boyfriend.'

'Not any more.'

'No, that's right.'

'He'll be back.'

'He won't. But if he does, of course I'll have him back. I broke our agreement. We'd just decided that we'd both work harder at making what we have special and the first thing I do is spend the entire weekend at work.'

'We're on the track of a serial killer.'

'That's not Lance's business. I've let him down.'

Natasha's phone rang. It was Lance.

'Of course I'll try harder,' she said into the phone. 'I promise . . . OK, what do you want? Chinese? Indian? All right, I'll pick up an Indian. See you. Love you.' She put the phone back and turned to Newson. 'Don't look at me like that. I think we owe it to each other to work at our relationship.'

'Is that what he said?'

'Basically, yes.' Natasha got up to leave and paused halfway. 'Ed? That thing about your using my name as your password? That's a nice thing, isn't it? I mean, that's how it was meant? Sort of like a compliment?'

'Yes, you could put it like that. Although of course you weren't supposed to know.'

'Right. OK. Bye, then.'

After Natasha had left Newson sat and thought for a while. One aspect of the case disturbed and intrigued him more than any other. It was the astonishing development that he *knew the killer*.

Once more he replayed the message that Christine had left on his mobile phone at a time that could have been only minutes before her death. '*Oh, hang on, that's the doorbell . . . Ju-ust checking through my little spyhole . . . Well, well, well! This is a surprise . . . Wow, Ed, will I have something to tell you. You'll have to come round now! Gotta go . . . Byeee.*'

Newson knew the man he was hunting.

Could he have saved her somehow? If he were a better detective might he not have guessed what was about to occur and shouted into the phone, 'Do not open that door!!' Except it had only been a message anyway. There was no one to shout to; by the time Newson had heard her message Christine was dead and long past saving. And how could he have known? It had only been Christine's death and the manner of it that had revealed to him the truth. Without the coincidence of the killer's choosing Helen's note to provoke his latest murder Newson would still be entirely in the dark. Was that a positive thing? Was there some way in which Newson could use that thought to give some meaning to her death?

No. Try as he might, he could not. An old friend was dead, killed by the very man Newson had been hunting. Christine Copperfield, who never stopped talking, had finally stopped. Stopped scarcely a handful of words after those that Newson now knew off by heart and which he would never fully expunge from his mind.

Byeeeeee.

26

The following morning Newson was at work by eight o'clock. He urgently wished to track down Annabel Shannon, and he needed to get his team on to the school records of the two remaining victims on his list: Warrant Officer Spencer and Neil Bradshaw. He was uncomfortably aware of his fast-approaching meeting with the chief superintendent, which was scheduled for ten that morning, and he needed as much information as possible to prove to his commander that progress was being made. Above all, Newson did not want to be taken off the case. Of all the cases he had tackled in his ten years dealing with murders, this one, for him personally, most required a result.

It proved easy to trace Annabel Shannon. The school she and Farrah Porter had attended kept excellent records and was proud of its old-girl network. They responded immediately to a police request for information, guessing correctly that it was to do with the Porter murder.

'You don't think that one of *our girls* was involved, surely, Inspector?' a very refined and extremely concerned secretary had enquired. 'We've never had any sort of scandal here, not even drugs.'

Newson thought about saying that the real scandal was that they had allowed appalling bullying to happen to girls in their care without seeming to notice it. However, he confined himself to assuring the secretary that his enquiries were routine.

Annabel Shannon, or Annabel Ahern as she had been known since her marriage, was a farmer's wife in County Kildare. Newson had hoped that Natasha would call Annabel Shannon. Natasha was an excellent conversationalist, she relished gossip and her sympathetic ear and chatty style had produced results from witnesses that Newson could never have hoped to open up. But Natasha was late, and, there being only junior women constables available to him, he decided to call Annabel Shannon himself.

A thickly accented voice answered the phone. 'Annabel Ahern speaking.'

'Ah. Mrs Ahern? I'm sorry to disturb you. My name is Newson and I am a detective inspector with the London Metropolitan Police.'

'A British police officer?'

'Yes, that's right. Of course, I don't have any jurisdiction at all with you, Mrs Ahern, but if you are amenable I'd like to ask you one or two questions.'

'I don't think my husband would approve of my talking to you, Inspector. If I'm honest, I'd have to say that he doesn't approve of the British in general and their police force in particular. Nor do I.'

'I'm sorry to hear that, Mrs Ahern. Of course I can speak to you via the Garda if you wish. We have excellent, mutually co-operative relations with the Irish Police, and they would without doubt put my questions to you if you would prefer it that way.'

'You're calling about Farrah Porter, aren't you?'

'Yes. Yes, I am. How astute of you, Mrs Ahern.'

'Hardly. I've had a number of responses from old girls to the letter I left on the Friends Reunited site. Not on the whole very enthusiastic responses, sad to say. I don't think it's the done thing to denigrate one's old school after one has slunk away, so to speak. Did one of them call you?'

'No, no. I looked you up on the site myself.'

'That was clever of you.'

'Oh, just a hunch.'

'It was a very good hunch, Inspector. I've been expecting your call, of course.'

'You have?'

'Well, after the papers got hold of the details of her death I guessed it wouldn't be too long before somebody made a link with what I'd written about what she did to me.'

'Really? D'you think it's that obvious, Mrs Ahern?'

'Well, clearly you do, Inspector, or we would not be having this conversation.'

Newson wished that it was Natasha who was having the conversation. She would have made friends with this woman by now, whereas the interview he was conducting was getting colder by the minute.

'You suffered greatly at Ms Porter's hands.'

'Yes, I did. And of course I killed her.'

'I beg your pardon, Mrs Ahern?'

'I said that I killed her.'

'Would you elaborate on that?'

'There is absolutely no doubt in my mind that I killed her. I've always believed strongly in the power of prayer, you see. It was that which sustained me through the terrible unhappiness I suffered at that dreadful school and it has sustained me ever since in dealing with the memories. Not a single day has passed in these last fifteen years or so when I have not prayed for Farrah Porter's death, not one single day. That's an awful lot of prayers, Inspector. You'd think that it might eventually bear fruit, wouldn't you?'

'Well, yes, possibly.'

'And in each prayer I took the liberty of asking the good Lord that he might see fit to arrange for her to die in a manner that befitted her sins. I rather cheekily suggested that some form of scourging might be in order. The papers seemed to be hinting that acid was involved. You have to hand it to the Lord, don't you? He certainly has a way with these things.'

'Um, yes. Mrs Ahern, d'you think you could possibly tell me what you were doing on the eighteenth of June?'

'That being the day when Farrah Porter went to hell?'

'Yes.'

'I know exactly what I was doing. My husband and I were attending a Noraid benefit in Boston to buy bullets for British soldiers.'

For a moment Newson was confused, knowing that Mrs Ahern was a staunch Irish Nationalist. Then he realized that these bullets were not intended to be offered as gifts. 'Ri-ght . . .'

'Your prime minister and those Judases in Dublin may think that the war ended with the Good Friday Agreement. I can assure you, Inspector, that it didn't.'

'Fine, good, well, thank you for your time, Mrs Ahern.'

'Not at all. Good day to you, Inspector, and God bless.'

Newson was grateful to put the phone down. As he did so he saw Natasha hanging her hat on the stand in the corner. It was another glorious sunny day outside and Natasha was always sensible about her skin. Her skirt lifted slightly as she raised her arm, and he admired the backs of her knees.

'Annabel Shannon, or Ahern as she is now, has a very good alibi. She was with a bunch of Boston Republicans plotting the defeat of the British Army and the unification of Ireland.'

Natasha turned to face him from where she stood. Her face bore a slightly bewildered but also defiant expression. One of her eyes was swollen black and bruised. 'I was mugged,' she said before Newson had time to comment. 'Last night, getting out of the tube station. Somebody tried to grab my bag and they whacked me.'

'Shit, Natasha, that's terrible! Are you OK? I mean, should you be in work?'

'I'm fine. It's a black eye. So what? Just wish I'd managed to grab the bastard, that's all.'

'Yes, yes, of course. Can I make you a cup of tea?'

'Lovely, thanks. Yeah, I could do with one.'

Newson got up and put the kettle on. 'Actually you were in your car last night, weren't you?' he said gently. 'You drove home.'

There was a pause before Natasha replied. 'Did I say tube? I meant I got whacked as I got out of my car.'

'Right. Of course.'

Natasha went to her desk and stared intently at the papers in front of her. She did not look up.

'So,' she said with a considerable pretence at good cheer, 'let's get on with it, shall we?'

'Natasha—' Newson said.

'I was mugged, Ed. Now can we please get on with our work.'

There was nothing more to be said and so they turned their attention to the school details of Neil Bradshaw, which had just been emailed to both their computers from colleagues working in the next-door office.

'Born in 1960, started nursery school at four,' said Newson, viewing the education record set out before him, which stretched all the way through to Bradshaw's postgraduate studies as an archivist. 'However, I think that what we need to be looking at is what his classmates thought of him around '72 to '74.'

'Glam rock?' Natasha enquired.

'Yes. That's what old Farmer "I pay my tax" Goddard said he heard wafting across the fields while Bradshaw was having his balls crushed in a vice. Great period: T. Rex, Slade, Mud, Sweet. Real speaker-blasting boulders of rock. Much underestimated because it never really caught on in the States. That's the problem with this country, we don't really take anything we produce seriously unless the Americans have sanctioned it.'

'Shall you log on or do you want me to?' Natasha asked.

'I'll do it,' Newson replied with a defensive smile.

Neil Bradshaw had attended a mixed grammar school in Leamington Spa, and once more a brief trawl through the various innocuous 'remember me' entries, which included Bradshaw's own, revealed another anguished soul who had elected to use the

Friends Reunited site to point an accusatory finger back across the years. The entry, which had been made a year before, was entitled 'An open letter to Neil Bradshaw'.

> I've often thought about going to the police and telling them about what happened to me. Even now, over thirty years later, I still dream of justice. But I suppose it would be no good. We were only twelve and thirteen, weren't we? It's all long gone now, isn't it? Except not for me. For me it's still as if it happened yesterday. Which is why I'm writing this now and putting it up on this notice-board. Just to tell the other kids in our year that if they were thinking of contacting you they should think twice, because you are a cruel sexual predator and I was your principal victim. It started with bullying, didn't it? You asked me out and when I refused you started to bully me. Your favourite trick was to steal my packed lunch from my bag and put it high up on the skylight ledge so that if I wanted to get it down I'd have to put a chair on to a desk and climb up on top of them. Then you'd stand underneath, looking up my skirt to see my knickers. And you'd tell the other boys what colour they were and make up stories about how they were dirty.

The details clearly recalled those of Neil Bradshaw's murder. Whoever had starved Bradshaw to death had forced him to die reaching up for food while wearing a schoolgirl's skirt and staring into a video transmission of the knickers he had been forced to wear beneath it.

'Fuck,' said Natasha, 'this gets sicker every day, doesn't it?' She did not turn towards Newson as she said this. She was clearly all too conscious of the bruise on her face.

> Then you got braver, and you started to wait for me on my way home. I used to have to walk along the canal towpath with the hedges by the side and that's where you'd lie in wait. Every day you grabbed me and pushed me into those hedges, groping me and

264

putting your hands into my bra and knickers, squeezing me and poking me. Sometimes you managed to get your fingers inside me. I expect that any classmates reading this will wonder why I didn't do something about it. I've asked myself the same question for three decades. Why didn't I tell my mum? A teacher? The police? I suppose there were the threats, that was certainly part of it. You said that you'd poison my cat, didn't you, and I believed you, I really really did. And then there was your power. You were such a teacher's pet, you were on every school committee and always got elected form captain. You really knew how to play everybody off against each other and always end up smelling of roses. Meanwhile, you were sexually abusing me. It was a short step, wasn't it, from staring at my knickers to bruising my body, particularly when you found out that you could get away with it, and then finally you raped me. We were both thirteen and you raped me, and that was when it stopped because I stopped going to school. I became an adolescent anorexic and was in and out of hospital for the next five years. The breasts that you so loved to squeeze as you forced me down amongst the twigs and brambles all but disappeared. As did I. Mentally and physically. I'm better now, but still not entirely well. I've never been able to get on with my life properly and I'm still single. Pathetic, isn't it? My closest relationship is still with you, Neil Bradshaw, and my hatred is undimmed. So if any of you old boys and girls were thinking of getting in contact with your old popular form captain, please try to remember Pamela White, will you, the quiet girl in the corner who left halfway through the third year. Because that bastard ruined my life.

When they had finished reading Newson printed off a copy and added Pamela White's name opposite that of Neil Bradshaw on his list of victims' victims. Natasha took the hard copy of White's essay from the printer tray and read through it once more.

'The more I learn about the people who got killed the more I'm on the killer's side.'

'You can't think that way, Natasha. It isn't helpful.'

'But Bradshaw deserved what he got in that seed shed!'

'You think so?'

'Yes! Particularly because he was still at it thirty years later. Remember what I found out about that teenager who worked in the bookshop, the one who was sacked when she refused his advances?'

'We don't have the death penalty in this country, not even after a fair trial, so let's not get misty-eyed about the deranged antics of a lunatic vigilante.'

'I'm just saying that what goes around comes around, that's all.'

'Natasha, did Lance hit you?' There. He'd said it. He wasn't even sure that he'd meant to say it, but he had.

'No!' Natasha exclaimed, too loudly and too quickly.

Newson did not reply and after a few moments Natasha got up and left the room. When she returned she had her speech prepared.

'It's not like you think it is, Ed. It's not typical.'

'What do you mean, Natasha? It looks like a typical black eye to me.'

'It's not a typical instance of what you think it is.'

'If you mean domestic violence, why don't you say it?'

'Because . . . because . . . Look, it's only happened once.'

'Oh, come *on*, Natasha. Listen to yourself.'

'He's only done it once!'

'So far! They've all only ever done it once the first time they do it. Whether he does it again is entirely up to you.'

'Look, Ed. Don't give me any speeches, all right? I've been in the police since I was nineteen. I know about this shit. I dealt with it every day for years.'

'Which is why you of all people should be aware that domestic violence is in most senses always typical and one of the most typical aspects of all is that the victim always tries to make out a special case for her abuser.'

'I just said I don't want any speeches! He was drunk—'

'Ah . . .'

'We were both drunk! He wanted to talk about us and I was too tired and I hadn't seen him all weekend and then I got home and I only wanted to sleep, and—'

'Natasha, please! *Listen to yourself.*'

'I'm just saying—'

'You're just saying that it was your fault that he hit you, that's what you're just saying.'

'I'm not! I'm saying that in a relationship both sides have to—'

'You're saying that it was your fault!'

'I don't want to have this conversation, OK? I haven't filed a complaint and this is not a police matter.'

'I'm your friend.'

'Then respect my right to deal with this in my own way.'

'Have you thrown him out?'

Natasha did not answer.

'*Have you thrown him out?*'

'No.'

'Then will you insist that he seeks counselling immediately?'

Again she did not reply.

'Will you make him seek counselling, and if he refuses will you throw him out?'

'I've just said I don't want to—'

'Then it's going to happen again.'

'It's *not* going to happen again.'

'Natasha, if nothing changes it *always* happens again. You *know* that.'

'Ed, we're seeing the chief in just over an hour. If you want to complete your list before then we need to find out what fucking nightmare Warrant Officer Spencer left behind him from when he was at school.'

And so, with a new and unfamiliar tension now existing between them, Newson and Natasha turned once more to the

Friends Reunited site to summon up the details of Spencer's years at school, which had lasted from 1980 to 1992, when he had left at sixteen in order to join the army.

They had no musical clue to highlight a particular year, and they were forced to read through Spencer's entire school career, which made up a grim catalogue of bullying and abuse. It seemed that he had formed the habit early.

Do you remember Denis Spencer? half a dozen different ex-pupils at Spencer's junior school had written.

> If you weren't in his gang you were in big trouble. If you caught his eye the wrong way, POW!, you got both fists straight in the face. If it was your turn to get it you crawled home on your hands and knees. If you got out of line he put your head in a desk and banged the lid down.

Again and again the same word came up.
Bully. Bully. Bully.

It was clear that Spencer had not been choosy about who he terrorized and by the time he got to his comprehensive school he'd really got into his stride. He was the number-one topic of discussion on the school's virtual noticeboard. An appeal had been made for good Spencer reminiscences and the replies were many and varied.

> He flushed my head in the bogs . . . He twanged my bra strap every day in the dinner queue . . . He'd just kick you as you walked by . . . He held me against the wall by my neck . . . He stubbed his cigarette out on my satchel . . .

A teacher had even made a contribution.

> I was so sorry and distressed to read of the way you all suffered at the hands of Denis Spencer. You must have felt that you should have been protected by the system. All I can say (and I cringe in

shame as I write) is that we too were scared of him. Spencer
was more than six feet tall by the time he was fourteen and he
had two older brothers, one of whom was a policeman and the
other a soldier. Spencer threatened me physically three times.
He was bigger than me and once he actually grabbed me by the
neck. He told me that he knew where I lived and that if I went
to the head I could expect a brick through my window. It would
have been no use going to the head anyway, he was weak
and scared himself. I don't know if you recall Ms Simpson
who taught art. She told me that he'd threatened her with
gang rape!

'My God,' said Natasha, 'what a thug!'
Eventually they found the letter they were looking for, the one
that linked an event in Spencer's past to the manner of his death.
It had been posted by a classmate called Mark Pearce.

I'd always managed to stay out of trouble with Spencer. Maybe it
was that that made him suddenly decide to have a go at me. They
do say bullies are cunning like that, don't they? Anyway, I'd never
have risen to his bait if it had been just me, but he was clever and
he had a go at my bird. I wonder if you're reading this, Mandy? Do
you remember what I suffered for you? It didn't make you stay with
me, though, did it? Not after I ended up in hospital with suspected
brain damage. You slag. One lunch break. That's all it took, and my
life got well and truly fucked. We were walking down the corridor,
me and Mandy, hand in hand. Mandy was fit and everybody
wanted to have her, so maybe Spencer was jealous or something.
Whatever it was, it wasn't my lucky day, because he and his boys
barred our way and surrounded us and he started lifting up
Mandy's skirt and saying to me that I should hand her over to him
for the lunchhour as payment for him not giving me a smack in
the mouth. Well obviously I had to try and stand up to him. I'd
have probably got done in whatever I did and I had to try and
defend my bird, didn't I? What would I have looked like if I hadn't?

269

So I told him to piss off and he said in that case I'd be the one who'd have to pay. So they sat me in a chair and started whacking me on the head with their atlases. Maybe you remember those books, of course you do, we had to lug them to geography twice a week, not that anybody ever learnt anything from them. Well, Spencer had his gang whack me on the head with the books for an entire lunch break, fifty-five minutes. Think about it. They hit me hundreds of times. By the end I was nearly unconscious and couldn't fucking walk. I had neurological damage, they said, and I was dizzy for months after. Luckily I was young and the brain is quite resilient when you're young, but I was still in bed for a month. I decided I wasn't going to let him get away with it, so I told on Spencer and his gang and there was a piss-weak investigation, and of course they all denied it so it was their six words against my one. They'd kept people out of the form room while they hit me, so no one else saw, not that anyone would have had the guts to speak out. Well, obviously after snitching on them I couldn't go back to school, so I had to go somewhere else, which really messed up my exams. What with that and the headaches that went on for years afterwards I ended up not going to tech, even though I wanted to be an engineer, but that was all fucked, obviously. I'm fine now, got a job and a life I like, but I had a very rough time for a year or two back then and all because I happened to be walking down the corridor just at the time that Spencer was looking round for a bit of fun. Well, that's my story but, Spencer, if you're reading this I'm telling you now that it ain't over. Oh no, it ain't going to be over till you get yours. I've got a plan, see. Want to know what it is? Don't worry, you'll find out soon enough. Oh yeah, and Mandy? Like I said, you're nothing but a dirty slag.

Newson's list was complete.

VICTIM	VICTIM'S VICTIM
Adam Bishop	William Connolly (compasses)

Neil Bradshaw	Pamela White (sexual assault)
Christine Copperfield	Helen Smart (tampon)
Angie Tatum	Katie Saunders (harelip)
Farrah Porter	Annabel Shannon (ginger)
Denis Spencer	Mark Pearce (book)

He was ready to attend his meeting with Chief Superintendent Ward.

27

'Good Lord, Detective Sergeant Wilkie. What the hell happened to you?'

'I was mugged, sir. I'm fine.'

'What a bloody awful world we live in, eh? Just what kind of bullying bastard would punch a defenceless woman like that?'

Newson did not look at Natasha, but he could imagine how much this comment hurt. His heart ached for her.

'All right, Newson, let's get on with it,' the chief said testily. 'This situation seems to me to be out of hand. We have a swathe of unsolved murders which you have chosen to presume are connected. One of these murders at least is highly media sensitive. I'm thinking in particular, of course, of the killing of Farrah Porter, which has caused alarm at the highest level in the Home Office. It's put me personally under a lot of pressure. I don't like having MI6 looking over my shoulder and badgering me for results. What's more, we now have to add to this catalogue of failure the grotesque complication of yesterday's death and your connection with both the victim and one of the suspects—'

'There's no complication, sir, I—'

'Don't interrupt me, Inspector. You can have your say when I've finished and not before. Now, what I want to know, before I take the decision to take you off this case and dump you somewhere in the depths of traffic, is whether you have anything concrete to go on.'

Newson produced his list and laid it on the chief superintendent's desk.

Ward glanced at it, unimpressed. 'What's this?'

'The progress you've been asking for, sir.'

'Does this list include the name of the killer or killers?'

'Possibly, but I doubt it.'

'Then could you explain what damn use it is, Detective Inspector?'

'It tells us that we're dealing with a vigilante, sir. A serial killer whose motive is revenge.'

'Revenge for what?'

'Just revenge, sir, not personal, but general.'

'I never knew a killer, serial or otherwise, whose motives weren't personal.'

'Well no, sir. The killer's *core* motive will be personal, deeply personal, but the murders he's committing are set at one remove from his own experience. I think he's taking a general revenge for a private hurt.'

'Meaning?'

'All the murder victims were bullies at school, sir,' Natasha interjected quickly. 'Every single one subjected their classmates to appalling brutality. It seems certain to us that our killer or killers are taking a belated revenge for what these people did when they were growing up.'

'Is this true?' Ward asked Newson. The chief superintendent was never very comfortable in conference with women. 'It seems pretty far-fetched to me.'

'Yes, sir, it's true. I don't think there can be any doubt.'

'What evidence do you have for this theory?'

'The killer murders his victims using the method of torture that they inflicted on others when they were at school. Look at the list. As you know, Adam Bishop was stabbed to death with a pair of compasses. We've discovered that forty-five years ago he nearly killed a classmate – William Connolly on the list – by stabbing him with a pair of compasses.'

For the first time Chief Superintendent Ward showed interest. 'What about Porter? She's the one I'm getting the pressure about.'

'She was murdered using an acidic bleaching agent that turned her tanned skin white, and her hair was dyed ginger. We now know for certain that during the late eighties, while attending a girls' boarding school, Farrah Porter made another girl's life a misery over her white skin and ginger hair. Her particular delight was to taunt this girl over the supposed presence of red pubic hairs on the soap. The *only* thing that the killer left out of place in Farrah Porter's bathroom was a single red pubic hair, which he carefully attached to a brand-new cake of soap.'

'Extraordinary.'

'In the case of the girl with whom I was acquainted, sir . . .'

'Yes, I've read Dr Clarke's report on how she died. Are you telling me that at school she forced a tampon down another girl's throat?'

'Yes, I am, sir. It's documented.'

'Where? Where is it documented? How the hell do you know what all these people did at school?'

'I read it on the internet, sir. Just as I believe the killer did before me. I believe that he tracks down his victims via an internet website called Friends Reunited, which is a site where old schoolfriends can re-establish contact and—'

'I know what Friends Reunited is, Inspector, I'm not a bloody idiot.'

'No, sir. Of course not, sir.'

'These others?' said Ward, looking at Newson's list. 'All the same? All dispensed with in the manner of their own previous cruelty?'

'Without a shadow of a doubt, sir.' And Newson went on to describe the grotesque mimicry perpetrated by the murderer on Neil Bradshaw, Angie Tatum and Denis Spencer.

'This really is the most extraordinary case,' concluded Chief Superintendent Ward at length.

'Isn't it?'

'And then there's your connection.'

'Coincidence, sir. I happen to have attended the same school as the bully and the victim in one of the cases on my list.'

'And you slept with them both.'

Newson was silent.

'The question is, what are you going to do about it?'

This was a question that Newson found difficult to answer. He had come a long way in his understanding of the murders but he did not feel that he was any closer to discovering who had committed them.

'I'll have to get back to you on that one, sir.'

The meeting over, Newson offered to buy Natasha a sandwich. As they were leaving the building, however, they discovered Lance waiting on the steps. He was holding a bunch of roses.

'All right, doll?' he said sheepishly.

There was an embarrassed pause. Newson did not know how to react. He wanted to arrest the man immediately for assault, but he knew absolutely that this was something Natasha must sort out for herself.

'I've been here since ten. Thought I'd have to wait all day.'

'Lance, I'm working.'

'You're always working.'

Newson tried to leave them to it, but Lance stopped him.

'Don't worry, mate, I'm going. You've got your precious murders to investigate, not that you ever seem to arrest anyone.'

'These things take time.'

'Yeah, all the time.' Lance turned back to Natasha and handed her the flowers. 'Look, 'Tash, these are for you . . . I'll see you later, all right?' He turned and headed for his motorbike. Natasha and Newson made their way to a nearby sandwich bar.

'Don't say anything,' Natasha said.

'He's a bully, Natasha.'

'I said don't say anything. What the hell does he think I'm

supposed to do with a bunch of flowers in the middle of a working day, anyway?'

'Stick them in the bin.'

'Don't be stupid.'

'Why's that stupid?'

'Because it must have taken a lot for a man like Lance to bring me flowers.'

'A man like Lance? What sort of man would that be, Natasha?'

'He's a proud bloke, Ed, and he's hurting.'

'How much did it hurt when he punched you in the face? And what did it do to your pride, for that matter?'

They were outside the café now.

'Look, I told you. I don't want to have this conversation, and if you can't respect that then I'm going. Understand? I'm going. I'll take a sickie and you can find this bloody killer on your own.'

'OK, I'll shut up.'

'Good.'

The café was small, and only a table for two remained vacant. Natasha was forced to place Lance's flowers beneath her chair.

'So,' said Newson after they had ordered their sandwiches, 'what do we know about our killer?'

'He's mad.'

'Yes, that's probably true, but what else? My guess is that he was a victim himself. These murders must have taken an enormous amount of planning, and considerable nerve. The psychological motivation to commit them would have to be absolutely compelling. He'd have to be a truly tortured soul.'

'Or perhaps he's the parent of a bullied child,' Natasha suggested. 'I mean, that's got to be the worst nightmare for a parent, hasn't it? Their child being bullied. It'd kill you, you'd feel so guilty that you didn't stop it. So helpless.'

'That's possible, I suppose,' Newson conceded.

'For me the problem with the idea of our killer being a victim is that he seems so cool and confident.'

'Cool?'

'Yeah, psychopathic but definitely cool,' Natasha went on. 'I mean, look, he's killed six people and we haven't got the faintest idea who he is. He pulled off these murders on his terms. He made life amazingly difficult for himself, but he managed it all the same. He's tough, resourceful, clever, he's got nerves of steel. How is someone like that ever going to have let himself be bullied?'

Newson looked at Natasha sitting opposite him with her swollen eye. 'You, above all people,' he said, 'should be able to see that strong, brave people, cool people, can still end up letting themselves be bullied.'

'I said not to talk about it, Ed.'

'Yes, that's right. I'm sorry.'

'But that was a nice thing to say.'

Natasha's hand was on the table top. Newson put his on hers and gave a gentle squeeze.

'I'm not very cool, Ed,' she said. 'I know you think I am, but I'm not. I'm an idiot.'

On their way back to the office Newson picked up a copy of the early edition of the *Evening Standard*. The front page was dominated by news of the death of a teenage girl attending a north London comprehensive, who had killed herself as a result of being bullied at school.

'My God, it's everywhere. We can't get away from it, can we?' said Natasha.

The story of Tiffany Mellors' suicide was doubly uncomfortable for Newson, because it reminded him of Helen Smart. The girl had gone into her bedroom while her parents were out, lit some joss sticks, put on some music and begun cutting at her arms. By the time she got down as far as her wrists she had generated sufficient despair and self-loathing to make the cuts deep enough to end her torment. She had left a note in her big girlish handwriting that simply said, *'The bullying killed me in the end.'* Her school had long been identified as one with a problem of bullying and the *Standard* carried an editorial calling upon the government and the teaching unions to do more to combat what they called the 'cancer in the classroom'. The article included a lengthy quote issued by Kidcall. Newson wondered whether Helen had written it.

'Bullying is a cancer. It eats at the souls of everyone involved, including the aggressor. It undermines the entire environment in which it occurs and in the long run diminishes us all. Our hearts go out to the parents of this beautiful young girl and I urge any other children who find themselves facing the same kind of despair to pick up a phone and call Kidcall. We can help. As for the government, we say the same thing that we say to teachers, parents and counsellors. It's not enough to stand around wishing these things did not happen. We all have a duty to do something about it.'

Newson thought again about Helen Smart. Damaged, self-destructive Helen, a bright, attractive woman who was crippled by self-loathing. He remembered the lout Kelvin slouching around her flat. What strange psychological point was she trying to make against herself by taking a man like that into her bed? Newson thought that perhaps it was the sexual equivalent of the cuts she made on her arm.

Tiffany Mellors' smiling face stared up at him from the front of the paper. The Kidcall quote had got it right. She was beautiful, with a big, twinkling smile. What kind of bullying could possibly have led a girl like that with seemingly so much to live for to take her own life?

28

The offices of Kidcall occupied a floor of Centre Point. Newson was visiting Kidcall because he had decided that he needed to understand more about the psychology of bullying and bullies, and this was the principal charity dealing with the issue.

'Everybody else does child abuse,' said the counsellor he had spoken to over the phone, 'but, you see, to us, bullying *is* child abuse. It just happens to be other children who do it.'

Newson had arranged to meet a senior counsellor and full-time employee of the charity. As he entered the offices he was relieved to see no sign of Helen. He'd known that by contacting Kidcall he ran the risk of bumping into her, but he felt he had no choice. He wanted to speak to experts.

The offices consisted of a phone room where four counsellors were permanently on call, a large administration office and a small office for Dick Crosby, the President.

'He's here quite often,' Henry Chambers said as they entered Crosby's office, 'but when he's not I get to use his room. So, Inspector? What can I do for you?'

'Well, Mr Chambers.'

'Please. Henry.'

'Henry. I'm interested in the psychology of bullying.'

'Well, you've come to the right place. That's our business. Bullying . . . Well, of course, I should say the prevention thereof.'

'Perhaps you could tell me a little . . .'

'You're a friend of Helen Smart's, aren't you?'

'Yes, I . . .'

'I mentioned you to her this morning. You know, said that you'd called and were coming round and she said she knew you. Small world, eh? To coin a cliché, ha ha.'

'Yes, isn't it?'

'She's a lovely girl, Helen.'

'Um, yes, yes, she is.'

'Best thing that happened to this charity, her coming to work for us. She's terrific on the phones, talking to the kids, you know. She's a great administrator and, well, just really, really nice.'

'Yes. I don't know her very well now. We were at school together.'

'That would have been nice.'

'What?'

'To have known her at school.'

It could not have been more obvious to Newson that Henry Chambers had a crush on Helen if he had written it across his forehead. Newson knew that grim habit of feeling the need to talk about the object of one's love and sing their praises to anyone who would listen because he recognized it in himself. He wondered if it was as glaringly obvious to Helen as it was to him.

'I'm trying to build up a profile of the typical victim of bullying,' Newson said.

'I'm afraid there's no obvious answer to that, Inspector. How long is a piece of string? What we've come to recognize is that bullying can happen to anyone. Kids who've never experienced it before might swap schools and get into trouble completely unexpectedly. Parents are often astonished when they discover that their child has been bullied. Look at the case in the paper today. The girl who cut her wrists. It's amazing how it takes a child to kill herself to get bullying on to the agenda at all.'

'Yes, amazing.'

'From what I've read, that girl wasn't a typical victim at all. She was popular, she was beautiful, which incidentally is another reason for the media interest. It's sad that we seem to find the death of a child more upsetting if that child is beautiful.'

'I suppose we're all attracted to beauty, aren't we?'

'Beauty and the appreciation of it are very subjective things,' Chambers said primly. 'Anyway, this girl Tiffany Mellors suffered in silence. Nobody knew anything about her torment and they were not on the look-out for it because she didn't fit any kind of victim profile.'

'But there must be some characteristics that are more common to victims than to others.'

'Obviously some kids are more vulnerable. Common sense tells us that. Kids who have problems physically are always targets. Slow kids, too, but also sensitive, clever ones get picked on. Helen could tell you more about that. You should talk to her. She was bullied at school, you know. Were you aware of it?'

'Not at the time, no.'

'You see, it's often a secret crime. Secret victims, secret motives, although in Helen's case it's pretty obvious that the other girls must have been jealous of her.'

Newson knew it was pretty obvious that this was absolute nonsense. Christine Copperfield had not been remotely jealous of Helen Smart, she had merely despised her and resented what she saw as Helen's feelings of superiority. But in Helen's case Henry Chambers was looking through the eyes of love and hence saw everything exclusively in that context.

'You simply can't tell who'll be the next victim,' Chambers continued.

A loud voice could be heard in the outer office greeting the staff. Newson recognized it immediately. Assured, confident, well-spoken but with the tiniest carefully protected hint of proletarian roots. Dick Crosby had arrived to pay a visit to his charity. He entered the office and recognized Newson before Chambers had even had a chance to introduce him.

281

'Are you following me around, Inspector? Should I be worried?'

'Not at all, Mr Crosby. Actually, I'm not here to see you.'

'And sadly you don't have your gorgeous colleague with you, either, so nothing in this for me at all, then.'

For a moment Newson was taken aback. How on earth did this man know Natasha? And then he recalled that when he had last met Crosby backstage at the eighties concert claiming to be on police business he had been in the company of Christine. Naturally Crosby would have assumed that Christine was a police officer too. Poor Christine. How she'd have loved to know that Dick Crosby had remembered her, that the first thing he'd done was bring her up in conversation.

'I never forget a face,' Crosby added, 'but in that girl's case I haven't forgotten the rest of her either. Definitely my kind of copper.'

Newson wanted to tell Crosby that Christine was dead, to smother his joshing in the thick blanket of sorrow that had wrapped itself around him. But he didn't. What would have been the point?

Henry Chambers spoke up from the corner of the room. He had removed himself from Crosby's desk the moment the great man had entered the room. 'Inspector Newson is investigating a case that involves bullying,' he said, sounding apologetic.

'Yes,' Newson added. 'I'm anxious to learn about the psychology of the subject.'

'Ah, tricky. Very tricky,' Crosby mused, crossing the room in a proprietorial manner and dropping elegantly into his chair. 'The only thing I know for sure about the psychology of bullying is that I don't know anything about the psychology of bullying. No two bullies are ever alike, no two victims either.'

'That what I said,' Chambers chipped in. 'How long is a piece of string?'

'Was there much bullying at your school, Mr Crosby?' Newson asked. 'I remember your speech at the benefit show in Hyde Park. It was very inspiring.'

'I suppose we had our share and I copped the usual quota. I wasn't a billionaire then, you see, just a scholarship boy at an expensive public school. We're always targets, us social climbers, aren't we? But, as you can see, I got over it.'

'I think perhaps that's something of an understatement.'

'I didn't expect to see you here today, Dick,' Chambers interjected.

'I came in because of this awful Tiffany Mellors business,' Crosby said. 'The media want some comment and I thought I'd do it here to give Kidcall a push. It would be good to get something positive out of such a tragedy. I looked her up, but she'd never contacted us. If she had perhaps she'd be alive now.'

Newson took his leave of Crosby and of Henry Chambers, intent on heading back to New Scotland Yard. However, on emerging from the office he saw that Helen Smart was waiting for him.

'Can we have a coffee?' she asked.

Newson had not wanted to have this conversation, but it could not be avoided. He accompanied Helen reluctantly to a nearby Starbucks, expecting further unpleasant recriminations or possibly a demand to stuff her orifices with white chocolate muffins and ejaculate into her skinny latte. Fortunately, however, she was in a relaxed, almost conciliatory mood.

'I wanted to apologize,' she said, attacking a bucket of mocha-flavoured soymilk foam. 'I've been acting appallingly.'

She still looked tired and unwell but she'd washed her hair and was nicely dressed, a contrast to the casualty she'd appeared to be when Newson had interviewed her at her flat only two days before.

'You reported me to my superiors, Helen. You said I was harassing you. I could've got into terrible trouble.'

'I know, it was a shitty thing to do. Totally shitty. But I was angry. I'm not angry now.'

'So what's brought about this change, then? Not that I'm not happy to accept the apology.'

'Well, they've put me on Prozac for a start, but that won't kick in for a while. In the meantime I'm doing my best with what inner resources I have.'

'So you did see a doctor, then?'

'Yes, she's given me medication and arranged for counselling, which I'm dreading. I'm suffering from depression, you know.'

'Yes, I rather think I'd worked that out.'

'But the point is that suddenly I can see that what I'm depressed about is myself. I'm my own problem. I have to get out of it my own way.'

'What happened, Helen?' Newson was now used to Helen's mood swings and he took nothing for granted.

'The kind of wake-up call only a mother can get,' she replied. 'It happened straight after you left on Sunday. Kelvin was really pissed off about cops being round.'

'Yes, I noticed. Who was Kelvin, by the way?'

'I'd met him the night before at a club in Camden.'

'I see.'

'I know, I know, picking up strangers, eh? Not a good look.'

'Certainly not strangers who look like Kelvin.'

'I did it after the Hyde Park show. After I saw you with Christine.'

'So, my fault again, then?'

'No, that's what I have to come to terms with. I mean, I still think it was a pretty shitty thing to do, turning up with her and all—'

'Look, I'm sorry but—'

'It doesn't matter, Ed. Like I say, I need to start recognizing that what happens to me is my responsibility. I've been acting like an angry schoolgirl. In fact, not *acting* like one. *Being* one. I've been a jealous, angry schoolgirl all my life.'

Newson said nothing. This was a new Helen, contrite, self-analytical. The edge of bitterness had gone. Was he meeting the real person at last, or was this just another paranoid creation from a disturbed mind? Was there any such thing as the *real* Helen? Had there ever been?

'I had a check-up by the way,' she continued. 'At a clinic . . . you know, after that evening we had together . . .' She stopped there. Neither of them was anxious to relive the details of that particular night. 'I felt I owed it to you. You know, to get checked up.'

'Slightly a case of locking the stable door after the horse has bolted.'

'Yeah, well, anyway the result was clean on all counts and you and Kelvin have been the only blokes I've been with in a long time.'

Newson was not at all sure he believed her about this, or what a 'long time' might mean. The sort of things that Helen seemed to feel the need to do and to have done to her were not urges that could be easily suppressed.

'So what about this wake-up call? What happened with Kelvin?'

'Short story. He was angry and weird about you guys being around in my flat and he was being a bit aggressive and then suddenly he got his works out of his bag and started free-basing. I told him to stop and that I didn't want that shit in my house but he just told me to piss off and kept right on cooking up just lying there on my couch, with no shirt on and his jeans unzipped, sneering and doing his drugs and refusing to budge, and I thought, oh my fucking God, another bully, I've gone and got myself another bully.'

'Trouble really likes you, doesn't it, Helen?'

'That's right, it does, doesn't it? But you make trouble for yourself. It's obvious. Anyway, I knew that Karl was coming back from his nan's at teatime. I had no food in the house and this aggressive stoned weirdo was hanging around doing the worst kind of heavy and highly illegal grade-A shit, and then he said that we should get back into bed and I thought I was going to be raped, so I started looking around for a knife and all I could think of was that I had actually brought this bastard into my home. Into Karl's home. I'd done it, it had been *my* choice, and I was the worst fucking idiot on earth.'

'Kelvin certainly didn't look like good news to me.'

'He looked shit even when I was pissed and stoned. And I picked him up in a crappy club and paid for a taxi to bring him into my son's home. But sober on a Sunday afternoon after a visit from the police and with no food in the house, he looked like the fucking devil come to take me to hell. And *I'd* picked *him* up! I mean, what's all that about?'

'I don't know. Lack of self-respect on your part?'

'Exactly. I hate myself and don't think I deserve any better.'

'That sounds like a reasonable analysis.'

'Anyway, that was the wake-up call. Don't worry, there's no punchline, thank God. In the end Kelvin ran out of drugs. I had no food, scarcely any money and I wasn't volunteering to shag him, and since there was nothing in it for him, being a man he just got up and staggered off. Didn't even say goodbye, like I gave a shit. When I closed that door behind him I nearly shouted I was so relieved. But after that, sitting around waiting for Karl to come home, all I could think about was what might have happened, if he'd turned violent, if Karl had come back with my mum to find me beaten and raped and robbed. Or even if Kelvin had still *been* there, Mummy's new bully doing drugs on the couch while Karl wanted his hot chocolate and a story. Shit, it doesn't bear thinking about. Anyway, that's why I went to the doctor. It's why I'm talking to you now. I have to get myself together. I've been a victim for too long. Twenty years, maybe all my life, and there comes a time when *you have to do something about it.*'

Newson noticed that Helen's fists were clenched, knuckles white. For a moment her eyes seemed to shine with a dark evangelical light. He'd seen that light a few days earlier, in the eyes of Roger Jameson as they'd stood together in the corridor at the Hilton Hyde Park discussing the brutal murder of a homeless New Yorker. Jameson had used the same phrase. *You have to do something about it.*

Had Helen done something about it?

He had dismissed the idea earlier but now he was not sure. Was that the reason she was suddenly emerging from her long darkness? Because she had turned out Christine Copperfield's light? Had she broken out of her prison of weakness and pain using Christine's choked and bleeding body as a battering ram?

'You do realize that when Kelvin walked out he took your alibi with him, don't you, Helen?'

She looked up from her latte bucket. There was froth on her lips. 'Ed, I didn't kill Christine Copperfield.'

Could she have done it? She certainly had a motive, her hatred of Christine, which had festered for twenty years. But what about the other murders? Could the self-loathing that Helen had worn like a coat ever since childhood have provoked such a cruelly psychopathic pattern of behaviour? She did work for an anti-bullying charity. Her life was devoted to the victims of bullying. Her working day involved a never-ending reliving of the pain that she had suffered as a girl.

'Ed,' she repeated in a strange, abstracted voice, 'I did not kill Christine Copperfield. I thought you knew that.'

Newson was not so sure. Had Helen been the surprising visitor whom Christine could not wait to tell Newson all about? It fitted, very neatly.

Because *Newson knew the killer.* How many mutual acquaintances did Christine and he share? Not many. Only their old classmates, Helen Smart foremost amongst them.

He looked at Helen, small, skinny Helen with her drawn face and scarred arms. Did those arms have the strength to haul a struggling woman round a cluttered room, forcing that woman's bleeding loins down on to one chair after another? Could Helen have wrestled Christine Copperfield's body through the bedroom door and on to the bed? It was *possible*, but not probable. And what of the others? Helen Smart couldn't have dragged an unconscious Adam Bishop up the stairs of his house, or gained entrance to that house in the first place.

Newson felt Helen's hand on his. 'I was sort of hoping that we could at least still be friends,' she said, gently squeezing his fingers. 'I mean, it's probably not on, but it would be nice, if you thought that some time or other you could see me again.' Her face was open, the eyes wide and sincere.

Newson smiled but removed his hand. Her eyes glanced downwards, disappointed but accepting. She smiled a sweet smile and then her eyes were on him again, now with a hint of an appeal in them.

'Well,' she said, 'you know where I am. I'll leave it with you. We all get lonely sometimes. I know you do. And we did have some fun that evening, before I spoilt it, didn't we? Weird fun, but fun. You enjoyed yourself. I know you did. I *saw* how much you enjoyed yourself . . . because, my, *my*! You are *hung*, Detective Inspector Newson. Oh yes. You can make a lady very happy.'

Newson could scarcely believe it, but out of the blue he was feeling that old familiar stirring. It was the *last* sensation he had been expecting to feel. Helen was weird, Helen was crazy. She was damaged and vulnerable. Perhaps the danger was part of her attraction. He knew that there was no way on earth he would ever go to bed with this girl again, but the fact that the thought had even crossed his mind was astonishing. Helen Smart knew how to appeal to a man, there was no doubt about that.

Could she have got into Adam Bishop's house that way? Was Helen Smart capable of springing a honey trap?

Looking into those eyes now, Newson thought that perhaps she could. Men were fools when it came to sex, Newson knew that all too well. How would big, bullying Adam Bishop have reacted if a little spiky-haired, puffy-breasted pixie like Helen had appeared at his door? He certainly wouldn't have suspected danger.

Could she have got Bradshaw into the van?

And tied Spencer to his chair?

In the space of a few minutes Helen Smart had made Newson do things to her and to himself that he had never done before, things that he had never *dreamt* of doing. He had been trying to prepare supper, poached trout in the microwave. She'd got him from fish to fisting in scarcely three minutes.

But what about Farrah Porter? How would Helen have got into Farrah Porter's sumptuous Kensington flat? She couldn't have. And Angie Tatum? Newson doubted that Helen Smart's kooky charm would have had any effect on that equally tough, equally damaged lady.

'Well, anyway,' said Helen. 'You've got my number.'

'Yes, I've got your number,' Newson replied.

Helen sat back in her chair. 'So you're looking for somebody who was bullied, then, aren't you?' she asked.

'Yes. Or somebody who was a bully. How did you work that out?'

'It's a bit bloody obvious, Ed, your coming round to get that idiot Henry to profile victims for you.'

'Idiot? You don't like him?'

'He's a creep.'

'I think he's in love with you.'

'You don't miss much, do you? God, it's a pain. He's always staring, you know? He thinks I don't notice, but I can sense him out of the corner of my eye, trying to look at my legs or down my front.'

Newson felt as if he had been kicked. Was that how Natasha felt about him? Because Helen could have been describing him in his own office, looking at Natasha.

'He always comments on what I'm wearing,' Helen continued, 'and pays me little compliments when we should be talking about work. It's a form of harassment, but of course if I brought it up he'd probably burst into tears or something. Either way I can do without it.'

Helen was describing his own behaviour exactly. *Was this how Natasha felt about him?*

'I'm really glad we got back in contact,' Helen said.

'Yes, me too,' Newson replied.

'Liar. Of course you're not. For you it was a bloody disaster.'

'No, no.'

'Don't be stupid, Ed. You ended up with a dysfunctional fuck-up

289

stabbing herself in your bathroom. No man wants that when he's looking for a quick shag. But for me it's been a catalyst. The truth is that if there is an answer to what's been screwing me up all these years it's not you and it's not poor, self-deluded, dead Christine Copperfield. It's me. Nobody else can provide the solution. You've taught me that.' She leant forward and kissed him on the mouth. He felt some of the foam from her upper lip transferring itself to his.

'Goodbye, Ed.'

'Goodbye, Helen.'

Helen turned and left. Newson picked up a napkin and wiped his mouth.

On the tube back to his office Newson resolved to seek out an opportunity to question Natasha about his behaviour in the office. He couldn't bear the possibility that she viewed him in the same manner that Helen looked upon the unfortunate Henry. How to approach it, though? Not easy to march up to a girl and say, 'Are you aware that I've been seizing every opportunity to look at your tits and if so I was wondering if you have a problem with it?'

When he got back Natasha was researching the last three names on the victim's victim list.

'I'm afraid Pamela White can't be of any further use to us,' she told Newson. She committed suicide thirteen months ago.'

'Ah, before Bradshaw was murdered?'

'Yes, but I've been talking to her mother and it does seem to have been the result of the note she left on the internet. I told you that Bradshaw was a slippery character, didn't I? Well, lots of people have very different memories of him at school.'

'She got hate mail?'

'Yes, and plenty of it. People wrote all sorts of things, calling her a liar and accusing her of making it all up because she'd been secretly in love with Bradshaw. Her mother thinks that Bradshaw orchestrated the replies amongst the girls who'd been in his thrall at school.'

'Jesus, the victims are certainly piling up, aren't they?'

'It's incredibly sad. That one bloke ruined Pamela White's life and was the direct cause of her eventually ending it. From the age of twelve or thirteen he basically *was* her life.'

Newson decided that it was as good a time as any to speak out. 'Sergeant, I was wondering, speaking of . . . well, speaking of nothing, really. Are you . . . are you entirely happy with my conduct in the office?'

'Sorry?'

'It's a simple question, Sergeant. One has to be very careful these days about these things . . . and quite right, too. I fully support that. So on that subject let us acknowledge that I am . . . a man and you are . . . let's face it, a woman.'

'Ri–ght?'

'And, you are, of course, without doubt, an . . . I mean it's clearly beyond dispute . . . um, any independent observer would accept the fact that you are an . . . *attractive* woman. Yes. That's it, that's the phrase I've been searching for. You are an attractive woman and as such will inevitably . . . in a sense . . . without any active promotion on your part . . . draw the eye. Yes. Draw the eye is a useful phrase and what I'm seeking to establish is—'

'Do I mind that I sometimes catch you checking me out?'

'Yes.'

'No.'

'Good. Terrific. Just checking, best to be sure. Now, the other two victims' victims that we were looking at . . .' Newson began furiously sorting through the papers on his desk, aware of Natasha's quizzical gaze.

'Katie Saunders and Mark Pearce,' she said.

'That's right, Katie Pearce and Mark Saunders. What about them, Sergeant? What can you tell me?'

'Both have alibis. Katie Saunders has gone to live with a cousin in the States. Her mum says that plastic surgery is in a different league over there and she's saving up for another operation. Those guys are expensive.'

'You're right there. New tits, that's the game to be in, all right.' It was the sort of vaguely humorous comment that Newson often made, but on this occasion it caused him a stab of pain and elicited no answering smile from Natasha. Christine Copperfield had made her contribution to enriching the business of plastic surgery. That fact must have been clear to everyone who had seen her corpse lying face up on the bed. Christine's artificial breasts had stood out from the blueing flesh and drawn the eye even more surely than they had done when that flesh had been living. Death makes a mockery of personal vanity and those twin domes had made Christine's corpse look silly, almost. Newson was painfully aware that she had deserved much better.

Natasha seemed to understand. 'It must be very hard for you,' she said. 'I mean, about your old friend.'

'Ah, so you're a mind-reader now, are you?' Newson replied, smiling.

'Well, I knew what you were thinking. I mean, that corpse . . . those breasts, they just looked so strange.'

'Yes, they did, didn't they? Very sad. Don't worry about me, though. I scarcely knew her, remember, even at school. I told you, out of my league.'

'Except obviously not.'

'No, not entirely, it seems. Poor Christine.'

'Yes.'

He pulled himself together. Christine was dead and her killer was still alive. Alive and very active.

'So what about the last one? Pearce.'

'He's the one I do wonder about. He works at a kick-boxing gym and when he isn't working he's training. The bloke I spoke to said he's a bit of a fanatic, crazy in the ring. Treats every fight like his last and treats the other guy the same.'

'I'll go and speak to him tomorrow.'

It was late in the day now and Natasha was gathering up her things to leave.

'What happened to the flowers?' Newson asked.

'I put them in a vase in the ladies' loo. Always nice to have flowers in the loo, I think.' She smiled. 'Don't worry about me, Ed. I'll be all right.'

'Yes, I'm sure you will. Just don't let him do it again, eh?'

'As if.'

After Natasha had left, Newson turned on the television to watch the south-east edition of the news. He had lost count of the times the media had more information on a case than he had and now he regularly watched the bulletins. The horrifying suicide of Tiffany Mellors was the top story as it had been in the *Standard* throughout all the editions of the day.

Watching the video footage supplied by the dead girl's family to the media, Newson found himself thinking once more of Christine Copperfield. Tiffany even looked a little like Christine, the same beautiful blond hair and golden skin, the same lithe figure. She had indeed been beautiful. A news editor's dream. There were a number of testimonials in the coverage, friends saying what a great friend she had been and teachers paying tribute to an attractive, spirited girl who had been such a credit to the school.

Then Dick Crosby appeared, speaking from his office with a Kidcall poster on the wall behind him, appealing for any other kids who found themselves in distress to just pick up the phone. 'Don't suffer in silence,' he said. 'Don't let the bullies scare you into keeping quiet. Pick up the phone, call us, we're here for you—'

Newson turned off the television. His phone was ringing.

'Hello. Chief Inspector Newson.'

'Ed,' said a deep American voice, 'it's Jameson. Roger Jameson.'

29

Newson met Roger Jameson in the bar at the hotel where Jameson was staying, a private establishment behind Marble Arch.

'They know me here,' Jameson explained after they'd been led to a pleasant table in the corner. 'I've been back and forth quite a few times over the last few years. This is kind of a discreet and cosy bolthole.'

'You like things discreet?'

'Who doesn't?'

'Well, it's very nice, anyway,' Newson said. 'I suppose they must pay pretty well in the New York Police.'

'For a long time it was more about exchange rates. For a heck of a while there the buck was real mighty. I used to come here all the time and feel like I was a king.'

Their beers arrived, and they drank for a moment in silence as Newson waited. Jameson had asked to meet him and Newson was going to let him get round to whatever it was he wanted to say in his own time.

'Great reunion,' Jameson said.

'Yes, quite a day.'

'I saw you leave. It looked like you'd gotten lucky with Christine for the second time.'

Newson said nothing.

'Listen, Ed, I heard about what happened. That Christine was killed.'

'I thought perhaps you must have done.'

'I saw the in memoriam note Sally Warren posted on our Friends Reunited page.'

'Oh, you were visiting that, were you?'

'Yeah. I wanted to see what people said about the reunion, and to thank Christine for organizing it. It was a great thing she did, particularly for me, giving me the chance to say all that stuff I said and all. I wanted to thank her, and to apologize for having kind of hijacked things.'

'My impression was that you made the party swing.'

'Well, whatever. I found out she's dead.'

'Oh yes, she's dead all right.'

'It was a big shock, and I guess I was also intrigued. Once a cop, and all that. Sally didn't give any information about how it happened, so I called a couple of pals. Your guys. London cops. CID.'

'You know officers in the Met?'

'Yeah, I did an exchange a couple years back. Spent twelve weeks over here. It wasn't a long time, but you know, bonds form quick in the front line.'

'You were on exchange with CID? I thought you said you were just a beat cop, a humble flatfoot.'

'Yeah, I did say that, didn't I? Truth is I did rise a little higher for a while one time. Not as high as you, Ed, but I made sergeant.'

'Detective Sergeant?'

'Yeah, that was me. I was a detective, too.'

'But not any more.'

'No, I got busted right back down to the pavement.'

'Why was that?'

'I killed a guy. Beat him to death. He was resisting.'

'Ah. Like the Somalian man.'

'Maybe a little. I got mad with him and didn't stop when I should've stopped. I think that's why when it happened again with the Somalian illegal I held back.'

'Or perhaps because a second occurrence of a similar offence might've got you life in jail?'

Jameson looked hard at Newson, his eyes narrowed over the rim of his glass as he sipped his beer, and for a moment Newson felt that he was thirteen again and that Jameson was the scariest person in his life.

'That was uncalled for, Ed,' Jameson said. Newson did not reply. 'Well, I guess it's to be expected. Just because I've decided to try and set the record straight don't mean everybody's got to suddenly believe I'm a good guy all of a sudden.'

'I did believe you when you spoke out at the party. Perhaps I still do. I'm just wondering why you bothered to lie to me.'

'I guess because I knew what you'd think. I really wanted to unload about the Somalian guy, see, so I just pretended the other thing never happened.'

'So why are you telling me now?'

'Because I wanted to talk to you about Christine, and I knew you'd figure out that I must have connections with your people to know what I do. Then you'd a gotten suspicious and looked up my FBI file on the net because every damn thing in the US in on the net and in the public domain. You were always the brightest kid, Ed, and you must be one hell of a cop because I never knew anybody make detective inspector at your age. I decided that if I was going to work with you I'd better be straight with you.'

'Work with me? What d'you mean?'

'Well, talk to you at least. Ed, do you think Helen Smart did it?'

Newson was taken aback. Clearly Jameson had been digging deep and seen things he shouldn't have. Unless, of course, he had other ways of knowing what had been going on.

'Why do you ask?'

'Oh, come on, Ed, give me some credit. I may not be the cop that you are but I ain't a fool either. I heard that Christine got choked on a tampon and that it happened only a week or two after Helen put that weird letter on the site saying what Christine did to her.'

'All right, then. No, I don't think it's likely that Helen Smart killed Christine Copperfield, but it's possible.'

'I don't think she did it. Any more than I think William Connolly killed Adam Bishop or Annabel Shannon killed Farrah Porter.'

It was fortunate that Newson had just drained his beer, because otherwise he would have choked on it at this point.

'Ah, I see we've been working on similar lines,' Jameson said. 'I hoped I wasn't making a fool of myself.'

'What do you know about Bishop and Porter?'

'No more than any guy who knows his way round the internet could discover. I guess I followed the same reasoning as you. When I realized that Christine could only have been killed by somebody who'd read about her on the Friends Reunited site, I wondered if maybe this wasn't the first time it had happened. So I went online with Google, looking for murders. You know, trawling the recent press archives, checking out the amateur sleuth sites. I was looking for out-of-the-ordinary stuff, murders where the most interesting aspect was the manner of death. Well, I wanted weird and I got it, two of the weirdest murders I ever heard of, and that's coming from someone who works in New York City.'

'Bishop and Porter.'

'Exactly. Next I found out where they went to school, just like I imagine you did. Then I went searching for them on Friends Reunited and, bingo, I had William Connolly and Annabel Shannon. Again, just like you did.'

Newson did not know what to make of it. Jameson knew so much.

'I'm right, ain't I?' Jameson asked. 'Someone out there is killing bullies?'

Newson could see no value in denying it. 'Yes, I think that's what's happening. Although it's only conjecture. What do you think? You seem to be as well informed as I am.'

'Oh, I doubt that. And don't go thinking I'm smarter than I am either. Anyone who read Helen Smart on the Friends site and then found out how Christine Copperfield died was going to start putting two and two together.'

'Perhaps not quite everybody, Roger. I think that to work out what you've done as quickly as you have shows extraordinary detective skill.'

'Whatever.'

'Either the NYPD lost a brilliant detective when you got demoted or they lost a clairvoyant.'

'No, I ain't that. But I admit I was good on a case. It's just that in the long run I had the wrong temperament. I'm impatient, see, and I got a short fuse. That ain't helpful when it comes to slow-burn cases. I want justice but I ain't prepared to wait for it.'

The waiter brought two more beers, despite the fact that they had not ordered them.

'They know me here,' Roger said for the second time. 'Don't worry if you don't want yours, I'll just neck 'em both.'

'No, I'll drink it. Long day.'

'Ain't no other kind for a cop.'

'That's the truth. Cheers.'

'Yeah. Cheers ... So why would someone be bumping off bullies? 'Cos they was bullied themselves, right?'

'The thought had crossed my mind, certainly,' Newson replied warily.

'I guess it's one theory.'

'You have another?'

'Yeah, I don't think you're looking for a victim, I think you're looking for a bully. I reckon this guy has to be worse than any of the people he's hitting just to do the stuff to them that he's doing. You see, in the long run I believe that people don't change. I believe that a man is pretty much set to be whatever he is going to be on the day he's born.'

Newson waited a moment before replying. When he did he

298

looked Jameson directly in the eye. 'You started off a bully, didn't you, Roger?'

Despite the fact that there was a waiter standing behind the bar and fellow guests in other corners of the room Newson found himself instinctively checking the exits.

'Yes, I did, I sure did, but, you see, I've come to accept that in myself and that makes a difference. If you understand a thing, you can control it. Focus it.'

'You weren't in control when you lost your stripes, though, you said so yourself.'

'That was all part of the learning process. Now I know why I do the things I do.'

'Why's that, then?'

'It ain't out of taking any pleasure in causing pain. It's kind of like a *need*. A need to be noticed, a need to be respected. I guess you could almost call it a need to be loved.'

'Is that why you beat a man to death for resisting arrest? Because you wanted to be loved?'

'You play hard ball, Ed.'

'It does seem like an obvious question, doesn't it?'

'Well then, OK. I think the answer is yes. When a man is on his knees in front of you begging for you to stop, pleading with you, promising you anything if you'll just take away his pain, that's kind of like the way a desperate lover might behave, don't you think?'

Newson did not reply. Natasha could most certainly take away his pain and he would without doubt be prepared to go down on his knees before her and beg her to do it.

Jameson continued. 'When you're about to kill a man he's totally dependent on you. His whole life is in your hands. You are his world and there ain't no room in it for no one else but you and him. Like a mother and baby. Or two people fuckin'. Ain't that like love?'

'I'd think that the differences outweigh the similarities,' Newson said, but he wasn't entirely sure. He was trying to find a confident, detached tone, but there was definitely something seductive about Jameson with his quiet drawl and his perverted thesis.

'Even back in the days when I was ruining Gary Whitfield's life I believe that I was doing it because I needed him, you know? I needed him to be obsessed by me, I needed him to be thinking of me twenty-four/seven. The more I bullied him the more I knew that I was on his mind every second of the day, from when he woke up to when he went to sleep, and even then I was in his dreams. He couldn't escape me. Ain't that like love?'

Newson knew that it wasn't, but he couldn't deny that Jameson had produced a pretty fair description of his own obsessive and debilitating feelings towards Natasha. When he woke up. When he went to sleep. And in his dreams.

'Why did your marriage break up, Roger?' Newson asked. 'What happened to that girl you met at the Springsteen concert? You said on the Friends site that it was pressure of work.'

'Plus the fact that maybe I'm gay, you think?'

'I did wonder, even when we were at school. Let's face it, your relationship with Gary Whitfield was pretty physical, wasn't it? In a robust kind of way.'

'And I loved to watch him cry.'

'You seemed to love to *make* him cry.'

'And I sure wasn't doing it for my health, eh, Ed? Yeah, you've got me all right. I always knew I had a thing about the boys, but it wasn't till I got married that I realized just how damn queer I was.'

'Bad time to find out.'

'Ain't that the truth?'

'And the big confession thing you did at the reunion? All the things you said to Whitfield?'

'Still trying to make him love me, I guess.'

'Do you think that perhaps the same thing could be said about the killer I'm seeking? That he needs to be loved?'

'I'm just saying that maybe you ain't looking for a victim, that's all. Maybe you're looking for a bully. A bully who wants to be top bully. A man who needs to feel significant. Who needs to feel respected. This guy's moved on from bullying victims. Now he's going after bigger game, he's bullying bullies. He's taking on the pretenders to his crown and he's laughing in their faces, 'cos he's showing them that there's only one *really* bad kid on his block.'

'It's an interesting theory.'

'Let me help you find him, Ed.'

'Why?'

'Because I want to get him.'

'Ah, you want to show him that there's an even worse kid around than him? You want to be the guy to outbully the *über*bully.'

'Partly, sure. Like I say, a man don't change much, but also I'm a cop and I'd like to be back in the saddle. Maybe if I can help get this guy, stop him before he kills again, it'll kind of make up for some of the stuff I've done.'

Newson drained his beer. 'I'm sorry, Roger, but it's out of the question. I'm not looking for a partner.'

'Oh, yeah. That's right, you got one, you're in love with her, right? You told me that.'

Newson had indeed told Jameson this and now he deeply regretted sharing the confidence. Everything about Jameson made him feel deeply uneasy. 'She's an excellent officer,' he replied. 'Anyway, I don't think my chief superintendent would approve of my teaming up with an American cop, particularly one who's on suspension.'

'All I'm saying is talk to me, Ed, tell me what you know, what you find out. I *know* the man you're chasing. He's the same as me.'

'Roger, I couldn't possibly make you party to a Scotland Yard investigation.'

'*I need to know*, Ed. I need this from you.'

'And what I need from you is a comprehensive list of your trips to the UK over the last two and a half years. I want to know when you were in England, Roger.'

Jameson stared hard at Newson. The easy smile remained but it was edged now with anger. 'Oh, I see. It's like that, is it?'

'I can always get the information from the passport office.'

'I suppose I should have guessed the way you'd start thinking, Ed. You're a cop, after all, ain't you? We're all bastards underneath.'

'I don't think so. I'd also like to know what you were doing on the day after the reunion.'

'Ah, the day Christine died.'

'That's right, the day Christine died.'

'Just chilling, Ed. Drifting around town. Checking out the Sunday papers, watching the world go by.'

'Was anybody with you?'

'Not a soul all day.'

'Did you speak to Helen Smart at all?'

'Helen Smart? Why do you ask?'

'Because I want you to tell me the answer.'

'No, I didn't talk to her.'

'What about emails?'

'Ah, emails. Maybe. I have emailed her. It may have been that day.'

'You've been in email correspondence with Helen Smart?'

'Not correspondence. I just wrote to her, that's all.'

'And the difference being?'

'Not much, I guess.'

'Why did you write to her?'

'To tell her that she needed to work through her demons. That she needed to get herself some closure.'

'I see. Did she reply?'

'She said she'd work on it.'

Newson got up. 'Thanks for the beers, Roger. I may be in touch.'

'When this guy gets in touch with *you*, Ed, come back to me. Like I said, I *know* him.'

'Oh, so do I,' said Newson. 'I mean, in a real sense. I actually do know him.'

'You do?'

'Yes, you see Christine Copperfield was on her mobile phone leaving a message for me when the killer turned up at her door. She looked through her little spy hole and when she saw who it was outside she concluded her message to me by making it clear that we were both acquainted with her visitor.' He was watching every detail on Jameson's face, looking for any sign of fear or panic.

'Well, I guess she didn't tell you who that guy was or you'd a pulled him in by now.'

'That's true. But whoever this murderer is, Roger, *I know him too.*'

Newson left, trying to walk the walk of a tough, confident, in-control cop.

As he got to the door Jameson spoke up after him. 'You know what? I think maybe your guy is doing the world a favour, kind of clearing away the trash, like that thing we do in New York, zero tolerance. How about zero tolerance for bullies, right? Has a nice ring to it, don't you think? I seen enough shit to know that sometimes it ain't good enough to sit round wringing your hands and saying how terrible things are. Sometimes you have to do something about it.'

That phrase. *You have to do something about it.*

Helen's phrase. Roger's phrase. Helen Smart. Roger Jameson. Quite a team. One bully, one victim, same school. Newson's school.

Newson knew them both.

Helen Smart could never have got past Farrah Porter's or Angie Tatum's door, but maybe Roger Jameson could. A big, handsome American cop. He might have persuaded them to let him in. On the other hand, Roger Jameson would be unlikely to make a man like Adam Bishop feel anything but nervous and defensive, while kooky, sexy little Helen would not scare him at all. Could there have been *two* people at Christine Copperfield's door when she made her final phone call? Then she really would have had a story to tell Newson.

30

The following morning Newson travelled once more to Manchester, where he had an appointment with Mark Pearce at the Fallowfield kick-boxing gym. He caught the 6.55 from Euston and having had breakfast, which to him always tasted better on a train, he thought it a reasonable enough hour to phone Rod Haynes, the Manchester pathologist. A woman's voice answered. A voice Newson recognised.

'Dr Clarke?'

'Who is this?' she answered suspiciously.

'Ed Newson. I was phoning for Dr Haynes.'

'Ah, right, of course. Silly of me to pick up the phone . . . It's just the kids, you know. I gave them this number.' She was clearly embarrassed. 'I'll just get him. It's pretty early, Inspector.'

'Yes, I know, I'm sorry. It was a medical question, actually. I was just wondering if someone suffers low-level neurological damage in their adolescence – if their brain was bruised – would that affect them much in later life?'

'That's a tricky question, Inspector. How do you define "low level"? And what do you mean by "affect"? Physically? Mentally? Psychologically? What was the extent of the initial bruising? How was it treated, and was that treatment effective? Surely, Inspector, you can see that you're being ridiculously vague.'

Having an affair had not caused Dr Clarke to lighten up.

'OK, a fourteen-year-old boy gets hit on the head repeatedly with a book for an hour, ending up nearly losing consciousness. He's treated in hospital for cranial bruising and then spends a month in bed, but he suffers from headaches for years afterwards. Fifteen years later, do you think he would still be affected?'

'Yes, of course he would! It'd impact in some manner or other on his whole life.'

'I'm talking about actual physical brain damage. Is it possible that an attack like that could have unbalanced the lad but not in a manner that was obvious, creating a sort of mental timebomb so that while he seemed to be getting on with his life, all the time the seeds of violence were growing and then one day he just flips?'

'And goes bananas?'

'Yes.'

'Sticking compasses in people and dyeing their pubic hair red?'

'Perhaps, yes.'

'Yes, it's possible. Not very likely, but anything's possible with the brain. However, there'd be no way whatsoever of telling without a scan and numerous neurological tests. The lad might be perfectly OK, he might be a Jekyll and Hyde. If you want to find out you'll need to section him under the Mental Health Act and have a really good look at him.'

'Right. OK, thanks. I doubt I'll find we have grounds for that. Anyway, just a thought. Thanks for your time. All well?'

'Yes, thank you.'

'So um . . . please give my best to Dr Haynes.'

Newson put down the phone. Dr Clarke was right, it had been a bit of a stupid question. He turned his attention to the papers. All the tabloids led on the tragic suicide of Tiffany Mellors. Most of the papers ran double-page spreads, simultaneously shedding tears for the tragedy of a young life cut short and glorying in the adolescent beauty of a teen queen. There was Tiffany grinning broadly in her little netball skirt, and in action wearing tiny shorts and a bikini top playing badminton on the beach. There were pictures of her at a school dance, gorgeous in a low-cut top, tummy proudly on display with the obligatory glittering belly button and the lowest-cut hipster trousers Newson had ever seen. Every paper pondered the same issue. If a girl like this could be driven to slash her wrists because of the torment of bullying, then we had scarcely begun to understand the scale of the problem. Newson read all the reports and he wondered. Tiffany Mellors had died like a Helen but she had lived like a Christine. Strange. He supposed the editorials must be right. With bullying you simply never could tell.

The train pulled in at Manchester Piccadilly Station in good time, affording Newson the luxury of walking to Rusholme. The placards for yesterday's *Manchester Evening News* were out in front of the newsagents as he passed by. They too had got bullying fever. The whole country was indulging in an orgy of soul-searching about lost innocence, flowers crushed and the general mental health of the children in its schools.

'It is only a matter of time,' the paper announced on its front page, 'before Manchester faces the tragedy of its own Tiffany Mellors.' And there again were the photographs. Some enterprising journalist had persuaded one of Tiffany's schoolfriends to produce a snap of the whole girl gang on a trip to the local lido. Five gorgeous girls bursting out of their bikinis, grinning over their ice creams with Tiffany at the centre, the gilded star of a golden galaxy, and yet, as she had informed the world herself just before she took her own life, *the bullying killed her in the end.*

The gym where Mark Pearce worked and trained was typical of its kind, rough, sweaty and intimidating. Men of all races were united here in the pursuit of physical perfection for the purpose of aggression. Six-pack stomachs and rippling biceps were standard. Newson noted, as he had had occasion to do before when encountering young men practising martial arts, that at some point an effort had been made to remind these disciples of perfection of the original spiritual routes of the craft they practised. There were posters on the walls featuring setting suns on still seas and prettily worded messages on the subject of harmony and humility. More recent posters, however, showed Van Damme, Bruce Lee and the Terminator. The men studying at the Rusholme gym were not doing so in order to learn about themselves and complete their spiritual journey to oneness. They were doing it so that they would be able to separate a man's head from his shoulders with a single kick.

Newson hovered in the doorway while an enormous bald man who seemed to be in a position of authority studiously ignored him, continuing to play the pub-style tabletop video kick-boxing game that served as a front desk. Eventually the game ended.

'They do a beginners' class at the Moss Side Community Centre,' said the man without looking up, 'but if I were you, mate, I'd just buy a gun.'

'I don't want to learn kick-boxing,' Newson replied. 'I'm here to see someone. Mark Pearce. I'm a police officer.'

Newson held up his ID, which the man glanced at with barely concealed contempt. 'Fookin' 'ell, *you're* a detective inspector?'

'Yes.'

'Fookin' 'ell, so southern coppers are as crap as your footballers.'

'Could you just tell Mr Pearce that I'm here.'

'Marky,' the man shouted at a young man who was currently in the ring unleashing kick after kick at the hapless head of a less-skilled opponent. '*Marky!*'

But the man still did not hear. He was lost in a world of his own where sweat, muscle and the broken body of the man opposite him represented the entirety of his existence. The man turned off the sound system, which was playing gangsta rap at full volume, and went to lean on the ropes of the ring.

'Fookin' *Mark!*'

Finally the man's name penetrated his brain and he stopped his kicking. The face that turned towards Newson looked be-wildered, aggressive and defensive all at once, like a dog that had been pulled from its dinner.

'There's a copper here from London says he wants to see you.'

Mark Pearce remembered now. Blinking through the sweat that was pouring down his face, he put a towel over his head and climbed out of the ring.

'Can't go out. Not got time to change an' that,' he explained. 'Only get three hours to train, after that I'm cleaning bogs, so make it quick, will you?'

'Three hours? You do that for three hours?'

'Fookin' right I do. Nobody fooks with me.'

They went into the locker room and Newson reeled from the smell. This was a male environment and it seemed to Newson as if he was breathing the soup-thick air directly through the sweat-sodden, greying jockstrap lying on the bench, where Pearce clearly expected him to sit, and which he was forced to brush off on to the floor in order to do so.

'How long have you been training?'

'Four years. It's great, it's my fookin' life. It's given me a purpose.'

'That purpose wouldn't by any chance be to give Denis Spencer a good kicking, would it?'

Pearce looked at Newson in surprise. 'What the fook do you know about me and Denis Spencer?'

'I read your entry on the Friends Reunited site.'

'Were you at school, then? I don't remember you.'

'No, I'm investigating his murder.'

'Whose?'

'Denis Spencer's.'

For a moment Pearce seemed not to understand. 'What do you mean? What're you on about? Who's been murdered? Not Denis Spencer? That in't it, is it?'

'Yes, Denis Spencer.'

'He's int' army.'

'He was. He was killed more than a year ago.'

'Fook off, no.'

'It's not something I'd make a mistake about. Denis Spencer is dead. I don't know why, but I presumed you knew.'

Mark Pearce's expression turned suddenly from bewilderment to despair. When he spoke again the noise he made could only be described as a howl.

'*No!* No, no, no, no. Fookin' nooooooo!'

'I'm sorry you're upset,' said Newson. 'I thought you'd be pleased.'

'Pleased?! Pleased?! I'm not fookin' *pleased*!' Pearce smashed a fist against one of the lockers, denting it considerably. He leapt to his feet and unleashed a series of kicks at the dead metal, making such a commotion that the big man from the door came in to admonish him.

'I'll fookin' dock your wages, you cunt! Dentin' my fookin' lockers.'

Pearce sat down again, his anger suddenly drained and replaced with despair. '*I* wanted to kill 'im,' he said. '*I* wanted to kick the bastard to death. *I* were going to go and do it the minute I got my black belt. Four years I've been training. Four fookin' years. He was my purpose. My goal.'

'Mr Pearce—'

'It were only when I decided that I had to kill him that I started to get on wi' me life.'

'Well, someone else has saved you the trouble, Mr Pearce, and also a life sentence for murder. I'd look on the bright side if I were you.'

'But *I wanted to do it.*'

'Mark, apart from the letter you put up on the Friends site, have you ever talked to anyone about what Spencer did to you?'

'No, it were between 'im and me.'

'Not even to a girlfriend?'

'Don't 'ave girlfriends. You can't trust 'em. They're all slags. I'm in love with kicking 'eads.'

'The person who killed Denis Spencer killed him by smashing him over the head with a book hundreds and hundreds of times. Can you think of anyone you know who might have felt like doing that on your behalf?'

'You're telling me he got killed wi' a book?'

'Yes. Somebody secured him to a chair and hit him over the head with a heavy book until he died.'

'That's . . . that's fookin' *mental*, that is. That's what 'e done to me!'

'Exactly.'

A big smile spread across Mark Pearce's face. 'Oh, that is sweet, that is. Oh, that's beautiful, that is. Dead fookin' beautiful. I don't mind that. That's all right, that is. An' there was me just goin' t' fookin' give 'im a kickin'. Oh yeah, somebody else has been thirstin' for revenge, in't they? He must 'ave done what he did to someone else, mustn't he?'

'It's possible.'

'All I can say, mate, is if ever you find out who did it tell him he's got a pal in me, OK? He's my brother, the bloke who done that to Denis fookin' Spencer. My fookin' brother! An' if you catch 'im and bang 'im up, I'll fookin' come and kill *you*!'

31

Mark Pearce had not known that Spencer was dead. Newson didn't consider Pearce the sharpest knife in the drawer and he was certain that he could not have faked his furious bewilderment at the news that he was too late to kill his tormentor. Staring at his list of victims' victims on the train home Newson felt reasonably confident in his mind that at least four of them had had nothing to do with the murders, beyond the obvious fact that they had unwittingly provided the killer with his targets and his methods.

Against the name of Helen Smart he put a large question mark.

Newson bought two cans of lager from the trolley, feeling angry with himself. He knew so much and yet he still knew nothing. He felt scarcely closer to identifying the killer than when he had first stood staring at the punctured body of Adam Bishop. Since then the killer had killed twice more and Newson had been powerless to stop him. What was more, the pace had picked up. There had been a number of months between each of the first three murders, and three weeks between the last. How long would it be before he was once more looking up Friends Reunited to unravel the wicked past of another corpse? Newson opened a beer and glanced at the *Manchester Evening News*. He was sick of bullying and yet he couldn't get away from it. Without really wishing to do so, he found himself reading the further coverage of the Tiffany Mellors case. As he read he began to realize that there was an element to the tragedy that did not feel quite right. All of the coverage had dwelt on the fact that nobody had had any idea that the bullying was taking place, and this was seen as the most disturbing aspect of her death. Something which must, without doubt, form a major part in any future policy-making on the subject.

The phrase 'invisible bullying' had been coined by the news talkshows and in the newspaper editorials. But what *was* invisible bullying? Newson had never come across it before. Certainly many a victim had suffered in silence but it seemed difficult to credit that a girl could be harassed into suicide without *anybody* being aware that there was a problem. He thought back to his schooldays. It was true that he'd been unaware of what Helen had gone through at the hands of Christine Copperfield and her friends, but he was certain that *someone* would have known about it besides the bullies and the victim. There must have been girls on the edge of it, people in the locker room who knew what was going on.

Newson read the paper thoroughly and thought back to the coverage he'd seen on the previous day. He realized that so far there had been not even the vaguest speculation about who the bully might have been. Tiffany Mellors was a victim without a persecutor, or at least without one who could be identified. And yet she'd been driven to the despair of self-mutilation and suicide. He could not help wondering if something was being missed.

Newson fell asleep at Milton Keynes and was jolted awake thirty minutes later by the train's arrival at Euston. He had nodded off determined to focus his brain on the facts of his investigation instead of speculating on the world of bullying in general. He woke up, however, with the conviction that the answer *had* to lie in the greater picture, in the psychology of either the victim or the bully. His killer had to be one or the other. Tiffany Mellors appeared to have been a girl with tremendous self-confidence until something drove her over the edge. Perhaps in her he would find the personality of his killer. On the other hand, if the killer had been a bully at school then he was a clever one, one who still knew how to cover his tracks, in fact an *invisible bully.*

If Newson could understand Tiffany and her mysterious persecutor then he would understand the killer. He was convinced. In the absence of any other obvious lines of enquiry he resolved that in the morning he would visit Tiffany Mellors' school in Ruislip to discover the psychology behind a confident victim and an invisible bully.

Newson did not find it easy to explain his thinking to Natasha the following morning when he asked her to go with him to the school.

'I just feel there's something there for us, that's all,' he said. 'Things we need to know, and you have to come with me. The victim was a girl. I'm not wandering round some school on my own trying to talk to a bunch of adolescent girls.'

'I hate schools,' Natasha complained. 'They remind me of school.'

'Well, imagine what it's like for me. I had six years of being ignored by juvenile females and now I'm going back for more.'

Natasha took a little mirror from her bag and for the fifth time in as many minutes she checked her reflection. Her bruised eye was looking better, but she was inevitably still self-conscious about it.

'How have things been with Lance?' Newson asked.

'Fine. Great. He's been really, really nice. I thought he was going to be furious because I didn't bring his flowers home with me, but he wasn't. He said he understood. Since then he's been lovely.'

'Natasha,' Newson said gently.

'What!' she snapped back. '*What?*'

'He hits you and now *you*'re grateful because *he*'s not angry.'

'You don't understand.'

'Yes, I do. Anyway, let's go.'

They were not the only visitors to the Aneurin Bevan Comprehensive that morning. There were still clusters of media hanging about at the gates along with the endless stream of local residents arriving to lay flowers and teddy bears at the base of the perimeter wall.

Inside the school things were nearly as crowded. Newson had expected the media presence and the flowers delivered outside. What he had not expected was the army of counsellors.

'There are so many of them,' Natasha said.

'We have a statutory obligation to provide grief support,' the school secretary explained. 'If any of the pupils were to become traumatized as a result of this incident, we could be held responsible.'

'Well, I think you've covered yourselves,' Newson replied.

They had. Every classroom had its own support group, grief counsellors and trauma counsellors.

'Shit, if this much effort had been put in beforehand,' Natasha said, 'Tiffany Mellors probably wouldn't be dead.'

'I doubt it,' Newson replied. 'There are always going to be bullies and there are always going to be victims. Being trained or prepared for it doesn't necessarily protect you.'

Newson had not meant this comment to reflect on Natasha's relationship with Lance, but she clearly took it that way. Her lips set firm and she went silent. Newson desperately wanted to backtrack, but he knew that he would only make matters worse. Besides which, whether he'd meant it or not, it was true.

The pupils, of course, were having a fabulous time. None of them had ever felt so important or found it so easy to skip lessons. Groups of girls hung about in the corridors hugging each other, red-eyed. Lads ran around the place looking tough and firm and clearly ready to deal with the invisible bully should he ever seek to try anything with them.

Natasha and Newson were given the use of the nurse's quiet

room in order to conduct their interviews. One by one Tiffany's classmates were brought before them.

First came her close friends, the members of the gang that Newson had seen pictured in their bikinis on the front of the *Manchester Evening News*. Newson was irritated with himself to discover that, despite the fact that he was now a senior police officer, he was as intimidated by fourteen-year-old girls as he had been more than twenty years before.

These were the pretty girls, the confident ones, their uniforms and faces all girlishly adorned to the limits of what the school would allow. Newson thought about his old classmate Sally Warren desperately trying to subdue a screaming toddler in a hotel foyer, no longer an object of desire. She'd been a golden girl once. All the boys had wanted to dance with her, but the last time he'd seen her she'd been dancing with her fatherless child. Newson wondered what kind of entries these fresh-faced girls would be making on Friends Reunited twenty and thirty and forty years on.

'She was great. The best friend ever. I'll miss her till I die,' said a girl called Nikki, echoing the sentiments of the previous three girls who had sat before Newson and Natasha. 'It's like, you know, she always knew the best stuff to get, right? And, like, you know, the party was always at Tiff's? And she'd say let's do something and we'd all just do it?'

'They were all jealous of her,' Natasha said after Nikki had left the room. 'I remember feeling like that. Some girls just have the lot. The boys want to have her and the girls want to be her. Tiffany Mellors was one of those girls. We had one in our class. I remember that I sort of loved her and I also secretly hated her because I knew that I was brighter than her and better than her but that if she called me and said come round I'd have dropped everything to be with her.'

'Did she ever call?'

'No, not for me. I was kind of halfway between the nerds and the cool gang. They sort of tolerated me and I got invited to parties to make up the numbers. But I wasn't at the centre, not like these girls. Not like young Nikki. I'll bet she's a right bitch, that one.'

'Ah, yes. We've met the class's golden girls. And Tiffany Mellors was the boss, wasn't she?'

'No doubt about that.'

'In which case it seems to me that everything that's being said about why she died contradicts who she actually was. I think a very major point is being missed here.'

'What's that?'

'I'm going to find out. And God knows, Natasha, I hope I'm wrong, because if I'm not what's happened here is truly terrible and what's more is going to happen again.'

The school secretary knocked and entered. 'Shall I bring up another group, Inspector?'

'No,' said Newson, 'I'd like you to bring back the ones we've just seen. I'd like to see Tiffany's closest friends again, please. Bring them in together.'

The four girls returned. One of them was destined soon to take Tiffany's place as coolest girl in class.

'Now then, ladies,' said Newson. 'I want to talk to you some more about bullying.'

The expressions on the girls' faces indicated that they had hoped for something more exciting. They did not think that there was anything left to say on the subject of bullying.

'We've told you,' Nikki volunteered wearily, 'we don't know who was getting at Tiff. If we did she'd be dead, right? 'Cos we'd get her.'

The other girls nodded in agreement.

'I don't want to know who you think might have been bullying Tiffany Mellors. I want to know who Tiffany Mellors was bullying.'

Newson let this hang in the air for a moment before adding, 'Who *you* were bullying, Nikki.'

The girls were dumbfounded.

317

'Come on,' Newson persisted. 'You look like a pretty cool bunch to me. You don't look like girls I'd want to mess with, that's for sure, and Tiffany was the boss, right? All the boys wanted to go out with Tiff, didn't they? All the girls wanted to be her, right? So what I want to know is, who paid the price for all that power? Who was on the receiving end? Whose life have you been making a misery?'

The girls did not reply. Nikki glared defiantly at Newson and the other three fiddled with their rings and stared at the floor. Clearly it was Nikki who was destined to inherit Tiffany's crown.

'I'm not saying anything,' said the girl who would be queen. 'None of us are saying anything,' she added, just in case any of her friends had had other ideas.

'Right, that's all I need to know,' Newson said. 'Thank you, girls. That'll be all.'

The four girls left and the secretary returned.

'Right,' said Newson, 'I'd like to see the rest of the class, one at a time.'

'Send up the girls first,' Natasha added, and then, turning to Newson, said, 'Save you a bit of time, Ed. You're looking for a girl, believe me.'

Both Newson and Natasha picked her out the moment she walked into the room. Tanya Waddingham was obviously a victim, or at least she'd been turned into one through being in the wrong year with the wrong girls. Her hair, parted in the middle, hung limply in front of her face, a face that was staring resolutely at the floor as she entered the room and which she scarcely raised at all as she sat down. She wore a long skirt and a big jumper that made it impossible to imagine what shape her body was, and her skin was pale and spotty. They stared at the greasy crown of Tanya's head as she sat before them, her chin stuck firmly to her chest.

'Tanya,' Natasha said, 'we want to ask you something and we'll treat the answer in complete confidence. Were you being bullied by Tiffany Mellors?'

The girl did not answer.

'Please, Tanya. It's very important. We need to know.'

After a few moments Tanya mumbled something.

'I beg your pardon, Tanya? I didn't hear that.'

'I'm glad she's dead,' Tanya repeated, still mumbling, but this time there was no doubt what she had said.

'Why are you glad she's dead?' Natasha asked.

'Because she was a bitch.'

Newson spoke. 'Tanya, would you roll up the sleeves of your jumper for me, please?'

Tanya did not move. It was as if she was frozen.

'I'd like you to show me your arms, please,' Newson pressed.

Still Tanya did not move. 'No,' she said.

'I'm afraid I'm going to have to insist,' Newson said.

'Can't make me.'

Natasha held up her hand to Newson so that she could speak. 'Tanya,' she said gently, 'we don't want to have to make you. You don't have to be scared with us, but whatever has been happening to you needs to be brought out. This is a police investigation, Tanya. Please do as the inspector has asked.'

Slowly and still without lifting her head Tanya raised the sleeves of her jumper. The pale, thin arms revealed beneath were marked by a crisscrossing of scars.

'Tanya,' Newson asked. 'Did you do this to yourself?'

The girl did not reply. After a few moments Newson repeated his question.

'No,' Tanya whispered.

'Did Tiffany Mellors do it to you?'

But Tanya would say no more. As far as Newson was concerned, she did not need to.

After the girl had gone Newson sent for the secretary and asked her to send up the next pupil. He explained that he would be needing to speak to all the other members of the class, including the boys.

'Why?' asked Natasha when they were briefly alone in the room. 'You've found your victim.'

'If we stop now,' Newson explained, 'Nikki and her little gang of hellcats will presume that Tanya told us what we wanted to know and Tanya's life won't be worth living. If we speak to all the kids, then our friend Nikki will have no reason to suspect Tanya. We can't just barge in here, turn that girl into an even bigger target than she already was and then bugger off again.'

'No, of course. You're right,' Natasha replied, then she gave Newson a hug. 'You're a good bloke, Eddie Newson. I hope you know that. A very good bloke.'

Newson did not reply, intent as he was on absorbing every detail of her brief, sisterly embrace. The pressure of her arms around his shoulders, the slight contact between her chest and his, the nearness of her mouth to his ear, the smell of her hair and the tiniest tickle as it brushed briefly past his cheek. It was over in seconds, but by that time Newson had managed to keep a piece of it locked in his heart to treasure for ever.

Newson passed no further comment on the interview with Tanya Waddingham until he and Natasha had left the school and were sitting together in his car, which was parked in a nearby street.

He opened the glove compartment, took out the notebook in which he had made his list of victims and the victims' victims, and added two new names to the bottom. *Tiffany Mellors* and *Tanya Waddingham*.

'What are you doing, Ed?' Natasha asked, and her voice shook with emotion. 'What are you saying?'

'I'm saying that our killer has moved from the past to the present,' Newson replied. 'I don't believe that Tiffany Mellors committed suicide. Tiffany Mellors was a bully and somebody killed her for it.'

32

Mounds of flowers were stacked up on the pavement outside the Mellorses' little terraced house. As Newson and Natasha walked from the car, a poorly dressed elderly lady in the process of leaving a little bunch of flowers stood up from the pavement and wiped away a tear.

Tiffany Mellors' mother opened the door and allowed them in. She had obviously been crying and was not overjoyed at the prospect of speaking to the police. 'I really don't see what there is to talk about,' she said, showing Newson and Natasha into her leather-furnished lounge. 'What the police should be doing is getting into that school and finding whoever it was that drove my girl to do this terrible thing. Not sitting here talking to me.'

'We'll try to make this as brief as possible, Mrs Mellors,' Newson told her. 'And please rest assured that we're as determined as you are to get to the bottom of what it was that caused this terrible tragedy.'

Mrs Mellors took a tissue from a flamboyantly embroidered box.

'Tiffany died some time after returning from school,' prompted Newson. 'You discovered her body when you got home at six thirty. Is that right?'

'Yes, yes, it is.' Mrs Mellors was having trouble controlling her emotions. 'I came home and called for her to help with the tea and when she didn't reply I went upstairs and . . . and . . .'

'Yes, Mrs Mellors, no need to go over that again. Just tell me: was it usual for Tiffany to be in the house alone after school?'

'Yes, me and her father both work, see. I get home at six thirty and he's back soon after that. Tiff had a key and unless there was sport or whatever at school or she was seeing a mate, she'd come home and let herself in.'

'So she was a responsible girl? You trusted her?'

'She was the best, that's all, Inspector. The best.'

'She'd get home, when? About four thirty?'

'Yes. She'd normally got her homework done by the time I got in. She'd get a Diet Coke and go to her room, and . . .'

Mrs Mellors broke down. When she had recovered Newson asked if they could look at Tiffany's bedroom. Reluctantly Mrs Mellors agreed.

'He wants to move out,' she said as they climbed the stairs, 'but this was her home. I can't just walk away from it.'

She opened the door on which there still hung a sign that said 'Tiff's place. No parents without permission.' Newson could see that Mrs Mellors was swallowing back tears. Inside was very much the bedroom one would have expected to belong to a teenage girl. There were boy-band posters on the wall, stuffed toys on the shelves and piles of celebrity magazines. The dressing table was covered in any amount of make-up and jewellery, and the mirror had notes and cards wedged into the frame. The only obvious thing that could be gleaned about Tiffany from a superficial glance at her room was that she was a very neat girl. Her magazines were nicely stacked and the make-up was all laid out in good order.

'Tiffany was proud of this room, I think?' Newson enquired.

'Yes, she was. She did it all herself and cleaned and vacuumed. I used to say it was the tidiest room in the house. She hated mess.'

'And yet she—' Newson stopped himself. He'd been thinking out loud. In front of the dressing table a little padded matching chair stood on dust covers, which had been laid over the carpet.

'We haven't decided what to do about the floor yet,' Mrs Mellors said, and she was crying now. 'I want to keep her room exactly as it was, but the carpet's all soaked in . . . soaked in—'

'We understand, Mrs Mellors,' Natasha said gently. 'Don't feel you have to speak.'

'Tiffany was sitting on the dressing chair when she died?' Newson enquired.

'Yes. She'd been looking at herself, I suppose, as she . . .'

Newson stepped forward on to the dust sheets and studied the little chair and table. 'They've been cleaned, have they?' he asked.

'Yes, my sister-in-law gave them a wipe down when she come over to be with us. Tiff loved her aunt, she did.'

Newson got down on his knees and looked at the seat back and the legs of the chair. It was the kind of fanciful chair that a Disney princess might have sat upon, painted in a rich cream colour with a crimson cushioned seat.

'She had that when she was eleven. I think she was beginning to think that she wanted something a bit different, a bit more grown-up.'

'I'll need to take this chair away with me if that's all right, Mrs Mellors,' Newson said.

'What do you want with it?' she said. 'What good can looking at her stuff possibly do?'

'I'm hoping that I may be able to shed some light on the causes of your daughter's death, Mrs Mellors. I'm afraid I'll have to insist that you let me borrow it for a day or two.'

'Do what you have to do.'

'There's a coffee cup on the dressing table, Mrs Mellors. You mentioned that Tiffany drank Diet Coke.'

'She had one every day when she got back from school. It was her treat.'

'Did she drink coffee?'

'Not at home. Starbucks, yes, she loved all that, but not much at home. Occasionally . . . I suppose on that day everything was out of character, wasn't it?'

Newson had seen all he needed to see. He put on his plastic gloves and picked up the vanity chair and the coffee cup and carried them downstairs. He assured Mrs Mellors once more that he expected shortly to have some explanations for her, and then he and Natasha left.

Newson let Natasha drive while he phoned ahead to the local morgue to ask them to expect him. Then he got hold of the pathologist who had attended the suicide and asked him to meet them at the morgue.

'I don't care if you're busy!' Newson snapped into the phone. 'No, it can't wait, and this is most definitely *not* a routine situation. You may have thought it was, Doctor, but I can only imagine that is because you are either blind or stupid . . . I'll take whatever tone I like with you, Doctor, and let me tell you that I have yet to decide whether to pursue you for gross incompetence. As it is I'll be advising the local police to find someone else to do their forensics!' He ended the call.

Natasha was surprised. 'Shit, Ed. You don't normally get angry like that.'

'I don't normally see unbelievable incompetence like this, Natasha. Because of this complete bloody idiot we've had Tiffany's aunt sponging up the evidence in what I'm quite certain was a murder scene.'

Newson got back on his phone and made two more calls summoning the local coroner and a member of the local CID to the meeting at the morgue.

'You never throw your weight around like this,' said Natasha. 'You should do it more often, it's a good look on you.'

They were the first to arrive and Newson asked immediately to be shown the body of the dead girl. The assistant wheeled out the corpse and pulled the sheet from it. Newson had never got used to being in the presence of dead children and teenagers, young and healthy people on the threshold of their lives. It was the worst aspect of his job.

He took out his eye glass and studied the girl's wounded arms, the only parts of the body that were not pristine. He needed only the briefest of glances to confirm what he had suspected. 'The man who declared this a suicide has definitely got to lose his job.'

At that point the offending doctor entered, accompanied by the local coroner and a detective constable from the local police station.

'Are you Detective Inspector Newson?' the doctor enquired.

'Yes, I am. You would be Dr Forrest?'

'That's right, and I'd like to make it very clear that I do not appreciate being harangued over the phone by stroppy detectives who think that just because they come from Scotland Yard—'

'Doctor Forrest,' Newson said, interrupting the doctor's angry diatribe, 'may I ask you when you last attended a teenage wrist-slashing in which the desperate and depressed adolescent in question had sufficient guts and anatomical knowledge to locate and to open *both* radial arteries?'

Dr Forrest was a large man. He had marched right up to Newson and was currently towering over him. Nonetheless Newson's tone stopped him in his tracks. 'What are you trying to say?'

'It's a simple question, Doctor, which I'll expand on: when was the last time you saw a fourteen-year-old suicide who had the presence of mind and the steadiness of hand to strike lengthways, *down the arm*, proximally to distally instead of crossways, which is of course the way most people would slash their wrists, but which is, as I'm sure you'll confirm, a far less effective manner of creating a fatal wound.'

Dr Forrest took a step back. 'Yes, it is, but—'

'All the other wounds are crossways, are they not?'

'Hesitancy incisions, Inspector. Very common in suicides.'

'Yes, I know, and even more common in suicide *attempts*, which is what most wrist-slashings, particularly adolescent ones, turn out to be. The subject probes and jabs, making small attention-seeking wounds. These so-called "hesitancy incisions" often do not develop into a genuinely traumatic wound, but when they do it will be a deeper version of what the person has so far attempted. A crossways cut, damaging only surface veins from which the blood will flow relatively sedately. In this case, however, an innocent, unsophisticated adolescent who has been pecking away with a knife up and down her arm in the usual cosmetic manner suddenly delved deeply into her wrist, located the main radial artery and parted the tough muscular tubing surrounding it, lengthways in a deep and traumatic cut. A cut from which her life's blood will *pump* in great dramatic arcs and which will kill her in minutes. Fourteen-year-old Tiffany Mellors does this not once but *twice*. Don't you find this surprising, Doctor?'

There was a pause. The big man's face was red, his fists clenched. 'Well, put like that I agree that this girl was unusually efficient. But there was a note and no sign of any struggle. I saw no reason to suspect foul play and I still don't.'

'I'll tell you something else of which there was no sign, Doctor. Blood. Blood on the walls, on the bed, on the ceiling. Almost all the blood went on to the carpet beneath where the girl was sitting. You and I both know what happens when a radial artery is opened. The blood is pumped as if through a hosepipe. When this kind of suicide is successful the whole room gets coated. The only way that all the blood would have sprayed in a single direction is if the girl's arms had stayed in a single position, hanging by her sides.'

'Which is how she was sitting when I attended the scene.'

'What are the chances of a girl who has done this to herself sitting rigidly in one position while she dies? Not very great, I suggest. Besides which, having made the first cut, she would have had to move the knife from one hand to the other and locate the second artery. During that time the first cut would have *had* to be pumping sideways and an arc of blood would have been deposited on the wall.'

'I did not attend the scene with a criminal investigation in mind, Inspector. What I saw was a suicide and I still believe that to be the case. There was a note which the mother confirmed was in the girl's own hand—'

'You are a *forensic pathologist*!' Newson almost shouted. 'Haven't you ever heard of duress? Where's the knife?'

'Well, I . . . I—'

'I read in your report that the girl supposedly killed herself with a knife taken from the family kitchen.'

'Yes, that's right. The mother identified it.'

'Where is it?'

'She asked me to take it away. I did so. I bagged it up and took it back to my office, and . . . I . . . I disposed of it in my sharps bucket . . . Inspector, the girl was alone in her bedroom. There was no struggle, there was a note . . . I just presumed—'

'Jesus!' Newson exclaimed. 'I'd have thought that the first, *the very first* principle of forensic medicine, even before disturbing nothing, is that you don't "just presume" anything.'

There was silence for a moment. Dr Forrest's head was bowed in embarrassment. The coroner and the local detective clearly did not know what to say. Newson looked at the body of the girl. It seemed strange to be having this discussion in her presence. He pulled the sheet back to cover her nakedness.

'What was the girl wearing when you found her?'

'Her school uniform, except she'd taken off her tie and blouse. She was in her bra and skirt, socks and shoes.'

'Where are these clothes?'

'We have them,' the morgue assistant replied.

Newson turned to the detective constable. 'I want the socks taken to the lab. My guess is that you'll find residual evidence of adhesive tape. If you study the vanity chair on which Tiffany was sitting when she died, you'll see that on both legs tiny bits of paint have been pulled off, as if a strip of tape had been wrapped around them and removed. The chair is in the boot of my car along with a cup, which I believe once contained coffee which Tiffany made for her killer, though sadly I doubt he'll have left us any prints or DNA. I also want Tiffany's upper arms examined, because I think amongst the scarring we'll find some evidence that she was restrained. Whoever did it didn't use tape, because he knew that would show heavily on the skin. I'm presuming some kind of cord was used, so there should be bruising beneath the cuts. Also please inspect her tongue. I'm pretty certain that she would have been gagged, and since there doesn't seem to be any tape marking on her face I presume that the gag was stuffed into her mouth.'

'Detective Inspector.' It was the coroner speaking for the first time. 'What on earth are you saying happened in this girl's bedroom?'

'Tiffany Mellors was subdued, gagged, secured to a chair and murdered.'

'But, Inspector,' the coroner asked, horror and bewilderment on his face. 'Why?'

'Read the note he made her write,' Newson replied. '*The bullying killed me in the end.*'

33

'Ed, *who is this man?*'

Newson and Natasha had left the Ruislip morgue and were heading back into town, battling the afternoon traffic which was clogged up with the three-thirty school run.

'I don't know, Natasha. I just don't know.'

'How does he get in? He always gets in, doesn't he? Every single victim just opens the door for him. I mean, this girl would be pretty streetwise, wouldn't she? Young women know not to open the door to just anybody. Yet he knocks, she lets him in, *makes him a coffee*, for Christ's sake, and half an hour later she's dead. How does he do it?'

Newson did not reply.

'Do you know what I've been wondering?' Natasha continued. 'I've been thinking that maybe it's got nothing to do with their knowing him at all. I was thinking that perhaps he holds a position of authority . . . Perhaps he's . . .'

'A copper?'

'Well, if he is it would certainly open doors and lull people into a false sense of security. You don't expect to be killed by a policeman, do you? And don't forget, Ed, *you know him*. Christine Copperfield said as much when she left her last message. You know a lot of coppers.'

'And let's be honest, a lot of coppers are bullies.'

'Well, a few, certainly.'

'Don't forget, Natasha, I know how many bullies there are at Scotland Yard.'

Their route back to town took them past the school they had visited a few hours earlier. The school was disgorging its pupils into the street. A great scruffy green-and-yellow mass of youthful humanity walking past the flowers and the two or three reporters who were still hanging about hoping for more stories. Suddenly Newson's attention was caught. He had seen someone he knew. A tall athletic figure in classic Ray-Ban sunglasses.

Roger Jameson.

'Speaking of coppers,' Newson said, 'there's one, an American one. I know him. We were at school together.'

Newson parked the car and approached his old classmate. 'What are you doing here, Roger?'

'Same thing as you, I imagine. The death of the girl who studied here has been all over the news. Everybody put it down to bullying and it was. But not the way they saw it, right?'

'I asked what you were doing here.'

'Oh, come on, Ed! You know damn well why I'm here. I'm trying to find out who it was that the girl Tiffany Mellors was cutting up. You've been in the school so I guess you know already. The moment I started reading about the lovely Miss Mellors I knew that she was no victim, leastways not until this serial psycho of ours whacked her, she wasn't. It's clear that whoever has been killing bullies has started to attack them at source. Now I don't know what it is, but somehow there's a connection between the kid that Tiffany was victimizing and the killer. Find that connection and we find him. So that's why I'm hanging round school gates, Ed, looking for the connection. Don't worry, I ain't added paedophilia to my various crimes against society.'

'You seem to have an uncanny nose for this investigation, Roger. It's almost as if you have inside information.'

'But you see I do, Ed. I told you. I *know* this killer. He's just like me. That's why I'm going to catch him.'

At this point Natasha joined them.

'Good evening, miss,' Jameson said, removing his glasses and fixing Natasha with a cool, easy smile.

'Hello,' Natasha replied. 'You were at school with Ed, right?'

'That's right. We're old friends.'

'But you're an American.'

'I am now. I wasn't then. Officer Roger Jameson, NYPD, at your service, ma'am.' Jameson held out his big strong hand. He was almost a foot taller than both Newson and Natasha, slim and powerful.

Natasha gave him a dazzling smile. 'Detective Sergeant Natasha Wilkie,' she said prettily. 'Her Majesty's Metropolitan Police.'

Natasha and Jameson laughed together.

Newson fumed. He could see that Jameson was just Natasha's type, big, handsome, sexy and a bullying bastard. 'Roger's gay,' he said.

'Oh,' Natasha replied, clearly nonplussed at such an un-expected and unsought piece of information.

Jameson was surprised too. His eyes narrowed angrily as he turned his attention back to Newson. He clearly did not like having his private life thrown open in such a confrontational manner. 'Yes, I guess that's right,' he said. 'Since you bring it up, Ed. Took me a long time to work it out too, but I got there in the end.'

'Yes, well . . .' Newson was embarrassed now, realizing how stupid and rude he'd been. 'Anyway.'

'So tell me, Ed,' Jameson continued, his smile still easy but his eyes cold. 'How long did it take before you worked out that you wanted to sleep with your sergeant here?'

Now Newson was taken aback. 'I don't know what—'

'Can't see any other reason for you looking at her the way you do—'

'I have no idea what—'

Natasha had turned bright red, but she made a good effort at nonchalance. 'This is a peculiar conversation, isn't it? I think I'll leave you boys to it. But we do need to be getting back to the office, Ed. Goodbye, Officer Jameson. It was nice meeting you.'

'My pleasure, ma'am.'

Natasha headed back towards the car.

'Cute,' said Jameson. 'Who whacked the face? The boyfriend? You said she was attached. I presume you went straight round and punched the bastard out. Except that ain't exactly your style, is it? You should try it. It'd probably get you laid.'

Newson was angry, with himself more than with Jameson. 'I must remember not to share confidences with you in the future,' he said.

Jameson sneered. 'Yeah, I could say the same thing.'

'I suppose that's a fair point.'

'Besides, Eddie, I don't need your confidences to know you. I know you anyway. It's a talent I have.'

'You may remember that I asked you to supply me with a list of your visits to Britain over the last two and a half years.'

'And I did. It's on your email. I hope you'll tell me if the dates check out.'

'What dates do you think those would be, Roger?'

'Ed, please. I told you that I wasn't stupid. I know you must have a number of other cases under review. You have access to the central crime computer and I don't. I'm presuming you've gone in there and reopened all the unsolveds and found some with our killer's hands on them. Now you want to know if I was around when the murders got done, because if I was then maybe I'm the killer.'

'Yes, I think that's a pretty fair summation of what's on my mind.'

'Or maybe I emailed Helen Smart and told it all to her. I can be very persuasive. Stay in touch, Ed.' Jameson turned and went, leaving Newson to join Natasha in the car.

For a moment they sat together in silence.

'Um . . . that remark Jameson made,' Newson said, 'about . . . ahem . . .'

'Wanting to sleep with me?'

'Yes, that one. Amazing thing to say. So silly, *such* a cheap shot. And complete rubbish, of course. You know that.'

'Yes, of course,' Natasha replied.

When Newson got home he found Roger Jameson's email detailing his trips to Britain as requested. Jameson had not been in the country when Adam Bishop had been killed. Nor had he been when Neil Bradshaw had been tortured in the seed shed. He had, however, been around when Denis Spencer had had his brains mashed with a book and also, more significantly, when Angie Tatum had been given her rough equivalent of a harelip. Newson already knew that Jameson had been in Britain when Farrah Porter had had her spine broken before being dumped in her acid bath.

There was also a message from Helen Smart. He opened it with little enthusiasm.

Hello Ed,

Can't get away from me, eh? You'll have to get a new email address. I'm home alone, well not alone of course. Karl's here, but he's six and watching Rugrats. I love him but he isn't the most stimulating conversationalist. Kids may say the darndest things but I'm here to tell you that they also say them about two million times. I'm naked right now. Just had a bath and I'm in the bedroom, my skin's still damp. You probably don't want to know that, or the fact that I thought about you while I touched myself beneath the warm water. So delete me. Delete me right now. Go on, scroll to the menu bar and delete me. Still reading? Thought you were. I'm sitting cross legged, by the way. The laptop's on my lap, that's where it was designed to go, I guess. It's a good position, it means I can type this letter one fingered and keep the other hand between my legs. One fingered, right? Did you look at our Friends site recently? That moronic slapper Sally Warren has created an 'In

333

Memoriam' page on the noticeboard. We're all supposed
to share our thoughts and our sadness about Christine
Copperfield's death. I did, I said that I THINK it's great and
I'm SAD it didn't happen sooner. Yeah, really, I am THAT fucked
up, Ed. But at least I'm honest. Don't tell me Sally Warren is
genuinely upset. 'A beautiful candle has gone out. A candle in
the wind'. Bollocks, she's LOVING it, the drama darling,
Christine murdered, how wonderful! That means Sally Warren
won. She wasn't quite as pretty as Christine and she wasn't
quite as popular but hey, she's not dead, she didn't get
murdered. That's got to put her in front.

   I'm angry tonight, Ed. No, don't get paranoid, it's not you.
I'm not coming after you with my nail scissors. It's a case I'm
working on and I've no one to talk to about it. Not Henry
Chambers, that's for sure. What a prick. It's disgusting.
There we are together in our office, dealing with the most
heartbreaking human tragedies and all he's thinking about is
putting his hands all over me. It's in his eyes every second of
the day. I can see his palms sweating when he comes near.
He'd do anything for me, you know. That man would do
absolutely anything to impress me. And I'd do anything to
avoid being within ten feet of him. Funny, eh?

Newson stopped reading for a moment, thinking about Henry
Chambers, Helen's lovesick colleague. Newson could remember
little about him other than the obvious fact that he was besotted
with Helen. A small, unthreatening, anonymous man. The sort of
person everybody knows but whom nobody notices.
The sort of person everybody knows.
Helen Smart thought that he'd do anything for her. Would he?
Anything? Could love do that to you? Unrequited love? Newson
was in love with Natasha and he certainly felt that he would do
anything for her. But would he really? Anything? Would he murder
for her? If there was someone in Natasha's life whose removal
would make her utterly happy, would he remove that person?

No. He would die for her, he believed that. He would also kill in her defence, he was sure of that too. But he would not murder for her. Of course he wouldn't. That was no kind of love, to nourish another person's madness, to pander to an obviously sick and corrupted agenda simply because you want to sleep with them, to share your life with them. If you love someone you try to make them strong, you don't endorse their weakness.

But then Newson was sane. He was in love with somebody sane. Was Henry Chambers sane? Was Helen Smart? In the latter case, not entirely. He wrote 'Henry Chambers' on his notepad and turned again to Helen's email.

So what am I angry about? Do you care?

Newson did care. Something made him care very much. Somehow Newson did not believe that Helen Smart's connection with his investigation was over yet.

I'm angry that there are so many little bastards in the world, that's what! Bastards like Christine Copperfield used to be before she got what was coming to her. They're all still out there, the bullies, ruining other kids' lives just like the dead bitch ruined mine. Every day I get another batch of misery to sift through, all lost souls reaching out, thinking that I can do something to help them. Thinking that I can do something about it! All these terrible stories of lonely little kids being attacked by other kids day after day. One boy is writing to me at the moment and you wouldn't believe what's happening to him. It's so terrible it makes me want to kill. Some little shit has been burning my client with cigarette ends. 'Client', eh? Huh! That's what I'm supposed to call him. He's not a fucking CLIENT, Ed! He's a young lad living in hell. It's been going on for months now and suddenly it's started getting worse. The boy's having his hand held in the Bunsen burners during science lessons, and it seems that yesterday the bully sat behind him on the bus and was flicking lighted matches into his hair. What kind of sick, fucked-up, low-life shit would want to do that? And how the hell do we stop him? We can't, it seems. It's incredible. If it goes on this kid is going to get seriously hurt, maybe killed. He's insane with worry about it, but no matter how many times I tell him to go to his teachers or the police, he's too scared. He lives in Brixton and there's not a lot of trust in the police down there. Surprise, surprise. After all, you're all shits, aren't you, Ed? Everyone knows that. Where this lad comes from, appealing to you lot would just make matters worse, make him a target of the gangs. That's how far you lot have got with your precious community policing policy. It's fucked. So the kid says nothing, his parents think he's been burning himself and are trying to make him see a psychiatrist, but still he won't tell. I'm the only person who knows the truth, but I'm not supposed to intervene directly, it's policy. Fuck! How's that, eh? I know it's going on, it's probably happening now, as I write this email, and I'm not supposed to do anything about it. I'm supposed to just sit here. And that's what I'm doing, sitting here thinking about how my life was ruined by bullying and that somehow I have to save this boy. Oh, fuck it. What do you care, Ed? Cops, eh? Bullies yourselves. Like our mutual mate Roger Jameson. Mind you, at least he recognizes his problem. At least he knows who he is. Do you, Ed? Do you know who you are? Are you the guy I saw sitting on his kitchen floor with a dick like a truncheon and his fist inside me? Did you recognize that guy when he appeared, Ed? When you met him for the first time? That was you. He's inside you, as much a part of you as your preferred version of yourself. The decent, amiable, steady copper. I preferred the wild guy. You should let him out again some time. I'm cold now, covered in goose pimples. All over. Except in my lap, the computer's warm on my skin. Hot, in fact. But the rest of me's cold. My nipples are fat and hard, Ed, there are rings of goose pimples around them.

They took the stitch out by the way. It's as good as new, thanks for asking. You'd hardly know it had your nail scissors in it. My teeth are starting to chatter. I should have towelled myself properly after my bath, shouldn't I? But I wanted to write to you while I was still warm and wet. I can't afford heating, you see. There's an electric heater in the sitting room where Karl is, but here in my bedroom it's cold. It's very, very cold. My mind's wandering. I keep thinking about that kid. Perhaps he's burning now.

Get Bad Ed to call me some time. Bye bye.

Newson turned off his computer. He couldn't understand how this girl, this person he'd known in happier days, as a complex but lovely person, had travelled so far from her centre. How had she got to be so scary?

Time, of course. That was all it took. Time.

Time had not been kind to Helen Smart. He wondered whether in the long run, in the very long run, time was ever kind to anyone.

That evening Newson sat alone and got quietly drunk, and as consciousness began to slip away he was forced to resist a sudden urge to call Natasha and offer to kill Lance for her.

He fell asleep in front of a late-night movie. When he awoke it was early morning. He'd slept all night on the sofa and felt like shit. The first local news bulletin of the day was on the television, and Tiffany Mellors' funeral, which was to take place that afternoon, was being heavily trailed.

'The family have requested a quiet funeral,' the reporter was saying, 'but police are expecting a large turnout from the local community.'

Well, they would do, Newson reflected, now that the time and location had been broadcast on television news.

'There is a great deal of heartache here, and also anger,' the reporter continued. 'Anger and confusion. How could this happen? People want answers and so far no one is able to supply them. It is expected that trained counsellors will be on hand to help those who find the scale of this tragedy all too much.'

Newson turned off the television. Answers? They didn't even know the questions. They thought that an angel had killed herself. Newson, however, knew that a bully had been murdered. What was more, he knew that unless his luck changed soon, more bullies would die. Bullies like Neil Bradshaw, who had clearly been a bad man, and like Christine Copperfield, who had been merely not entirely good.

But Newson knew that he had to do more than rely on his luck changing. He simply had to. Despite what the psychopath he was chasing might think, none of the victims had deserved to be murdered. *Nobody* deserved to be murdered. Newson was firmly against capital punishment. He'd seen far too many miscarriages of justice to think anything else. Unfortunately, his adversary was not, and his adversary definitely had the upper hand.

Newson drank some coffee and took a shower, during which he resolved to join the insensitive throng who would surely deny the Mellors family's request for privacy and attend Tiffany's funeral that afternoon. Perhaps the killer might turn up? Newson's heart sank to realize that his investigation, which in some ways had begun to progress, was now so deeply mired that he had no better plan for the day than that.

He'd been on to something with Friends Reunited. All of his murders were connected by the site, until Tiffany's. Tiffany's class would not feel the tug of nostalgia for at least a decade. Most of their school memories had not even happened yet and in Tiffany's case never would. This time the killer had decided on his victim by another means.

The answer when it came to him struck Newson as being so obvious that he cursed himself for not having worked it out the moment he had seen the cuts on the arms of Tanya Waddingham, the girl whose life had been immeasurably improved by Tiffany Mellors' death. She was there at the funeral with Tiffany's entire class, red-eyed with the rest of them, and overcome by the solemnity of the occasion. Only Newson knew that Tanya's tears were not what they seemed.

But it was not Tanya at whom Newson found himself staring as he stood in the crowded churchyard, behind the police cordon, scanning the faces in the crowd.

It was Henry Chambers. Helen's unwanted admirer. Her fellow worker at the offices of Kidcall. Kidcall: help online for the victims of bullying.

Online. Just like Friends Reunited.

The crowd stirred. The funeral cortège was arriving at the front of the church. Every gawper gaped as Tiffany's family followed the coffin through the old iron gates. Newson had never seen a pink coffin before.

Once more he scanned the crowd, standing on tiptoe and shuffling about in order to do so.

'Oi,' said a voice behind him. 'We all want to see, mate.'

But Newson ignored the voice. Nobody in the crowd wanted to see as much as he did. Or had better reason. The faces around him were grim. Some were weeping, others were angry. But they were all grim – except one.

Henry Chambers was smiling.

He wasn't grinning. Nor was he gloating. In fact, his smile didn't seem to be a happy one at all. There was no joy in it, but it was a smile nonetheless, a small, determined smile that seemed to contain within it a hint of satisfaction.

'So you came for Tanya?' Newson said, approaching Chambers from behind as the black Daimlers drove away and the crowd began to disperse.

Chambers turned round in alarm.

'I'm Detective Inspector Newson. We met at your office.'

'Yes, I remember.'

'I said that you came here for Tanya Waddingham.'

'Yes, I heard you.'

'Tiffany Mellors was bullying her.'

'Yes, she was.'

The churchyard was almost empty now, and the two men stood facing each other amongst the gravestones.

'And Tanya Waddingham appealed to Kidcall.'

'I'm afraid I'm not at liberty to—'

'Don't be so bloody stupid, Mr Chambers. Of course she did. You're here at Tiffany's funeral, for God's sake. Why did you come?'

'Because Tanya was a client. Her case had moved me . . . And now it's over with.'

'Yes, it's certainly over with.'

There was silence for a moment.

'Why did you come here, Henry?' Newson asked.

'I don't really know. Not to mourn, certainly. I suppose I . . . it just all seems very strange, that's all.'

'Yes, it does, doesn't it?'

'That girl killing herself.'

'You don't believe she did kill herself, do you, Henry?'

'What? Of course she killed herself, there was a note. It's in the papers—'

'Did Helen know about this case, Henry?'

Chambers looked at the ground. There was a long pause before he answered. 'She knows about all the cases. We're a small office.'

'Was she upset about Tanya's distress, like you were?'

'Of course she was. How could she not be? Helen's a very caring soul, she feels the pain of our clients very deeply . . . Too deeply, I think. I try to help her but she doesn't seem to want it.'

'Whose client was Tanya? Yours or Helen's?'

'As I say, we share them, but—'

'Whose client was she?'

'Helen's.'

'You say you try to help Helen with her pain, Henry. But Helen doesn't want your help. Do you find other ways of helping her?'

'I don't know what you're talking about.'

Henry Chambers scurried away through the church gate. Henry Chambers, in love with Helen Smart, whose personal experience of bullying had given her such pain, who felt the pain of the victims she dealt with at Kidcall as keenly as she felt her own.

He'd do anything for me, you know. That man would do absolutely anything to impress me. That was what Helen had written in her last email and now here was the very same man attending the funeral of a girl murdered for being a bully.

Newson called Natasha and instructed her to get a warrant to impound Henry Chambers' computer. 'You're looking for any mention of Friends Reunited. Also check him out for the date Tiffany Mellors was murdered. See if he has an alibi.'

'You think it's the bloke from Kidcall?'

'I don't know. Maybe.'

As Newson made his way back to his car he wondered. Henry Chambers was unprepossessing. His face could pass unnoticed and be instantly forgotten. Could that face have got him close to Bishop? To Porter? Was it possible that so unthreatening a demeanour could effectively mask the most terrifying of threats? With each step he took, Newson felt that he was getting closer and yet equally it seemed to him as if his quarry was moving away.

He feared that the killing was not over yet.

When Newson arrived home there were two messages on his answerphone. One was from Helen Smart.

'What the fuck's going on, Ed? Some coppers just turned up and took away Henry Chambers' computer. Call me.'

The other was from Roger Jameson.

'Did you check out the news yet, Ed? Things moving a little fast for you, huh?'

Newson turned on the television to Sky News and had only moments to wait before the quarter-hourly headlines revealed what Jameson was referring to.

The news led with yet another adolescent tragedy. A boy had been deliberately burnt to death.

A big boy. A tough boy. On this occasion there was no suggestion that an angel had been returned to heaven. Trevor Wilmot was a known local thug, a major player in the inter-school gang wars that were a feature of the south London comprehensive which he sporadically attended. A known bully, it seemed that he had fallen victim to others of his kind, and in the most brutal manner possible.

Some time that afternoon a person or persons unknown had spirited Wilmot from the streets of Brixton as he made his way home from school. They had taken him to a lock-up garage and then set him on fire.

Newson sat watching the television, trying to make sense of the suspicions spinning around in his head. What had Helen written to him only twenty-four hours before?

> Some little shit has been burning my client with cigarette ends
> . . . It's been going on for months now and suddenly it's started
> getting worse. The boy's having his hand held in the Bunsen
> burners during science lessons . . . flicking lighted matches into
> his hair . . .

Newson turned on his computer and scanned the email that Helen had sent.

> I'm the only person who knows the truth . . . Somehow I have
> to save this boy.

The telephone rang. It was Roger Jameson.

'So you're back, then,' Jameson said in his lazy drawl. 'Did you see the news? Your guy is picking up the pace, huh? Better get him quick, my friend, before he knocks off half the kids in London.'

'If you're talking about the boy burnt in Brixton, Roger, why would you think that his death is connected with my investigation?'

'Ed, come on! You gotta be thinking what I'm thinking here. It's just too big a coincidence. You ain't going to tell me that you're not asking yourself if the kid that our old pal Helen's so upset about ain't connected with the bully that just got burnt and is all over the news.'

'Helen wrote to you about that?'

'Nah, not this time. Hey, I should be so lucky to get e's like she sends. *Hot babe*, Ed! Damp skin, one finger on the keys, one in the bush, goose pimples round her fat, hard, cold nipples. *Nice prose*. Did you whack yourself off, Ed? Course you did. Man, I thought about it and I'm gay.'

Suddenly the scales fell from Newson's eyes. How could he have been so stupid? 'Have you been reading my emails?'

'Da-da! He twigs! Of *course* I've been reading your emails, Ed. Jesus. What, did you think I really *was* fucking clairvoyant? Did you think I had a *crystal fucking ball*? I ain't half the detective that you've been giving me credit for, but I gotta tell you that compared to what we have in the States, your computer security is pitiful.'

Newson's emails were routed through the Scotland Yard machine. His and those of thousands of other policemen like him. Relatively secure from the outside but not from within, not if you had friends who used the same computer. Friends who shared the same basic address.

'Did your old pals in CID set you up an address on the Scotland Yard mainframe?'

'Hey, it's no big deal. Like I say, in America everybody gets to look at everything everybody else does by law.'

'You realize that I'm going to arrest you for this.'

'You won't find any proof, Ed.'

'I'll impound your laptop.'

'Don't have one, Ed. I work out of internet cafés. It's more sociable. I just sit there with all the other lonely geeks. I get my cup of coffee, I type in my false name and your access code and I check out what my old pal, the best detective in London, is up to.'

'What do you want, Roger?'

'The killing is speeding up, Ed. He's leaving less gaps. He needs it more and more. I'm fascinated. I'm a part of this. I want to be in at the kill.'

'Are you sure that you haven't been in at the kill already?'

'Ah, still hanging on to that old theory of yours, huh, Ed? Did the Yank do it? I can see some merit in the idea. I was a bully at school, that's for sure.'

'You're a bully now.'

'Yeah. Like I told you, Ed. Nature and nurture. People don't change. That was a cute little picture Helen Smart sent you of herself, wasn't it, Ed? Weird tits, though, huh? You like those? Looking at your little sergeant yesterday I had you picked for a boob man. And of course Christine had those nice big new ones, didn't she? Shame for her. If she'd known she was going to get killed she could a saved the money. Were they good, Ed? Nice to hold? You know those implants will still be lying in the ground long after the rest of her's rotted away. Crazy thought, huh?'

'I'm going to make you pay for this, Roger.'

'I doubt it, Ed. You don't have it in you. After all, you ain't a bully like me, are you? Although who knows? Perhaps you'll surprise me. After all, I gotta tell ya, if anybody would a told me that *Ed Newson* of all people, the ginger minge, would end up a big detective and get to fuck not one but *two* of our old chicks, straight off the internet inside a fortnight, *and* have one of them sending him porno shots of herself! Wow. I gotta tell ya, Ed, I'd have said they were crazy. I mean, according to her email you *fisted* that little girl! Sat right down on your kitchen floor with a dick like a truncheon and gave her the long arm of the law. Classy! Yeah, you sure are a surprise to me, Ed. So who knows, you may get me yet. First, though, you have to find out who killed the kid in the Brixton garage.'

'I intend to do just that.'

'What was it little Helen wrote to you . . .? I'm looking at it right now on my little McDonald's screen here. *It's so terrible it makes me want to kill . . . I'm the only person who knows the truth . . . I have to save this boy . . .* Maybe she did just that, eh, Ed? You wondered about her before, after Christine got killed. I bet you've been wondering since. Now here she is again, right at the centre of it all. Don't tell me it hasn't crossed your mind. Ha. That'd be a laugh, wouldn't it? Top tec screwing serial-killer bitch. That'd be a nice little addition to your currently spotless police record.'

'I have to go now, Roger.'

'Don't you want to know why I'm in your face like this, Ed?'

'I know why, Roger.'

'You do?'

'Because you're jealous of me.'

Jameson did not reply. For the first since the conversation began Newson felt the balance of power shift slightly. 'Who knows, maybe you're a serial killer too but you're jealous of me. I was the class nerd and you were the biggest, toughest kid in the year. Now you're a failed cop trying to dodge a murder rap and I'm the youngest inspector on the Met. Why wouldn't you be jealous?'

Jameson chuckled quietly. 'Oh, so you don't get it all, then. I was *always* jealous of you, Ed. That's the one thing you never understood. You weren't the class nerd. Sure, you were a little weird and small and you had that red hair and all. But you were actually cool, oh yeah, you'd better believe it. Everybody knew that you respected yourself and in the long run that's all it takes, right?'

Newson remembered the note he'd left for the boy in Scotland, making exactly the same point.

'That's why you got to get a piece of Christine Copperfield when you were fourteen years old and it's why you got to fuck her after the reunion, when all the guys had been hoping to, 'cept me and Gary Whitfield, of course. I look good on the outside, but inside I'm fucked and I always have been. You, on the other hand, ain't no Brad Pitt but inside you're cool. You're focused. You got

345

a *centre*. That's why I hate you, Ed. That's why I'm on your tail.'

'You can't bully me, Roger.'

'Oh yeah? Try this. That sergeant of yours. Sweet little Natasha Wilkie with the sharp tongue and the big tits. I've been reading her emails too.'

Newson made no sound and yet he knew that Jameson was aware that his shot had struck home as surely as if Newson had gasped and swore.

'See, Ed? Us bullies know the weak points. It's an instinct for us.'

'Goodbye, Roger—'

'No, no, don't hang up for a minute. You're dying to know, so let me tell you. You make her skin crawl, Ed. She thinks you're a sick, irritating little dog on heat and if you ain't careful she's going to report you for harassment, you horny little fuck. But, hey, you can't be sitting around yakking to old friends like me, Ed. You need to be getting down to Brixton.' Jameson hung up.

Newson swallowed hard. The pain of the blow that had just been dealt him was excruciating, but for the moment, at least, he must endure it, ignore it. He had to concentrate on the case. He dialled Helen Smart's number. He heard her outgoing answerphone message. The moment the beep sounded he cut in.

'Helen? It's me, Ed. If you're there, pick up the—'

'Ed! What the fuck's going on with Henry? Why have they taken his computer?'

'Listen, Helen, I don't have a lot of time. You sent me an email at about five thirty yesterday evening.'

'Was that the time? God, that means I must have started drinking at five. Oops. Naughty me. That's right, I had wine in the bath. My little treat. Then I wrote to you. Sorry about the rude bits.'

'Your email, the story of the boy getting burned. Do you know the name of the persecutor? The boy who's been flicking the matches?'

'I can't tell you that. It's all confidential.'

'This is a police matter.'

'Well, I'll need to see a warrant.'

'Just tell me his fucking name! Was it Trevor?'

There was a pause. 'My client calls his tormentor Trev.'

'Thank you, Helen. I can assure you this is very important. What were you doing this afternoon?'

'What?'

'Look, Helen, if I have to send a squad car round I will. What were you doing this afternoon?'

'I've been at home. Karl's sick.'

'Can anyone confirm that?'

'Only Karl.'

'Right. Thank you. We'll be in touch.'

Newson could hear Helen's voice protesting as he put down the phone. Feeling worse than he could ever remember feeling in his life, Newson left his house and headed for Brixton. On his way he left a message for Natasha to meet him there if she was available. Whatever she might feel about him, she was still the second most senior officer on the investigation. He would have to come to terms with what he now knew about her feelings towards him later.

34

Tensions were running high outside the lock-up garage in which Trevor Wilmot had died. The murder had been gruesome even by the tough standards of the streets from which Wilmot came. The various factions and drug dealerships in the neighbourhood were already lining up for a showdown. Everybody, including the police, presumed that the killing had been a deliberately provocative attack designed specifically to spark trouble within the community.

Newson had travelled to the scene by tube, it being an easy trip from West Hampstead and a lot quicker than driving. A group of youths had called him a ginger cunt as he rode the escalator at Brixton High Street, but Newson was so cut up inside about Natasha he scarcely noticed.

The stench of petrol and burned flesh in the lock-up was over-powering. The supervising officer filled Newson in on what scant details had so far been established.

'The killers played music while the boy died. That's why no screams were heard. Loud drum and bass is not an unusual sound around here, so nobody took any notice.'

'No, I suppose not.'

'They must have tethered him to that block of concrete. Most of him is burned now, but you can still see where the manacles were attached.'

'Yes, that's pretty clear,' Newson agreed, 'and the boy was conscious while he burned.'

'How can you say that?'

'Look at the scraping marks on the concrete. He was struggling to free himself in his agony and managed to drag that huge anchor a good few inches across the floor in the process. He was a strong lad.'

'Jesus. The bastards.'

'I don't think that you'll find that this was the work of a gang, Sergeant. One person did this.'

'With respect, I don't think so, Inspector. Trevor Wilmot may have been only fifteen, but like you say he was an enormous lad. He got picked up on his way home from school. Just lifted off the street. No one could have done that to him on their own, not without a huge fight.'

'Unless he knew his killer. Or trusted him for some other reason.'

'I suppose that's true, sir, although I don't know what other reason he could possibly have.'

At that point Newson noticed that Natasha had arrived at the crime scene and was hovering on the edge of the forensic group. In the drama of the moment Newson had briefly not thought about the terrible truth he'd learned from Jameson, the devastating revelation that Natasha despised him and was thinking of making a complaint against him. He had long since resigned himself to the idea that he would never be the object of Natasha's affection, but it was almost unbearable to know that he was in fact the object of her contempt. He felt doubly wounded, because he felt that he did not entirely deserve her derision. After all, he had only recently asked her if he needed to moderate his behaviour, and she had assured him that he didn't. On the other hand, Newson knew that he was her boss and that she would always feel constrained in what she was able to say to him. It was his job to censor his manner, not hers, and now he had ruined everything.

For the time being, however, that would have to wait. All that mattered now was to catch the killer, and for the first time Newson believed that he was truly on the trail.

'Thank you for coming down so promptly, Sergeant Wilkie,' he said.

'That's OK,' Natasha replied, but it didn't look as if it was OK. She looked tired and not at all well. Newson wanted to ask what was wrong, but he no longer could. His relationship with Natasha was over in all but the most strictly professional sense, and with heavy heart he knew that even that must end soon.

'Sergeant,' he said. 'I want you to arrange for Helen Smart and Henry Chambers from Kidcall to be interviewed. We need to find out their whereabouts at the time of all the murders under review.'

'Shit, Ed,' she said and Newson wondered why she called him that when she disliked him so much. 'You think the Kidcall workers are killing bullies?'

'No . . . well, maybe . . . It's possible. We certainly need to rule them either in or out. All I do know is that our killer has taken to sourcing his victims via the Kidcall computer. And Henry Chambers attended Tiffany Mellors' funeral.'

'Wow. Really?'

'And Helen Smart wrote to me only yesterday about the . . . Well, I'm pretty certain that the boy who was burned here was in the habit of burning another boy at his school – someone who'd appealed to Kidcall for comfort.'

'Your girlfriends just won't keep out of this case, will they?' Natasha said. Newson did not reply.

They left the crime scene together, and Newson accompanied Natasha to her car. As she stooped to get in he saw her face contort with pain.

'Natasha, you're hurt. What's wrong?'

'Nothing. Nothing at all,' she said and closed the door.

Perhaps before, Newson would have pressed the point and insisted that she explain. But not now. Not ever again.

Newson asked the local police to take him back into town. He felt an enormous sense of urgency now.

Your guy is picking up the pace, huh? Better get him quick before he knocks off half the kids in London.

That was what Jameson had said. He seemed so sure about it, too. How much did Jameson know? What was he up to? Newson felt strongly that he needed to speak to him, once more to confront the ex-New York detective face to face.

'Rossiter Hotel, Marble Arch,' he told the driver.

During the drive Newson tried to concentrate on the murders, attempting to give form to the suspicions swirling around his brain. Thoughts of Natasha haunted him, though, and the private loathing that she had been keeping as her secret while he had been falling deeper and deeper in love.

She thinks you're a sick, irritating little dog on heat and if you ain't careful she's going to report you for harassment, you horny little fuck.

How could he have got it so wrong? He racked his brains to think of clues that Natasha might have given him and which would have helped him to modify his behaviour, but he could think of none.

Once at the Rossiter, Newson let his squad car go and asked at reception if Jameson was in. It seemed that he was in luck. The night porter, who had just come on duty, reported that Jameson's key was not in its box and that he must be in his room. However, when the porter phoned up he received no reply.

'Perhaps he's asleep,' the porter suggested.

'Then wake him up.'

'Oh, I couldn't do that.'

'This is a police investigation. Let me into his room.' Newson produced his credentials and soon they were on their way up to Jameson's room.

'Just give me the master key and return to your desk,' Newson said. 'I'll bring it down when I've finished.'

Reluctantly the porter did as he was told and Newson let himself into Jameson's room, which was in fact a small suite consisting of sitting room, bathroom and bedroom.

'Roger,' Newson called out into the darkness of the heavily shaded room. 'Roger, are you there?'

There was no reply. Newson turned on the lights and stepped further into the room. He checked through the suite. Jameson was not at home.

Returning to the sitting room, Newson approached the desk, which was covered in numerous handwritten notes and annotated photographs. More were stuck to the walls and mirror with Blu-tack and Post-It strips. Newson knew an amateur surveillance exercise when he saw one and his blood ran a little colder as he recognized in Jameson's research material various elements of his entire investigation.

There were photographs of groups of girls from Tiffany Mellors' school; a number of faces had been circled, including that of Tanya Waddingham. There were newspaper clippings and computer printouts detailing the Farrah Porter case. Attached to one of these was a telephoto shot of her neighbours Mr and Mrs Lloyd, and their Australian nanny. Photographs of her other neighbours, the Geldsteins, were scattered alongside images of the seed shed at the Goddard farm and the barracks at which Warrant Officer Spencer had served. Files and boxes lay on the floor and underneath the desk. Newson pulled out the first of these, marked 'Bishop'. Inside he found a comprehensive dossier on the Willesden murder, together with copies of his own emails on the subject. At the bottom of the box he discovered an old-fashioned school compass.

Newson sat down at the desk. The question was, had Jameson assembled this material after the murders as a part of his jealous interest in Newson's affairs, or *before* the murders as a research and background brief in order to commit them? Then he realized that he was staring at what was probably the most important clue of all.

Sitting on Jameson's desk, lid closed, half concealed amongst the clutter of photographs and notes, was an Apple Macintosh PowerBook.

Jameson had lied. He did not need to visit internet cafés to go online; he owned his own computer after all.

Newson opened the lid on the machine. The screen came instantly to life, displaying a fishtank screen-saver. He noted that the remote access icon was flashing. Jameson had broadband in his hotel room. Newson scrolled down the menu bar, chose the search programme and typed in his own name. Numerous hits appeared, the first of which was a folder marked 'Ed'.

In the folder was a search icon and further files marked 'Downloads'. He pressed the search icon and immediately arrived at his own email access page. Newson pressed 'get mail', and sure enough his most recent messages appeared immediately before him. There was one from Dr Clarke, another from the office of the chief superintendent and a third from the builder with whom Newson had been discussing a new patio. Jameson had a window on his life. Newson did not read the emails, instead opening the file marked 'Downloads', and there he found every message that he had sent and received in the previous two months: messages, documents and jpeg reproductions of forensic research. One of the jpegs was titled 'This is me'. Newson double-clicked it and sure enough once more Helen Smart stood naked before him.

He closed the file and swallowed hard to contain his anger. Time for that later. There was something else he needed to do.

He pressed the search icon again and typed in the word 'Wilkie'. At the top of the hits that appeared was a file with contents laid out in a similar fashion to his own, including an internet icon that would no doubt lead him to Natasha's email folder and a file marked 'Downloads'.

Newson moved his finger on the track pad, and placed the little arrow over the file icon. For a moment he hesitated. Just because Jameson had been illegally snooping on Natasha's private correspondence did not give him that right too.

But he did not hesitate for long. He had to see for himself the terrible truth. He needed to discover from the tips of Natasha's own fingers how little she cared for him. Besides, he still loved her. He'd spent so many months hoarding the tiniest fragments of knowledge about her, and now the whole story was only a click away.

Jameson was an efficient voyeur and his Natasha file differed from his Newson file in as much as he had decided to divide her correspondence into two groups: 'police' and 'Ed'. Newson opened the second file with a shaking hand. It contained one document, again titled 'Ed'. He clicked on the icon and focused on the page of cut and pasted quotes from different emails that appeared before him. Jameson had clearly been hoarding any information he could find about Newson.

Screwing up his courage, he read the first.

What can I tell you, Pru?

Newson recognized the name. Pru was Natasha's younger sister.

Ed's the same as ever. He's so funny, it's obvious he fancies me. The other girls laugh about it all the time, and I honestly believe he thinks we don't know . . .

Newson's eye flicked down the page.

Ed and I have this weird relationship where we talk about all sorts of private stuff but never the one thing I know he's really thinking. I ought to be annoyed, but actually I think it's sweet.

Hope began to surge through Newson's body.

It certainly makes a change from Lance. At least Ed seems to give a shit how I feel . . .

Jameson had lied! The bastard had lied and if Newson had not discovered Jameson's computer he would never have known the truth. He would have moved Natasha on from his team as quickly as possible and believed for the rest of his life that she despised him. Relief flooded over him like a warm bath, combined with rage that Jameson's intentions could have been so cruel.

He heard a sound behind him. He spun round, trying to remember the attack and defence stances from his brief and unimpressive efforts at aikido training while fumbling in his pocket for his personal alarm. There was no way on earth he could fight Jameson, he knew that.

It was the hotel manager. 'Inspector,' he said. 'The night porter told me that you were looking for Mr Jameson. I wonder if I might trouble you again for your ID.'

Newson offered his credentials, which the manager studied with great care before saying, 'Mr Jameson was on the squash court. He asked for it to be opened late. I suppose it's possible he may still be there; we have a steam room and there are refreshments. Would you like me to take you there?'

Together they descended into the hotel basement.

'Who was he playing?' Newson enquired. 'Did you see him?'

'No, the gym and court are open to non-residents if they join our health club, and there is an entrance directly from the street.'

'The door can be opened from the street?'

'Not in the evening. Mr Jameson would have had to let his guest in.'

Newson knew that he should call for back-up. If Jameson was still there he intended to arrest him immediately for IT crime and information theft, but Jameson was aware that he was under suspicion of murder. If he was guilty he might fight. He would certainly run. Either way Newson knew that he should wait.

But he couldn't. He had to confront the bastard. Newson and the hotel manager walked along the basement corridor and approached the door marked 'Health Club'. It was only then that he heard it.

There could be no mistake.

Everybody wants to rule the world.

Tears for Fears, *Songs from the Big Chair*, 1984.

Newson sprang forward, grabbed the handle of the door and pushed. It was locked. Inside, the song was ending. He commanded the manager to produce his master key as another song began.

'The Power Of Love'. Frankie Goes to Hollywood, *Welcome to the Pleasure Dome*, 1984.

Someone was playing an early-eighties compilation album.

'Open it,' Newson instructed, 'and wait here.'

The manager unlocked the door and Newson entered the club. The squash court was to his right, behind a perspex wall. It was empty. To Newson's left was a gym with weight-training equipment and treadmills. It was also empty. At the end of the corridor a T-junction pointed to the pool and spa, and the changing rooms, male and female.

The boys' changing rooms. An alarm bell rang in Newson's head, competing for his attention with the sound of pop music from two decades before. The pop music of his schooldays. And of Jameson's.

He rushed past the gym and down the corridor, turned the corner at the end and pushed open the door of the male changing room.

Jameson was dead.

His hands and feet were tied and his entire body, from neck to toes, was a bloodied pulp. He lay on his side on the floor, his face turned upwards. Somebody had written on his forehead 'I am queer', just as Jameson had once done to Gary Whitfield.

Newson's phone rang. It was Natasha. 'Ed, I've spoken to Helen Smart and Henry Chambers and asked them to check back over the dates I've given them . . .'

'Call them back and tell them not to bother,' Newson replied.

'The ground has shifted again, but this time, thank God, it feels a little firmer beneath my feet.'

'What?'

'I finally have a theory.'

'Oh, good.'

Newson asked Natasha to join him at the Rossiter Hotel, and then alerted the murder team to Jameson's killing. He secured the scene, and returned to Jameson's room and his computer. He typed the name 'Helen Smart' into the search engine but found no connecting icon to show that Jameson had been accessing her communications. There was one small folder but it contained only a copy of the same jpeg of Helen naked and one email, the message that Jameson had himself admitted to sending, in which he had advised her to find closure. Jameson and Helen were not connected. What was more, since Natasha had spoken to both Helen and Henry Chambers that evening, it was clear that neither of them could have had anything to do with the murder of Roger Jameson.

Helen Smart was not the killer. Newson was glad, for her sake and her son's. He had never really believed that she could have been. Jameson had seemed a much more likely contender. Newson had genuinely suspected him, but now Jameson was dead. It would probably be little consolation to Jameson's immortal soul, but he was off the hook.

'First on the scene again,' Dr Clarke said across the bloodied corpse of Roger Jameson, which lay on a cold slab in the West London Police Mortuary. 'You seem to be making a habit of this, Inspector.'

'I intend to ensure that Jameson's is the last murder in this particular series,' Newson replied.

'Let's hope so. Anyway, it's the usual story. This man was chemically overpowered by means of a spiked drink.'

'Yes, we found the glass, beer and a small dose of Rohypnol.'

'Small is right. There's very little in the stomach. He probably wasn't even rendered unconscious.'

'Just woozy enough to be unable to prevent himself being bound.'

'Yes, he wouldn't have been able to defend himself.'

'So the killer gave him a light dose because he was in a hurry and didn't want to risk Jameson's being unconscious and missing the fun.'

'Hypothesis is your department, Inspector,' Clarke said. 'As I have told you many times, I prefer not to speculate.'

Dr Clarke seemed much more her old self. Newson preferred her like this, brisk and bossy. Glancing at her hands, he noticed a wedding ring through one of the bloodied translucent gloves. On their previous meeting she had not been wearing it.

'All right, Doctor. Speculation aside, how did he die?'

'His neck was broken.'

'With what?'

'Some kind of heavy whip. You can see that there are two or three massive weals on his upper shoulders and the back of his head. I'd say the killer delivered five or six blows and one of them broke his neck, finishing him off.'

'And the other blows?' Newson was referring to the fact that Jameson's entire body had been whipped raw.

'Incredibly painful, but not life-threatening. Basically, Jameson was given a savage whipping, which resulted in the massive skin trauma that you can see all over him. Then the killer switched weapons and broke his neck.'

'And the whip – the first weapon?'

'Ah, now that's interesting. There's a huge number of fibres left in the wounds, so we can be quite certain what the killer used for a whip. Take a look at this—'

'I don't need to look,' Newson said. 'I know what he whipped Jameson with. Wet towels.'

'Goodness gracious. How could you have guessed that?'

'Because it's all described on the Friends Reunited site. Twenty years ago Roger Jameson tormented a boy by whipping him with wet towels. Then he wrote "I am queer" on the boy's forehead. The mills of God, eh?'

It was after one o'clock in the morning when Newson and Natasha left the mortuary.

'He killed twice in twenty-four hours. He thinks he's invincible,' said Newson.

'Isn't he?' Natasha replied.

'No. Not any more.'

'He doesn't have a lot of respect for you, though, does he?'

'Ah yes, you've spotted that, then.'

'He's killed two of your classmates now.'

'Yes, I think we can put the first down to coincidence, but the second was definitely personal. This man has supreme self-confidence, we've known that from the start. Look at the little details he puts into his murders. He wants to show that he can do whatever he likes whenever he likes.'

'And of course he can.'

'Yes, that's true. So far he's pissed all over us from a very great height. His vigilante campaign has been a stunning success and he's moved on to sourcing his victims via Kidcall instead of Friends Reunited. However, when he found out that I was leading the hunt my guess is that he remembered my name from the Christine Copperfield internet exchange. Having made that connection he would have recalled that there was a second bully in my class, and he couldn't resist dealing with him too. Just to make it absolutely clear who's boss and that in our shared lives I might be the policeman but he holds the moral high ground.'

'Wow. One mad fuck.'

'Exactly. The fact that we've started to investigate people at Kidcall must also have rattled his cage. I think he wanted to hit back.'

'So you think the killer has only recently become aware of you?'

'Yes. Just as I've become aware of him. Can we get a coffee somewhere? Perhaps a sandwich?'

They got into Natasha's car, Newson noting once again how

she winced as she stooped to get in. She drove them to a twenty-four-hour service station and parked in the air and gas bay. Newson picked up a microwave coffee and two chocolate chip cookies.

'So,' he said when he was once again sitting beside her in the car. 'I think I know who the killer is.'

'Good work, fellah!'

'Unfortunately I don't have a shred of proof.'

'Ah.'

'So I'm afraid that we're going to have to entrap him. The problem is, he knows me.'

'I see. So what you're saying is that *I'm* going to have to entrap him.'

'You don't have to do it. In fact, I can't believe I'm asking you. After all, this bloke is certainly the most efficient killer you or I have ever encountered.'

'That's all right. I'm used to dealing with bullies.' Natasha shifted in her seat.

'Natasha, did Lance hit you again?'

Suddenly her face was furious. 'Yes, he did! All right? You said he would and he did! And I'm the fucking moron who took him back and let him do it. The bastard fractured two ribs. You were right. I was wrong. Hooray. I've let down the whole of womankind. Whoopy ding-dong.'

Newson did not reply and they sat in silence for a while.

'Sorry,' said Natasha at last.

'That's all right. No problem.'

There was another brief silence. This time it was Newson who broke it. 'So what did you do? You know, after he hit you—'

'After he *kicked* me.'

'After he kicked you?'

'What do you think I did? I arrested the little prick.'

'You didn't!'

'I fucking did. I nicked him for assault.'

'But that's fantastic! Did he come quietly?'

360

'He was furious. Couldn't believe it. I mean, he was white with rage and I could see his fists clenching, so I reminded him that he was under arrest and that if he hit me again it wouldn't be a domestic any more, it'd be assaulting a police officer, which was just a little bit serious.'

'Fuck.'

'Then I called for back-up and they took him in. End of story. Fuck him.'

'Natasha.'

'Yes.'

'Nothing.'

'What?'

'Nothing.'

'*What?*'

'Will you have dinner with me?'

'I thought we were going to catch a killer.'

'After that.'

'Maybe, I'll think about it. Who's the killer?'

'Well, it's obvious, isn't it?'

'Is it?'

'Yes. The key is that everybody trusts him. Even Roger Jameson let him in. *They always let him in.*'

35

On the evening of the third day after Trevor Wilmot and Roger Jameson died, Natasha sat alone in her little flat.

'Third time lucky, eh?' she said. 'Hope you can hear me.'

Down in the street Newson sat in his car with a small receiver in his ear. 'Yes, I can hear you, Sergeant,' he replied, although he knew that she couldn't hear him.

Somewhere, circulating in the surrounding streets, was an anonymous van in which six more police officers waited for Newson's instructions to move in. They had been there on the previous two evenings, but so far the man Newson suspected of being the serial killer had failed to rise to the bait.

The bait consisted of a series of urgent and desperate appeals to the Kidcall website. A young female police constable was being terrorized by her supervising sergeant, Natasha Wilkie, an evil bully of a woman.

I know that you're really only interested in schoolchildren, but I'm only eighteen and I don't know who else to turn to. I was bullied at school too and I partly joined the police because I wanted to learn to stand up for myself. I never expected it would be worse here, but it is, much worse. I work at New Scotland Yard, seconded to one of the murder squads. I just do filing and stuff, but I thought it would be so exciting. Instead my life has been utterly ruined. The truth is that I'm seriously thinking about killing myself because I just don't want to get picked on any more.

The funny thing is that the team I'm with are working on a bullying case! There he is, high and mighty Detective Inspector Newson, trying to catch some killer who's obsessed with bullies, and he doesn't even bother to stop what's going on in his own team.

Newson had concocted his story carefully, wanting to appeal to the killer's vanity, sense of drama and distorted views on fair play. He felt sure that if the killer believed that he, Inspector Newson, was turning a blind eye to bullying, it would make the bait all the sweeter.

I haven't told the inspector, of course. If I did I think Sergeant Wilkie would kill me, but he must know what she's like. She makes all the girls' lives a misery, but particularly mine because I'm small and new, I suppose. Every single day she gets me in the ladies' and pushes me around, pulling at my clothes, deliberately laddering my tights. I don't know if it's sexual or whatever but her favourite thing is to flush my head in the toilet. I can hardly bear to type the words. I feel so humiliated. I know I should stand up for myself and make a complaint, but I can't. Everybody's scared of her and it would be her word against mine. She's so cruel, it's as if she lives to torment me. She loves Westlife and I tried to make her like me by telling her I was a Westlife fan too, but she just said that they'd never look at a little slut like me and then made me stand in the middle of the office and sing 'Flying Without Wings'. She's always trying to think of stuff to torment me. What can I do? What can I do?

Natasha had objected to the bit about the toilet. 'He'll come round and shit on my head or something.'

'I've got to make it tempting. I think it'll intrigue him. He hasn't drowned anybody yet.'

The fictitious teenage constable had been sending messages all week, sometimes dropping little hints that the evil Sergeant

Wilkie lived alone. Now all Newson and his team could do was wait.

Shortly after eight thirty they were rewarded. An inconspicuously ordinary car pulled up outside the entrance to Natasha's apartment block and a man got out, carrying a case.

Newson watched as the figure pushed one of the bell buttons on Natasha's front door. 'Fuck, I think this is it,' he heard Natasha whisper. There followed the sound of Natasha crossing the room.

'Hello,' she said.

Newson could hear the voice of the visitor coming through Natasha's intercom.

'Natasha Wilkie?'

'Yes. Who is it?'

'This is Dick Crosby.'

'Who?'

'Come on, Natasha, you know me. Dick Crosby. Geeky guy with beard. Billionaire, you know the one. I've got some good news for you.'

'This is a wind-up, right.'

'No, not at all, Natasha. You probably know I own the Telecom network. Well, the last call you made on your phone was kind of a lucky one, because it was the billionth one since I took over, and you may remember that I pledged a million pounds to my billionth caller.'

'I don't believe it!'

'Well, you'd better had, girl. Come down and see. I always promised that I'd do this anonymously. Of course, if you let me use it publicly that would be nice, but it's up to you. I have your cheque right here. I want to be able to give it to you personally.'

'I'm coming down to see if it's really you.' Natasha was playing the part well, trying not to appear too eager. Any girl would clearly need to see the person claiming to be Dick Crosby before letting them in. But the moment anyone actually laid eyes on the great man all their defences would evaporate instantly. He was the ultimate celebrity. *Everybody knew him.* Everybody would be pleased to see him.

The figure at the door waited for Natasha, glancing about, nervous lest he be seen. That, of course, was the downside of his celebrity. He would need to be very careful approaching the houses of his victims. Newson noticed that Crosby had taken the precaution of wearing a hooded top.

The door opened. Natasha stood for a moment in front of her visitor. 'Oh, my *God*!' she said.

'That's right, it's really me,' Newson could hear Crosby reply. 'Are you going to let me in or what?'

'Yes, yes, yes! Can I ring my mum?'

'Let's have a chat first, eh?'

Newson could hear them going up the stairs. In a few seconds he would alert his officer.

'I need to talk to you about this cheque. A million pounds is a lot of money to suddenly be given. You need to think about this carefully,' continued Crosby smoothly.

Newson heard the door of Natasha's flat open.

'You mean it! You really mean it! I've won a million!'

'Yes, you have, Natasha.'

The door closed.

'This is just amazing. I mean, it's like a dream—'

At that point Natasha gave a muffled gasp. There was no mistaking the sound. Something had been pushed against her mouth.

Newson grabbed at his radio and was on the point of triggering his men to move when the door of his car was wrenched open and he was pulled out into the street and thrown to the pavement. The radio clattered to the ground. Newson found himself lying on his back, staring up at Lance.

'You're stalking her, you bastard! I'm gonna call the cops.'

'Lance, I—'

'She always said she thought you fancied her, you little fucking

365

ginger cunt! It's you that put her up to saying she'd nick me, in't it! She listens to you! You're what's fucked us up! You fucked us up so you could try and get her for yourself!'

Newson reached for his radio to alert the back-up team to Natasha's danger, but Lance kicked it from his hand, sending it spinning into the road.

'You ain't radioing no one! This ain't police stuff, this is man to man, it's between you and me, you bastard. Get up, you cunt! Fight me for her!'

Newson staggered to his feet. 'Lance. Listen to me very carefully. I am a police officer—'

'You cunt! You cowardly fucking bastard! Hiding behind your bleeding badge! You think just because you're a cop you can nick a bloke's bird! Well, I don't care what you do to me, you've had this coming for a long time!'

'Lance! Listen!'

'Tell her I love her! Tell her I'll always fucking love her.' And with that Lance nutted Newson. Newson blacked out and his knees buckled under him as he collapsed once more on to the pavement.

When he regained consciousness he was lying in the gutter and Lance was gone. For a moment he could not remember where he was. Then he heard music, very close to him, almost inside his head.

The wire with which Natasha had been communicating with him was still in his ear, the receiver pack in his pocket. The music was Westlife's 'Flying Without Wings'. It was playing softly and as he tried desperately to orientate himself he heard a voice.

'It's a terrible thing to bully someone you know, Natasha. You don't just create pain for the moment, you create pain for life. Nobody forgets when they've been bullied, not ever. All their lives they dream of revenge. It's my job to make their dreams come true. Don't struggle, Natasha. In a moment or two you'll be past struggling for ever, so relax, enjoy your final breaths . . .'

Newson staggered halfway to his feet before collapsing to the pavement, a massive throbbing in his head.

And that voice. Crosby's voice.

'*I was bullied, you know. A little scholarship boy at a posh school, helpless at the hands of the rich kids. I suppose I should be grateful. That which does not kill me makes me stronger, as they say, and it could be that bullying made me what I am. Because that lonely boy, isolated and despised, ridiculed, abused, burnt, beaten and buggered by a shit from hell in a public school dormitory . . . that boy became me. Rich, powerful, all-conquering. Maybe I should thank him.*'

Newson was on his feet, desperately searching for the radio. Now he saw it, in the road where Lance had kicked it, crushed, destroyed beneath the wheels of a passing car. How long did he have? The van with its six police officers was somewhere nearby, but it was on the move to avoid attracting attention. There was not enough time to find it.

'*Perhaps a certain little teenage policewoman will thank you one day. Thank you for making her stronger through your despicable cruelty. But most of all, I think that lonely abused little girl will thank me. Not personally, of course. She'll never know who it was that liberated her from your wicked clutches, you bitch. Only you and I will ever know that . . .*'

Newson grabbed a truncheon from his car and ran towards the apartment-block door. He could hear Natasha's grunts and gasps as she was dragged across the room.

'*But she'll thank the man, whoever it was, that came to your house one night and drowned you in the toilet. I blocked it, by the way, while you were unconscious, and filled it to the brim. Not with water, I'm afraid. Oh no. I brought with me a caseful of slurry from the septic tank of one of the cottages on my estate. I'm going to drown you in the shit of a farm labourer and his family so that you will never, ever hurt anyone again . . .*'

Newson heard in his earpiece a muted gasp of terror and then the sound of what could only be described as a muddy submersion. He smashed desperately with his truncheon at the reinforced-glass window of the front door. When he could finally get an arm through he reached in, flipped the latch and bounded up the stairs. He knew the number of Natasha's flat and having located her door on the third floor he hurled himself against it with all his might.

The door was not as weak as Christine Copperfield's had been, and it took blow after blow before it gave way. Suddenly he could hear the sounds of the struggle for real. Ahead of him was a corridor at the end of which was the open door to Natasha's lavatory. Crosby was leaning over Natasha, whose hands and feet were bound, and he was forcing her head into the toilet bowl. The music was loud inside the flat, and such was Crosby's concentration on subduing the desperate girl that he did not notice Newson's arrival.

As Newson rushed towards them he could see that Natasha's struggling had almost ceased.

Crosby turned to face him and Newson raised the truncheon above his head and brought it down with all his might. There was a crunch of cracking bone and Dick Crosby fell forward. Newson pulled Natasha's head from the toilet and pushed it over the side of the bath, turning on the shower and washing away what mess he could before laying her limp body down on the floor beside Crosby's. Then he turned her face to his and administered the kiss of life.

Even under these circumstances with the profusely bleeding body of a serial killer lying next to them and Natasha coughing septic slurry from her mouth into his, Newson found himself reflecting that his lips had met Natasha's for the very first time.

36

Newson woke up in his hospital bed knowing that the game was not quite over. He and Natasha had been treated for severe stomach disorders caused by ingesting slurry. Natasha now lay in the next room. They had spoken briefly after having their stomachs pumped, and she had almost forgiven him for rescuing her only after she had spent three whole minutes with her head immersed in the contents of one of Dick Crosby's septic tanks.

'I can't believe you were outside fighting Lance while I was being murdered,' she said.

'I wouldn't call it fighting. It was more of a mugging.'

'You'll have to prosecute him.'

'Maybe. I'm not sure. Bit embarrassing, really. I mean, I didn't even land a blow. Besides, I have some sympathy for him.'

'*Sympathy!*'

'Yes, he may be a nasty bully, but he's a sad one. Sad and pathetic. And he's definitely in pain. He loves you, you know, in his own inadequate way.'

'Well, whatever. I still say you should nick him.'

'I'll think about it.'

And now, alone in his room, Newson knew that he hadn't finished. He had most certainly stopped the serial killer. Chief Superintendent Ward had even been moved to send a note of congratulation along with a modest bunch of carnations. Of course there would be an inquiry into Dick Crosby's death, but Dr Clarke, who had been waiting with the emergency response team and attended the scene, testified that Sergeant Wilkie had been very close to the onset of brain damage, and that Newson's prompt actions had saved her life.

But the case wasn't over. Something was missing. Newson sat up in bed, pain gripping his bowel and stomach, and knew what it was.

What had Crosby done about his own bully? The one who'd made that lonely little boy so miserable that he'd turned into an embittered killer?

Newson begged a nurse to bring him in a laptop and a phone line. With trembling fingers he dialled up the online *Who's Who*. There was Crosby. Next, Newson went to Friends Reunited and entered the name of the public school that Crosby had attended as a scholarship boy from the age of thirteen. Crosby was not listed, but Newson hadn't expected him to be. Instead Newson typed in a name that had lived at the back of his mind for two whole years.

Scanlan-McGregor.

He was there! The mysterious peer who had disappeared without trace had attended the same school as Dick Crosby, and at the same time. Newson jumped from his bed and grabbed his trousers. He struggled down the corridor, pulling them over his pyjamas and dialling into his mobile at the same time.

Natasha called after him.

'Where are you going? We're ill!'

But Newson was already speaking to Scotland Yard. He needed sniffer dogs and an emergency search warrant. 'If you can't get a warrant just bring a sledgehammer.'

The team were to meet him at the London residence of the deceased billionaire Dick Crosby.

As he drove in a squad car to Crosby's Belgravia house, Newson despatched teams to investigate Crosby's country mansion and shooting lodge in Scotland. But something told him that if his hunch was correct the answer lay in London. Scanlan-

McGregor's body had never been found, yet Crosby had made no effort to hide his other victims' corpses. Perhaps Crosby had hidden the body in order to avoid the possibility of his connection with Scanlan-McGregor's being discovered. *Or perhaps he had not killed him.*

If Crosby had not killed him, then he had decided to keep him. And Newson imagined that a man like Crosby would keep the things he valued close to hand.

It did not take the dogs long. In the beautiful basement kitchen of Dick Crosby's London mansion a false wall was soon discovered, behind which lay what could only be described as a torture chamber. This tiny cell had been Lord Scanlan-McGregor's home since his kidnapping eighteen months earlier. It would later be discovered that during that time Crosby had subjected Scanlan-McGregor to all the tortures he had used on his other victims. The unfortunate peer had been the guinea pig for Crosby's carefully planned assaults: he had been bashed over the head with books, had had his upper lip cut and stitched, his nipples had been crushed, he'd been jabbed with a pair of compasses, the skin on his chest had been bleached, and his pubic hair had been dyed red. He had survived, however, and as the door was kicked down and Newson pushed his way through, Lord Scanlan-McGregor raised his head, blinking in the unaccustomed light, and in a hoarse voice that nonetheless revealed the plummiest of accents, said, 'You took your farking time. Where's that little bastard Crosby? I'm going to kill him.'

'Too late,' said Newson. 'I did that.'

Scanlan-McGregor re-entered the House of Lords six weeks later, just in time to vote against a ban on foxhunting. He would later remark that attending a public school was excellent training for being trapped in a torture chamber by a sadistic lunatic.

'Old Scanlan-McGregor may be a bastard, but he's a stylish bastard,' said Natasha while perusing the thick leather-bound menu at the Savoy Grill.

'Natasha,' said Newson.

'I'm going to have a bloody big steak,' she said. 'I think my guts can finally handle it.'

'Natasha,' repeated Newson.

'What are you having? Got to celebrate. We caught a serial killer and no longer have gastroenteritis.'

'*Natasha*,' said Newson rather too loudly, causing those at nearby tables to turn and stare.

'What?'

'I don't think we can work together any more.'

'Why not?'

'Because I'm in love with you.'

'Ah, that's a shame.'

'What? That I'm in love with you?'

'No, that you don't think we can work together. Couldn't we risk it?'

'So . . . it's not a shame that I'm in love with you? Or is it?'

'I don't think it is at all. I think it's great. You don't know me, of course, so you'll probably change your mind, but—'

'Never! Bloody never. Look, Natasha. I know it's very early days, but will you—'

'You see,' said Natasha, 'as always you're right. It *is* early days. Let's order. I'm starving.'